AT GONZO STATION

"Colonel?"

"Yes, Frank."

"Two Migs, climbing through twenty thousand feet, heading straight for the Korean."

Standford rushed back to his desk and glared at his displays. "I knew it. I knew it. If we're not careful we are going to have some major trouble here. Willis, keep trying that Korean. Jack, get hold of Bahrain. Update them on what's going on and tell them to get some cover up. Then call CINCPAC. I'm not going to let some Oriental joy-rider ruin my day!"

"Right, sir."

"If we don't contact them in ten minutes, we'll need all the help we can get." Standford flopped down at his console, ran his fingers through his hair and shook his head to himself. "Don't those idiots know where they are?!"

Black Alert
AT GONZO STATION

by

Julian Hudson

**Commonwealth
Publications**

A Commonwealth Publications Paperback
BLACK ALERT
AT GONZO STATION

This edition published 1996
by Commonwealth Publications
9764 - 45th Avenue,
Edmonton, AB, CANADA T6E 5C5
All rights reserved
Copyright © 1995 by Julian Hudson

ISBN: 1-55197-03-9

This work is a novel and any similarity to actual persons or events is purely coincidental.

Designed by: Danielle Monlezun
Cover Illustration by: Richard Connor

Printed in Canada

Dedicated to the memory of Dennis, who opened my eyes to life; and to the officers and men who gave their lives aboard the USS Stark.

I wish to thank my mother Muriel for her vision, my wife Elvira for her loving devotion, Argie, all the folks at the Village Pub in Breckenridge, Colorado, Roy, Fish and Tim at the McKee Bridge Restaurant, Oregon, for their encouragement, and our Lord for my inspiration.

Acknowledgments: Ron Bauford, Author of <u>*The Puzzle Palace*</u>*; and the Department of the United States Navy.*

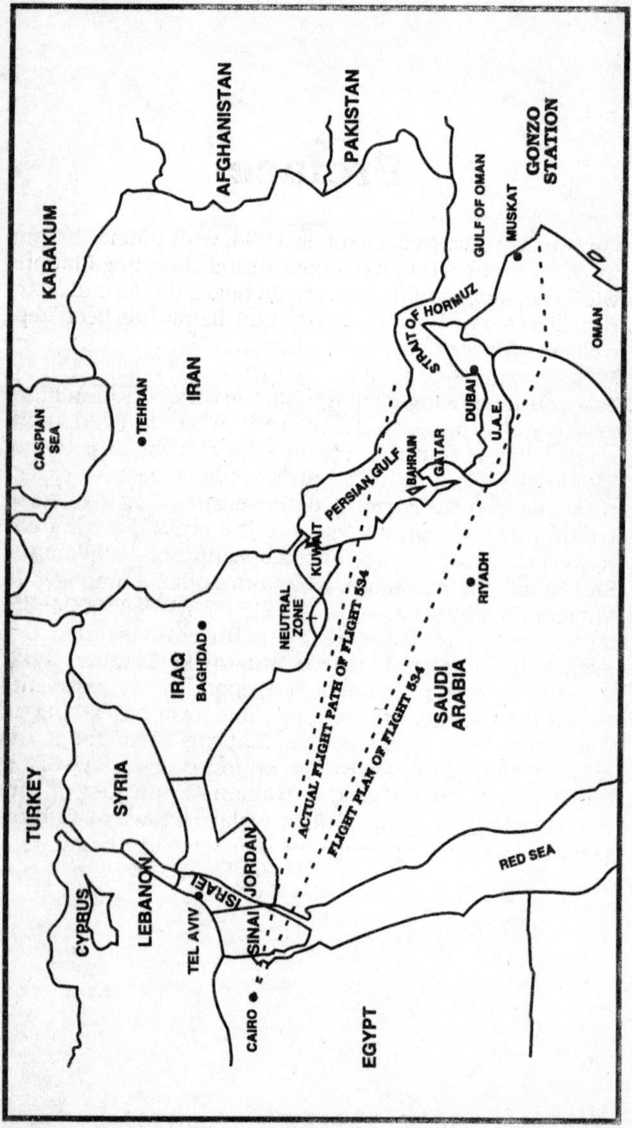
KARAKUM
CASPIAN SEA
TEHRAN
IRAN
AFGHANISTAN
PAKISTAN
GONZO STATION
GULF OF OMAN
MUSKAT
STRAIT OF HORMUZ
OMAN
DUBAI
U.A.E.
QATAR
BAHRAIN
PERSIAN GULF
KUWAIT
NEUTRAL ZONE
RIYADH
BAGHDAD
IRAQ
SAUDI ARABIA
ACTUAL FLIGHT PATH OF FLIGHT 534
FLIGHT PLAN OF FLIGHT 534
TURKEY
SYRIA
JORDAN
ISRAEL
LEBANON
CYPRUS
TEL AVIV
SINAI
RED SEA
CAIRO
EGYPT

Preface

On Sunday the 9th of October, 1994, with the no-fly zone in effect and NATO forces continuing their negotiations with Iraq, an incident occurred on board the Aircraft Carrier *USS George Washington* that until now has been kept a closely guarded secret. The fact that the circumstances surrounding this incident have not been made known earlier is surprising, considering the numbers of military and civilian personnel involved. What is even more remarkable is that the repercussions to the direction of military design for future hardware have been so severe that major rethinking of defense spending has been continuing without any leaks to the press. Fortunately, however, during the routine inspection of a diplomatic bag on a flight to London, a custom's official managed to intercept a copy of the Pentagon file, 37NGW1850004F35, a confidential document detailing the entire sequence of events that occurred on that Sunday in October. What follows is a reconstruction of that report, with adjustments to put the text into a more readable form describing all the events that took place on that day throughout the military community, with special focus on Group Six, a battle group circling in the Arabian Ocean just off the entrance to the Persian Gulf at a place known as Station Gonzo.

Chapter One

Assuming you remembered your way between the explosive hazards that remained long after the clean-up and that you no longer trusted the glue holding the bombed out bridge together over the river Jordan just north of the Dead Sea into no-man's land, you would still decide to travel at night. But even if you made it in by day, you'd never make it out. The prerequisite for any clan destined to initiate an illegal activity was to meet halfway between their side and ours, at night, alone and unarmed.

The new moon was low, half smiling as if in approval of the agreed exchange. The small, rough-looking soldier carefully climbed out of the jeep he'd parked between the sand dunes and waited for the signal. A seasoned informer, he had traveled this excuse of a road enough times to know most of its twists and turns. Although he could have safely navigated his way in the middle of the night, the hour was early enough to allow him some sense of anonymity with the evening traffic, yet late enough for his unlit vehicle to travel out of bounds without being seen.

The soldier stood there surveying the horizon, his heart drumming out the secret message. A flashlight winked three times. Crunching footsteps started their plod in the sand toward the front of the jeep and no sooner had they arrived than one big army boot raised itself from the desert and took refuge on the bumper. The unmistakable sound of a metal-cased liquid gas lighter flicking open and the roller flinting its flame was to the soldier, if nothing else, a token of trust. Experience teaches that forced words can bring death. In such meetings body language speaks volumes. A voice that breaks under stress can throw the balance of arbitration in the other's favor. A smile can confirm that all is well, yet hide the betrayal if there is one. Even the New Testament describes Judas pointing Him out by using the sign of kissing him on the cheek rather than uttering a word; a word that, in its effort to hide the fear, could reveal the lie. The eye has difficulty in picking up any such irregularity on its own, but speak, and the well-trained ear can add enough depth to the understanding to perceive any such deceit.

The new visitor raised a virgin cigar to his mouth, bit off the end and sucked it into life using the luminescence, as much to allow the soldier to see the smile on his face, as to generate heat. The soldier was confident that the distant flame hid his surprise at being met by such a young adversary. What mercenary delights could a nineteen year-old boy have mastered to achieve the rank of Major in the Palestinian army, if indeed he was a Major or in fact a recruit of the army at all, he thought to himself. If death at this point was to be the final handshake, they would have sent someone older. If his curiosity showed the Major never let on. The young officer puffed on his cigar, continuing to allow the flame to do its work in the night. Keeping his eyes firmly fixed on the soldier's gaze, he slowly and deliberately lifted his hand to his inside pocket. Gently, a large envelope was pulled and placed on the front of the jeep. The soldier reached over, picked it up and counted its contents. He took a small step closer to the Major's ear. Though Israeli was his native tongue, he spoke in English.

"An army truck carrying a Colonel and a driver will arrive in the city no earlier than ten-thirty this evening. That's just about two hours from now. They will join with an escort for the remainder of the journey as they leave the suburbs, I cannot be sure exactly where. Are you ready for them?" The Major did not reply. He just stood there examining the soldier's face for any little detail that would give him cause to doubt the accuracy of the information. It was as though he were waiting for the pointers on the machine taking the pulse and respiratory responses to quiver their announcement. None came. The soldier's heart jumped as the Major flicked shut the lighter's lid. In the second it took for his eyes to become accustomed to the darkness once again, the visitor was gone. Money in hand the wealthy soldier jumped to his jeep and started it. He backed around and sped off into the darkness, determined not to turn his lights on until he'd at least reached the bridge. It took him all of twenty minutes. On each of the five previous occasions he'd agreed to trade like this, he had pondered the chances of getting out alive. Now that he was again successful, he smiled to himself that his demands for a higher fee were accepted. This was his biggest payment yet and it was not getting any harder. The more that he survived, the more valuable he knew he became. They needed him and his information more than they feared betrayal. However, he could have charged five times as much for this particular exchange and they would have paid him gladly. They knew that while he was a bargain the risks for now were relatively cheap.

The jeep finally made it safely over the bridge, and eighty miles later, drove up to the main gates of the Israeli Research Center at Rehovo.

Chapter Two

Thanks to the continued benevolence of the tiny sovereign state of Bahrain, the United States had for some time enjoyed a great deal of access to the southern portions of the Gulf. The airfield at Al-Muharraq, generally known as Bahrain Air Force base, due more to its proximity to the Straits of Hormuz rather than its stature, still maintained the second highest number of take-offs and landings of any airfield dedicated to Gulf interdiction. The rows of bulging hangers and aircraft wings crowded around the taxiways was, at least, a testament to efficient parking. In bay five, with its large radar dish above another version of the highly successful Boeing 707, the 320B turbofanned E-3B stood awaiting its turn in the skies. The eyes and ears of the Persian Gulf region was the Airborne Warning and Control Squadrons. By overlapping shifts with the Saudis or by prolonging individual duties, an incredible 150,000 hours of continuous watch had been accumulated.

To help maintain the crew's high levels of performance, each aircraft was fitted with a fully stocked minikitchen, refrigerator, three bathrooms and even a fold-down cot. Yet all this was nothing compared with the rest of the equipment aboard one of the most costly aircraft operational in the world today. Indeed the equipment installed aboard AWACS 24 cost more than the aircraft itself to build. Rotating at six times a minute the thirty-foot Westinghouse APY2 Roto-dome is the most powerful airborne radar aloft. With over-land and over-water capability, its dish-like structure is carried on pylon struts high above the fuselage. On the back of this antenna are the other antennas for IFF; Identifications Friend or Foe. The APY2's range can be increased, at the cost of elevation, to stretch its normal working shadow some two hundred and forty miles in all directions. It can even track hostile electronic signals in a passive mode, receiving data when not transmitting. The standard compliment of fifteen or so operators sit at the situation display consoles laid out in rows of three. Using light pens they talk to their on-board IFF and AIDS, Automatic Identification Systems, on friendly and non-friendly aircraft alike, keeping the operators fully informed by displaying each designation against their contact points. Using GPS; Global Positioning Systems II, and the Joint STARS; Surveillance Target Attack Radar System, virtually nothing within range goes unnoticed. The current status is routinely sent directly to Bahrain, commanders, pilots in the area, and via satellite back to the Pentagon. This highly sophisticated network of equipment has also been "hardened"; a term used for encasing all the hardware in shrouds that protect against energy intrusions generated in large quantities during a nuclear attack. The AWACS, working in harmony with the rest of the military community, is the best of its type anywhere in the world.

Four E-3B's and one E-3C were stationed at Bahrain but their movements were not the only flights arriving and leaving what had become one of the few reliable and secure allied airports in the region. The Royal Saudi Arabian Air Force, with a great deal of support from the United States, had been helping the Bahrainians improve their air force strength. The AWACS aircraft, though operated by American crews, were bought and paid for by the Saudis, and apart from one squadron of F-15D's, all the rest were USAF. Long before Iraq looked beyond its own borders for financial security, aircraft had been flown into Bahrain to help with Persian Gulf surveillance and protection. The official policy had been that the RSAAF was required to provide as much support for what was then SAC and TAC. After many attempts however, to secure the skies above the Gulf, the Pentagon realized that the Saudis just didn't have the capability to cover such a wide area.

Early in 1994 while the war was still going on between Iraq and Iran and with Group Six some five hundred miles to the south, it was obvious to the Joint Chiefs that something more was necessary. Under the guise of 'Cover Charge', operations were increased.

The compliment called for by General Wilson was as follows:

a) Two squadrons of F-15Ds, including three F-15MTDs. These Maneuvering Technology Demonstrators, with movable canards mounted forward of the wings to increase lift and reduce drag, were also fitted with rectangular jet nozzles to allow for vectored thrust for take-off and in-flight maneuvers. All part of the 67th TFS of the 18th PACAF.

b) One squadron of F-16C Fighting Falcons and one squadron of F-16E Agile Falcons. The latter have larger composite wings and stronger power plants than their earlier counterparts. This unit was officially a Demonstration Squadron from the 496th TFS. On location to persuade the RSAAF to make additional purchases, the Falcons were also expected to show off their capabilities to the Egyptians who were thinking of expanding their F-16Bs at the time.

c) Two EC-135As and one EC-135C 707-320B Stratotankers.

d) One EC-135K. A converted -135A, fitted with extensive communications equipment to support command and control missions from the CINC.

e) One EC-135N ARIA, (Advanced Range Instrumentation Aircraft), a recent arrival operated by the ASDs 4950th test wing as a voice and telemetry relay station to act as adjunct to the land and sea receiver stations for NASA and DoD.

f) One EC-130H of the 41st ECS, Electronic Command Squadron, "Compass Call", a refitted C-130 designed as an enemy communications jammer.

g) Three CH-3B helos.

h) Two C-130 transports.

i) Two Sikorsky UH-60G Black Hawks and

j) Two HH-3E Jolly Green Giants.

On top of this list various other types made visits for one reason or another including a brand new CV-22A, which at the present time was undergoing some minor modifications in one of the six hangers at the far end of the airfield.

Earlier, each member of the AWACS crew had mailed off a postcard or two, finished off a hearty meal and received their orders. The briefings were very similar to the other air force pre-flights, except that the most senior rank of record commanding the flight was not the pilot; in AWACS Squadrons a higher authority is present. A Lieutenant Colonel or equivalent rank heads up each shift and is responsible for all aspects of the mission. Direction is given to the flight crew as to what course to fly in order to maintain and improve a specific vigilance. It is this vigilance that the 28th Air Division, 562nd AWACS of the 9th Air Force is particularly proud of.

As Captain Michael O'Grady and his crew walked out under the lights onto the tarmac past a row of helos and beyond to the four E-3s at the north end of the base, no-one suspected that this particular shift was to be anything other than routine. That is, if one assumed the monitoring of a no-fly zone south of the thirty-second parallel, the tremendous tank build-up around the marshes of southern Iraq and the annoying, if not hazardous, movement of Iranian aircraft throughout the region was routine. Each six hour shift performed by the AWACS squadrons was arduous and stressful. Once the recommendations had been passed down by the Armed Forces Select Committee on the tragic shooting down of the Iranian Airbus and the disastrous friendly fire incident during a recon mission in the Iraqi no-fly zone, the sharing of contact identification between AWACS missions and the various information gathering entities had been much improved.

O'Grady, a short man in his early forties joined his Plane Captain for his walk-around inspection while the rest of the crew clambered aboard. While they began their pre-flight checks, each member of the group within the main body of the aircraft took up their assigned stations, and as the in-board generators came on line the crew began their start-up procedures. O'Grady gave the thumbs-up to the ground crew and Lieutenant Bill Gwynn, in the right seat, pushed forward on the throttles to start their roll down the taxiways.

The captain turned on his headset. "Tower, this is flight 24, checks completed and awaiting clearance," announced O'Grady. Though born and raised in the States, his Irish brogue was still unmistakable.

"Good evening, O'Grady," came the familiar reply. "A beautiful night everyone. Winds around twelve knots, visibility over a hundred, clear skies, no weather likely."

"It sounds good but which way do I turn? You know I can't find me way in the dark without a map."

"Look, O'Grady, you've taken that old bucket of bolts out more times than I've had hot dinners. You should be able to do it in your sleep by now."

"Well okay, but if I get lost out here and I find myself pulling into a terminus somewhere you're going to get billed for a very expensive parking ticket."

"When you arrive at the north-eastern end of forty-eight, O'Grady, hold your position we have an Eagle on finals."

"Roger tower." As the E-3B pulled up to the edge of the runway, O'Grady turned off his headset, leaned forward and peered to his right. Out where the runway ran to grass scrub for the long run to the water's edge, out where the runway lights ceased their glow, a twin seat, F-15E of the 555th TFTS came quickly into view.

"Look at that, Mike," said Gwynn. "Letting it all hang out. Landing lights on, wheels down, flaps down and air brakes out. Boy, what a sight. Just once I'd like to get a chance to fly one of those puppies."

"You wish. Come on boys! Let's get this tub in gear."

"Boy, you in a rush or something?" said Gwynn, noting the tinge of jealousness in O'Grady's voice. As the wheels of the Eagle touched down softly in front of the 707, waiting patiently its turn on the strip, a cloud of dust and a scattering of gulls flew into the air.

"That should make our run a little cleaner," O'Grady said matter-of-factly as he switched back to the tower. "It was a nice show, now can we get off this Island?"

"That's a rodge' O'Grady. You are cleared to six-zero, local gusting at fifteen knots south-westerly, no ceiling. Have a good trip."

"Well thank you kindly, tower, I thought for a moment there you didn't mind much what happened to us."

"Just take good care of Bob Standford and his boys."

"Don't I always?" said O'Grady switching to Colonel Robert Standford's set. "We're all set up here Colonel, how about you?"

"All set. Thank you, Mike."

"Okay then, hang on to your bobblies." He nodded at Bill and a nudge on the power rolled the aircraft on to the apron with the pilot steering to the left. O'Grady loved taking off at night since this final turn, with the rows of yellow and blue lights interspersed with an occasional red bursting into view, always reminded him of turning on the lights of the Christmas tree at home. "Give me full power." Both Bill Gwynn and his engineer Alan Trent pushed the throttles as far forward as they would go and the power-plants roared into life.

As they started to pound down the runway Gwynn called out the speed. "50 knots... 60... 80... 100... 120... 160... V-one... V-R rotate... V-two." O'Grady pulled the stick back firmly and AWACS 24 was airborne. Gwynn hit the undercart and O'Grady began the long sweep to the right to meet his incoming counterpart, AWACS 21, some one hundred miles to the north. Ten minutes later at twenty thousand feet O'Grady switched to 128 megahertz.

Although Colonel Standford had been in touch with his opposite number on board AWACS 21 from the moment he had felt the wheels leave the tarmac, O'Grady had taken his time before checking in with his opposite number. "Lima-Lima this is Zulu-Camp.

"Lima-Lima this is Zulu-Camp. Do you read me, Turney?"

A few seconds later Captain William Turnable's familiar voice crackled in his ears. "This is Lima-Lima. Been waiting for you, Mike."

"You boys ready to head home? You sound a little tired, William."

"You would be too if you had had a day like we've had, O'Grady. Those two frigates the Iranians have in the Straits have started to mess around again. There seems to be some activity down at the Silkworm sites on the coast. There's a couple of Migs flying up and down the Gulf as though they own the place and, just to make things interesting, I'm nearly out of gas."

"Never thought I'd hear the day when you'd run out of gas, Will, you've always got something to say," O'Grady remarked cheerfully.

"Not me you idiot, the tanks."

"Situation normal, right?"

"Yes, but watch out Mike," said Turnable seriously. "It's very easy to spend a lot of time keeping an eye on the no-fly zone, but watch your rear end, someone out there is turning up the volume."

"Well I'm sure our two chiefs have things well in hand."

"Right. I could do with a cold one."

"Have one for me, and then get some kip."

"I will. My chief tells me she's all yours, so see you in the morning, Mike."

"Right-oh, Lima. We've got her. It's your turn to buy."

Little did O'Grady know that he'd have to wait a little longer to have that drink in the bar this day.

Chapter Three

Captain Mantu Lu was late. The airline had already put enough pressure on their pilots to accept certain changes to maintenance standards to keep their aircraft flying, but now there was a push on to maintain the new tight time schedules.

Inside the crew's offices, Captain Lu, a short, dumpy, expressionless man had briefly checked the cargo weight and passenger list. He was just about to re-work the fuel requirements for the haul to Seoul via Delhi when the local chief walked in and asked him, somewhat curtly, why he was not already on board. Lu was then reprimanded for his tardiness, as Flight 534 had already been given the first call for boarding. After a few words of apology, Lu signed the aircraft out and, still grumbling under his breath that he should never have been spoken to in such a manner, made his way to the concourse, joined enroute by his co-pilot. A fifteen year veteran does not need to be told how to run his affairs and he considered it a tremendous loss of face to be spoken to in such a fashion. Although there may have been some truth in what his chief had said, Lu was well respected by his colleagues and in all his years of experience this was the first time he had been warned that a tardiness report would be placed on his record.

By the time the captain arrived in the cockpit his engineer would have normally completed all the data input to the INS computers. So Lu assumed that, after handing out a few conciliatory gestures of greetings to the chief steward, all he needed to do was to strap himself in, complete a quick preflight check and away they would be. Eight years on 747s had taught him what a reliable and dependable aircraft it was and he could catch up on any other business that still needed to be attended to after they were rolling. Unfortunately, on this night, rather than arriving some forty minutes before the flight was called, his engineer had also been late and was rushing the entries into the Internal Navigation System.

There were three systems on the flight deck. The pilot's, co-pilot's and his own. A series of checks and rechecks by the designers had eliminated all but the most deliberate of errors. The system's memory contains a detailed map of the entire globe including distances to and from each way-point, and this knowledge permits the INS to navigate completely independently. Today, western airlines require that all data entry is carried out by all three crew members simultaneously, but there are still a few that leave the chore to the engineer alone. All he has to do is to enter the correct series of way-point identification numbers marking the intended route and leave the rest to the INS. Once engaged, the INS will fly the aircraft to the first way-point and on to the second and so on. Only seven way-points can be fed in at any one time. Therefore in a flight requiring twenty or more settings, the engineer would wait until one has been reached before replacing it with the next on the list. Although the procedure for entering these co-ordinates was simple, the key to its success is to accurately tell the system, while still parked at the terminal, exactly where the aircraft is before it takes off. That is, to feed the exact latitude and longitude of the airport's location into the computer against its reading of 'zero'. Then the INS can read the next way-point from this zero and determine the flight path necessary to get there.

The equipment itself has built-in mechanisms that can help a diligent engineer spot errors and correct them long before the rest of the crew comes aboard. First, the engineer sits in the left seat and feeds the "zero" and the way-point identifiers into the pilot's INS unit and waits for acceptance. Then he moves to the co-pilot's unit and repeats the operation. If there are one or more entries that don't exactly correspond with his first inputs to the pilot's unit then the INS system will not accept the co-pilot's data, producing a corresponding warning signal and audio identifier. In these circumstances the engineer is then required to repeat the procedure until the two units match. Once they do he moves to his own seat and repeats the entire procedure for a third time before completing the flight's navigational pre-flight requirements.

Today however, Lu's engineer for this flight, Denny Typi, was in a hurry. Unlike western crews where good communication and help is available from the captain on down, the oriental hierarchy does not permit questioning one's superiors about decisions or asking them for help if time is pressing. Typi, upon entering the second computer's data, received a warning that the information did not match those of the pilot's. Instead of refeeding the co-ordinates, he over-rode the warnings, canceled the pilot's co-ordinates, and re-routed the co-pilot's set back to the first INS unit so that they both matched.

Just at that moment the captain and co-pilot arrived in the cockpit. Typi moved back to his own seat, dialed up his own INS, among other chores, and decided to keep a quiet eye on all three during the flight for any discrepancy. Formal greetings were shared between the three crew members as they assumed their respective positions, just as a knock sounded at the door.

"All boarded and doors locked, Captain," said the chief steward, poking his head in.

"Thank you," responded the Captain looking at his watch. "We'll do our preflights on the way out. Let's go."

The aircraft took its turn in the congestion that evening and by the time the wheels actually left runway 22—RIGHT, the flight was already sixteen minutes late.

Although this fact was considered during the investigations the following day, history was to record that it was minor in contrast to the events that forced the downing of flight 534.

Chapter Four

The *USS George Washington*, having been commissioned only a few months earlier, was the latest nuclear-powered Aircraft Carrier to take up position in the Arabian Ocean. Her three hundred and thirty yards of flight deck is one of the longest afloat, and the GW, as she is affectionately known, is regarded by all six thousand three hundred crew members as the most sophisticated sea-based aircraft platform built to date.

On deck, it was business as usual. The night-shift Red shirts were loading armament. Yellows were directing traffic while the Greens were hooking the next launch up to Cat two. The Blues were ensuring that aircraft didn't roll off the edge as Purples fueled up. The Whites were making sure crews were following correct safety procedures and the Air-Boss was in charge as usual. Blue Thunder was coming to a close and the entire ship was alive with activity. Three F/A-18 Hornets had already returned. Four F-14D Tomcats were lining up on finals thirty seconds apart, and the rest, two tankers and a Hawkeye, were not far behind. As the wires did their best to catch every hook that presented itself, the handlers parked each aircraft in turn away from the flight deck proper as quickly as possible. The wind was howling down the deck at thirty-five knots, and there was plenty of opportunity for the flight-deck crew, head-phones alive with activity, not to hear an aircraft behind them, slip on the fuel-soaked deck or just get in someone else's way. From the Air-Boss's windows high above the melee the evening session may have looked like a disorganized panic, but the entire landing sequences went smoothly. With a new video concert being held in the mess that night, it was not surprising that the crews performed effectively and efficiently. No-one wanted to be given extra duty.

In complete contrast to the crowded, noisy atmosphere top-side, the hangers that contribute to the two and a half acres of below-deck work space were rela-

tively quiet. Chief Technician Jim Spreg was just finishing the removal of one of the data recorders from an
F/A-18 when Commander Brian Davis, a seasoned veteran of two campaigns, walked quietly up behind Spreg
and tapped him on the shoulder.

"What do you think, Joe?" said Davis, showing some
concern.

"Not sure, Commander," said Spreg. "The ouija
board's looking pretty busy at the moment but I reckon
you'll get another go around if you want."

"That depends on whether we can get this damn
thing to stay operational for more than two seconds."
The two walked toward the clean room where avionics
are examined and repaired.

Spreg was shaking his head. "It was fine this afternoon, again!"

"Well Joe," said Davis, "this is the third time we've
put her through her paces down here and she checks
out okay."

"That's why I'm pulling the tapes. Maybe it'll show
us something we've missed."

"Maybe. You going to copy it now?"

"Yes, sir. There's no time like the present," said Spreg
keenly. "I want this puppy to work just as much as you
do. My brother was one of the best pilots in Vietnam
and if he'd had one of these gadgets in his F-4, I reckon
he would have made it. If in some small way I can help
you save a few lives and perhaps a few of our beloved
aircraft at the same time, then I'll do whatever it takes,
even if it does mean missing Madonna's concert."

"Is that on tonight?" Davis said sarcastically. "I
wouldn't want you to miss..."

"It's all right Commander," Spreg interrupted as he
stripped the cassettes from their housing. "A friend of
mine managed to sneak into the control room two days
ago and rewire the VCR to not only show it on the big
screen but to dub a copy onto one a friend gave me at
the same time." Commander Davis smiled at Joe's ingenuity. "And besides, every seat in the place had been
booked weeks ago when we knew we was going to get
it."

"I thought everybody got a seat."

"They did; including me, but I lost mine." Spreg looked at Davis, not sure whether to smile or not.

"Now how could anyone on the GW lose one of the most valuable tickets to come our way since Hefner came aboard with some of his bunnies?"

"Well don't worry about it, Commander. I got my money's worth."

"You sold it?"

"No, I exchanged it."

"Well I hope you got a week's pass back home for it or you were robbed."

"Not quite, but as good as. I exchanged it for a broken down old VCR that yours truly tweaked and stroked back into life. In exchange for that show I'm missing tonight, I've got my own copy of the tape plus a fully operational VCR to boot."

Davis congratulated his engineer for his good fortune. "Good work, but how did you know you were going to be able to fix that machine after you'd traded the ticket for it?" Spreg had finished extracting the two digital tapes and plugged them into a decoder attached to laptop and a printer. The F/A-18's data recorder copied every instruction that the recent additions had given during the first thirty seconds of the in-flight test carried out earlier that evening, and it was now up to Spreg to run a hard copy of all the data to be analyzed by Davis and his staff.

"Well Commander," Spreg continued. "When a pilot has a problem with a piece of gear like a VCR on a remote island like the GW, they can't drive down to their local TV repairman to get it working again, so they generally bring it to me to see if I can fix it. Well, he did, and I couldn't. See what I mean?"

"You mean you didn't, but you could've?" said Davis a little confused. Spreg didn't say anything, just broke into a smile. So did Davis as he realized that they'd been joined by his chief assistant, Lieutenant Commander Peter Hunter.

"Brian, thought I'd catch you down here. You ready?"

"Actually Peter, I think I'm going to give tonight a

miss if you don't mind," Davis remarked, pulling a ticket out of his pocket. "I think I better stay here with Joe and see if we can work out a solution to all of this."

"I don't mind at all. I keep trying to tell you, Brian, that that poor, overworked, over-pampered little box of tricks of ours just needs a swift kick in the pants. If you want my opinion, all you have to do is increase the sensitivity and start around seven rather than the two or three that we've been running at up until now. You'll find she'll get stuck right into the job at hand and bring that baby down right on the money. Besides, I've been offered a weekend stay at a wonderful retreat high in the Colorado Rockies for one of these babies," said Hunter taking the ticket from between his Boss's outstretched fingers. "You two can stay here if you like, but if you ask me, you won't find anything except a rather nervous switcher or two."

"You may be right, Peter. But we're going to check it out just the same."

"Are you still planning to test it tonight?" asked Hunter somewhat surprised.

"Sure am," replied Davis. "The weather is perfect, far as the eye can see and not a breeze to be found."

"Isn't that pushing things a little, considering we have yet to keep it working for more than two minutes during the day?"

"Perhaps, but I promised the Admiral that we'd have it running by the weekend and besides, maybe a night landing will be just what we need to get the adrenaline pumping."

"It'll do that all right. I'll come and find you after the show. At least my end of things is up to speed," said Hunter as he left .

"Why didn't he go to the earlier showing?" said Spreg, tapping away at the terminal keys.

"He thought the late show would be a little less rowdy that the earlier ones."

"If that's the case, he's in for a shock. While the rest of the hordes have been flocking in to have their hour of fun, the rest of the evening shifts have been working overtime to ensure that there's no reason for any sadistic officer to stretch their duty. Since they're the last ones to witness the temptress in all her glory, the place is going to be torn apart."

"Come on then, Joe. Let's see what this can tell us." The two read the printout and after a couple of minutes of close scrutiny, Davis suddenly pointed at a particular spot on the page. Spreg ran back to the aircraft where he pulled a board from one of the two housing units under the port wing and brought it back into the shop.

"Commander," said Spreg, "if you were to sit yourself up in the cockpit and run the simulations again with the buffers increased by fifty, I bet you'll find she's ready for duty."

"You've said that before!"

"I know, but this time I'm dead sure she's a winner."

"Sounds good," agreed Davis. "I'll go and climb aboard while you plug her in."

An hour or so later they were ready to try it for real.

Chapter Five

The movement of army vehicles throughout the state of Israel had always been numerous and varied. Following the fall and rise of Kuwait, however, all military personnel had been placed on full alert. This resulted in a vast increase in the number of small army trucks that could be seen coming and going. Colonel Ashmere had been given instructions to join a series of tank maneuvers taking place in the Negev. Although he had been softened over the months by the Research Center's air-conditioning he was anticipating his mission, even if it did mean 120 degrees in the shade.

His young driver had spent most of the early journey south toward Tel Aviv going on about how many miles he'd driven recently, how he'd like to get more than one day's leave in ten and how the army was depriving him of his wife and children. The Colonel grunted sympathetically once in a while in response, but his thoughts had drifted to why he, the recognized local expert in artillery support repair, should be ordered down to the desert to watch over boys in tin cans trying to dodge each other in the sand. A series of dodges that had been carried out on many previous occasions with only his chief assistant, Major Liefstein, sufficient to monitor the situation. He ruled out the importance of the few rounds of ammunition they carried in the back of his canvas covered truck and the importance of his driver. So his curiosity had been aroused. It was only a matter of time before he would know whether some new interesting twist had been placed in his charge or just another wasted trip to watch the watchers.

Shortly, the driver's attention turned to the ever-increasing volume of traffic he now encountered as they entered the outskirts of the city. At each set of lights the traffic became more congested. Large tractor-trailers blocked streets as they swung wide to negotiate their turns. Police officers on duty did their best to keep everything moving smoothly, but ten minutes after entering the suburbs of Tel Aviv, the traffic was bad. The one-way street system, five lanes wide, would drain of vehicles ahead. Then, as the lights turned green, everyone would jockey for position as they charged the next hundred feet, only to grind to a halt again. With each attempt it seemed the surrounding traffic was getting closer to the Colonel and his driver. At one such junction they had stopped behind a tall van for the third time when two large articulated tractor-trailers pulled up, one on each side. Another big van had stopped right behind them boxing them in so tightly that it was practically impossible for anyone outside, save those with a helicopter handy, to see anything of the small army truck at all. The Colonel reached for the radio and started to call in his predicament but somehow his transmission was being jammed. Suddenly both doors flew open and the occupants were dragged from their vehicle before they could reach for their weapons. From the underside of the trailer on the left something unusual began to happen.

First, two load-bearing arms buried themselves in the tarmac, as a low mobile table appeared, sliding under the Colonel's truck. Four large jacks then proceeded to lift the vehicle from the road's surface just sufficiently for two sets of runners to slide under the wheels; one for the front and the other the rear. These runners now carried the weight of the truck as it rose to the level of the trailer on the right. At this point, the other trailer's entire side seemed to fold into itself revealing an empty compartment, save for a small winch, cable and hook. As the runners reached the height of the floor of the trailer, a hook was attached, a motor started, and the truck dragged on its runners into the compartment.

The whole operation had taken just over a minute. As the lights changed to green, the big door slid shut, the hydraulic table disappeared underneath the trailer from whence it came, and the driver and passenger were bound hand and foot inside the van in front. As the traffic continued its temporary dash for freedom the large vehicles went their separate ways disappearing in the confusion. It took another twenty minutes before the impatient escort, located some ten miles south of the city, dialed up their radios to locate the tardy Colonel and his truck. By then, like every sober witness who saw nothing, the trail was stone cold.

Chapter Six

Two things woke Vice Admiral Pat Swanson from the sofa in his office that day. Although it was a Saturday, the Office Commanding Gulf Operations for the Navy never closed. He had decided to use his lunch hour to catch up on some of the sleep he'd missed the night before. The first was the noise of the alarm he'd turned on only an hour earlier and the other was Lieutenant Commander John Latchkey, throwing open the curtains to let the afternoon sun brighten the room. As Admiral Swanson began his ablutions at a small sink in an adjoining cupboard, Latchkey began straightening out the room while filling him in on the latest.

"Waking you before two o'clock, sir, as requested. Black coffee and a blueberry muffin on your desk with the afternoon takes. I have that file on previous Carrier operations inside the Persian Gulf. It's pretty thin. As you know, sir, we hadn't really considered taking any Super-Carrier inside prior to Desert Storm due to the limited turn-around space available and the risks from mines in the area, and though the *Independence* is the only one on duty at this time, she is coping with the situation satisfactorily. Admiral Tyson has made it quite clear that, apart from another Desert Storm, he won't agree to another Carrier entering the area while mine-laying activities continue." Swanson finished toweling his hands and sat down behind his desk in his large swivel wing-back chair. "At ten tomorrow you have a meeting with Bob Dewey, noon lunch with Colonel Chips and Mr. Welesley would like you to call him to set up a meeting with yourself and the chief."

John Latchkey, a bright, efficient officer with blonde hair and a broken nose that he had suffered in a diving accident, having finished his brief update, stood in front of Swanson's desk. His overall function was to take care of the Admiral's needs, and as his best friend from the academy put it, he "did that admirably". At the personal request of Swanson, John Latchkey joined his staff

two years earlier, just after the Admiral had been promoted to the Pentagon. Latchkey had been Swanson's
Chief of Operations on his last ship and Swanson had
made it obvious that he considered that the Lieutenant
Commander had brought him luck from the moment
they were first introduced. Stories run that, after the
introduction party prior to sailing that first night, somehow Latchkey had ended up driving Swanson home via
the pretty route when a multi-car pileup in fog occurred
at the same time on the road Swanson would normally
have taken. As they were leaving the dock two morn-
ings later Swanson, leaning out over the side, failed to
notice that someone had not properly secured the gate
on which he was leaning. The pin holding the gate
snapped open under the pressure and just as Swanson
was about to fall into the harbor, Latchkey's hand was
there to catch him. There had even been rumors that
after a couple of days out to sea Swanson had com-
plained about the temperature a few bottles of his favorite beverage had reached while undergoing delivery to
his quarters. While transferring some of the Port wine
to a small cut-glass decanter he kept in the board room,
he had noticed that a couple of them were warm. So,
later that day, he sent a comment to the Master Supply
Sergeant mentioning the fact. An apology returned with
a simple note asking the Admiral to specify the required
temperature in degrees Fahrenheit that he desired.
"PORT 30," came the reply. The story finishes with Lieutenant John Latchkey heading off a rather dangerous
change of course. That was the clincher. Ever since then,
wherever you were to find Vice Admiral Pat Swanson,
John Latchkey was not far behind.

It wasn't that the Admiral really needed much watching. If he was watched at all it was to see what masterful moves he would make next. He stood six foot three
in his socks with a full head of silver gray hair, a match-
ing beard and eyes of blue; a man anyone would turn to
in times of crises, and they often did. He had won praise
earlier in his career by ignoring incoming shells and
permitting many, who would have otherwise perished
at the Bay of Pigs, to find safety on his ship. He had

commanded the Sixth Fleet that had sailed inside the so-called 'line of death' into the Gulf of Sidra off the coast of Libya to, as Tyson had put it, "test the waters" and redraw the line. In his opinion, Gaddafi had no more right to those waters than the whales but until then no-one had dared call the Rebel leader's bluff. The records describe Libya sending out their best pilots to push the fleet back into the Mediterranean, and losing. Pat Swanson had proven to be a leader as well as a great sailor and was promoted to Vice Admiral and given a post inside the Pentagon.

Since then, he admits he has slipped occasionally when the pressure was off but when it was on, he was masterful. His greatest attribute, as many around him have been eager to point out, was his ability to move on hunches and act on instinct rather than go by the book or play the percentages. Many a shipmate has watched him go against the odds and come out ahead. After two years behind a desk he had gained a great deal of respect from his colleagues in the Pentagon and Executive Branch. Swanson's clear vision has been credited for preventing many a disaster, with his ability to point to a submerged rock, in a plan that many could only see plain sailing.

He looked up at Latchkey and asked, "Anything else, John?"

The Commander knew what was on his mind. "No, sir. I'll let you know the moment we hear anything."

"Okay then. That'll be all." Latchkey left Swanson's office not by the main door, but a small side door at the other end of the room beyond the board room table and chairs. The Lieutenant Commander's office was small but very well equipped. Messages were sent via the official communication channels one floor down and they in return sent all relevant materials to Latchkey for Swanson's attention. If necessary however, the Commander could send, on the Admiral's behalf, direct orders to anyone in the field and receive same on special frequencies. As Latchkey returned to his duties Swanson sat down at his desk, picked up the half eaten blueberry muffin, turned his decoder to scan the NAVCOM feeds and proceeded with some unfinished paper work.

Chapter Seven

It had to be timed perfectly. Any miscalculation by the team and the mission would be scrubbed for the night. The *Jardavian* had been monitored taking out supplies from the oil rig *Tazmania* to the *Sabalan*, one of two former British frigates the Iranians operated primarily in the Straits of Hormuz. She then proceeded at full speed for about an hour to the middle of the 'up' channel used by tankers heading to the oil wells in the north. Slowing to ten knots she then performed a one hundred and eighty degree turn and spent the rest of the time cruising back. This kind of operational procedure had been discussed many times throughout the course of the peace talks between Iraq and Iran, but proving that any vessel's movements inside the Gulf were anything other than acceptable ship movements was difficult at best. The *Jardavian* was a typical case in point. Small by Gulf shipping standards, she weighed in at about one thousand tons with all the superstructure located in the rear. The open cargo space forward was empty all the way to the bow doors. Doing about fifteen knots she held her straight-line course oblivious to what lay ahead.

The small blob that bobbed and weaved just below the surface ahead of her was an inflatable dinghy, but how it inflated and the kind of power plants on board made this anything but standard issue. Power is provided by batteries in watertight compartments, which gives the electric stern-drive ample propulsion on the surface. Four other shrouded props located above the water-line and beyond the four corners of the boat provide momentum beneath. The two in the rear are connected by a cross member providing a fixed straight-line forward push. The two in the front are steerable in tandem in any direction. Upon command the boat can be deflated quickly, and as it begins to drop below the waterline, the stern-drive is shut down and the four props started up. The seven crew on board switch to breathing apparatus as the driver increases negative buoyancy, points the front props downward so that the bows increase their dive angle and completely submerge the boat and its occupants. Even with its eight knot under the surface, and twenty knot above, its range is still considerable with some six and a half hours available. From compressed air tanks the boat may then be inflated again to positive buoyancy, the bow thrusters angled upward until the divers' heads just break the surface. Additional air pressure is provided to surface the boat and the stern-drive restarted. With practice, the transition can be made smoothly and most importantly with hardly a sound. Developed in Australia and tested in Loch Ness, the "Din-jy", as it is euphemistically pronounced by those who use it, is a perfect addition to *Gold Seal*'s inventory. An inventory that is second to none for a team regarded by the other colors as 'The Cream'. Each navy seal team is given a color to designate the kind of activity they have been specialized for. Red Seal's work with nuclear installations while in this case gold has been chosen for its 'Special Operations' capabilities and it is commonly accepted that they, like cream, will always float to the top.

The problem that had faced Admiral Swanson a month earlier was how and where to place *Gold Seal* and their equipment where they would be the most effective. Their task had been to acquire some Iranian prisoners by catching them in the illegal act of minelaying. To accomplish this, *Gold Seal* would need a base close to the channels. The nearest available was Bahrain, but due to the large distances involved from this port, no team could be expected to execute captures successfully without being detected. Swanson asked for and received permission to proceed with an idea he'd had for a long time. With all the listening devices located below the waterline all around the Gulf, no ship movement could go undetected easily, and since he wished for the final destination to be kept secret, he instigated the first phase of his plan. What he needed was a supertanker with twin screws and a captain and crew who could follow strict instructions without question. Swanson knew that many tanker crews had been reduced to about twenty and with two-thirds of them either off-duty or sleeping, it leaves only seven members actually involved at any one time running the ship. If the shifts could be arranged so that the chief engineer was on duty alone prior to the accident, the captain could time the shut down accurately and control how much assistance the engineer would need for repair.

Fortunately for the Admiral, the San Bernardino was en route to the Gulf with orders to fill up at the recently reopened refinery on the Saudi coast, so the American Oil Company had been subsequently contacted for permission. They consented to allow the navy to use one of their company helicopters to fly a naval officer, dressed as one of their senior employees and carrying a letter of introduction, to drop in on the San Bernardino and visit with the captain and chief engineer under the pretense of a spot inspection. Once aboard, after observing protocol and a tour of the ship, the agent asked the captain to call for his chief engineer to meet them on the boardwalk, a near mile long gangway to the bows, where they could talk privately. There, after various credentials had been examined, they were told that the real reason for the visit had been to ask them to fake a breakdown.

Though it was made clear to the captain that no reason could be given for this action, it was revealed that by carrying out the navy's requirements a much tighter grip on the Iraqi and Iranian movements inside the Gulf would be possible. Upon reading the letter of confirmation from their head office on the understanding that their actions would not endanger the lives of anyone on board, they both agreed to follow any and all instructions. The letter indicated that they were to shut down the port engine and drive-train just before entering the Gulf, under the pretense of some failure, leaving the ship to continue its journey on the starboard screw only. From then on they were to remain on the one engine until they reached a set of coordinates halfway up the Gulf. This position on the west side of the Gulf was very close to an oil rig that had been brought in by the Saudis six months earlier. Since many tanker crews favor the west side channel, all would appear routine. The engineer was asked to create the kind of failure that would require about four hours to fix, following which the port engine would be restarted to continue the rest of their trip up the Gulf. The ship's log should record the visit but not the intent nor especially the breakdown, for it must appear as though the ship had both engines running for the whole trip. The rest of the crew should be kept busy. If there were any reports of unusual noise such as rumblings, vibrations, or sightings of jetsam, they were to carry out a cursory examination and then dismiss them. Under no circumstance must there be any reports out of the ordinary.

After a few further incidental questions were answered, both the captain and the engineer agreed on the plan and the naval officer climbed aboard the Jet Ranger for his flight back to Bahrain leaving the two behind to retire to their cabins. One would record the visit in his log while the other, with ten days in front of him to work things out, prepared to make things happen.

Upon confirmation of this meeting Pat Swanson sent word to the *Louisville* at Station Gonzo supporting Group Six in the Indian Ocean to receive a visiting officer with a personal message for the captain. The following day a CH-3 touched down on the *George Washington*, and, while refueling commenced, Swanson's messenger visited with the Vice Admiral and Captain on board to discuss the plan. Though two submarines were standard Task Force operating requirements it was agreed that the *Philadelphia* could handle the duties alone until a second boat, the *Topeka*, already en route, could join them. The CH-3 then carried the officer over to the now surfaced USS *Louisville* and prepared to lower him gently to the hull waiting below.

To make the transition easier Captain Barrow had brought his boat to a dead stop and a-beam so that the Sea King, while head-on into the wind only a few feet above the foredeck, could lower its passenger quickly and cleanly into the arms of the waiting submariners. Above, high on the sail, Captain Barrow watched his visitor climb up to meet him.

"Lieutenant Commander Mike Latchkey reporting, sir. Permission to come aboard."

"Given, Commander. Good trip?"

"Yes, sir. No problems at all, thank you," replied Latchkey shaking the outstretched hand.

"Do you have any relatives in the service, Commander?" asked Barrow peering through the shadows that half covered his visitor's face.

"Yes, sir. My older brother works for Admiral Swanson."

Barrow nodded. "I thought the name sounded familiar. I couldn't believe the Admiral would send his right hand man all the way over here just to see me."

"Yes, sir... I mean, no sir," said Latchkey with a grin. Captain Barrow moved away from his executive officer keeping watch on the lights of the fleet and turned to look at Mike Latchkey. Tom Barrow had been introduced to John Latchkey a couple of years ago at a launching ceremony and from what he could remember it was as though time had stood still. Standing before him was John Latchkey as he was some two years earlier. Tall, fair skin, straw head of hair, lean but tough looking. The kind of sailor you'd expect to see as bowman on *Stars and Stripes* or hanging out on a Hobie Cat. Whether you had Mike or John at your side, if you were to lose out on the race course, it would probably be because you yourself made an error or you were racing a much faster boat.

"So what's all this about, Mike?" Barrow asked, as though he didn't know.

"Well, sir. You should have received a copy of the general orders directly from Admiral Swanson."

"I did. The orders are clear enough, though it certainly looks as though our time aboard has been extended."

"Well Captain, maybe not. Admiral Swanson has ordered me to let you know that the compression chamber, inside the door of the eastern most leg of the rig, is now operational. So that may mean some of your men can rotate, sir. But more importantly, *Gold Seal* will now be able to move off the *Louisville* undetected. Much of their equipment can also be stored inside the same leg. A compartment has been built for that purpose. The rig carries a crew of forty-two to maintain drilling operations but five of the men have been planted by us to perform extra duties when required. The rest of my instructions are to confer with you as to the arrival of *Gold Seal* on board in about three days and to confirm the commissioning of the tanker *San Bernardino* to take you in."

"Even if we can literally stick our sail to the hull of that ship, isn't anyone going to hear us, especially on the run through the Straits?"

"Admiral Swanson is willing to give it a try if you are, sir. Our equipment is sensitive enough to distinguish one screw from another miles away, but he is confident that by shutting down the port engine on board the *San Bernardino* before the mouth of the Gulf, the combined sound of the *Louisville's* screw and the tanker's would not be far off the desired effect, especially to those untrained eastern ears out there."

"It's worth a try," said Barrow, raising an eyebrow as though anticipating some close order drills. He was not to be disappointed.

The seven members of *Gold Seal* arrived on schedule and just over a week later the *Louisville* made the rendezvous off the stern of the *San Bernardino* as she entered the Straits of Hormuz. Right on time Sonar announced that the port screw had stopped and Barrow took his boat right in underneath the hull of the empty tanker. The *San Bernardino* was cruising at twelve knots preparing for the long left turn around the narrow Straits when the *USS Louisville* moved underneath, slowing to keep their prop at the same location as the one above them. It was long, arduous duty. The levels of concentration necessary to maintain four hours of close maneuvering can tire many a good man very quickly but the entire crew of the *Louisville* were up to the task. Above, the captain of the *San Bernardino* watched from the bridge as they slowly cruised by the *Sabalan* and her sister ship the *Sahand*, waiting for anything that might give a sign that they had been found out. He was very familiar with the type of wake his tanker normally generated and as he watched it change and the apparent speed of his ship increase about half a knot, he guessed what the navy was up to. A captain becomes very accustomed to the rumble beneath his feet and though he was minus an engine and some twenty-five floors above sea-level, he could feel the heightened vibration of the intruder. From then on the captain remained on duty making his turns slow and deliberate maintaining constant revolutions to keep the disparity between the two screws to a minimum. About four hours later, after stripping down and rebuilding a perfectly good pump, the engineer called the bridge and confirmed that the repairs had been completed and that the *San Bernardino* was ready to restart the power plant.

Captain Barrow, who had run a quiet boat ever since they joined with the tanker, let the *Louisville* slip silently and softly down to the bottom. Shutting down all power he let the boat sink slowly under her own weight with the very minimum of ballast blowing. During the six minutes that it took for the submarine to finally come to rest, it was necessary to play with the bow planes to swivel the boat in an effort to find level bottom. The last thing any of the crew wanted to deal with was spending weeks, months if necessary, living aboard a submarine that was listing twenty degrees.

After a couple of days of digging in *Gold Seal* donned their deep water diving gear, left the *Louisville* through the forward hatch and swam over to the rig some two hundred yards away. Although the visibility was poor to non-existent due to the drilling activities, Digger lead the team directly to the far side of the platform's nearest leg and began searching upward for signs of a door. Within minutes, about forty feet from the floor, they found the recessed handle that took four strong hands to turn. The huge door, stubborn against the mass of water inside and out, eventually swung open. One by one the seven divers made their way inside and ascended the remaining distance to the surface. The leg, some thirty feet in diameter, although reminiscent of the training tanks the navy used to simulate rescue missions, was unlit and already thick with algae. As they surfaced it was apparent that someone had been there before them. Taking up half the available space with a ladder down to the water's edge, a large floor had been constructed complete with racks, hangers, and storage trunks containing an entire array of underwater equipment. The team climbed on to the make-shift platform and after turning on the lights began examining some of the interesting items.

"A regular home-away-from-home," said Phil to no-one in particular as he checked out the compressor.

"Right," replied Bill going through the pile of wet suits and breathing apparatus. "Everything but the kitchen sink."

"Hello," said Buddy looking at a notice someone had taped to the ladder leading up. Digger joined him and read the following:

"This hand-operated elevator only goes to the penthouse suite and is for emergency use only. It comes out in a storage room hidden under some large empty crates. Do not use the receptacles while the train is standing in the station. The phone must not be used to make personal calls. Please sign out any and all equipment you intend using. Turn out the lights and put the seat down before opening the door to your right. As you can see it is six feet above sea level (depending on the tide) and must be used with caution. The employees of the rig have not been informed of this addition. If a tug has been arranged to take you ashore, wait until you see the low handle turn before opening it. The tug will off-load any cargo first and will then swing around under the rig making a brief call at this door. Exit quickly and go below so as not to alert anyone above and close the door behind you. Since there is no handle on the outside, if you wish to re-enter use one of the keys provided."

Doug had found some more wet suits. Canny was checking the radio equipment and just as Chancy was diving through a chest of weaponry, Phil pulled the tarpaulin from a pile of gear on the far left of the flooring.

"What do we have here?" said Phil picking up a shroud. The others gathered around.

Buddy picked up one of the other shrouds that was laying on top and said, "Hello, hello, hello. Just what I've always wanted." Taking in a deep breath, they all joined in with one laughing exclamation. "A Dingy!"

Just after midnight, with the choppy and oily waters of the Gulf lapping gently against the hull, the *Jardavian* continued its steady trundle at fifteen knots. Canny, had given just enough positive buoyancy to the Dingy for all seven masks to break the surface. In contrast to the consistent light and smooth travel below, the Dingy began rising and falling with the waves. Like the Great Lakes, this stretch of water can turn nasty at times and it took quite a touch to keep the boat below the surface. Even if someone had been peering at the radar aboard the *Jardavian*, *Gold Seal* were still too low in the water to be seen.

Canny brought the boat into perfect position about thirty yards ahead, just off the leeward side of the oncoming hull. The nearer they came, the closer Canny steered to the ship. With about fifty feet to go the Dingy and its occupants were at their most vulnerable as they now entered the window of danger. If the ship were to change course and turned right at them, there would not be enough time to submerge or to get out of the way. But the danger passed as the rough-looking vessel maintained her heading. Canny hit the valve, filling the sides with compressed air, shut down the four props as they rose above waterline and kicked in the stern-drive. He only increased speed to ten knots allowing the *Jardavian* to overtake them and then waited for midships to pass completely before pushing the throttle a little more. The crew was tearing off their bottles and masks and hitching large clips to their left boots. The wash from the hull threw the tiny craft around but the team paid little heed. The stern was closing in on them when with a quick flick of the wrist, the Dingy was quickly cruising at fifteen knots aft of the superstructure.

Digger and Buddy, each with a crossbow, fired carbon-fiber grabs attached to lines up over the rear deck rails. No sooner had the hooks taken hold than Phil and Buddy clipped their foot brakes onto the lines. Each brake consisted of a clip affixed to the instep of the left boot. A hole in the clip opened to allow the line to slide into it. Once the clip was closed, the user stood up and the brake, or wedges, dug into the wet lines taking the weight. A small ledge on the top of the brake permits the right foot to add more pressure to the wedges. When the arms pull the legs up, the ankle, is rotated away from the line releasing the grip, then the ankle rolled straight applying the brake once again. This motion is similar to watching someone on a pogo stick. But instead of bouncing up and down on the ground the body makes its way cleanly and quickly up the slippery line. In a matter of moments Bill and Phil had reached the top railings with the four others close behind. Canny remained behind to handle the Dingy. Two sets of eyes peered between the railings. All seemed clear. Digger and Buddy pulled their knees up, released the clip, and jumped quietly onto the deck, quickly making for the shadows. Bill, Phil, Chancey, and Doug followed in silent succession.

Bill and Phil, born William and Fillmore, generally took the "heavy" roles. They were small in stature but hard as nails. Whenever knives or silencers were in service these two had a knack of knowing what the other was doing. They seemed to work like twins, in tandem. From the moment they were introduced at Annapolis they knew the other was going to be a Seal and had worked as a team, thought as a team and, as proven by their final assault scores, they excelled as a team. From 'clearing'; forced entry quietening any resistance for the rest to come through, or 'cleaning up'; staying behind to give the others time to clear the area, these two were the best the navy had. Digger was glad he had them, especially now. Taking ten to twenty men is not that difficult. They had captured groups larger than this many times before in training. The danger here however, lay in the unknown numbers that were spread over eight decks in numerous cabins. Anyone of them could sound the alarm for the others to rally. Therefore since some were on duty, some were not, some were sleeping and some were working below, not one slip-up could be made. The risk of some radio operator sending a distress, the engineers digging in, or the workers getting out a back door, presented Digger and his six man team some unique problems.

One thing that was going to give *Gold Seal* a big advantage in this task was having spent the last two days memorizing the layout and familiarizing themselves with every stairway and corridor until they could walk the ship blind-folded. Nevertheless, since the orders had requested that the prisoners be taken alive, the biggest obstacle that stood between success and failure of such a mission, was trying to secure the ship without killing anyone. First, one had to know who was where at the crucial moment of surprise. The first few hits had to be made in unison and safely. That's why Bill and Phil led the way, it was one thing to locate everyone on board. It was something else to capture them all alive. Although knives were preferred, the aim of any weapon used should be low and accurate. Even if the knees or thighs were hit some wandering hand could still reach for a pistol or knife. Working in twos, the leader of each pair confirms the hits on a given party and then moves on while his partner stays long enough to check for firearms, handcuff the prisoners to something solid and follow. Later, hopefully, all aboard would be moved to the mess on the third deck to be secured.

The fifteen knot breeze moving across the decks of the *Jardavian* acted as a silencer to the soft footsteps that moved around the ship. The team split. Bill took the starboard steps to the bridge, Phil, the port. Digger and Buddy found the side door and made their way down to the dungeons while Chancy and Doug made for the berths. At the given moment Bill and Phil made their move. Bill took a quick glance through the door's small window into the dimly lit control room that constituted the bridge. An officer was leaning up against the back wall. Behind the wheel a young helmsman was staring into the compass with a possible third shadow somewhere behind. Bill checked the tightness of the silencer on his pistol, tried the handle and, feeling the door give, swung it open. He fired off a round at each of the three individuals he saw in quick succession, then backed out and closed the door. The captain, helmsman and second mate let out a few groans, grabbed their legs and tumbled in a heap to the floor. Phil darted in from the port side, checked briefly on the incapacity of the injured and ran to the radio room two doors away, just as his partner jumped back in to secure the area.

Meanwhile, below, Chancey and Doug had made it to the crews quarters and picked two of the seven doors. The corridor was narrow, dark and quiet save for the deep rumble of the engines coming from astern and a slim sliver of light under one of the doors at the far end. Armed with air pistols that fired gas pellets they made their way past each cabin to where the light squeezed out into the hallway. Bill reached for the handle and as Phil stood square to the entrance, Bill pushed the door open and dived in, nearly crashing into the bucket and broom that someone had left just inside the cupboard. Bill grabbed and clawed for wall space so as not to knock anything off the shelves and ended up lying on the floor with his face inches away from a rather disgusting looking mop. Phil looked down at him with a big cheesy grin and stretching out his hand, lifted him to his feet. He turned the cupboard light out while Bill made for an adjacent room ignoring the silent jokes. Each disappeared into a berth and a few thuds later came out again and smiled at each other as two eight year olds would after raiding the candy jar. Picking another two doors the process was repeated and a moment later another couple of thumbs up. Twice more the two Seals took care of business. After regrouping at the far end of the gangway, Bill reloaded his pistol. Phil received one of those "What's up?" looks and shook his head in reply. Bill nodded towards their next target and they made their way down to the engine room.

By now Digger and Buddy were in the basement, well below waterline. They had a good idea where the operations would be carried out, if they were being carried out at all. Whatever intelligence reports may confirm, the only way of knowing that the *Jardavian* was indeed laying mines was to go aboard. They found it off the back of a dark storage room about as deep in the heart of the ship's stern as they could go. The door with the light shining under it and the sound of two crew members talking confirmed their suspicions that their objective was near. The hiss of air escaping under high pressure heightened their expectations. Digger and Buddy put their ears to the woodwork for a second to try and make out whether there were more than two divers inside.

Gold Seal's team leader looked at his friend and smiled. They had worked well together for many reasons. One was that Digger was the lead and Buddy had no aspirations for that kind of responsibility. Buddy felt that his own talents were best used watching the back door, securing their retreat, locking up afterwards, turning lights out and so on. Taking care of all the fringe things that needed to be done allowed Digger to manage the main task at hand.

Maybe it was because Digger was engaged to Buddy's sister. She had asked each of them, in turn, to take care of the other because she loved them both equally. She loved Digger because as she put it, "he was the best", and she loved Buddy because, "he was the greatest". Perhaps the biggest reason they worked so well together was that they were the closest of friends. Friends in a way everyone wants to have a friend. Trusted and admired, respected and loved as brothers love, and they believed in each other. Digger, though born an American had spent most of his time in Australia, growing up with sheep that needed constant feeding or sheering. As a consequence, whenever the pressure started to build or after a couple of beers, he would start to let slip some of his Australian dialect. Buddy, on the other hand, came from the Bronx, and was proud to make it out of his neighborhood alive. His maxim was, "the best place to be is the navy and all the rest is gravy." When he was about ten years old his father had taken him to see the movie Goldfinger. From the moment he saw the opening few frames of James Bond swimming into a harbor just under the surface, wearing a cap with a duck stuck on the top of it, he knew what he wanted to be; a diver that plays tricks on people. His last name was long and foreign enough for Digger to nearly always mis-pronounce, so his closest friend, and soon everyone else, called him what he was and always would be... their buddy.

Digger tried the handle to the door. It wasn't locked. Still just the two voices coming from within. They took a deep breath and burst in. In front of a large pressure chamber, working at a table full of detonators, stood two fat, bare-chested Iranians who froze just long enough for Digger to get close enough for accurate aim. He waved to them to put their hands up. While Buddy moved quickly around behind the two workman, searched them for weapons and pushed them away from the table before checking the other two doors. Digger looked around. A cot lay in the corner next to a wooden chest where three used coffee cups and a smoldering ashtray sat waiting to be trashed. Buddy nodded and made his way around, taking up a position behind the entry door with clear sight of the cot. Digger waived the two prisoners over to it and after ensuring that they were sitting comfortably, moved over to the chamber, hid his hands behind his back and faced the half swinging door. A few moments passed before they heard the noise of someone approaching. The door swung back and in walked a third member. He took a quick look at the black-suited stranger and walked over to the two on the cot making some expletive statement about visitors, not noticing the door swing shut behind him. It was all over as quietly as when it started. Digger snapped two sets of handcuffs on their wrists, joining the three together and without a fuss they followed him upstairs with Buddy bringing up the rear.

By now the engineer and his mate were also climbing the ladders. As each crew member hobbled or stumbled their way into that dining room, Phil, acting as Maitre d', seated each of them in turn and fastened their handcuffs to a table. Digger waited until Bill had arrived to confirm that there was no-one left on board unattended except those fast asleep in their bunks. Leaving the rest of his team to watch the room fill with unwilling guests, he climbed up a flight of stairs and walked out on deck. Digger always enjoyed the satisfaction of a successful mission, and with the wind and salt spray adding to the fact that no-one had been seriously hurt, this one felt particularly good.

Digger reached into his water-tight pack, pulled out his radio, checked the settings and said, "Swallows to Bird Dog, Swallows to Bird Dog, over."

"Swallow, this is Bird Dog, over," came the reply.

"All secure here."

"Roger Swallows, five minutes."

"Swallow clear." Over the salt spray he could already hear the sound of the two General Electric T-700 turbofans. By the time he had climbed to the bridge and slowed the ship to a couple of knots, the Black Hawk thundered into a hover. Two lines fell out its door thirty feet above the deck and nine marines slid quickly down into the empty cargo space of the *Jardavian*. They spread throughout the ship, some to the mess, some to those still sleeping in their bunks, and two quickly moved toward the bridge to meet up with the Seals. Just as well, there was no-one there. *Gold Seal* had already left.

Chapter Eight

Aboard the six year old Boeing 747-200 thirty-three thousand feet above the northern desert of Saudi Arabia, everything apparently was fine. The passengers were ordering drinks and making their choices for supper. Engineer Typi, figuring that the headings shown by his Litton laser gyro-compass were as close to prescribed parameters as to make no difference, continued to monitor the way-point settings as they tripped over. To this point all was going well. The co-pilot, sitting quietly awaiting the Captain's return to allow him some moments of privacy in the forward bathroom, was on oxygen. By chance the upper lounge was full of fellow officers of similar rank from different airlines, all of whom had accepted a seminar and various accompanying tourist trips from an Egyptian travel agency. Since the captain's position in the company afforded him a great deal more leeway regarding sharing the work load and overseeing procedures than western pilots, he had decided to socialize extensively. Although his activities might have been decided by some as high profile, he nevertheless enjoyed the freedom to spend hours at a time away from the flight deck. After the way he had been treated earlier, he considered that he had earned some time to relax, especially after saving the company a considerable amount of fuel on the trip out from Cairo. Following clearance from Cairo airport at six-zero Captain Lu, attempting to make up for his tardiness, decided not to switch to his INS system immediately. Instead he chose to lay in a compass heading and set course directly for way-point two and avoid the use of way-point one altogether. Some pilots follow this routine to score points with the operations director as it saves both time and fuel and under normal situations would have allowed Flight 534 to make up for the late departure and arrive in Delhi as scheduled.

The flight corridor for this trip takes commercial flights down the west coast of the Persian Gulf, around the tip of Iran and on north-east to Delhi. Overflying Iran itself had been restricted ever since the war with Iraq had started ten years earlier. Unfortunately for the passengers engineer Typi was confident all was well with the navigation. Though the possibility of making this type of error has been eliminated on all of the latest Boeings, little did they know that he had indeed transposed two digits of the 'zero' for the location of Cairo airport at the gate, causing the INS to believe it had taken off some hundred miles west of Cairo airport and was now compensating for the fact by pushing the aircraft ever eastward. After flying directly to way-point two, the INS had been engaged and proceeded to fly a course where it thought the way-points to be, a path much closer to the Iranian border than permitted. Many FAA inspectors believe that generally accidents occur due to a series of errors or decisions rather than one major failure. Already the count against flight 534 was standing at strike one. The entry deviation should have been picked up at the second way-point at the latest. Now, with the captain's corner-cutting, the use of the INS was delayed and the discovery by the co-pilot of this new route was to occur much later in the flight. Instead of the first way-point rolling over perhaps three minutes later than it should have, it had now been by-passed altogether. So when the INS was turned on to fly directly to way-point two, everything appeared to be fine. It wasn't until passing the fifth way-point that the co-pilot became concerned as to their correct location. Under normal circumstances, he would have notified the pilot immediately of the discrepancy.

However, what with the disgrace of allowing the error to go this far without being discovered and the possible wrath incurred by disrupting the Captain's social activities, he did nothing. The consequences of which were to start a chain of events that were to lead the ultimate detective to discover at least the 'how' of one of the most devious and premeditated acts of cunning to hit the United States Navy since Pearl Harbor. The resultant repercussions caused devastating effects that are still rocking the boat of reason in Washington. Although the trail of decoys and red herrings throughout the day ran deep into the heart of naval intelligence, history would record that flight 534 was a key ingredient in the story surrounding the Station Gonzo Incident.

Chapter Nine

Commander Brian "Hotrod" Davis looked left out of the canopy of his F/A-18 Hornet at the lights of the fleet sailing toward him. He passed the stern of the *George Washington* on the starboard side at two hundred knots, at two thousand feet, just as two F-14D Tomcats and a EA-6B were being loaded into the chutes to take over the evening watch for the next four hours. They would be clear long before he was ready on finals. As Davis ran the internal checks for the umpteenth time, the call came through.

"Viper One this is Mother."

"I read you Mother," he replied.

"We are ready for you, Viper."

"Let's give it a shot."

"Handing over to Commander Hunter now." Davis dialed up Commander Hunter's numbers and waited for his project assistant's calm voice to give him the go-ahead.

"We're all set here if you are, Rod." said Hunter, chopping his call-sign as usual.

Davis checked his instruments. The cockpit looked the same as any other Hornet, the two large visual displays updating the pilot on all the functions of the aircraft, except that now Davis reached for one of the recent additions to the push button array in front of him and dialed it in. Immediately the HUD took on a new look. There was the prerequisite aircraft altitude, speed and altimeter monitors, but now additional information was available. A small bright moving dot in the center pointed the aircraft's heading. Outside of this a larger circle adjusted in size and position as the aircraft closed in on the Carrier deck, with a fixed square in the center with four separate readouts located around the border. The two above and the two below ran in degrees high and low of the required flight-path. The two on each side, indicated the angle left and right of center. Situated as high on the panel as possible just below the

HUD, a red light started to flash warning Davis that the aircraft was located, or had wandered, outside the parameters required. It confirmed that the system was on and running waiting for the Hornet to reach the point at which the pilot would look up, locate the Carrier deck and 'Call the Ball.'

Davis took one last glance out of the canopy at the lights flickering by. The sky was clear and the quarter moon bright but the sense of remoteness and vulnerability was heightened by the fact that he was preparing to take his hands off the controls. "Going for the flight controller now, Pete."

"With you all the way, Rod," said Hunter. In a dark corner of the Combat Information Center deep in the heart of the *George Washington*, the Commander scrutinized a complete duplicate of the Hornet's HUD on the screens in front of him. He also studied a complete set of the aircraft's parameters, altitude, engine speed, flaps, air-brakes and fuel reserves. Although Hunter couldn't actually fly the plane remotely from the comfort of his swing chair he could at least make certain adjustments to the sensitivity of the F/A-18's systems, remotely, to compensate for cross winds, throttle and flap settings and wave-off procedures. In case of emergency, if any part of the aircraft were to fail, Hunter could even fire the pilot's ejector seat.

Both Davis and Hunter studied their respective displays as they came on line. The systems checked the motors and pumps, the up-and down-links to the Carrier and finally an internal examination. Davis's green confirmation came from the center cowling next to the flashing red light as he began the calls to his assistant confirming the motion of the aircraft and calling moves that he would have made had he been the actual pilot.

"All systems go here," said Davis, a little surprised at the amount of excitement in his voice.

"We've got a go down here, Commander."

"Let's do it." Davis took his hands and feet off the controls. For the first time in Carrier operations an aircraft with its own on-board auto-pilot was going to navigate to that final turn and then fly right down onto the deck, including undercarriage/hook deployment, momentary full throttle and shut down.

Davis began to call the play."Two thousand feet... heading 120... 200 knots... Turning left. Speed brakes deploying. Hey, looks like she's going to run for real this time. Flaps deploying. Throttles to idle. Half flaps. Heading to zero-eight-five, still turning. Speed dropping to 160... altitude 1200. Around to heading 280, straightening up. Three quarter flap. Throttle up. Heading 280. Gear down. Wings coming level. Thirty degrees flap. More throttle. Speed 150. Down to eight hundred feet. Coming up on finals now. Smooth ride. Altitude six hundred. Turning left. More throttle. She's a little late, raise the sensitivity, Peter."

"Taking it up two notches," Hunter confirmed.

"Rounding nicely, right on the money." The green light came on and the red ceased to flash as the nose of the Hornet lined up on the stern of the Carrier. The large circle that up until now had remained still, closed in size and started to wander around the HUD. As the aircraft constantly adjusted its position the small dot made moves toward the border of the ever shrinking circle. Just as the Hornet had leveled out, a gust of wind blew the aircraft sideways, momentarily and the small dot rushed beyond the safety limits. The left side indicator began showing digits in the minus column indicating that the Hornet had wandered beyond the safe landing window in that direction. The green running light went out, the flashing red came back on and a tone sounded. If the dot remained outside the window for more than three seconds, the system would abort the landing and apply full throttle, but it quickly swung back to center. Kicking the rudder and applying more power the system brought the little bright spot back to the middle and the warnings ceased. The circle, now shrinking ever smaller as the Carrier grew closer, required the system to work harder to keep the parameters in shape. Davis continued. "Good recovery, right on the ball. Heading 120. Full angle of flaps now. Speed down to 140. More throttle. More brake. Down to 500 feet." The system confirmed it had automatically switched sensitivity to level nine for the final few seconds of flight.

Peter Hunter watched in anticipation as everything continued to run smoothly just as they'd hoped. He'd have loved to have been up top, watching the touchdown visually but he left that to the rest of the crew. As many as fifty extra pairs of eyes behind the tower were glued on that Hornet, peering out from behind the hoses and extinguishers in front of them. The crew of the *George Washington* had awaited this first nights testing, with much anticipation. It was the culmination of hundreds of hours of work and extra duty. Now, a lucky few watched the Hornet's lights bob and weave their way toward the deck.

Davis's adrenal glands began to pump faster as he eyed the Meatball. "Down to 400 feet. Speed down to 135. Getting into glide-slope now." The window of flight requirement had now shrunk to the size of a silver dollar so that the bright dot was now constantly flirting with danger, but the Hornet continued undaunted. With each touch the dot made on the fringe, the lights flashed and the tone sounded, but the system managed to somehow remain within limits. "300. Nose down. Dropping right wing. 250 feet. Straightening up. Speed 130. Looks good." Again the lights and tones. The deck lights, only yards away, rushed headlong at Davis, his voice raising in pitch as the deck loomed large in front of him. He was finding it difficult to keep his hands off the stick and throttle but he ran through the checks. "One-two-three, Gear down and locked. Visual Slats. Stab Shift and Boards are out. Hook is down. Skid Pops are off. Hook Bypass Set. Ready to come aboard. 200 feet! Dropping starboard again! Rudder kicking over! Wings level! More brake! 150 feet! Nose up! 100 feet! Wings level! Over ramp. Full throttle! Touch-down! Good catch! Brakes! Throttle zeroed!" Davis suddenly realized he had been holding onto the grab bar so tightly that it took a few seconds to extricate his fingers.

"Great job, Brian," shouted in his ears.

"Thanks Pete. See you shortly," said Davis trying to calm down. He acknowledged the directions of a Yellow

Jacket signaling the release of the cable, engaged the 'wings-fold' gear and increased power just enough to taxi to the starboard side. Unfortunately he found that his legs were shaking so much that the intense feeling of momentary fear returned as he recalled his first few night-landings years ago. Maneuvering the aircraft under power on the slippery surface after a night landing, especially near the bows can actually be more dangerous than any other part of the flight. He settled himself down and took his time rolling to starboard. As the canopy rose above him the sound of cheering and applause from the foredeck crew filled the cockpit. Davis waved back his appreciation. A ladder was rolled against the side and a familiar face appeared.

"Great job, sir." smiled Barry, one of the Hornet's Plane Captains. "The Captain would like a word with you in CIC when you have a moment, Commander. I think he wants to take the next one himself."

"Yeah," said Davis with some doubt. "Say Bazle, keep all hands off her until we've given her the once over, okay?"

"You bet, Commander. I'll keep the souvenir hunters at bay." Davis climbed down into the arms of the many well-wishers wanting to shake his hand.

Suddenly the air-boss's commanding tone sounded over the flight deck. "Okay everybody give Commander Davis some breathing room. Back to your stations. And be quick about it or we might install auto-pilots in all our aircraft and put some of you guys out of business." The crowd dispersed hissing and booing as Davis made his way quickly below to see the Captain. Every uniform that he passed on his journey through the gangways gave him some form of congratulations before he finally set foot in CIC.

Out of the shadows of the darkened room stepped Admiral Lodgers. "Good morning, Davis. I wanted to be here when the LSO gave you his report."

The Landing Signal Officer stepped forward. "Commander Davis, number 303," he remarked, checking his clip-board. "We like a fifty-five second pattern, you came in at sixty. Too low. Too much power. High on the Ramp.

Third wire. Good pass." There was a silent pause then all the lights went on and the huge crowd that had gathered burst into a round of applause.

"Thank you, Admiral, but it's Pete you should be thanking."

"We all know Pete's done a marvelous job," replied Lodgers shaking Davis's hand. "But this has been your baby from the start. Besides, this gives me a chance to open a couple of bottles of our best bubbly. We've been watching our backs so much recently that it's good to have something to cheer about. Tony?" Lieutenant Tony Cliffard passed Davis a paper cup. "Here's to ALARMS. May God keep her and all who fly in her." The fifteen crew members gathered drank to the toast, put down their cups and returned to their posts as the Admiral took Davis to one side. "You didn't touch the controls once on the way in?"

"I was sure tempted a couple of times, sir. But no, Pete had her under control all the way in."

"Well congratulations. Your hard work has certainly paid off." Admiral Lodgers took Davis over to where Hunter was standing. "Pete, Brian here keeps insisting that you should carry out the next test."

Hunter shook his head. "Oh no, sir. I'll help design 'em, build 'em, install 'em and run 'em, sir. But I fly only keyboards. I leave all the glory to the experts like Brian here. Besides, I joined the navy to sail. If I'd wanted to fly I would have joined the air.., as a pilot, Admiral."

"All right, Pete. We all know your dry sense of humor," Lodgers said with a grin. "But I wouldn't go round broadcasting that kind of attitude too loudly. You might wake up one morning and find yourself being loaded into the rear seat of a Tomcat. But seriously, Brian, how much time will you need before you give it another shot?"

"Depends on the data. Pete and I will go over it tonight to see if there were any problems. If not, I don't see why we couldn't have another go round tomorrow. Pete?"

"Sounds good to me."

"Great," echoed Lodgers. "The sooner we get this

thing past preliminary testing the closer we'll be to making ALARMS operational. Right Brian?" The tone of his voice was back to normal, firm and positive.

"Yes, sir," Davis looked to Hunter for confirmation but the Admiral didn't wait for a response.

"Good. It'll be a while before you'll top the honors you both received today so I'll leave you to it."

Rear Admiral Bill Lodgers turned, gave a quick glance around the room to assure himself that everyone was back at work and left CIC. Although it was Commander Davis's engineering talents that kept him alive and well during the testing of the Automatic Landing And Remote Management System, it was his sheer guts that everyone would soon be admiring.

Chapter Ten

Aft of the forward torpedo rooms the seven members of *Gold Seal* had just finished filling their tanks with Helix mix when Captain Barrow walked in.

"Just received word from head office. They want me to give you guys a congrat's on a job well done."

Digger wiped his hands on a towel and shook the captain's hand. "Thank you, sir. The whole team did a great job. What will happen to the prisoners?"

"I'm not sure, Digger. I do know they were taken to the lock-ups in Bahrain, but where to from there is anybody's guess. Anyway, if you boys aren't busy at the moment I'd like to buy you some supper before you pack your bags."

"Are we leaving, sir? I thought we were here..?"

"So did I, but let's discuss this further over a bite to eat." The Seals put their chores on hold and followed Captain Barrow through the narrow gangways to the dining room. It was empty save for a couple of propulsion engineers finishing off some pancakes who, upon seeing the Captain and the divers come in, quickly downed their few remaining mouthfuls, and left.

After choosing from some of the finest fare offered anywhere on a navy ship the team sat down at one of the long tables to listen to what lay in store for them.

"What are your strengths?" said Barrow sampling some strawberry pie. "Apart from the obvious, I mean."

Digger did the rounds. "Buddy here is our navigator. He can fight with the best of them and though the rest of the team would probably take issue with me, he's probably the strongest swimmer here. Bill and Phil, down the end, are our experts on armory. They tell me what weapons we'll need and they're also point men. They take the lead in close quarters to clear the way for the rest of us. Canny there, he's our equipment guy. Whatever equipment we decide to take on a mission it's his job to make sure that it works and that we don't leave it behind. Plus he's also our driver and radio operator. He can pilot anything with a steering wheel and many times he's got us out of some serious problems safely. We thought of naming him 'Can't-he' but he succeeds more often than not. Chancey, a nick-name given for our resident risk-taker, and Doug are our deep diving duo. We can all handle extreme diving conditions but if it only warrants two of us going real deep then these two volunteer."

"And what about you, Digger?" Barrow asked finishing his plate.

"Me? Well I handle most of the explosives. I've been trained on all the various equipment we use plus much that we find in the field used by the East. If the team is in danger I'll even have a try defusing some of them. But mostly I just fix them and turn them on."

"How are you at fixing and turning on a new type called a Porcupine?"

"Well I've read about them, sir, but I thought it would take another six months or so before they would be cleared for field use. I've never set them myself but they can't be too difficult to handle, especially since we've planted many of the sensitive Dingers in the past."

"Okay. Who's the climber here?"

"The best climber we have is Doug. He's taken us up some pretty straight-up stuff, sir." Captain Barrow wiped his mouth with a napkin and took a sip of coffee. "Why the questions, Captain?"

"We're getting very concerned about some Silkworm movement overlooking the Straits. It appears that they're getting ready to use them. It really doesn't make much difference whether it's against us or some foreign shipping, we still need to keep control of the situation, especially since all our attention has been turned to the northern coast line. If they do decide to use them, we couldn't retaliate with an air strike without escalating Iranian friction and using sea bombardment would only give them an excuse to shoot at anything that floats." The Captain studied the reaction of the divers before him.

Phil joined in. "So?"

"So. What we, or should I say our leaders, want you

to do is to go in and plant some nasty little devices on those Silkworm launchers to give us an edge in case someone gets trigger happy." There was a long pause as Barrow surveyed the fit and strong young men in front of him.

"Sir," said Digger. "Don't confuse the silence for a lack of volunteering spirit. It's not that any of us want to balk at a challenge, far from it. It's just that we need a little more information."

"Of course," said Barrow pulling a sheet of paper from his inside pocket. "Look, here's a list of the number of Porcupines we think you'll need, their weight, and a list of the various hazards you're expected to encounter. The most serious is a sheer rock face you will have to climb immediately upon reaching the shore. It's straight up and it's as smooth as glass with no apparent protrusions to assist any climb. That's why the Iranians don't have any lookouts posted over there. They feel there's no way anyone can get up it, not without a helicopter I mean."

"How much time do we have to look this over, sir?" said Digger sounding low key.

"About an hour." Barrow stood up. "I'll leave you to it. If you need me you can find me in my cabin." He smiled and left the others to discuss their options. They gathered round their leader.

"Get us the topo on this area, will you?" said Digger and Chancey left the room.

Bill sat down on the corner of the table. "Is there anyway we can use our harpoons to get a cable up that rock?"

Digger checked the sheet that Barrow had left for them. "The face is listed here as being one hundred and eighty feet high, so, no. We are required to carry nine Porkies across the channel, up the cliff, across three miles of sand and rock, with marginal cover of small clumps of trees, locate the two Silkworm launchers situated about three hundred yards apart and plant a Porky on each of them plus two stock-piles close by."

Doug leaned forward to join the discussion. "How do you feel about those new, Porkies, Digger? I hear they're real sensitive and since they're new the receiver will have to be checked after they've been set to ensure good reception. We don't want to go to all this trouble only to throw the switch and have nothing happen."

"Right. I feel comfortable enough I guess but the problem they've been having is that some have detonated as the sensitivity was being turned up. I'm not sure I want to be part of a test." Canny came in with the map and spread it out before them.

Digger looked at Buddy. "What do you think?"

Buddy leaned over and examined the terrain. "It looks as though they've chosen launch sites in two clearings in a clump of trees close to an underground spring. The cover should at least give us a chance to survey the scene undetected once we get there. Getting there and back is another story. For the first mile there doesn't appear to be much cover at all. You can see here where they've located two high towers to watch the coastline, but as the captain said they monitor the coastline well south of the cliff. They start up again where the cliff ends north. Though they have clear line of sight up to and including the beach head, it does appear that we can get by. The ground level is hilly with some cover, so the good news is that if we're careful we should be able to get in and out. The bad news is that climbing that rock is going to be really tough and very time consuming."

Digger rocked back in his chair. "It's going to be a bear all right. Anything else?"

Buddy turned to Canny. "Do you think we'll have a problem securing the Dingy?"

"No. Once it's totally deflated she should stay put. The trick is, mooring far enough out so that the outgoing tide doesn't reveal its location. One thing is crucial though. Considering that the whole journey plus a time zone would have to be made submerged, we would have to make the crossing from the closest point on the west coast. That would put us on the northern most tip of Oman which means we'll need a vehicle and supplies for the trip there and back.

"That means we will have to make our move in the

next hour or so," replied Buddy looking at his watch.

"Right," said Digger folding up the map. "Buddy and I'll go talk to the skipper." The two headed to the captain's quarters as the rest put their plates away.

The room was tiny, even by navy standards. Captain Barrow was sitting behind his small singular desk pouring over some papers as they peered in the open door. "Come on in gentlemen. May I offer you a drink?" he said gesturing to a couple of bottles sitting on the sideboard.

"No thank you, sir. We might be leaving soon."

"So you've decided to tackle it?"

Digger sat down in front of Captain Barrow leaving Buddy standing by the door. "Not exactly, sir. We think we have it down except for a couple of points."

"The cliff?"

"Yes, sir. Without a high degree of confidence of scaling that thing, it just isn't on."

"Well supposing the navy has come up with a solution to that, is their anything else?"

"We'd need a truck or something for the trip down the coast. A drop from a helo would draw too much attention. To be frank, sir, I haven't seen anything to indicate that we've overcome the predetonation problems that those Porkies still have."

"Good point, Digger," Barrow acknowledged as he referred to the clock on his wall. "All I know is this. If you're willing to tackle it, Admiral Swanson will help you as much as he can. First, in about forty-five minutes, a boat will pull up alongside the platform on the rig to take you and your men to shore. You will be dressed as rig workers changing shifts. The boat will take you to Bahrain where the riggers normally disembark. There you will be met by Lieutenant Charlie Fielding in a truck. On board will be all the equipment you need to get over the channel and up that rock."

"And what about the mines?"

"Lieutenant Fielding has just completed training on Porcupines and will be able to demonstrate how you should set them."

"Captain, this trip is dodgy enough without taking

some regular navy type along?" The captain frowned at him. "Oh, sorry, sir. No disrespect intended. But after all is said and done my guys work as a team."

"We understand how you feel, Digger, but he's just going to get you all up that cliff, that's all. So it's either go with him, or don't go at all."

Digger thought for a moment. "Do you mind if I talk it over with the men?"

"Not at all, but don't take too long. High tide is at two-thirty in the morning if you want to use it and for about ten minutes the surf does just cover the entire beach area. It'll be up to you how much of the morning light you want to deal with."

"Yes, sir," said Digger joining Buddy at the door.

"Anything else you need just let me know."

"Right, sir," said Digger and the two left Captain Barrow to his paperwork. As they walked back to the men preparing their tanks for the journey to the rig, Buddy smiled. "So, even the skipper was considering the tide, eh?"

"Yeah, but what worries me is that if we're to meet the boat up top in forty minutes, it must have left the dock about ten minutes ago. And if there's a Lieutenant waiting for us with all the equipment we need, they must have packed the truck hours ago. It seems as though someone is ahead of us, mate."

"Yes, Digger."

Fifteen minutes later, dressed for the deep, they left the warm dry confines of the *Louisville* and swam the two hundred yards to the rig. After entering the leg they made their ascent to the surface, each stopping momentarily on occasion to allow for decompression. Eventually they climbed onto the storage platform where they toweled themselves down and climbed into their assigned dry clothes that someone had neatly laid out for them. When everyone was ready, Digger turned out the lights and slid the cover back from the small peephole in the door. Right on schedule a flashing green light was bobbing and weaving its way closer to the leg. As the sound of the single diesel grew louder Digger opened the door, watched his men jump aboard, followed suit and swung the door shut behind him. Two crew members were there to meet them but apart from a hello or two, nobody said very much. They were waved below as the boat pulled away from the rig and there they stayed until they docked, not in Bahrain but at a small jetty adjacent to the air base. The tiny harbor annex was quite gloomy as the Seals climbed the ladder to the dock. A few hands were shaken and Digger led his men down the jetty and into the dimly lit parking lot beyond. Between two rusty old trucks sat a sandy colored, six-wheel drive, twin rear axled Range Rover covered in road dust. The extended rear and the roof rack were loaded full of gear. As the team walked by the vehicle the driver's window slid down to reveal a warming smile.

"Want a lift?" said a voice invitingly. Digger left the rest admiring the vehicle and approached the window. She had the dark smooth skin of Asian descent. About twenty-five, her deep eyes bordering on pure black looked up at Digger with a squint of acknowledgment. "Say Digger, why don't you and your men climb in and let's go for a ride?" Her voice was cool and calm with a purr of sophistication that matched her good looks.

"And who might you be?" Digger responded.

"Charlie Fielding. I was told you and your men wanted to do some hiking and were looking for a guide?" Digger reluctantly signaled the men to climb in as he walked around to the passenger side. The increased length of the Rover had permitted an extra bench seat to be fitted in the rear while still maintaining ample room for gear. Fielding fired up the aluminum V-8, switched on the headlights, pulled out of the parking lot and turned toward the bridge that took them over to Bahrain proper and on to the causeway that links it with the mainland.

Digger took a couple of moments to watch her at work. She was taller than he first thought with shoulder length jet black hair that seemed to shimmer in the lights. Wearing gray worker shorts, her legs looked long and lean with her small feet capping off a pair of Birkenstocks. Her dark green shirt, unbuttoned down halfway, had that look of a uniform with pockets and tabs everywhere. She must be used to working in extreme temperatures, thought Digger, since the air-conditioner wasn't turned on and there were no tell-tale wet patches under her arms. With her window still down and her sleeve flapping in the breeze, Fielding knew she was being scrutinized. It didn't seem to concern her much though, her eyes on the road. Glancing at the five rear view mirrors often, she allowed Digger to get the full picture.

Digger swallowed some of his Australian pride and said firmly, "I wasn't told."

Fielding, smiling at her own expectation of Digger to question the obvious, continued to ignore her passenger's wandering eyes. "You can't blame Captain Barrow for that. He was kept in the dark just as much as you were. The Admiral felt that if you knew you may not have decided to come."

"And he was probably right."

"Can you speak Farsi, Digger?" asked Fielding squinting a little from the oncoming lights.

"Speak what?"

"Iranian," Fielding clarified somewhat sarcastically.

"A little in a pinch."

"I can, fluently, and you might need it."

"If we need it, then we failed in keeping a low profile," said Digger coldly.

"Perhaps speaking the language could be considered keeping a low profile," replied Fielding. As Digger chewed the point over in his mind the interior of the Rover fell silent. Having entered the city proper Fielding made a left hand turn, followed the signs to the air base, pulled up at the main gate, and, after various identification procedures had been completed, drove out to where a C-130 Hercules sat silently under the floodlights. A female Lieutenant flagged them down and examined Fielding's papers. After a few brief words on her mobile phone she nodded at the driver. They drove around to the rear to be met by open doors just as the four power-plants coughed into life. A female airman asked them to walk up the ramp as she took over the wheel. In the time it took for all eight passengers to tighten their bench belts, the Range Rover had been secured, the ramps raised, the doors closed, and the now ancient, ubiquitous transport was clawing its way into the air.

Digger turned to Fielding, who by now had hidden her locks under a cap, and smiled. "Looks like this operation has been planned for quite a while?"

Fielding nodded. "At least since yesterday morning." She pulled open her left breast pocket and pulled out a sheet of paper.

"What's this?" Digger asked taking it from her.

"I'm sorry Digger, but we have two tasks in front of us. It's all laid out there for you." Digger began to read. "Look," she continued quietly. "I know that you don't really need any help in securing those Worms and I'm sure if you were pushed you'd get the job done without too much trouble. After all, you are the best in the business. But I'm here to give you assistance getting up that rock and to show you how to arm the Porkies. I'm not here to get in the way." He turned to her as he folded the orders into his pocket.

"You checked out on these things?"

"Sure am."

"They must have fixed the problems then," he said as if to himself.

"Well, not really," said Fielding interjecting. "They can still detonate prematurely, but not if you follow proper procedures."

"Then why are we using them if they're so dangerous?"

"Those Worms have a very fast launch speed. We needed something that would be quick enough to catch the weapon before it left the ramp. From the moment of ignition the Porky only has a hundredth of a second to sense the launch and stop it dead in its tracks."

"But we have tons of stuff that can do that," said Digger, a little confused.

"Yes, but these are designed to distinguish the difference between a firing and the general shocks that can come from driving the launcher to another site. They will be set to destroy them if they are used, not if they are moved, although we have that capability too.

"I still don't understand."

Fielding pointed to the Rover. "In my pack I have a transceiver. I can dial them to detonate for launch only, first shock if we don't want them moved or in fact, fire them at will. Yes there are risks, but how we handle those risks is up to you. After we get everyone up that rock you can choose to leave me there to watch over the gear while you press on or you can take me with you all the way and I'll just stand by in the shadows in case you need me. You have a well-oiled, closely knit team. Where as I, well, I'm replaceable. To be frank with you I think the navy feels they would rather risk me than any one of you. If anyone were to get hurt in this it should be me. I have identification that can easily be traced to various Iranian groups and, as you noted, the paramount importance of your mission is to get everyone, with the possible exclusion of myself, out alive. Even if it means abandoning the task at hand, you have to maintain total security. Your reputation in this is a matter of record. That's why *Gold Seal* was chosen rather than the Marines. So just look on me as an expendable member of your group." She sat back and stretched her arms above her head in relief.

Digger watched the buttons take the strain. "That may be harder than you think."

Fielding reached for one of the bags and pulled out an irregular shaped block with a hole in the side. "Here," she said, "there's enough explosive here to blow this plane to a million pieces. And this," she continued, passing him a small cylinder, "is the receiver and sensitizer." Taking the small tube from Fielding Digger examined it carefully as she unclasped her bench belt and slid a little closer to him, unaware that her very slight perfume began to fill Digger's nostrils. "Here, in the middle of the tube are the settings. As you twist the top counter clockwise you turn on the power to the receiver. Push it all the way in and then tighten it against the threads, again, counter clockwise. The finger hold on the top of it should now be below the surface of the mine, which will be hidden as it is placed magnetically against any metal surface. If anyone does manage to remove it from the vehicle without detonating it, they'll have to remove the detonator and will probably fire it off as they either pull on it or screw it counter clockwise." Fielding took both pieces and put them back in her bag. "Any problems?"

"If I think of any I'll let you know," said Digger yawning. "For now I think I better catch up on some shuteye." Fielding considered the decidedly frosty reception the other men had given her and looked over to see the remainder of the group were already resting. Some were sleeping against the airframe, while two were on the floor and one, Buddy, was watching Fielding closely. It wasn't so much of a stare but a look of close observation. Fielding returned a quick smile and moved forward to the cockpit leaving the team to their dreams.

Chapter Eleven

Captain Chuck Fulton, when offered the duty of escorting tankers up and down the Gulf a year ago, gladly accepted without a moment's consideration. It had been a while since he'd seen action in Vietnam and Korea so he was keen to roll his sleeves up and get working again. A short man, balding above his big round face, he constantly sported one of those grins that has spent hundreds of hours out in the elements studying the horizon, in everything up to full gale force winds. A good man but one who spoke his mind often, and although it had brought him trouble in the past, he still stated his case with the best of them. Right now what was uppermost in Fulton's mind as he stood on the bridge eyeing the lights of the *Mishtosh*, was the condition and position of the three tankers in his charge. Ever since the Saudis had reopened their port, tanker traffic had increased substantially with the US Navy resuming some of their escort duties. Heading south toward the Straits of Hormuz the convoy consisted of the British Mine sweeper *Lipton*, having taken the point some two hours earlier, followed by the tankers *Rajah Queen*, *Mishtosh*, and *Shkirto* with Fulton's frigate, the *USS Stork*, bringing up the rear.

Captain Fulton put down his night glasses and glared out of the window in front of him. "Will someone get on the horn to those damn foreigners and tell them they've got to stay in line! They're supposed to be in convoy, not drifting about all over the Gulf! And tell that translator of ours to put some grit in his teeth. If we can't keep these guys in line by asking them nicely then I'll bring out the sledge hammers. Where's my coffee?" His Executive Officer rushed off to have a word with Communications as Fulton noticed his mug staring up at him from the sill. The crew didn't mind their skipper mouthing off once in a while, especially since most of the time they agreed with him. It was just difficult for some of them to keep the smiles from their faces. "A fine show of force this is," Futton continued. "Here we are relying on the British to sweep the Gulf before us because someone, somewhere, ten years ago, decided we didn't need to build anymore mine sweepers of our own. We even let the tankers go up in front because if there is a hit their hulls can deal with a mine better than we can! A fine Frigate of the American Navy we are!"

His Executive Officer, Don Carlton, came back on the bridge. "Excuse me, sir. The *Mishtosh* reports that she's having some trouble with her steering gear. It's all she can do to maintain her heading." Fulton ran his fingers through the few remaining strands of his hair, picked up a half smoked cigar butt lying in an ashtray on the window ledge in front of him and lit it. He puffed a couple of times trying to receive some relief for his jangled nerves and, as though he had found some, blew a big puff of smoke right at the window and settled back on his heels.

"Well tell them they had better have it fixed by the time we reach the channel or we'll have to leave them behind. We don't have anyone spare to stay with them, so they're going to have to make it through. I'm just not going to have a ship of that size going through the Straits, running aground due to steering problems and block it up for the rest of us. Those Iranians would just love that. How long before we get there?"

"About two hours, sir."

"Good. If that gives me enough time to shower and shave then it should be enough for the *Mishtosh* to fix that rudder. Stay on top of them, Dan. When I say fixed, that's what I mean." Fulton handed Carlton his mug as though he expected him to refill it and made a move to leave. "Any news on those Silkworms?"

"No, sir."

"What about the gun boats?"

"No, sir. After their initial movement they have taken up positions either side of the channel. But there's still plenty of room to get through."

"Good. But you come and get me if there's any change. I don't care if I'm only wearing a towel. Got it?"

"Yes, sir."

"Once we're out the other side we should have at least a couple of hours before taking the next group back in. That should give Willy enough time to fix that oil pump he keeps nagging me about." He left by the starboard door and took a look at the sky. Off in the distance he heard the sound of two small boats being chased down the Gulf by the flood lights of the Topple. The fast and agile boats were highly maneuverable but were no match for the navy's SRH (Surface Resistant Hydrofoil). She had ridden high out of the water on her four skids and must have been doing at least fifty knots when it passed by the *Stork*. Carrying one Phalanx and a launcher she skimmed over the water like a long-necked crane coming in to land. Her two extended turbo-shafts churned up an incredible wake as she bore down on the Iranian rafts. Fulton went below wishing that the Iranians would give the Topple some excuse to send them to the bottom once and for all.

Chapter Twelve

Commander John Latchkey put the phone down and, in that simultaneous routine one develops when serving a senior rank of the armed forces, knocked on his boss's door. Without waiting for a response he turned the handle and walked in. His chief, wearing half spectacles and with his hands clasped behind his head, was seated at his desk staring into space.

"Admiral, Lieutenant Fielding just called in to say that *Gold Seal* was on their way."

"Did you tell her about the extra duty?"

"I did."

"Very well. What do you think their time frame will be?"

"Assuming that they don't have any major hiccups along the way, I estimate that camp will be established in about an hour from now. If all goes well they should be on their way out to the channel by zero-two-thirty."

"Fine. How about a quick drink before we go?"

"Yes, Admiral." Latchkey walked over to the bookcase, slid back the small glass door, opened the small refrigerator and poured out half a glass. The phone rang on Swanson's desk.

"I got it," said Swanson punching a line. It was Tom Lasier, assistant National Security Advisor on naval affairs. "What's up, Tom?"

"Look Pat," said Lasier. "I don't know how important this is or whether anything will come of it but I've been asked to pass this along to you as quickly as possible because some people over here think that it could be legitimate." Latchkey put Swanson's small scotch on the desk and returned to his own office.

"You know I'm always willing to voice my opinions when asked, Tom," continued Swanson.

"Thanks, Pat. This isn't really navy stuff but the clan is meeting at seven to discuss this matter further and I'd like to have your gut reaction to all this beforehand."

"Okay, what is it?"

"Would you believe that the Iranians may just be prepared to shut down any and all anti-American activities in return for aid and comfort?"

"You can't be serious?" said Swanson rubbing his forehead in dismay.

"I am serious. An Iranian official on behalf of his chief loonies in the Gulf, has sent us a proposal. I just wish I'd been there when it came in but I had this stupid survey to look over. Anyway, it appears that they're now admitting that the wars with Iraq has taken its toll on their resources, and although the talks are still going on, they seem to be resigned to making some kind of peace with their neighbors and are willing to set up preliminary talks with us. They have completely run out of spare parts for the few Eagles we sold them way back when, saying in fact that their whole air defense capability is apparently pretty much dead. Apart from the nuclear deal, Yeltsin has closed the door for the moment on extending any old military deals they had and they're looking to us for some dough. Now get this. They've suggested that if we were prepared to finance a large portion of their internal rebuilding program plus provide American personnel and know-how, they would be prepared to cease all antagonistic activities with us. Supposedly they would clear the Gulf completely for safe shipping operations and, apart from keeping a strong guard on their own border with Iraq, lay down their weapons and join a positive effort to bring total peace to the region including the Israelis. Isn't that fantastic?"

Swanson put down his glass and sighed. "I'm sorry if I haven't grasped the full implications here, Tom. It has been a long week. Surely no-one is taking this seriously?"

"Well, yes they are," Lasier went on. "Apparently a few top brass are saying that they can't afford not to. If there is any credence to this at all, we would be foolish not to make every effort to use it to our advantage."

"Look, I don't mean to be such a skeptic, but hasn't anyone up there been reading the newspapers in the last hundred years? I mean it's just got to be a fake.

Have you checked with the embassy to verify its authenticity?"

"Yes, and it's legitimate."

"Tom, this had better not get out," said Swanson leaning back in his chair. "If his countrymen hear that some high official is trying to make this kind of offer, he'll be hung up by his thumbnails for sure."

"All I know is that enough people think it's worth pursuing, especially since the Chair is ordering those bombers into Bahrain. With the possibility of nuclear weapons on your doorstep, wouldn't you want to tread softly?"

"Treading softly is one thing. Making deals with your sworn enemies is another."

"Maybe they're just getting war weary."

"Right, and maybe you can put wings on a dog and teach it to fly."

"To be frank, Pat, I don't know what to think. Maybe when they see our B-1s arrive their government might just be prodded into giving us a foot in the door. Who knows?"

"Tom, let's suppose for a minute this letter is genuine. What's the Iranian Government going to do? Go to their people and say, 'thanks for all the lives your families have given up over the generations kicking out the Shah, but now we're going to let the Americans come back in with the big money and big western ideas and I want you all to treat them as friends? It's just not going to happen. And even if by some miracle it did, they must know that we'd put forth so many provisos that they would have to become the fifty-first state before we'd actually hand over any real hard cash." Lasier didn't answer.

Swanson was beginning to feel as though Tom, like the others, just wanted to believe there was some truth to the proposal at the expense of sound reasoning. "Here's what I think. It's either a ruse to find out if we really are as dumb as we sound sometimes, and actually get some help without us making too many conditions, or it's a trick. Knowing how little they trust us and how tight-lipped our guys are I think that they hope it's going to get leaked to the press. And as we try and make their government look stupid, then they must have some way of turning it around ten times more so. Just by taking it seriously we could do a lot of harm to what's left of our credibility. My guess is that it's some kind of delaying tactic. Apart from their continual mine-laying operations we haven't seen them try anything really stupid for some time. So I think they're cooking up something for us. What, I don't know, but it all sounds extremely suspicious to me, Tom."

"You may be right. That's why I asked for your opinion. You know these guys as well as anyone. Do you mind if I pass your comments on?"

"Not at all. I know they've pretty much agreed to stop fighting the Iraqi's for the time being, but why would they be willing to change their entire philosophy against the West now? They've been short of funds before. And to mention the Israelis, well, that's just too much to swallow."

"We'll see. I do appreciate your input, Pat."

"That's okay. It'll all be irrelevant soon, anyway. By the time we've finished with kicking the Iraqis' butt, no-one in the whole region will dare try anything."

"Good evening, Pat." Swanson gently put the phone down to find John Latchkey by his side topping off his drink. "Thanks John. Not too much, it's a little early."

"Sir, *Green Seal* has confirmed they will be arriving in Bahrain in six hours to replace *Gold Seal* on the *Louisville*."

Swanson nodded. "At least we're running a smooth ship. I wish I could say that for the boys upstairs."

"Sir?" Perhaps it was the lack of sleep but Admiral Swanson had always maintained a very loyal approach toward his superiors even when he totally disagreed with them, so Latchkey was somewhat surprised at his chief's comments.

"Nothing, John," he said picking up his glass.

"By the way, our new prisoners are fine and kicking their heels in the lock-up."

"Very well, John. I'm going to pop over to my place and get a shower. I should be back in a couple of hours."

"Yes, sir." Commander Latchkey turned the Admiral's personal line off so that it would roll over to his own, waited for Swanson to don his coat and scarf and close the door before returning to his own office. Latchkey was looking forward to his racket-ball match that evening with one of his counterparts. Unfortunately for him his match, as well as an appointment with a bowl of sweet and sour pork, would all go by the board.

Just after 9:30 that evening when the phone rang to let him know that the panic button had been hit, Latchkey dropped everything and made his way as quickly as possible back to his office, only to find the Admiral and nearly every other chief who was immediately available already gathered round the board-room table.

Chapter Thirteen

She was on duty alone. From the moment the *Louisville* left for the Gulf the *Philadelphia* had been pulling double duty. Not that it meant too much extra work, for the waters beneath Group Six had been quiet for a long time and save for a Russian or two observing them from long range, there wasn't too much going on. Captain Harry Davidson had spent two-thirds of his life under water with the last promotion to Captain of the *Philadelphia* coming four years ago. Although he was a tough man he looked relatively skinny as sailors go with that sallow complexion that comes from being without sunlight for a long time. With an aristocratic gleam in his brown eyes he exuded that air of confidence that is a prerequisite for any skipper of one of the world's deadliest of weapon platforms. In fact only two or three of his crew had ever seen him smile. Davidson said that working a submarine was not a funny business and although he didn't mind his men having a good time and letting off steam in the mess once in a while, he insisted on total professionalism while at work. The unusual thing about this regimentation was that he himself was the consummate humorist. Although his crew kept the smiles from their lips, his wit and comments kept a lighter atmosphere aboard the boat which did nothing but help ease the tension of long hours on duty. He was a man of relatively few words but his men enjoyed being in his company. When Davidson first took over the *Philadelphia* he had decided to share a meal with some of the crew to get to know them a little. They found out that he had a love for motorcycles though it was not something that he'd enjoyed from childhood.

When he was young many of his class-mates had tried to rile him into action by calling him names and the one they most favored was 'Harley'. Ever since then he had grown up with a dislike of those machines and everything they stood for, especially with the reputation that they enjoyed in the sixties.

But one day a friend had offered to give Davidson a ride to the airport, and since this wasn't the first time this offer had helped him out, he had accepted gladly. Just one hour before the flight was due to leave his friend rolled up at his front gate, not in his car but on a brand new Harley Davidson. He didn't have time to make alternate arrangements, and although Davidson was pretty upset with him for not giving him any warning of his impending ride, he donned the spare helmet gracefully, and hung on. By the time the then Chief Executive Officer stepped off the machine outside the terminal, he was sold, not on Harleys specifically but on bike-riding in general. In the following ten years, he had amassed one of the largest collections of Trumpets anywhere in the north east.

From the beginning of this voyage, the crew referred to their captain as 'Harley' and although they were sure he didn't mind, they never tested it within earshot. Davidson had overheard the name being used once or twice but it didn't bother him as it had during his younger years. He acknowledges that the initial visit with the men had brought them closer together and he continued to make a point of eating with the crew at least once a week.

Corporal Beadle watched as his SAPS jumped into life. "Conn, Sonar."

Davidson reached for the button. "Sonar, Conn."

"Contact bearing one-two-five. New contact designated Tango-two-two."

"What do you have there, Beadle?"

"Typhoon class doing about thirty knots, heading straight for Group Six, sir."

"Very well. I'll be right there."

"Sonar, aye."

Davidson buzzed Lieutenant McClusky. "McClusky?"

"Cap'n?"

"Put the kettle on the boil will you? We might be needing you shortly."

"Fission, aye." McClusky's job until now had been

fairly routine, keeping the 'kettle' on simmer. But in Davidson's book for "kettle on the boil" read, "be prepared for high speed maneuvering." Within minutes the rods would be raised to increase the heat and the whole boat would know of the anticipated activity.

The captain made his way forward to find Beadle monitoring the tracking of the contact. "How's it going Corporal?"

"Definitely Typhoon, sir, and she's not alone."

"Interesting." Davidson leaned in to examine the thin green tracks. "Does the Library have anything?" whispered the captain quietly in Beadle's vacant ear.

"I think I hear at least three others. System's confirming now."

"Curiouser and curiouser."

"Yes, sir. Confirmation of three others. One Typhoon and three Foxtrots designated tango-two-three, two-four and two-five," Beadle entered the relevant data.

"Very well, Beadle." Davidson straightened his back and asked somewhat sarcastically, "Keep an eye on them for me will you?" He turned to see his Executive Officer, Commander Mike Young, standing in the doorway. "Take us up to the ninety's will you, Mike. We need to call this in." Young nodded and left.

As the antennas broke the surface the messages rushed their journey to Vice Admiral Lodgers aboard the *George Washington* circling ten miles north of them. Much to Davidson's chagrin the reply simply stated that the *Philadelphia* should maintain her position, watch, wait, and keep the Admiral informed.

Chapter Fourteen

This was no ordinary Jeep. Although it looked standard issue the two or three extra pieces of inventory made this vehicle very different indeed. Although its original color was obscured by the 30,000 miles of accumulated dust and sand the profile had that distinctive look, as did all jeeps, making it difficult to tell where the outside stopped and the inside began. Purporting to be part of an original shipment purchased for the Shah, it was, in fact, driven into Iran by Barton about six months previously. The optional extras had been fitted by the Army Corps of Engineers before leaving the States and although not available to today's purchaser of the C.J., they were indeed highly sought after. To the man in the field the biggest problem had always been how to provide secure radio traffic when calling home. Although the use of codes have at least permitted the messages to remain somewhat obscure, the location of the sending unit is difficult to hide. Any listening post worth his salt can locate the bearing and range of most signals and invariably that last, desperate call has signed many a good agent's death warrant. To this end Research and Development had come up with a new procedure. First they designed a small compartment concealed behind the spare wheel in which several small transceivers were stored. They then converted the front hose or tube, which was used to allow the engine to breath while crossing streams, to be part of a directional transmitter. Instead of this tube being raised to the vertical position, it could be elevated and pointed to any reasonable angle forward of the jeep. Once one of the small transceivers, a mini version the E-Systems EHF 44L unit was turned on and placed upright in the sand, the jeep was driven some ten miles away. The tube was then pointed in the general direction of the transceiver and, using a miniature phased-array antenna, allowed to home in on its location. Although the radio on board the jeep received messages directly through the AM/FM unit mounted under the dashboard, the transmissions could now be sent via the remotes placed in the sand. Using very high UHF frequencies it was possible to transmit directly to the unit yet made it virtually impossible for anyone to eavesdrop unless they were in the direct line of sight. The signal was then converted and sent on its way by a powerful but short-lived cell which enabled the message to be received by AWACS and SATCOM. Any direction-finding equipment would then track down the remote's location rather than the jeep's. When the Iranian security guards arrive to investigate the area, they would find nothing except a large hole in the ground where the unit had detonated into fragments. The driver received uninitiated transmissions directly using conventional methods. The oil light would flash to tell him someone was sending and if he was alone he would write down the repeated message and decode it later.

The Corps then fitted an updated version of GPS II. The standard GPS unit consists of a receiver only, permitting the user to track his position to the nearest twenty feet. The "dash-II" incorporates a transmitter, permitting Commanders to have precise information as to the location of the users. To this agent its use would be considered as a blown cover and emergency procedures would be instigated, since opposing forces can also track GPS transmissions . And finally, located inside the jeep's front and rear lights, were listening devices with the yellow directional indicator light dedicated to inform the driver of any homing transmitters being used within a five mile radius.

Since the United States Government had gone to a great deal of trouble developing this vehicle and getting it into Iran without being discovered, they weren't going to entrust this mode of transport to just any field agent. The driver of this unique vehicle was lying on his stomach on the edge of an overhang a thousand feet from the desert floor, watching a long string of lights trundling north in the distance. He wore a thin mustache and a nasty looking scar down the left side of face. His sunglasses sat up on the brim of a uniform of a Field Colonel in the Iranian Special Forces Group. Night glasses in hand and a cheroot between his lips this man looked mean and aggressive. His brown eyes squinted occasionally as though, like the tail of a wildebeest, they tolerated the flies and bugs that hovered around his face.

Born in America of Iranian descent, trained by the Navy and given the rank of Major by the service he was now on loan to, the Department of Military Intelligence—Asian theater, this driver was ideally suited for the task at hand. He had developed a crusty flavor to his un-shakable Iranian dialect. He had studied the inner work-ings and methods of the local patrols and, though he hadn't set foot inside Iran before, he looked and acted as though he'd been a member of the Iranian Internal Security Forces ever since he was old enough to write his name. A name that resided proudly in the files in Washington. A name that he had chosen after running away from home at the age of ten; Leonard Michael Barton.

He lay on that cliff edge as he had countless times before watching the tanks and trucks come and go from their border with Iraq. His instincts turned up the range of his hearing. A sound of an engine approaching com-ing from the dirt road behind him caught his attention. He rarely hid his jeep since he favored the use of his credentials to get him out of trouble rather than con-cealment. He had learned the hard way, early on, that Security Force Officers are brash, loud and obvious and would never stoop to hiding their vehicle.

He got up, pulled a small metal tube from his pocket, stuck it in the ground and walked toward the road drop-ping his sun-glasses onto his face as he went. As he arrived at his jeep two large trucks pulled up in front of him, their headlights causing him to shield his eyes. The good news, the Major thought, was that there was no jeep heading up this parade, indicating a lack of sen-ior officers present. So he went through his routine of bluffing a standoff. He walked over to the giant radiator looming large in front of him and just stood there, legs apart and arms folded. If there were any important rank inside the leading truck they would soon be out to ques-tion him. Instead, as he began to be aware of a number of troops chattering away in the rear of the vehicle, a window rolled down and a voice shouted in a southern Iranian dialect.

"Is there a problem, sir?"

The Major walked around to the drivers door, climbed up on to the running board, took a deep draw on his cheroot, and blew it in the driver's face. "What the hell are you boys doing on this road? Don't you know this whole area has been restricted to essential personnel only? How are we expected to monitor escape routes by our chicken hearted brethren if we allow trucks like this to just come and go as they please?!"

"Ah, yes sir," came the driver's nervous reply. "But we do have orders," reaching inside his tunic. Before the driver had a chance to pull the papers out he felt the barrel of a Russian S209 being pushed into his skull.

"Easy does it, soldier."

"We're just on our way to Khartreen!"

"Ah ha. Let me see those, slowly." The Major took the papers, stepped down from the truck, and walked back to his jeep, apparently to make a call. He knew that the truck had a radio and that they might try and tune in but he had to try and handle this in such a way as to make it look routine, with emphasis on ensuring that his visit would not be revealed to anyone once they arrived at their destination. He reached in and grabbed the handset. Now that he had made it clear to them that he was going to call in and check up on those orders, Barton reached into his pocket and pressed a small switch. A blast sounded not far away. Barton ducked down in front of his jeep as though avoiding enemy fire and smiled to himself as a few of the men, including the driver, came running out with guns in hand to see what had happened.

"Are you all right, Colonel? What was that noise?" the driver asked.

Barton stood up and brushed himself off. "Thank you Lieutenant but I'm okay. I must be getting jumpy in my old age," and as he put his arm round the Lieutenant's shoulders he proceeded to laugh. "I've just been planting some mines in this area and one of them must have taken it into its head to detonate prematurely. You know, some of the equipment we've been receiving recently must be defective. I sometimes think we are becoming so poor that we are stealing our ammunition from the Iraqis." Now everyone joined in. They walked back to the truck together laughing and chatting. "Listen. Stay close together. I'm here because there have been reports that enemy forces have used areas like this one to ambush trucks such as yours. You carry a lot of guns and ammunition, right? Enough to arm a small group of insurgents. Be careful." The driver nodded in approval as he climbed back in his seat.

"Thank you, Colonel, and you too."

"And by the way," continued Barton handing the Lieutenant back his papers, "the fewer people who know what I'm doing out here, the better. No point me laying mines if no-one's going to show up, eh?"

"Yes, Colonel, we understand."

The leading truck ground itself into gear and moved off. As the second truck rolled by the soldiers in the rear leaned as far out as they could and gave their obligatory defiant salute which Barton returned in kind as the lights disappeared from view. Quickly he jumped in his jeep, fired up the V-8 and drove off in the opposite direction toward the valley below. He knew he had to get a message off about the convoy he'd seen, but there was something more. He was unable to pinpoint it right then but something was making the hairs on the back of his neck talk to each other and that wasn't a good sign. His plan was to follow the cliff road as far as he could before it began to descend. There he could plant a transmitter, drive down to the main road, make his call and hide in the convoy. The column he had seen trundling north was comprised mostly of regular army troops so there shouldn't be any problem.

As Major Barton sped off down the mountain he was unaware that his pair of night glasses weren't the only set being used on that ridge that night. A few minutes after Barton's jeep had left the ridge another engine started up and casually drove off in the same direction. Barton, now up to speed, checked his dashboard and noticed his little yellow tell-tale light had started to flash.

Chapter Fifteen

Colonel Robert Standford rose from his desk twenty-nine thousand feet above the Gulf, surveyed his troops, adjusted the fit of his headset, looked down at his displays and watched for a moment the various flights moving gently and quietly across the screens. Tall, slender with a little gray in his dark hair, Standford wore a small military style mustache, the ribbons of the Vietnam, Korean, and Desert Storm campaigns and an independent remote unit enabling to him to talk to any member of his team while roving around the aircraft. His team of technicians sat in rows of three across the cabin each with their own CRT and communication sets. All were quietly busy with the task in hand, to monitor the skies above the Persian Gulf.

This mobile, survivable, flexible and jamming-resistant surveillance aircraft is one of the most sophisticated in the world, with Command and Control, Communications Systems (C3), Antijam and Communications Counter Measures (C3CM), Computer and Communications Security (COMPUSEC AND COMSEC), and the austere maritime surveillance system. All was at the command of Colonel Standford, a man who was at his best when spending a day at the office.

"Colonel?" said Sergeant Jennings.

"Yes, Frank."

"Two more Migs coming up from Shiraz."

"Is that five now?," queried Standford making his way over to where Frank sat.

"Six, sir. Five Migs and the one Eagle."

Standford glanced at the time-zone clocks on the wall before peering over the Sergeant's shoulder. "Bit early for Morning Glory isn't it?"

"A little, but we have seen these routine border checks as early as oh-three-hundred, Colonel. Remember two months ago when we saw eight Migs in formation doing the tour?"

"Yeah, but these guys are wandering all over the

place. It's as though they're preoccupied with something other than early morning patrols.

"Perhaps they're just going to do some local communications checks, to see how their border guards are doing."

"They might also be looking for something." Standford stood up and looked back toward his own desk.

"Colonel?" interrupted Communications Technician First Class Jim Wallis.

"Yes, Jim."

"Just received orders to head further south. Apparently there seems to be some Russian sub activity developing south of Group Six and although the ASW's have everything well in hand at the moment, they want us to keep an eye on things down there. You want to speak to Colonel Barker yourself?"

"No, that's okay. I'll go and check with the driver." Standford made his way back past the isles to the flight deck. "O'Grady?"

"Yes, Colonel?" said O'Grady warmly.

"Some red subs are getting a little close to Gonzo so about face, O'Grady, and get our butts down there as fast as you can." Standford left without waiting for a reply.

O'Grady banked the 707 to the left, pushing the heading back down below the two-hundreds. "Call my wife and let her know I'm going to be up here all night, again!"

"Doesn't she believe you," asked Gwynn, "when you tell her you've been flying around the skies all night long?"

"Na. She thinks I find some gambling joint out on the edge of town somewhere and spend half my money on wine, women, and song."

"So," Gwynn went on, "why don't you tell her to come along one night and see what you really get up to?"

"What, and lose my self respect? You've got to be joking." O'Grady looked back at his engineer and said, licking his lips, "I think it's about time to break out the sarnies, Trent."

"Right. Meat or cheese?" Trent asked reaching for the cooler.

"Both. Do I have any mustard left in that there ice box of yours?"

Trent stretched his neck to peer down into the freezer. "Sorry, Mike. You used the last of it up on our last trip. Bologna I think it was."

"Great. Bologna is right. I think someone's been dipping into that fancy of mine while I'm not looking. Just what I need... a lovely night, work to do, and no mustard. When we get back grab a couple of pots for me will you?"

Trent passed a couple of packages forward. "Get your own jars, O'Grady. I have enough problems with remembering my pickles without worrying about you."

"Pickles? Well that's just fine. I'm sure a couple of those dills of yours will pick this lot up just great." His engineer reluctantly passed over the jar while Gwynn called the new heading into Bahrain.

Back in the rear Sergeant Frank Jennings was logging in a new contact. "I've picked up a commercial a little off-course."

Standford sat down at his own radar and took a look.

"Verification?"

"Coming up now, sir." Jennings dialed up the commercial identification frequency and touched his screen with a light pen. A couple of seconds later the information appeared next to the inbound on his screen. "Korean flight, 747 out of Cairo."

"I got it," said Standford. "What's his heading, Frank?"

"Zero-nine-four or there abouts," Jennings replied.

"That'll take them straight over the tip of Oman, across the Straits and on into the heart of southern Iran," said Standford flatly.

"Right."

"How long do we have if they don't change course, Frank?

"About ninety minutes."

"Okay then. Keep an eye on them for the time being

and see if they wake up to where they really are while I find someone who knows how to read the frequency charts."

"Colonel," Jennings continued, "another couple of Migs coming on board, -29 Fulcrums. Pretty border-line, sir. Range three hundred and twenty miles, just about to make the end of the Gulf heading south. Turning into a busy morning."

"You're right there."

"Back from some sight-seeing perhaps. Hitting their own border now. They're not too tightly grouped either, sloppy formation as usual."

"Yeah maybe. Boy, the nerve of those guys. Okay, get sharp everyone, I don't want this getting out of hand."

Back on the flight deck O'Grady leveled out and turned on his mic, "Colonel, on course."

"Thank you."

"Skipper, 26 has just been scrambled to take over duties in the north," said Gwynn.

"That's a bad sign, looks like we could have a long night in front of us."

Gwynn took out a handkerchief and wiped his brow. "Boy, what I would give to go for a nice long swim about now."

"Oh, yeah, Bill? Trent, did I ever tell you about the time Gwynn and I took some leave in Spain a few years ago?"

"No," Trent replied leaning forward.

"The first evening Bill and I took the quarter ferry boat across San Antonio bay to the 'big city.' Earlier we had finished what was to become our "evening consti-tutional," of which I was more the winner than loser whether I was white or black. We walked by the small outdoor pool on the patio at the rear of the hotel del Mucho and found some change. Following twelve min-utes of rock and roll in a row boat shorter than a cot, we made it safely on terra-softa once more and headed straight for the game room. Although speed limits throughout Ibiza were less than a hundred kilometers, both him and I splurged twenty potatoes on thirty min-utes behind the wheel of a three hundred and fifty mile-per-hour Ferrari. With finger on the metal and thumb on the brake the two miniatures hurtled around the track and sometimes hurtled around the room. We bought a round of drinks at the local meat market, signing away our lives on credit with a piece of paper that even made the early parchment the inn-keeper used to open a tab, to ourselves, partners in thirst. Finally it was on to the floor and ask some dolly whether she was out for a good time, oh, 'do she wanna dance,' and, 'can you speak any English at all?' Only to find that one of the few that said 'Yeah' to one of the above, actually came from a small continent south of Canada. In fact her parents lived in a small town about fifteen miles away from where I grew up. Boy, those travel agents were really on to a good thing persuading us to spend all that money to travel three thousand miles so that we can dance with a girl who lives above the local chish and fip shop. And I thought I was going to let my hair down with some locals. What a let down!! Anyway, to cut a long story off at the knees, I finally dumped her, found Gwynn here sitting rather painfully on the wrong end of a bar stool and tried to find out whether he had had enough. 'I'm really not smashed,' he said trying to pull one of his toes out of one of the four staples that was an excuse for the joinery work that kept the stool in one piece. 'How many beers have you had?' I asked trying to find where the bloodshot stopped and the face started. 'Only one, but you're right, Micky, it's time to head back.' At this point his head fell back on the bar. I took the gallon can from his fist and dragged him to the door which opened right out onto the esplanade. 'A pier!' I cried. 'No thanks, I still got one going,' he replied. I laughed, he smiled. I laughed more and he changed color. He threw up and I changed color. He laughed and I threw up, and we ended up walking home. I'm not going to say it was late but the ferry boat driver was already eating breakfast by the time we made it back to the small but difficult flight of step that led back on to the patio at the del Gruncho. 'I know,' said he, which, lets face it, must have been a first. 'I'm going to take a refreshing swim in the pool.' Gwynn proceeded to walk toward the raised area. 'Don't be silly,' said I, which again was asking for a change of a lifetime of commitments. 'You'll get all wet and I'll have to come in and get you.' He made an attempt to climb the other long flight of step to the pool area when I grabbed Bill and dragged him back inside. We entered the lobby just in time to wave good-bye to the parting guests, witness the lights being turned off and his stomach being emptied. Later that morning we got up, showered, and went to breakfast about three P.M. out on the patio. To our amazement, there was a big Spanish guy. He must have stood four-foot-five if he was an inch, which he probably was. With garden hose in hand he was filling the pool up with water. The pool had been drained the night before for cleaning. At dawn, when he and I arrived back, the only thing in that pool was some miniature livestock and some rather questionable remains. You, my friend," said O'Grady pointing to his Co-pilot, "would have had a very nasty fracture of the face had you taken the plunge."

In the ribbing that followed Trent dropped a tomato down between his switches, Gwynn spilled his soda all over the floor and O'Grady was wiping dill pickle from his shirt.

"O'Grady?" said Colonel Standford in O'Grady's ears.

"Yes, Colonel?" he mumbled trying to swallow his food and talk at the same time.

"Sixty-five fifty and twenty-five even, got it?" The food in O'Grady's mouth was beginning to choke him.

"What, Colonel?" asked the Pilot as pieces of sandwich began spurting out from his teeth.

"The coordinates, O'Grady! the coordinates. We've got tons of Migs up and about at the moment so you better sharpen up. Things could get real sticky around here."

"They already are," O'Grady replied looking around him.

Chapter Sixteen

The small secluded beach was empty, not because of sharks but because of the many land-mines buried deep in the sand. Although the northern tip of the Oman coast and the accompanying islands were very close to the boiling waters of the Straits, all was very peaceful. Although the Oman troops were friendly they had made this part of the coastline very inhospitable during World War II. Now, only the local forces were allowed to catch fish and watch the ships coming and going through the Straits of Hormuz. The morning dawn was still over a couple of hours away. The warm seas lapped against the long rocky coastline and no-one was there to witness the shaded headlights of the Range Rover gently bump and weave its way down the hiking trail just above one of many tiny coves.

A while earlier the eight passengers aboard the Hercules had sat as quietly as anyone could have under the circumstances awaiting the moment to disembark. The Range Rover's wheels were secured fast to the wooden platen and the large chutes, to be ejected first out of the doors, had been prepared. *Gold Seal* donned their free-fall gear and chutes while the pilot closed in over the drop zone at ten thousand feet. The doors opened and the cool night air rushed back into the fuselage to greet them. The red light turned green and in one quick motion eight uninvited guests dropped onto Oman soil. Free-falling during the day can be dangerous enough at the best of times, but here, in the dead of night, with just a small electronic alarm to signify twenty-five hundred feet, the lack of vision only intensified the incredible adrenaline rush that pushed all of the senses to the limit. The wing-shaped chutes opened as each team member felt that enjoyable snatch as the belts grabbed between their legs and slowed their descent. Digger had been first out and, by counting an additional three seconds before pulling his cord, was also the first to feel the sandy scrub under the spring in his legs. Before grabbing his chute in Digger pulled out a small lamp with a two inch shroud above the lens and stuck it in the ground pointing skyward. It was just bright enough for anyone above who was looking for such a signal to see it clearly and direct their sideways travel toward it. By the time Digger had pulled in his lines, the soft thumping of other feet in the desert signified the rest had made it down safely. Digger turned off the lamp as a hole was dug to bury the reliable transports. As soon as their task had been completed he turned the lamp back on again and pointed in the direction of the C-130.

The rugged transport had now dropped to three thousand feet preparing for its run about two miles to the south. The Hercules dipped its nose and began a steep dive toward the team's location. Its flaps down, running lights off and the rear doors open, it made a gentle swoop towards Digger and his colleagues awaiting the delivery, they hoped, of a fully packed Range Rover in perfect condition. The Hercules continued its approach as though it was attempting a landing. But instead of lowering its undercarriage it charged onward, the power plants dancing their beautiful song in the breeze. Suddenly it was upon them no higher than twenty feet off the scrub. The huge chutes burst out of the rear door, took a second to fully deploy, and in one giant tug took hold of the wooden platform and dragged it into the chilly evening air. By the time it hit the ground the chutes had already slowed it to fifty miles-per-hour, and before the inertia could throw the vehicle off in one direction or another, the bumpy landing brought the Rover to a dead but dusty stop in about thirty feet. The C-130 was already climbing away in the distance, the soft rumble fading from the ears as *Gold Seal* rushed forward to check for damage. As the straps holding the Rover down were being torn off, the steering and suspension were given the once over. The engine burst into life at the first turn of the key and the gauges quickly confirmed the twin tanks were all but full and that everything was in good working order. Doug checked that the slit eye covers over the headlights were secure while Buddy gave the gear on the roof a final inspection. There was plenty of clearance for the six wheels to roll off what remained of the landing gear and once everyone had boarded they were on their way following their noses toward the narrows.

The rocky coastline with its interweaving trail, dodging rocks and boulders along the cliff edge, made for an adventurous journey. The risks and hazards of slipping into the Gulf were little compared to what lay in store. Canny was at the wheel with Digger as navigator. Fielding was wedged between Doug and Buddy with Chancey, Bill and Phil in the rear.

Digger, keeping his eyes glued on the small area of road that the lamps flooded, considered some questions. Would they be stopped by an over-zealous night patrol or border guard? Would they be discovered during the journey across the Straits? How tough would the cliff face turn out to be and how long will it take to get the team and equipment to the top?

As the Rover bounced around through the darkness with its shielded headlights doing their best to spot the next protrusion or pot-hole, each member had withdrawn into that solitude that every good military man and woman has learned to accommodate. An outsider could be forgiven for assessing these eight silent travelers as returning from some drunken party or the core of a baseball team coming home from a major loss, each of which couldn't have been further from the truth. Some might call it 'calm patience', or some 'a withdrawn consciousness'. But to those who use it and rely on it in those moments before entering the storm, it's a welcome relief. For some it's a chance to shut down the questions and doubts about how it will go, an opportunity to still the constant stream of data that swirls around the mind attempting to anticipate those moments when the ability to make good judgments will be tested.

It wasn't long before the Rover had ducked low around the outskirts of the coastal city of Al-Khasab, navigated its way to a small sandy trail that took them out to the headland and headed north-east toward the tip of Oman. Forty minutes had passed since they had first set foot on Oman soil and as Canny brought the Rover to a halt in a dip off the left of the road, a sense of relief filled the air. The passengers piled out as Canny shut the engine and lights off. They knew roughly what the terrain and the hazards would be from the aerial photographs Fielding had handed out during the flight while they changed into their black suits, but now to get a first-hand look. They made their way over to the edge of a rocky crevice and crouched down behind a clump of small scrub overlooking the cove. All was not what they had expected. Bill was pointing down to a leeward crag just under the face of the gentle drop to the beach, and there, half hidden off to the right, was a small makeshift lean-to.

"How long has that been there?" whispered Digger to Fielding.

"I don't know. It certainly didn't show up on the aerials."

"How long ago were they taken?"

"I don't know, but it's there now so what do we do about it, go somewhere else?"

"Perhaps not." Digger clambered over to where Phil and Bill lay looking down at the cove. "Do you think you can get down there and check that hut out?"

"No problem," Phil replied.

"Very well, but don't take too long."

Bill and Phil had a quiet word with each other followed by what appeared to be a coin toss. After checking their equipment the two slipped away into the night while the rest went to work. The Rover was unloaded as Doug and Canny started to cut as many long scraggly branches as they could find to not only cover the netting but also to brush away their traces.

Meanwhile down on the beach, to the two recent visitors the lonely hut, at least from a distance, looked empty. It was made of a mixture of corrugated iron and driftwood using part of the rocky cove as one of the walls. A large hole in the rear looked out onto the grassy slope that ran down to its base while the door gave access directly to the beach. Bill had made his way around the slope to come down immediately behind the wooden structure, staying high enough to retain a clear view of his team mate. Phil had approached from the side keeping his feet off the beach as much as possible. Having reached the closest point to the entrance Phil lowered himself flat to the sand. He reached into his belt pack and pulled out what appeared to be a radio with head-phones. Pushing the miniatures into his ears he plugged the tiny cable into the top of the radio and switched it on. Any onlooker would have been forgiven for assuming that one of *Gold Seal's* crack scout team was going to take a break from the action and catch up on the weather forecast or listen in to his favorite overnight talk show host. Phil stretched the device out in front of him about two inches from the sand and began to sweep it slowly back and forth in front of him. Inch by inch Phil crept his way closer to the door. On about the twenty-fifth sweep he froze for a moment, shifted his position a body width to the right, and continued his sweep.

Above them the work was going well. Considering the amount of equipment they needed it was amazing to everyone that so much gear had been squeezed into and onto that Rover. Apart from unloading the normal range of diving gear, tanks, radios and weapons, there were three other bags.

"I'm surprised you managed to get all the gear on here," said Chancey, struggling to get the largest off the roof rack. Chancey would not normally have trouble sin-gle-handedly unloading a piano.

"It's a new version of the Dingy." said Fielding matter of factly.

"New?" questioned Chancey.

"Yes, more range."

"Good, we'll need it with all this stuff."

"But what about Digger and Doug?"

"We've brought two MUTs, but be careful, they're the only two we have." Chancey shrugged that look of disbelief as though anyone would doubt his capabili-ties. One by one the various bags, large and small, were carried over to the head of the trail down to the beach. The large irregularly shaped canopy the last bag contained was unfolded and thrown over the roof of the Rover. In just two minutes the vehicle had been swallowed into the terrain, and after the brambles had secured the corners it would have been easy to believe that the Rover could have remained undiscovered for months.

Back on the beach Phil repeated his maneuvers, circling to the side of each obstacle three more times before making it to the open gap in the front of the hut. Bill watched keenly from above the roof line strapping his flashlight to the barrel of the Stoner M-63A lightweight machine gun. Phil made it to the entrance and slowly peered around the corner into the gaping void sweeping his sounder out over the entrance. Satisfied that all was safe and secure, Phil climbed to his feet, put away his radio and headphones, reached for his flashlight and silencer and took a step to the side of the hut to check on his colleague. Bill had climbed down the few remaining feet to the edge of the slope and held up five fingers. They both counted down. At four, Phil made his stride back to the entrance. At three, Bill moved back and crouched down under the window. At two, Phil flipped the safety catch on his automatic. At one, they both took a deep breath and tightened their grips. Zero. Bill shone his narrow beam directly through the gap in the rear toward the rock as Phil shone his in, aiming directly at the far corner. A cot, a couple of wooden crates, a propane stove, a black pot and a mug greeted the squinting eyes of the two intruders. Immediately the flashlights were turned off again as the two relaxed. Phil gave another quick flash of light to the floor just inside the hut and thought he saw a glint. He ran his hand down the side and came across a tiny thin thread that had been strung across the entrance about a foot off the sandy floor. Stepping in cautiously, he studied each side of the entrance to see what the line was connected to and then checked out the pot and mug. He returned quickly, stepping over the line once again to find Bill waiting for him.

"What do you think?" whispered Bill.

"Whoever is using this hangout hasn't been here for a while. The mug's stains are old and the pot's cold. I'll signal the others and clean away the tracks while you go and give the others a hand." Bill returned the way he had come, brushing the soft sand flat behind him as he went. Phil flashed two long and one short up to where Digger and Buddy were waiting.

Immediately the rest of the group grabbed handles and began moving the gear down the soft slope. Digger was already halfway down with one of the bags when Bill reported in. "All's well. Empty, at least for the time being."

"Okay Bill, thanks. Phil?"

"He's clearing a way across the beach."

"Good." It took about ten minutes to get everything down to the beach. They finally took up position just out of sight of the shelter around the windward edge of the cove just the other side of an outcrop of rock. Doug was put on watch as the others broke open the bags and began building their transport. In about five minutes the Dingy II was ready. It was longer and narrower with a small shroud over the nose improving its drag coefficient. Then they turned to their own needs, donning their suits, tanks and masks.

"May I, Digger?" said Fielding as she handed out some energy bars to everyone gathered around the raft.

"Go right ahead," agreed Digger folding his arms.

Gone was the smooth talk and the winning smile. Here was a woman, the oldest member of the group, about to run through a few details concerning the extra gear they were to carry. No-one knew that she was dating a man back in New York City that was ten years older than she was, a broker that had enough financial security that she could have easily bought herself an entire beach full of male models, and had behind her enough dangerous missions successfully completed to last a life time. Yet here she was, completely forsaking the comfort and safety of her Long Island home to face a very professional group of young men about to embark on probably the most dangerous mission they had undertaken so far as a team. For the first time they looked into the eyes of a very determined woman. No make-up, good looks stored in some vanity case, the team began to see a different side of Fielding. A woman who did what she did because she was good at it and enjoyed being so.

Fielding scanned the probing glances. "Listen. I volunteered for this job but so did many other guys. I admit I didn't go through the dive training at Little Creek or attain the high levels of combat readiness that you guys have. But the very same gentlemen who chose you to take this mission chose me out of thirty-five of the navy's best to provide you with a climbing detail. In fact, I had to score a few on top since this is classified as a front line job. Technically my being here is illegal, but you need to climb a rock and plant a few Porkies and I'm here to help you do both." Fielding quickly undid the zip down the front of her dry suit and pulled back both sides of the top to reveal two perfectly formed, round, naked breasts. She thrust them forward and let the whole team have a good look. "Just because I have two of these doesn't mean that I won't hold my end up, and I'm sure your ends are no different than countless others I've seen." Before anyone could cover up their surprise at Fielding's gesture she zipped up again. "I can be just as crude as the next guy, so now you've seen them both we can get on with the business at hand. If at any time in the next six hours any of you feel that I did not perform my duties as you expect, then you have my full permission to write it up and send it directly to Admiral Swanson. I believe business should never be mixed with sex so rest assured gentlemen. Because I'm here on this mission none of you are going to get a chance to know me. I'm the best at what I do and the real reason I decided to volunteer for this duty was because, if I was chosen, I would be working with the best Seal unit the navy has, and that's you. I'm putting my life in your hands, just as much as you're putting yours in mine."

Having had her say she looked over at Digger who appeared as others did to be a little embarrassed over the situation and at the silence that followed.

"Ah, yes, well, what else do you have for us?" he replied somewhat sheepishly.

"In these bags here are the two Miniature Underwater Transports, MUTs. They are much smaller and lighter than what you've been used to but just as fast and twice as efficient. Both the motors and batteries have been reduced in size considerably as you can tell, and, Digger, you can use them safely anywhere in the Gulf including close quarters without fear of being heard. They're very quiet." Pointing to a small pile of bricks in the sand, she continued. "These here are the Porkies, or Piggies as we call them. On the hike in we will each carry one of these in the belts provided. These two packs here are the climbing equipment we'll need. There's two packs of radios, two packs of Stickers for the gun-boats and two packs of supplies." She handed Digger the Stickers and loaded the other pack under a strap in the center of the boat along with the rest of the gear. The team stood and watched as the last straps were tightened. Digger glanced at his watch, turned and looked up at his friends, friends he had worked and played with for the last four years, friends he didn't want to lose.

"Okay gentlemen, here it is." They all moved in closer. "We've made good time. The tide has just started to turn so you won't have to run at full speed. Buddy says that a heading of zero-nine-three should take you straight to a small beach at the foot of the cliff.

You will be able to travel on the surface until you reach the far side of the channel. We'll leave it up to Canny as to how much allowance has to be made for the current. Doug and I will join you over there. We have another little chore to take care of first. Any questions?" Digger looked around at the faces quickly disappearing behind the black-face they were spreading over their skin.

Doug decided to break the ice. "Dig, have you been told exactly how many men we're supposed to encounter?"

"No, not exactly. Could be ten, could be twenty, I don't know."

Then Fielding spoke up. "Is everyone wearing their dog-tags?" They all turned to look at her.

"We took ours off hours ago," said Bill with a smug expression.

They stood there watching her silently, all except Digger. "Fielding took hers off before she even left the States." A series of questioning looks flitted across a few faces as Canny broke up the awkwardness of the moment.

"I've got one for you. What's going to happen when we do get back here and find the resident of Cabot Cove here has just moved back in? From what I've seen there's not too many other places we can get out of here."

"We'll just have to cross that one when we get to it," Digger answered. "Anything else? Okay then, play it by the numbers everyone, the Admiral is counting on us." *Gold Seal* donned their masks, adjusted their supply, checked their watches, dragged the Dingy into the water and, leaving Digger and Doug on the beach, climbed aboard, started up the stern drive and slipped silently into the darkness. Digger dragged the two MUTs into the surf while Doug smoothed out the sand. Quickly rejoining his colleague in the murky wash, the two turned on their bubbleless breathing apparatus, fired up the MUTs and headed off for the two Iranian frigates waiting quietly three miles out in the Straits of Hormuz.

Chapter Seventeen

"No change, Captain. Total of one Typhoon class and three Foxtrots still maintaining heading. Range five miles." Beagle was surprised at the calmness in his own voice. Only once before had his systems monitored four contacts simultaneously and that was in the North Sea two years earlier, where groupings of more than two were understandable being so close to their northern ports.

Captain Davidson returned to the Conn and lifted the handset from its holder. "Good morning everyone. This is your Captain speaking. I know the Grams are due to be delivered but I want everyone up and ready. We have four Russian Boomers heading this way and even though they may be here for a spot of fishing, we're not going to take any chances. Rig for red." The gongs and red lighting brought men scampering to their stations. He put back the handset and turned to his Executive Officer, Commander Mike Young. "Okay, so what do you think?"

"Not sure," Young replied. "Some kind of heavy patrol. They might just be coming over to sniff around a little."

"Four of them?"

"I know," said Young nodding his head slightly. "Maybe we can find out if this bunch has been monitored in this formation before now?"

"Right. I think we should also check to see if we can do some sniffing of our own." Young left the Captain deep in thought to make the call to the Admiral. Meanwhile in a small room ten feet forward of the bridge, Corporal Beagle was keeping his eyes glued to the tracking of the four bogies as he ran diagnostic checks on all of his support equipment. Apart from the two IBM BQQ6 Sonars, Beagle also relied on the Raytheon BQS 13 spherical arrangements for the BQQ6s, the Ametek BQS 15 active/passive for close H.F. work, the Raytheon BQR 19 active for navigation H.F. and, the Western Electric BQR 15 passive towed array. On top of all this, he had one more system available. Although not fully operational he couldn't wait to turn on the new addition he'd been working on and demonstrate it to his captain. Since radar cannot be used from submerged vessels this new GE 375 computer was designed to give Beagle and the captain at the Conn a color display of the tactical positions of the *Philadelphia* and any other vessel, taken from all of Sonar's systems. Displayed three dimensionally on a 2048 color monitor, Beagle was confident that it would change the course of submarine warfare by demonstrating the actual locations of proximity to the *Philadelphia* from a tactical point of view. From the moment the *Philadelphia* had put to sea some three months earlier Beagle had spent every spare moment writing and rewriting the programs. Even though he was giving the current situation his fullest concentration, he had the feeling that somewhere in the deep crevices of his subconscious the last few pieces of the puzzle were falling into place.

Just at that moment, as if his Captain had obtained some higher forms of understanding, Captain Davidson, with Commander Young in attendance, appeared behind him and asked loudly enough to be heard through head-phones, "Any chance of trying out our new toy, Corporal?"

"Not yet, sir, I still have some work to do on it."

"How much time do you need?"

"Not sure, sir. I think I've got a handle on why it keeps hanging up. I think it has something to do with..."

"Spare me the details, Corporal, get Thompson in here to cover for you while you get on and finish it."

"Aye, Cap'n." Beagle picked up his intercom as Davidson and Young left.

Just as they arrived back on the bridge the chief of the boat, Bob Danwall, handed him a communiqué. "Flash traffic, Captain," handing him the copy.

Davidson read it quietly while reaching for the intercom. "Corporal, get on that right away will you?"

"Right away, sir," Beagle confirmed.

"Mike, let's go see if we can get the Admiral to give us a little more time." Davidson sent off another request to the *George Washington* and returned to his cabin.

As Davidson flopped down in his miniature version of an arm chair, he asked himself what these former enemies of the west would want with him and his ship-mates aboard Group Six. Why would four boats link up and approach them, not in single file obscuring their numbers, but spread out in formation giving his systems ample opportunity to pick them up and monitor their movements early on? And why now? During the staggering heights of the Cold War when tempers ran high during close monitoring activities, the obvious threats to western shipping that could have warranted grouping such as this, would have been excusable, if not acceptable. But now, with eased tensions between the new Russian Republic and the U.S and with both old adversaries joining in efforts to apparently bring the nuclear threat to its knees, the Russians were trying desperately to convince the U.S. to send more and more money for aid and assistance. So why would any com-mander be permitted to put together such a show of strength as this?

He sat for a moment staring up at a painting of the great Nautilus hanging above his desk, remembering again what his father had said to him the day he left for what turned out to be his last tour of duty. 'David,' he had said, calling him by the name he had used in those moments when he wanted to get his son's attention. 'If you ever decide to become a submariner there will be moments where you will be confronted with decisions that are based on nothing but hunches. We sail in the dark using our ears for eyes, and no-one can tell you what that uncertain feeling of doubt can do to the clear-headed thinking a captain needs... that clarity that is necessary to overcome adversity, until it happens. But all I ask is that if you ever find yourself in that situa-tion, remember a few well chosen words that were passed on to me by an old friend. You never knew your Uncle, my brother, but he was a sub driver from way back, fifteen years older and a lot wiser. He received his third promotion before I'd even graduated and although I speak of him rarely, he is often in my thoughts. I never knew my father and Tommy took to the role as though it was his purpose in life. He raised me as if I was his own son and just before he left on that tragic journey it was like he knew something was going to happen. So he took me to one side, sat me down just as I am with you now and gave me one small piece of advice. It is this advice that I pass on to you. 'The cheeks of my backside and the cheeks of my face have been bruised and punished more times than I can recall. They bear the scars of countless moments where one after the other they have been turned in the face of pain. But I will die with a smile on my lips for all the death their endurance prevented and for the joy and relief that the warm handshakes that followed, gave me'.

The Submariner gave his son a long hug before leaving the bench to walk down the jetty for what was to be the last time and Davidson now pondered, as he had thousands of times before, whether his father, like Tommy, had felt that impending doom was close at hand. And each time he recalled the moment he wondered if he too would ever have that similar feeling and a similar chat with his own son. Davidson smiled to himself. What chance had he to have a son. He couldn't even get enough shore time to find a wife. Maybe he hadn't tried hard enough. Maybe he didn't want one. Perhaps that one conversation he avoided in his mind so much that he would do anything to prevent it happening, including getting married. Even the occasional search for a loving companion had become a thing of the past.

A knock on the door jolted Davidson from his thoughts. Mike Young came in without waiting for response. "Sorry to trouble you Captain but I think you'd like to know. They've changed course. Now heading zero-zero-five."

Chapter Eighteen

Rear Admiral Bill "Lucky" Lodgers was standing on the flag bridge one floor up from the main bridge watching the launch of two ASW S-3G Vikings ordered out to keep a close eye on the recent visitors, when a rating brought another communiqué. It was the third in fifteen minutes.

> Z031012ZOCT
> FM: PHILADELPHIA
> TO: CINCARA.
> //POOOO2//
> REQUEST PERMISSION TO GO AND MAKE EARLY CONTACT WITH OUR VISITORS. DAVIDSON.
> END...

The rating left as Lodgers laid the message on his desk and opened one of the large starboard windows. He stared down to where the new moon danced a thousand little dances on the crest of the ocean below, down to the depths where the *Philadelphia* was awaiting its confirmation to go in. Could he seriously justify preventing Davidson and his men from protecting the Group as much as they could? He pictured Harry Davidson sitting at the chart table, quietly but impatiently waiting for the reply. He would never allow his men to see he was keen or eager but knowing him as well as he did, Lodgers could see the glint in Davidson's eye in anticipation of the chase. Not that Davidson would reveal anything that could be classified as eagerness, but at least enjoying the responsibility of providing protection for the Admiral. How could he refuse him the task at hand?

As the breeze and salt air filled his nostrils he reflected on the conversation he had had before leaving Admiral Walter's office.

"Bill, here are your sealed orders. I'll be having more

meetings with Gerry Tyson and I'm sure once we've finished clearing the mines we'll be giving you the go-ahead to enter the Gulf. Remember, those Iraqis are just itching to have a go at their peasants in the south and even though we've shut down their airspace for the time being, they might just try something stupid again. If you are threatened, of course you must repel borders. But until we can notify you accordingly, your posture must remain defensive only, at least for the time being."

"Looks like a busy time ahead, Sandy."

"Yeah, better keep your sleeves rolled up just in case."

"Don't worry, we'll keep our eyes open."

"Well, good luck, Bill," said Walters holding out his hand.

"Thanks, I have a feeling we're going to need it." Lodgers shook hands with his chief and made motions toward the door.

"Even so, I wish I was going with you."

"You know something Sandy, so do I. See you."

Lodgers refocused his attention on the waters cruising by below. He searched his feelings as if to recapture the trepidation that he experienced in Admiral Walter's office. None came.

"Admiral?" It was his aid, Marine Corporal Billings with some hot coffee.

"Thanks," said Lodgers cupping the mug in his hands. He began sipping it slowly as the distant lights of the coast of Oman made their long sweep across the bows to the right, part of the ever circling motion required to maintain constant air speed over the flight deck.

Billings made way for Captain Brad Gurney, a giant of a man who easily filled the door frame as he entered the Admiral's bridge. "Admiral, Davidson is due south of us about eight miles out, and he's still requesting permission to close on the four contacts. He reports that the Russians have changed course to zero-zero-five and would still like to intercept them before they get too close."

"Any word from the ASW's?"

"Yes. They sent them a wake-up call with a few so-nar buoys about five minutes ago."

"Have you sent this all back to Admiral Swanson?"

"I have."

"Well what do you think, Brad?"

"I know we're down to just one boat, sir, but in my view this kind of situation is exactly what we need sub support for. If they get five hundred yards off our bows and surface we might have to do some serious maneuvering. So while we still have some time why not give the *Philadelphia* some room to work and go have a look see? At least we might find out what their intentions are before they get too close."

"And what if they split up? We'll need the *Philadelphia* right here."

"Perhaps, but if their plan was to surround us and play some kind of pressure game, I don't think they would have arrived in wide formation as they did. They know we have them in our sights and although there's a good chance they also know that we only have one boat, I don't think they're going to try anything. Their course of action, I'm sure, was agreed on long before we lost the *Louisville*. They'd expect us to be prudent and draw in our skirts so let's do the unexpected. Send Harry out to have a chat with them. We can also make things a little easier all around by putting some distance between us and those subs and make all speed further north into the mouth of the Gulf."

"Okay Brad, I'll go along with that, but make sure Davidson keeps his nose clean. He's got a great reputation for keeping his cool in confrontations but a four-to-one ratio is making me nervous."

"I have complete confidence in him, Bill, and besides, with two Vikings ready to pounce at any moment, any move on their part would spell certain disaster."

"I hope you're right." Captain Gurney left the Admiral to his own thoughts once again. Now, as Lodgers looked back out of the window once more, he became aware of a nervous feeling of foreboding that he'd felt a couple of times before. He still had time to rescind the order, but why? Because of a hunch? Because a gnawing feeling in his gut was trying to tell him something? Many a good decision had been made on a hunch. Maybe the face-off would provide some insight as to their intentions that he could act on sooner rather than later. Lodgers closed his window and returned to his desk still sipping on his coffee. He picked up his intercom to the main bridge.

"Yes, Admiral?"

"Everything in order?"

"Yes, sir. Thirty-five knots, visibility eight miles, all secure Admiral."

"Thank you, Commander." He gently laid the telephone receiver back on its hook and whispered to himself, "It's true what they say. It sure is lonely at the top."

Even though he would see the *Philadelphia* again, for the rest of his life he would curse the day he let her go. Before he would speak to Captain Harry Davidson again he would have spent the most harrowing three and a half hours of his life aboard the *George Washington*.

Chapter Nineteen

Barton brought his jeep to a halt again. He waited and listened. The night air was still, not even a bird called to him over the creaking exhaust. Each time he stopped, he turned his engine off and listened. Either his warning device was faulty or they were running without an engine. He ran back up the road briefly to peer over the last crest but no lights, no noise... nothing. He ran back to his jeep, lifted the rear wheel from its latch, and pulled out a transmitter. Quickly pacing off to the side about fifty feet, he stuck the remote in the dirt, extended the antenna, and turned it on. Upon returning to his jeep he disengaged the parking brake and let the four wheels give in to gravity to roll off down the incline in front of him. After about a minute of this Barton threw it in high gear, leaving the lights off and let the engine kick over as she gained momentum to thirty miles an hour. Following five minutes of sharp left and right turns he reached the flats and drove out from the cliff some two miles. Here he pulled over to the side of the road, spun the jeep around, pointed the nose toward the direction of his remote and turned off the engine. He flicked a couple of switches and an electric motor began its soft whine, raising the horizontal tube from its mooring on the left front fender. Another switch and it rotated to the left and up toward the direction from which he'd come. The tube hesitated for a moment, wandered up and away from the vehicle, and once it had found its target, locked on. Barton picked up the radio's handset and spoke quickly in English.

"Rhinestone to Black Beauty. Rhinestone to Black Beauty."

Immediately his speaker crackled with the reply, "This is Blue Note. Go ahead Rhinestone."

"Force ten gale moving west, imminent. High winds could cause much devastation. High pressure system following. Temperatures in the mid eighties. Frontal system expected in your area in three hours accompanied by heavy air pressure. Will check as far west as possible. Am watching closely. That's all."

"Black Beauty, Blue Note out."

Barton reached down and fired the detonator. The tube wound itself back to its former position and Barton rushed the jeep on from the face of the rock toward the long row of lights in the distance that continued to rumble north in the moonlit dust of North-Western Iran.

Chapter Twenty

"Colonel?"

Standford looked up from his desk. "Yes, Frank?"

"That Korean commercial is still maintaining its heading."

"How large is the course deviation?"

"Well sir, her heading is zero-nine-four when it should be one-six-nine plus. She crossed the eastern border of her flight corridor some eighty miles ago."

"Okay that's enough. Corporal Willis?"

"Yes, sir?"

"Find out what frequency that Korean is using and tell them that in about twenty minutes, no, make that ten minutes, they'll be flying over Iranian air space. They are to turn south on heading one-eight-zero for fifteen minutes before turning east. Got that?"

"Yes, sir," replied Willis.

"Colonel?" Sergeant Jack Berenson sounded concerned.

"Yes?"

"Just received a message from Rhinestone, sir."

"Hold on." Standford stood up and walked round to where Berenson was sitting, took the sheet from him, read it quickly, and handed it back. "Okay, pass it on will you."

"Right, sir. Do you want me to let Rhinestone know they've got something up?"

"No, Johnny, I'm sure he knows. Besides he's probably got his hands full."

"Sir, I can't raise the Korean," said Willis.

The Colonel walked back to the rear of the aircraft to the final row of technicians. "What do you mean you can't raise them?"

"I've checked our manuals, sir. As you know there's one main and five possibles they should be using depending on altitude and location. I've tried them all and there's nothing."

"Try them again," ordered Standford.

"Korean seven-forty-seven from Cairo do you read me, over?" He turned up the small speaker in front of him so that his chief could hear. "Nothing but static. That's all I get on all frequencies. Either their radio's broken, they're asleep at the switch, or, they have it on some other setting that we don't know about."

"How long would it take for you to try them all, Willis?"

"Ten minutes, maybe less. Maybe the pilot's left the cabin and the co-pilot doesn't speak English."

"That wouldn't surprise me either, but even if his English was rusty he'd at least acknowledge us even in Korean. Besides, they must have seen their IFF indicators being set off. Just keep trying."

"Yes, sir," Willis replied.

"Colonel?"

"Yes, Frank?"

"If the Koreans continue the heading they're on now it will take them right over the Silkworm launchers the Iranians have positioned just off the Straits."

"Thank you, Frank. That's all I needed to hear. Anderson?" Standford looked over to the main communications desk.

"Sir?"

"You been listening to all this?"

"Yes, sir. I've got a call in now to their main office in Seoul."

"Good, perhaps someone there can tell us if their boys use a radio at all. We have about thirty minutes before the Koreans really get into trouble so there's still time to warn them off. If you think of anything, let me know. I'm not going to have some stray Korean give those idiots a chance to keep the ball rolling so get to work! And someone get me General Wilson on the line!"

Chapter Twenty-One

Gold Seal had made good time across the Straits and were now submerged.. Meanwhile, even though they had been fighting the tide somewhat, the MUTS with Digger and Doug aboard had made good progress. Digger continued across the middle of the channel to the *Sabalan* while Doug closed in on the *Sahand*. As Doug began his ascent the thick oil that had accumulated from the multitude of tanker traffic that this valuable stretch of water had seen over the years began to stick to his mask. As his head bobbed to the surface he shut the motor down and took off his mask to give it a wipe. About a hundred yards away looming large in the early mist was the *Sahand*.

The aging frigate, purchased by the Shah some fifteen years before, had seen plenty of action in World War II. Although mechanically her years were beginning to tell, outside, reflected in the mass of lights, she proudly displayed a new coat of paint, battleship gray. Doug took one more quick look and then slipped the mask back over his head, fired up the MUT once more and headed off in the direction of her rudder. Although the paintwork didn't look more than a couple of weeks old the Stickers he'd checked before leaving were the same color as the hull. He returned to the task at hand and ran over the procedure to himself, visualizing any problems he might face; come alongside into any prevalent current... steer close to the hull at surface level without banging into the hulk... reach into his chest pack... pull it out... turn it on... face it against the hull... wait for the surface swell to bring him higher... and reach up to place it well clear of the waterline.

The shadow began to take shape in front of him and he followed the procedure precisely. Just as he was about to reach above the waterline and place the device close to the propeller a loud clanging noise nearly made him drop it. At the very moment that Doug was about to place the magnetic base of the mine to the outside of the hull someone had decided to start up one of the Vosper engines. Doug took stock of the situation, waited for his heart beat to slow down, reached up, and placed it on the hull around where the curvature was gentle. The first one was easy. The current was pulling him away from the hull. Repeating the procedure on the other side of the ship where the swells could push him closer to the aging ship, would take a little more concentration. But he completed his mission without incident, glanced at his watch, checked his bearings and headed off down the channel, across to the cliffs where hopefully his teammates would soon be setting up shop.

Chapter Twenty-Two

Davidson had positioned the *Philadelphia* four hundred feet down and about a thousand yards directly ahead of the four Russian boats when he called for Battle Stations. The gongs sounded and additional crews arrived at their posts in a matter of seconds, firing up their targeting equipment.

"Conn, Sonar."

"Conn."

"I'm not totally confident, sir but I think we can have a go at the three-seventy-five."

"Good."

"Would you turn the extra monitor the chief installed in front of you on and give me a couple of moments? I'll try to have something for you in about five minutes, Captain."

Davidson stared at the large, blank monitor inset in the console in front of him. "Well don't delay. If ever there was a test case where this piece of gear of yours just might come in handy, this is it."

"Aye, sir."

"Captain?" shouted the voice of Beagle's right hand man.

"Yes, Thompson, I can hear you."

"They're slowing down to fifteen knots."

"Still in formation?"

"Aye Cap'n. Four spread across two hundred yards. Still slowing. Down to ten knots. Still slowing."

"Chief, give me ten knots and thirty degrees of rudder to the right, I want my stern tubes bearing on this bunch."

Young moved closer to his Captain. "Captain, what about the others?"

"If they turn and run that's fine. But if they charge I want to be facing in the right direction. I'll let the Vikings take care of the others if they turn away." Just forward of where the captain stood the chief of the boat called for thirty degrees of right rudder with just enough steerage to make the one-eighty turn without losing too much of the blocking position they represented.

"Conn, Sonar."

Davidson reached for the button. "Conn?"

"Sir, three of the boats have stopped."

"The fourth?"

"The lead boat is still making ten knots."

"Heading?"

"The same, sir, zero-zero-five."

"Distance?"

"Five hundred yards and closing."

"Beagle? You ready with that tracking yet?"

"Just about, sir."

"Well enough of the 'just abouts,' fire the damn thing up."

"Aye, Cap'n. Coming up now." Everyone stood there waiting for something to happen. The chief was calling out the degrees of turn as the boat listed hard to the right. It took two minutes for the turn to be completed.

"All stop."

"All stop, aye," echoed the order. They stood there for a good minute and just as the captain was about to reach for the intercom one more time the screen flickered into life. First nothing but junk and distortion. But then suddenly, as if kicked by some upset user, the monitor burst into a full tactical display. There, on a blue background, a white profile of the *Philadelphia* appeared facing the bottom left hand corner. Behind it, moving ever closer, was the black boat of the closest Russian.

Davidson was impressed. "Nice job, Corporal, take ten bucks out of petty cash. Now, where's the others?"

"Hold on, sir. Going tactical." Slowly the whole perspective moved as the black and white subs, without changing their respective positions to each other, moved around so that the display presented a frontal shot. The two silhouettes in the foreground were now joined by three other black boats off in the distance.

"Great work, Beagle. What choices do I have?"

"You call it, Captain. Overhead?" The graphic display moved the five boats around and rolled them over as though looking down from above. "Inverse tactical?" Again the picture rolled around to look down the stern tubes of the rear guard. "Anywhere you like, sir."

"Give me the front again will you?"

"Aye, sir. Just one thing, Captain."

"Yes."

"This display, though accurate, is delayed. It's not like a GPS system where the images are only a moment or two behind. The information is based on a combination of SAPS, Sonars and all of our other environment-sensing equipment, water temperatures etc. and then averages out the information. The system therefore can run up to as much as 15 to 30 seconds behind."

Before the captain could answer, Thompson came back on. "Conn, Sonar?"

"Thompson?"

"Sorry to interrupt, sir, but if you can see what I see here, the lead boat is coming along side about fifty feet off the port side."

"Thank you, Sonar. What's her speed?"

"Five knots, Cap'n."

"Very well."

"Sonar, aye."

"Chief, give me five knots and keep pace with her. Weapons, give me firing solutions on Tangos two-three, two-four and two-five, and I want Mark 48s in the rear tubes."

"Rear tubes to be armed with Mark 48s, aye," echoed Fire Control. Bob Danwall returned to his seat behind the steering station and brought the *Philadelphia* up to five knots.

"Steer zero-zero-five."

"Steering zero-zero-five, aye, Cap'n."

"Quick quiet." Davidson signaled to Danwall to take the Conn as he and Young went forward to Sonar where Beagle and Thompson sat side by side.

Beagle was the first to speak, bending his head as though he couldn't quite believe what he was hearing. "Sir, I can hear them talking."

"Good. Can you put it on the speaker?" Beagle switched the audio on. There was nothing but strange wallowing and hissing sounds at first but then, quite clearly, they heard a voice talking.

"It's in English, sir," said Thompson somewhat surprised. "And they're not just talking, they're speaking to us."

"Hello, over there," said the voice. "Can you hear me okay?" The language was English but the accent definitely Russian.

Davidson's voice was soft but urgent. "Corporal, run tape on this lot will you. I'm going back to get as close to the left side as I can. Hopefully I can not only hear him, but he'll hear me." Young followed closely behind. They moved to just aft of the bridge and stood there for a moment.

From the speaker overhead came that question once again. "Hello over there. Can you hear me?"

Davidson took a deep breath and yelled toward the side of the boat. "Hello over there. We can hear you."

"Is this Captain Barrow or Captain Davidson to whom I am speaking?"

Davidson turned, gave his colleague a questioning look and whispered, "Is he serious?" Young shrugged his shoulders. Davidson again took a deep breath and yelled back. "And who shall I say is calling?"

"There is no need to shout Captain. I can hear you quite well, thank you."

Davidson again whispered, "Who does this guy think he is?"

Beagle appeared before him. "Captain," he said very quietly, "the other three boats have started to follow us."

"Same course?"

"Yes, sir. Same course, same speed."

Davidson nodded and just as Beagle was about to leave, his skipper grabbed his arm and asked softly, "Can you hear what's going on over there?"

"Well, funny you should mention it, but I think I hear one or two them laughing once in a while."

"Laughing?"

"Aye, sir, like it's all a big joke?" Davidson nodded once again and Beagle returned to his post.

Once again the distant voice asked a question. "Do

you have any problems, Captain?"

Davidson decided to sound relaxed. "You didn't answer my question."

"You didn't answer mine," came the reply.

"My name is Barrow," said Davidson confidently.

"Okay Captain Barrow, my name is Dubrovney."

"What are you and your colleagues doing in this area, Captain Dubrovney?"

"We are here to complete some training. Do you have a problem with that?"

"Yes, as a matter of fact we do. You know very well we have a Carrier group up ahead that is located in the Gulf of Oman to assist our shipping."

"Yes, we know about Group Six. But what has that to do with us?"

"Your course and heading demonstrate you intend to close in on our group. As you know that is a restricted maneuver."

This time the sound of laughter could be heard quite distinctively. "Ha, ha, Captain, what is this no-no?"

"Captain Dubrovney, you know very well what I mean. We don't close within one mile of your navy and you don't come within five of ours." Although Davidson's forehead still looked calm and dry Commander Young's appeared to be making up for the two of them.

"You know as well as I do we have both come very close to each other many times before this."

"Maybe, but this time there are four of you. That makes us nervous."

"Yes, especially since there is only one of you. Where did your other one go, Captain?"

Davidson gave in and smiled at the Commander. "Boy he's sharp eh?" He turned to continue his dialogue. "Captain Dubrovney, do you expect me to believe that you and three other boats have decided for the first time to pick our location to carry out some training?"

"I do."

"If the roles were reversed and I wanted to carry out maneuvers close to one of your Carriers, would you let me continue?"

"Good question, Captain, but these are international

waters and we will continue our operations. I will tell you this though. We are friends now, right? I mean there is no friction any more between our two nations. Our intentions are strictly peaceful. We will not get too close to your Carrier. But we will finish what we came here to do and then we will leave peaceably.

"How close do you intend to get to our Carrier, Captain Dubrovney?"

"I don't know for sure, maybe two thousand meters, maybe one."

"You can't tell me exactly."

"I'm sorry Captain that's all I can tell you. I have my orders you know."

"Yes, and I have mine. I will accompany you on this training exercise."

"We would rather you didn't but again, to be fair, I suppose we can't stop you either." Again there came some laughter from beyond the bulkhead and it was beginning to grate on Davidson's nerves.

"Very well. We will follow and watch but Captain, do your best to remain beyond one mile of our Carrier or I will be forced to intervene."

"Intervene? Ha ha. You will not need to intervene Captain. We mean you and your colleagues no harm, just as I am sure you mean us no harm. Nice to meet you Captain Barrow." This time it was the turn of the *Philadelphia's* crew to burst out laughing, but it quickly returned to silence after a quick glare from Davidson who turned to Young quietly and said, "Mike, I want you to follow as close to this barrel of goo as you can. But first take us up just long enough to notify the Admiral. Be quick about it. I don't want this joker pulling any fancy stunts right before our eyes and getting away with it. I'm going to have a few words with Corporal Beagle."

"Aye, Cap'n."

Chapter Twenty-Three

Admiral Pat Swanson felt fresh and clean from his shower and change of uniform as he entered his office. He turned on the lights, closed the door behind him and was hanging his hat and scarf in his closet just as John Latchkey came in carrying a fresh cup of coffee.

"Just received word from Rhinestone, sir."

"Good news or bad?" Swanson inquired, returning to his desk.

"Good and bad," Latchkey replied, with more emphasis on the latter. "It confirms our satellite recons on replacing their border defense positions. It reads, 'Largest convoy seen for some time. Heavy, repeat, heavy artillery, up to eight thousand troops amassing from his direction, about three hours from the Iraqi border.' There's one more thing. He's being followed."

"Is it serious?"

"Not yet, but in the six months he's been over there this is the first time he's mentioned it."

"Where's he headed?"

"To the coast, probably up around Hendijan."

"Anything?"

"Not really, sir. The only close option we have is the Pave Hawk on the *La Salle*."

"Well, let's come up with a pick, John, something that can get in and out fast. And in the mean time, give them a call, will you, and make sure she's ready just in case."

"Right, sir."

"Tell me as soon as you've come up with something so we can let him know we can get him out when necessary. I recommended him for the job after we'd worked together in Libya, so the least I can do is provide some help in his time of need."

"Right, sir," replied Latchkey and returned to his office.

Swanson reached for his mug. As the warm caffeine brought color back into his cheeks, Swanson's eyes wandered to the picture frame that took pride of place on the corner of his desk.

Admiral Swanson's apartment was located only a couple of miles away and although he enjoyed its proximity, he tried to get home as often as he could. His official residence was listed as San Diego, California, and despite the long, arduous journey necessary to make it back to the west coast, he endured it as often as he could. Even though the rooms of his cliff-top ranch had been quietened upon the departure of his two daughters to college and silenced by the death of his wife three years ago, he still longed to sit at the workbench out on his porch overlooking the Pacific and continue his hobby. His mind took him back to his last visit home.

He was slipping the plastic sheet over the hull and deck rigging of his fiftieth scale three masted schooner, making a promise to himself that before he left home next trip at least the sails and mast rigging would be completed. So reluctantly as the taxi driver rang the door bell, he carried the model in from the afternoon sun, locked the patio doors, grabbed his briefcase, turned the security alarm on, took one last long lingering look at his masterpiece, blew an imaginary kiss to his wife, Diana, and turned out the lights. It was as if he had spent his life saying good-bye to someone or another. If he wasn't saying good-bye to his family he was leaving behind a crew, and no sooner was he greeted with a welcome home, then it was off to duty once more.

The phone rang on his desk bringing him back to reality far quicker than he would have liked. "Swanson here." As he listened to the voice ramble on about some interdepartmental problem involving funding and appropriations, his eyes fell once more on the photograph.

"Hello, hello. Admiral, are you there?" sounded in his ears.

"Uh, yes, I'm here. You were saying?" Swanson grunted and the monotone caller continued its dialogue. Pat Swanson would make good on the promise he had made to himself and complete the rigging on his next trip to San Diego, but not before a few more gray hairs and a couple more wrinkles had appeared in the mirror.

Chapter Twenty-Four

Major Barton was having difficulty keeping the jeep on the road. The vehicle's somewhat non-standard 300 H.P. V-8, pushing him along at 85 miles-an-hour on the long winding trail up to Route 72 to Ahvaz, was coping fine with the speed. It was Barton's own preoccupation with the rear-view mirror that occasionally allowed the wheels to wander from their path. Ahead, the huge convoy of trucks, tanks and armored vehicles trundled along toward the heart of the southern border with Iraq. Their dim headlights shone from the left, brake lights to the right. His plan upon joining the convoy was to somewhere make a left turn and head toward the coast. He was confident that he could out-run his pursuers unless they had some kind of artillery. Once he had increased the separation to five miles or more he felt they would have difficulty stopping him. If only he could find a short-cut to the coastline and lose them in the desert. Perhaps the patrol he had come in contact with up on the ridge had called in and did some checking or perhaps some mean-spirited security officer came across his tracks while searching for some AWOLs. Whoever it was certainly had a bead on him now. The yellow flasher had been continuing its duty for the past twenty minutes.

Barton brought his jeep to a stop about a hundred yards from the junction. The convoy, perhaps some 20 miles long doing about 35 miles-an-hour was tight, leaving little or no room to squeeze in. But then to his left he noticed a larger than normal gap between two trucks as they approached the junction where his jeep waited patiently. He threw it into gear and hit the junction just as the opportunity presented itself. Cutting the corner off slightly Barton and Goodyear managed to complete a 20 foot right hand skid at 30 miles-an-hour without sliding out into the oncoming traffic. Accelerating to sixty he pulled out and began overtaking the trucks and tanks in front of him. Every now and then a pair of headlights would come screaming up to him from around the next bend and he would dive for cover behind the next vehicle.

Around him, from the quiet peace of the back country, the noise and fumes of hundreds of diesels pushed the overdrive button of his adrenal glands. As if he wasn't already wired from the picture of those chasing him boring into the back of his neck, Barton was now dealing with some heavy traffic, the senior officers located in jeeps throughout the convoy and the few security officials that travel incognito within the ranks, all while keeping an eye out for a good left turn toward the southwest.

As if this wasn't enough to keep the average grade-one infiltrator's nervous system at red line, Barton turned his attention briefly to the dark moonlit sky above. There, over the thundering wheels and squeaking axles, above the pounding four-cylinder diesels, came the shrill roar of jet engines. A traveler making his way across country comes upon many points of interest, but sometimes the speed of the moving bus or train or the stubborn impatience of the driver can make these visits very short. And when the eyes are lucky enough to fall upon some unidentified flying object they are decidedly reluctant to stray from their target. Perhaps a quick glance out of a window catches something unusual, the left hand trying to locate the casually placed camera, the voice crying out to the driver attempting to buy more time. What was its range? How big is it? In just a few fleeting seconds even the trained observer, when asked later to recall precisely all the relevant facts, can find it difficult to describe accurately the shape and form of the brief encounter. How many observers have asked themselves afterwards why they didn't have a camera handy, loaded and ready to shoot. What post-mortems have served commitments to always keep an instant 35mm format close to the right hand, only to never again meet the chance of a lifetime?

Barton knew he only had a second or two. He took his eyes off the fifty or so men hanging out the back of the truck in front of him for a quick glance upward as the deafening roar consumed him. As the aircraft flashed overhead, his memory, like a computer, went through their trained routine. Quantity—Two. Type—Mig-29 Fulcrums. Speed—About 250 knots. Altitude—100 feet. Heading—South-East. Ownership—Iran. Armament— Each carrying two Exocets. Destination—Unknown. Additional information—Each carried two long range fuel tanks. Neither had their external running lights operating. Correction. They just turned them on.

As quickly as they had arrived they disappeared. The raw sound from their nozzles crackled for a moment then died to a whisper as the two Fulcrums roared off into the night sky. As Barton's memory hit the 'save' button a couple of times and the prerequisite BAK just in case, his attention returned to the task at hand. He gave a quick glance at the men sitting quietly in the back of the truck in front of him doing their best not to lose their seat on the rough road beneath them, stood on the accelerator and made a dash for the next truck further up the convoy. Truck after truck, tank after tank, he sped by them all. Some of the men he passed would wave at him or hold up their rifles in defiance and on each occasion Barton acknowledged their gestures. The more vehicles he overtook the more confident he became, and even though he was willing to accept the risks of making it to the lead vehicle, he was determined to find a turn-off. If there were any high ranking officers commanding this armada of trundling troops he would find them up front. It wouldn't take much for them to flag him down and question his orders or confirm his identification. One quick call to the wrong official and his cover would be blown. But Barton had been in spots like this before, tricking his way through, sliding his way out from under to safer havens where he could continue his work.

Suddenly there it was, about thirty yards ahead... a break in the left gully of the road. Barton, seeing the way was clear ahead, pulled out from the column, jammed on his brakes and turned south-west on the sandy trail throwing up a cloud of dust as he went. As the speedometer once again began to climb up toward the sixties he took stock of the situation. He had radioed in the troop movement, made it out of the mountains, joined and subsequently left the huge army heading toward Iraq. As the lights grew dimmer in his mirrors perhaps now he had finally shaken his pursuers. With each bend and twist in the road, with each mile of dust he placed between him and the turn-off, the greater chance he had of losing them altogether. As the wind began to howl off the windshield he reached up and rubbed the hairs on the back of his neck. The feeling was leaving him. The reflex action of constantly wanting to look back for some stray headlight was fading, only to be replaced by something new. Something that began to knock at the door of reason. What was it he thought. It was something he had seen but not noticed. Something his senses were questioning. It was something about those Migs. He allowed his auto-pilot to take the helm as his 'transfer-load' began to play back the brief encounter. They were certainly loaded for bear but they were heading south-east probably back toward their base. They had flown into Iraqi territory and were now on their way home. That was okay even though they carried armament the cease-fire prevented them from using. They had violated Iraqi air space, yes, but as long as they didn't blow anything up it would be considered as reconnaissance. The Iranians did the same thing to the Iraqis all the time. Why weren't they being pursued by Iraqi Migs? Maybe their local radar was on the fritz again. They were flying so low anyway it wouldn't have surprised Barton if even the American's had found it difficult to pick them up. They carried Exocets, but these were mainly anti-shipping weapons not normally used outside the Gulf. They flew low over their own tank and truck convoy glad to discover that their colleagues were once again preparing to harden their border defenses. So what could it be. All he knew was that something was wrong, seriously wrong. But he just couldn't figure out what it was. He trusted his instincts totally. When they cried out for Barton's reason to work on a problem he rarely questioned whether it was necessary.

As the information began see-sawing its way back

and forth across his mind, as though some internal sieve was hoping for a chance find, a little glitter of gold that would make all the work worthwhile, Barton returned his attention to the clear road in front and the task ahead. He checked his gauges. He still had two hundred miles of fuel available without touching his reserves. Engine oil and temperatures looked okay and nothing was behind him. So Major Barton, happy that even his warning light had now ceased to flash, sat back and prepared for the long drive ahead.

Five miles behind him another set of wheels, having had to wait seven minutes before they could find their own gap in the convoy, also ground to a halt. After momentarily examining the freshly dug wheel ruts in the sand they too turned toward the coast.

Chapter Twenty-Five

The level of noise around Colonel Standford had built over the last thirty minutes to a buzz as operators continued to try and call in the Korean flight.

"I'm sorry, sir. Still no response," Willis reported apologetically.

"Well, keep trying. Jack, anything?"

"No, sir, not yet. I'm still talking direct to Korean H.Q. in Seoul. At first they had trouble finding someone who could speak English well enough to understand who I was and what I was saying but finally they put me through to their Director of Operations, however I've been on hold now for some five minutes. They're having difficulty finding anyone who knows anything about it."

"Colonel?"

"Yes, Frank."

"Two Migs, climbing through twenty thousand feet, heading straight for the Korean."

Standford rushed back to his desk and glared at his displays. "I knew it. I knew it. If we're not careful we are going to have some major trouble here. Willis, keep trying that Korean. Jack, get hold of Bahrain. Update them on what's going on and tell them to get some cover up. Then call CINCPAC, I'm not going to let some Oriental joy-rider ruin my day!"

"Right, sir, "

"If we don't contact them in ten minutes, we'll need all the help we can get." Standford flopped down at his console, ran his fingers through his hair and shook his head to himself. "Don't those idiots know where they are?!"

Chapter Twenty-Six

Denny Typi was now beginning to sweat. Senior officers do not like to correct other crew member's mistakes and it would certainly go bad for Typi upon arrival in Seoul. He sat there quietly trying to figure out whether he could get by without mentioning it at all. He knew that since there was a long left turn around the southern coast of Iran, the INS unit would return the aircraft to its correct course on the run in to Delhi. All he had to do was to estimate how much of Iranian air space they would actually fly over. After considerable deliberations, he made a decision. He reckoned that flying fifty miles further east wouldn't cause the Iranians that much concern and since he'd heard other engineers back in Seoul talk about some of their trips over Iranian air space without causing their careers too much damage, he decided to remain silent.

Unfortunately for him that decision was to prove to be a costly one. Little did two of the crew know that there were two Iranian Migs heading straight for them and that someone had switched the radios to the frequency used by Korean airlines local to Delhi instead of Bahrain air traffic control. Strike two.

Chapter Twenty-Seven

Captain Davidson accepted the hot mug of coffee from Young and took another look at the brand new GE 375. He watched his monitor closely as the three Russian submarines to the rear began to maneuver. The Sonar tracking demonstrated that the middle boat was increasing her depth. In the foreground stood the white and black silhouettes of the two larger lead boats doing five knots side by side. To the rear, the bottom boat continued to dive deeper as the left sub moved into the heart of their sandwich.

"Conn, Sonar."

"Go ahead," replied Davidson reaching for the intercom.

"They are changing formation, Captain."

"So I see. Sweep of all contacts."

"Sir, Typhoon alongside to port, three Foxtrots astern, Group Six to the north. No other contacts, sir."

"Very well." The silhouettes, in their new formation lining up directly to the rear of the *Philadelphia*, began to increase their depth and just as they moved lower on the tracking display the bottom of the three moved out to the left and the other two descended past it. Davidson scratched his head for a moment. "What the devil are those guys up to?"

Chief Danwall who had been watching the display with Beagle, returned to the bridge. "Could this lead boat be a blind, taking us away from where the action really is?"

Davidson kept his eyes firmly fixed on the monitor. "Possibly, but while we're all staying in relative close quarters I'm going to stay with Dubrovney." Davidson paused for a moment. "Look at this. The two lower boats are going deeper." The crew stationed to the immediate rear of the bridge had a clear view of the latest addition to the Conn. But slowly, without officially moving from the posts, others began peering and stretching their necks to gain a glimpse of the system in action.

Davidson reached for the switch again. "Sonar, Conn."

"Yes, Cap'n."

"Beagle, how deep can the bottom boat go before this tracking system will start to have difficulty maintaining this view?"

"Shouldn't be a problem, Captain. The more spread out they are, the smaller the images become. Right now I'm working on the range parameters. When I add them to the display you will be able to read out the distances between you and the various contacts."

"Sounds good, Corporal, how long will that take?"

"Hopefully no more than about an hour."

"As quick as you can, Beagle. Oh and one more thing."

"Sir?"

"Any chance you can change the color?"

"Color, sir?"

"Yes. We may regard ourselves as the white in shining armor, but I think Red rather than Black would add a touch of realism to the other boats, don't you think?" The entire room nearly collapsed in laughter but they all managed to hold on to protocol.

"Sonar, aye."

Chapter Twenty-Eight

"Scramble, scramble, scramble! Tags scramble." The blaring tannoys shattered the tranquillity of the aircrews sitting quietly in the 'Ready Room'. Some had been reading, some playing cards, some catching a few extra moments of sleep, but all were dressed ready to go. As the noise filled the room they grabbed their helmets and ran straight out onto the tarmac and into the adjacent hanger, climbing quickly into the three F-16 Falcons of the 555th. Each aircraft was equipped with six soon to be phased out Sparrow AIM-7Fs and six AIM-120 AMRAAMs. The air crews ran the ladders as the ground staff pulled the generator support lines, the cups and pins from the missiles and the chocks. Within seconds the Pratt and Whitney F100-PW-220s roared into life.

Major Dan 'Fink' Hinkley completed his quick start-up procedure and led the other two F-16s out from the bright lights of the hanger into the darkness of the pre-dawn morning, their power-plants whistling softly in the cool morning air. Within seconds their wheels turned toward the end of the runway some fifty yards away.

"Tags aboard?"

"Tag two rolling."

"Tag three rolling."

"Tower, this is Tag one and company, ready and requesting clearance."

"Roger, Tags. Runway clear, gusting at five knots." Cleared to ten-zero, your Delta one-five-zero."

Major Hinkley, followed closely by his two team mates, brought the nose of his Falcon out onto the end of the runway and pushed the throttles forward with his left hand, felt the notch of the afterburner slot and thrust it forward as far as it would go. "Tags rolling. Delta one-five-zero."

"Roger Tags. Targets are two -23 Floggers and possibly two -29 Fulcrums.

"Copy." Afterburners blazing, the three F-16s lifted into the night sky, pulled their wheels up behind them and banked right toward the Straits.

A fresh voice took over, the ever calm voice of the Sentry. "Laser-one this is Yankee-three. We have two bogies heading for a Korean commercial that has just wandered into their air space over the Gulf of Oman. Make for intercept Delta-three-seven. Do not intercept the Migs. Do not cross into Iran. Further instructions to follow."

"Roger, Yankee-three."

"Will advise you accordingly."

"Any contact with the Korean yet?"

"Negative Laser. We are working on it."

"Roger, we're on our way."

Major Dan Hinkley considered his foe. The -23 Flogger and the -27 Flogger looked exactly the same. Weighing in at 16 tons the variable geometry wing single-seater replacement for the -21 Fishbed had few avionics and a Tumansky R-29B turbofan engine developing 27,500 lbs of thrust. With a range of 900 kilometers and a maximum speed at 36,000 feet of 1190 knots, she carried 4 weapon pylons and two 23mm cannons. Her air-to-air Pulse Radar was very poor by today's standards and at best the platform had fair maneuverability. Typically she would carry AA-2 and AA-8 missiles with a couple of AA-7 radar homing. Its greatest attribute is that the huge production runs ordered made the -23 one of the cheapest air combat fighters and the -27 one of the most inexpensive ground attack variants available. Compared to the -29 Fulcrum for example, the Russian equivalent to the F-16, the -23 cost about half.

"Tags, keep it tight," and the two wing men tucked in closer.

Chapter Twenty-Nine

"Colonel, I've got someone from Korean Headquarters in Seoul on the line." Colonel Standford stood up and looked over at Jennings.

"What do they say, Stan?"

"They don't know. The only frequencies they use are those standard to the corridor. Willis has been going through all the permutations but still nothing."

"Great. Tell them to keep the line open. And tell them if anything happens here we'll be sending out a whole team of investigators to find out why a captain of one of their flights has decided to turn his radios off!"

"Right, Colonel. The two Floggers are about thirty miles from the Korean and closing."

Standford sat down and examined his displays. "Damn cloud cover! If nothing else they could've seen how far off course they've gone."

"Colonel?"

"Yes, Jack."

"Tags one, two, and three on their way, sir, plus two Tomcats from the *GW*."

"How long?"

"Tomcats should be close within ten minutes."

"Have you updated them yet?"

"Yes, sir." Just as Colonel Standford was about to call O'Grady, his Irish brogue sounded in his ears.

"Colonel?"

"Ah, O'Grady. We need to keep a surveillance on a situation that's developing over Station Gonzo."

"Okay, Colonel. I called to let you know that it looks like we might have to pull a double shift. A KC-135 was dispatched the moment all this started. They will assist the fighter support and top us off when we need it."

"Any idea of the problem, Mike?"

"Not sure, Colonel. 21 developed a problem after it arrived in the hanger and the other's got a bug in the main generators."

"But what about the other two?"

"20's still going through the refit, and 25 was sent up to cover for us up North."

"Okay, thanks, Mike. It's probably just as well. Anyway, we'd like to see what happens here and follow it through." Standford turned his attention back to his team. "Listen up everybody. Looks like we might be up here for a little longer than usual, so if you think you need to use the head or grab a sandwich from the bin, do it in the next few minutes. If the Migs do approach the Korean I want everyone glued to their seats." Colonel Standford sat staring at his display, watching many of the contacts as they charged toward the Korean. As if by some hidden curiosity that sprang up from the depths of his experience, he hit the print button on his terminal. Within moments the broad sheets rushed from their rollers, spitting out the relevant data of all the contacts being monitored at that moment. Standford ripped it off the machine, pulled a pair of reading glasses out from his pocket and examined the information:

AWACS 2-4COLONEL ROBERT STANDFORD COMMANDING

TIME: 00:52GMT   ALT: 20,300 FEET SPEED: 353 KNOTS
DATE: 1:10:91HEADING: 1-0-1
POS: LONG 26:15 / LAT 55:58
TURN: <<
CLIMBING/DESCENDING : /\ /\
RATE OF CHANGE :110 fpm.
FUEL REMAINING:62,254 pounds

CONTACTS:	HEADING:	POSITION:	IFF:
747 KOREAN COMM	0-9-6	26:08/59:09	KN2CHQG
MIG-23 IRANIAF	1-7-1	27:20/57:30	IRA1M23L
MIG-23IRANIAF	1-7-1	27:20/57:30	IRA1M23L
F-16C USAF	0-8-9	25:88/54:60	USBM15V
F-16C USAF	0-8-9	25:88/54:60	USBM15V
F-15A IRANIAF	2-7-2	30:05/57:12	IRA0M15L
KC-135C USAF	0-9-2	26:02/57:15	USB7-100
MIG-23 IRANIAF	1-1-5	29:69/52:58	IRAM23L
MIG-23 IRANIAF	1-1-5	29:70/52:57	IRAM23L
S-3G USN	2-0-3	24:41/61:02	US6MS2-

S-3G USN	3-4-92	24:40/61:01	US6MS2-
E-2C USN	2-8-8	24:45/60:44	US6ME2-
F-14D USN	1-3-5	24:30/59:12	US6M14-
F-14D USN	1-3-5	24:30/59:12	US6M14-
A-320 INDIA COMM	2-3-6	25:87/65:04	INDC32L
MIG-29 IRANIAF	1-3-6	27:20/54:00	IRAM29+
MIG-29 IRANIAF	1-8-2	27:20/54:01	IRAM29+
MIG-23 IRANIAF	1-9-2	26:05/60:15	IRAM23L
MIG-27 IRANIAF	1-9-2	26:05/60:18	IRAM23L
MIG-23 IRANIAF	1-9-2	26:04/60:18	IRAM23L
MIG-23 IRANIAF	1-9-2	26:04/60:17	IRAM23L

As the tapes continued to record all aspects of the AWACS operations, a few other events were taking place far below the watchful eye of the huge dish. Three tankers with two Frigates escorting them were about to enter the Straits of Hormuz. In the Straits were two Iranian gun boats, one on each side of the channel, and under the Straits two groups of divers were closing in on the rocky coast of Iran. Group Six had ceased circling and were now heading north deeper into the Gulf of Oman. Further out, three hundred feet below the surface were five submarines, four Russian and one American.

Though the latter information was not recorded on the AWACS contact recorder, it was part of the sensitive intelligence information gathering process that was correlated and centralized by the staff of the Officer Commanding at Bahrain, Major General Larry Pullman, who passed all the relevant intelligence back to Washington via NAVCOM II. All of those concerned admitted, at the final debriefing a week after the incident at Station Gonzo, that upon examination of the contact recorder data of AWACS 24, together with the GPS runs for eight minutes to one o'clock in the morning of October the ninth, the decisions and actions of the officers on duty would have been totally different if they had known what was about to happen. But the final pages of the report of that day concluded that hindsight is twenty-twenty, and that no-one was to blame for what happened, no-one was reprimanded for not examining the situation more closely. It was also noted however, that if, by some good fortune, someone had foreseen the events of the next ninety minutes, they could have still averted the incident up to the time the above printout was originally recorded.

But now, as the scheming wheels of misfortune laid down by those enemies of the United States were about to hit the USS *George Washington* as well as the other surface ships that constituted Group Six, time had run out. This moment is regarded by many involved in the ensuing investigation as the remaining few seconds allowed to Allied Forces, which, had defensive tactics been enacted, those actions could have prevented one of the most premeditated and devastating attacks on the United States Navy since Pearl Harbor.

Chapter Thirty

High above the clouds and the sandy dunes of Gulf theater of operations, thirty-two thousand feet above the fresh shadows of dawn the upstairs lounge of the 747 was busy. Much gold braid and heroic stories filled the room as company employees were enjoying showing off to their lessor mortals. Captain Mantu Lu, perhaps the loudest and most affected by the situation was just having his glass refilled at the bar when a steward spilled some orange juice all over his sleeve. Lu turned and barked some remark when he realized it was not the steward's clumsiness that caused the accident but a sudden shift of the aircraft's attitude. One moment flying straight and level, slightly nose-up and the next a hard bank to the right. Lu ordered everyone to resume their seats and rushed in through the cabin door. He found his engineer, Denny Typi, shaking in a cold sweat and his co-pilot, likewise, still on oxygen banking the aircraft to starboard. Lu was about to yell some obscure Korean obscenity at the crew when his co-pilot turned his head revealing a pale look of fear.

"Captain, Captain, look!" cried Don Lee, ripping off his mask and pointing out the window. "Look, jets, Iranian I think. They are going to shoot us down!"

"Ridiculous," yelled the Captain climbing into the pilot's seat. "Typi, where are we? We shouldn't be anywhere near Iran."

"The INS must have taken us over their border but they have no reason to get this close," Lee yelled back.

"Well, they think they do." Captain Lu brought the course round to one-seven-zero. "Lee, what course were you on before you started the turn?"

"I'm not sure, zero-nine-five I think," he said trying to pull a handkerchief out of his pocket.

"Zero-nine-five?" He glanced to his left out of the window to see the silhouette of a Mig, its running lights blinking at him for a moment and then another Mig appeared behind the first. They were certainly crowding him, pushing him to the right. He dropped the right wing a little further and brought the aircraft level once again, but the Migs were still there nudging him once more to the right. Each time he turned further West and straightened up the Migs were there crowding him over some more. It was on the fifth occasion, after he had turned to a heading of one-eight-five just over ninety degrees from his original course, that the skies finally appeared empty. He ran through a very brief cockpit check when he noticed his radio settings. "What is this radio...?" stopping in mid sentence. "Who has altered the settings on the radio?" Both Lee and Typi denied touching the radio but Lu didn't bellieve them. Before any of the crew had a chance to look out of the window to see if the Migs had returned, their attention was suddenly drawn to the loud clanging of an alarm. Above on the main engine control panel, a red light flashed its fire alarm of number one engine.

"Fire! We have fire on board," yelled Lee.

"Shut down the throttle on number one," Lu yelled back as Lee grabbed the throttle and pulled it back to idle. The captain reached up, grabbed the red flashing cover over the extinguishing controls, pulled it down, and pushed the button. "Extinguisher now employed on number one," he said, trying to calm himself as he shut the alarm off.

Lee still sounded distressed. "Did they fire at us. Were we hit?"

"I don't know," said Lu. "Take control of yourself and get on the radio. Find out where the closest airport is."

Just as Lee was reaching for his book of frequency usage for that part of the world another gong sounded.

Lee shouted again. "Fire, we have another fire. Engine number four."

"Thank you Lee, I can hear," shouted back Lu. "Reaching for extinguisher on number four," and he went through the routine once again. "Shut the throttle down. Do I have to tell you everything?" Lee pulled back on the lever closest to him. "Now get on that radio before we run out of engines."

"But Captain, I'm sure they are shooting at us," said Lee nervously.

"Did you feel anything?"

"Uh, no."

"Look out your window. Do you see any damage. Is our starboard wing running-light still on?"

"I see the light but it's too dark to see any damage, Captain."

"Lee, just do as I say."

"Captain," shouted engineer Typi. "We are losing fuel."

"How much?"

"I'm not sure."

"Then work out how much flying time we have. Or do I have to come back there and do it myself!" barked Lu.

"Uh, as long as we make for the nearest airport we should be okay."

"Why do your estimates not make me feel happy? There will be an investigation into all this by our superiors and I am going to make sure that whichever of you put us in this position will make statements that will clear me of all blame."

Lee attempted to make his case. "Captain, the aircraft was on automatic pilot, I couldn't have..."

"Be quiet and get on that radio while I get us down to fifteen thousand. We still have two good engines to land on so calm down and do your duty." Lu pushed the nose of the 747 lower and watched as the altimeter began winding off.

"I knew it, I knew it," mumbled Lee to himself as he desperately thumbed the pages of the reference guide. "They fired at us and hit our engines."

"Keep your comments to yourself," Lu reiterated.

"I got it, one-one-two point three."

"Well dial it up and get someone, will you?" No sooner had the numbers come up than both pilot's ears were filled with chatter.

"Korean commercial, Korean seven-forty-seven, do you read me, over?"

"Yes, this is Captain Lu of Korean Airlines. We are

in trouble."

"Finally!" A big sigh of relief sounded in the Captain's headset. "You are seventy miles inside Iranian air space."

"What?!" cried Lu.

"Just continue on your present heading. Are you okay?"

"No, we are not okay. We had fires in engines one and four and are losing altitude. We need to get to an airport quickly."

"How much damage do you have?"

"Controls are okay but we are losing some fuel. Turning will be slow but we should be able to make it down safely if we can find somewhere. Who are you?"

"This is the United States Air Force. Now listen carefully. We have contacted Muscat airport and they are getting ready to receive you. You will need to maintain a heading of one-eight-five losing altitude to six-zero over the next thirty minutes. Do you understand?"

"Yes, thank you. Course one-eight-five for thirty minutes dropping to six-zero."

"Right," said Willis.

"Have those Migs gone away?" Lu's voice still sounded nervous.

"Affirmative Captain Lu. The Migs are returning to their base. Do you know whether they fired at you or not?"

"I don't know," replied Lu. "We didn't feel anything hit."

"All right. Now we are bringing in two Tomcats of the United States Navy to escort you in to Muscat, so remain on this frequency. They will be contacting you in a couple of minutes."

"What about you?"

"We will be monitoring all radio traffic to and from your aircraft so just take a deep breath for a moment, concentrate on your heading and altitude and get your aircraft down to Muscat in one piece. Okay?"

"Yes, thank you! Thank you very much."

Lu sat back for a moment and surveyed the scene. He was proud of himself. He had remained calm and cool without revealing how frightened he really was of being shot down. He had kept control of the aircraft and crew and with two good engines there should be nothing to prevent him from bringing his passengers down safely. And what was more important, there was a possibility that his good deeds from here on in might outweigh any reprimand, especially if he could get either of his crew to admit to wrong doing before they landed.

Lu suddenly realized that he had forgotten to fasten his straps when he had first sat down and so proceeded to do so as he picked up his intercom for the forward steward station.

"Yes, captain? What is happening, we...?" said the steward hastily.

"Now be quiet and bring me up a glass of orange juice and a cup of black coffee." Lu switched over to the cabin's public address system without waiting for a reply. "Fellow captains, ladies and gentlemen. Please accept our humble apologies for alarming you in this fashion but we have had a slight malfunction with two of our systems. We will be landing at Muscat airport shortly so please return to your seats immediately and fasten your seat belts. Again, our apologies for the disrupted flight but Korean Airlines will do what it can to get you all on your way as soon as possible. Thank you."

The steward came in with Captain Lu's drinks. Both Typi and Lee took advantage of this visit to also order some refreshments. Lu continued to maintain his new heading as requested, preparing in his thoughts for the risks involved in trying to land his 747 at night on two engines at Muscat airport. He knew non-nations had to deal with Oman's custom's officials and their increased tight security and bothersome rules and regulations but for those of eastern or oriental origin it was a particularly harrowing experience.

"Captain Lu, this is Lieutenant Commander Dailey of the United States Navy."

"I hear you, Commander."

"We are here to escort you in to Muscat."

"Are the other jets gone?"

"Yes. Do you still have control of the aircraft?"

"Yes, but I have to be careful of my turns. I'm down to only two engines."

"Are you sure you weren't fired upon?"

"I'm not sure about anything, Commander."

"We will be with you about five minutes after you cross back over the Iranian coast-line. We'll do a visual and see if we can locate any external damage."

Lu sounded surprised. "We are still over Iran?"

"Yes. Just stay on your existing heading and we'll be with you shortly. Once we are sure you don't have any major external damage we will give you Muscat's numbers, okay?"

"Okay," sighed Lu.

"Your radio does work doesn't it, Captain?"

Lu's face turned a bright red.

Chapter Thirty-One

Colonel Standford stood behind his console at the head of the room responding to the demands of his team.

"Two Floggers seem to be zeroing in on the Fulcrums," said Sergeant Jennings, studying his monitors keenly.

"What do you mean, zeroing in?" asked Standford, glancing quickly at his own.

"The -23s are about a 100 miles behind the two -29s heading toward the Straits but whenever the leading two change course the other two follow suit as though they're trying to close the distance."

"Okay, duly noted. Maybe they're trying to form a larger formation together which would mean they have something up their sleeves. Those Tomcats taken over escort duties?"

"Just about to, sir."

"Good. For the time being, we'll let them play their own little games. What's more important is that the Korean is crossing the coast line with the navy in attendance. Did we get any Infra-red confirmation of the Migs firing?"

"No, sir, but they were so close they may have used live ammunition."

"Well thank goodness their aim leaves a lot to be desired, we could have had a real nasty one on our hands."

"Colonel?"

"Yes, Willis?"

"Muscat would still prefer we steer the Korean back to Dubai."

"Tell them the Korean has next to no steering, losing tons of fuel and will be landing there shortly. Tell them that if they try to close the airport or do something stupid like that the two Tomcats of the U.S. Navy escorting the Korean will re-open it."

"Yes, sir."

"Colonel, it looks as though the two Iranian gun

boats are on the move again," said Sergeant Jennings urgently.

"I have them." Standford eyed the contacts flickering in front of him and it was obvious that the two frigates were making for a point right in the middle of the channel. "Willis, notify Captain Fulton immediately."

"Colonel, the radio traffic is revealing some pilot chatter that I think you'll find interesting," said Jennings.

"Okay, plug me in," Standford ordered. In his ears came a multitude of Iranian yelling and shouting. "Good grief, undisciplined bunch aren't they? What am I supposed to be listening for, Frank?"

"Just listen to the tone of their voices."

Standford listened to the babble that ran without pause from one pilot to another. "Sounds like a long string of profanities to me. You getting all this, Salter?"

"Absolutely, Colonel."

"What are they saying?"

"It's garbled, sir. They're not using their normal jargon. Something about big disagreement. It's difficult to tell, their accents are pretty thick."

"Keep on it. I want to know what the hell they're squawking about."

"Yes, sir." The tapes kept rolling and so did AWACS 24.

Chapter Thirty-Two

Commander John Latchkey took a sneak look at his watch as he stood patiently in front of his chief's desk. Admiral Swanson put down the latest communique on the desk, sat back in his chair, and looked up at him.

"Four boats? What in heaven's name do they think they're doing? We usually have to go and search them out, not the other way around." Swanson got up from his desk and walked over to the computer terminal on an adjacent table. After a few seconds of data entry, the system pulled up a list and confirmed that there had been thirty-five reports of four or more boat contacts in the last two years. "Just as I thought, everything from exercises to training. They do spend a lot of time on rescue and recovery, don't they?"

"Yes, sir. But why give us an opportunity to watch this close?" said Latchkey as the Admiral returned to his desk.

"Good question, John. Whatever the reason, let's hope Davidson gets as much footage as he can. Get ahold of the *Nebraska* and *Cleveland* and tell them to make top speed to Gonzo. Shouldn't take them more than six hours. Let Admiral Lodgers know help is on the way and that I approve of his move into the Gulf of Oman. We should be getting the go-ahead to move him inside the Gulf shortly anyway. I'll leave it up to Gerry Tyson to see what can be found out from the Russian Ambassador."

"Yes, sir."

"One more thing, John. I need to know if they definitely fired on that Korean or not. Get ahold of General Wilson's office and see if you can get copies of the tapes. If they make it to Muscat, great. But if she comes down in the drink then I'll need all the hard evidence we can get. The last time this happened we came out with egg all over our faces and I promised the Secretary of Defense that while I'm head of Gulf Operations we will only issue statements that are true and factual. Even if the press has to wait another day, I want it sewn up." Swanson started to hand the copy back to his assistant when he changed his mind. "On second thoughts John, this is something I better deal with myself. It's getting late and I'm sure you've got other plans."

"It is Sunday, sir. I can cancel if you think it's necessary." he replied.

"No, that's okay. But take your pager along just in case."

"Yes, sir. I can be here in fifteen minutes. A quick bite, then down to the club."

"Okay, John. Have a good game," said Swanson sincerely.

"I will, sir," smiled Latchkey as he returned to his office to make a couple of quick calls before grabbing his hat and coat.

Admiral Swanson sat staring at the door for a moment as it closed behind the Commander. Then, as if by some subconscious desire, his gaze began to wander around the walls of his office, finally coming to rest on the large, framed photograph of his wife that took pride of place on the corner of his desk once again. She looked young and beautiful, but yet so far away. Pat Swanson looked down upon her warm and friendly smile and longed for it to move, to suddenly spring to life. Although it had been just over a year since her soft grip slipped from his for the last time that night in the hospital room, it seemed like decades. How is it, he thought to himself, that memories can be so long suffering while at the same time lose the very essence of pain and pleasure? It was as if the swelling of sadness that began to build inside his chest was doing its best to forget the comfort and security he had always felt when she was around, paying little heed to the one small tell-tale tear of confirmation that slid down his cheek. If time could heal all wounds, he pondered, why couldn't it also heal the guilt that hid under that noble responsibility that was born from pride and duty? How can everything he had worked so hard for slip from his fingers so quickly, just as Diana's did on that fateful evening?

Her long fingers curled as she turned her head toward him.

"Pat," she had gasped.

He leaned forward so that his ear wouldn't miss a word. "What is it, Annie?" he said squeezing her hand back in encouragement.

"Pat, you will be okay." Her voice now just a faint whisper. The bountiful joy, the exuberant tones of her southern heritage all but gone as she gathered every ounce of energy to speak to her life-long love. In return, her husband of thirty-five years held his breath for fear that the sound of his breathing may drown out what little volume she had left. "It's not your fault, Pat. I don't want to go knowing that you think it's all your fault. It's not. Our Lord has taken care of us and our children for so many years. Thank him for that. Don't let guilt walk all over the great times we had." Her voice began to fade, to disappear down that long tunnel of emptiness. He had been dreading this moment for the past three months ever since they had discovered the cancer. She had been out at the supermarket and just as she picked up a bottle of the Admiral's favorite pickles her arthritis grabbed at her knuckles preventing her from maintaining her grip on the jar. It fell to the floor, shattered and in her eagerness to avoid the flying glass, she slipped on the contents and fell. Diana Swanson hadn't broken any bones and save for a nasty bruise on her hip, thought that after a few days rest she would be fine.

She wasn't. The bruise healed and her life returned to normal but after a couple of weeks she started to feel edgy. Her appetite disappeared and Mrs. Diana Swanson, in the space of a few short weeks, went from a wonderful shining star in the life of her Admiral to a dark cloud about to pour her last few tears of substance on his long and meaningful career. Somehow the fall had vitalized some dormant cancer, a cancer that could have remained so for another twenty years, to spring into its deadly commitment. So quick and lethal was its progress that all the medical help the navy could provide proved hopeless in its cause. From a well endowed one hundred and forty pounds she now lay a mere skeleton of her former self, forcing her last gasps of reassurance at the only man she ever loved. "Pat, my dear," she gasped. "You have given me the best years any woman could ask for. Thank you. Now, say that you'll be okay and kiss me."

Pat Swanson looked longingly in her eyes and said gently, "I will be okay, my darling Annie." He kissed her softly on the lips, saw the attempt of a smile, and felt her hand slip out of his. As he sat by her bed wishing that some magic wand would wave and bring her back, Swanson reflected on how wrong she had been. He had spent so much time at sea, so much time away from San Diego to enhance his position, that the actual time the two of them had spent together enjoying each other's company was in fact infinitesimal.

His career had always come first and now that retirement was just a few years away, his purpose in life had left him. Why hadn't he spent more time with her when he had had the chance? Why had he taken the extra duty when it was offered? Because Annie had said it was alright. She'd said that they'd have time to travel together later and that she was a patient woman, willing to wait. Now, he was the one who would wait. Wait for the end of his duty and look forward to nothing.

During the months following the funeral Vice Admiral Patrick Swanson had shaken his depression and decided that if his wife could devote her life to him, then he was going to devote what remaining time he had to do the best job he possibly could. Not for Annie and not for the navy, but for himself. However selfish he thought it might sound, he had summoned up all the determination he could muster and projected it all into the task at hand.

Just as he put his handkerchief back in his pocket the phone rang.

"Yes?"

"Sir, Major Hughes here."

"Yes Major, I was just about to call the General," said Swanson clearing his throat.

"Got a message from Commander Latchkey that you

wanted all the hard data on this Korean thing?"

"That's correct."

"Well, Admiral, I've just got off the line with General Wilson in the Med. and the word is we don't know. The Korean pilot didn't feel anything and we've just received word that there is no visible damage to the exterior of the aircraft save for the two engines that caught fire."

"Which two?"

"One and four."

"Would you let me know when our Sentry has confirmed a safe landing?"

"Certainly Admiral. Will that be all?"

"Uh, no. Next time you talk to him, ask him if he wouldn't mind us sending a couple of investigators local to Muscat to check this thing out on the ground. If we go through channels it'll take forever to gain State Department permission and we don't want to waste any more time on this thing than is absolutely necessary."

"You have a team in the area, sir?"

"We do," said Swanson.

"I'll let the General know, Admiral."

Swanson put the phone down and pulled a blank order form from his desk.

Chapter Thirty-Three

Canny had brought the Dingy and its occupants as close to shore as possible without breaking the surface, but with the limited depth and swirling current beginning to buffet them around the time had come to shut the motors down. Following Canny's signal, the divers let go of the straps and waited for the boat to settle to the bottom. Bill and Phil worked on the anchor lines while the rest unloaded the four bags and swam the few remaining yards to shore. The cliff, set back in the cove and shrouded in mist and spray, rose tall and straight in front of them like a fortress. The team, a little awed by the cliff's overwhelming size and flat face, began divesting themselves of all the air tanks, masks and flippers, changed into their walking clothes and began passing out the climbing equipment. Buddy looked up into the night sky and noticed briefly a series of twinkling lights heading west at about fifteen thousand feet. He pondered before shrugging himself back to his duties why three or more aircraft would be flying in formation. He crunched through the wet sand up to the wall of rock and started to feel around for the pits and crevices necessary for grip, but the more he looked at the face the more impossible the climb appeared. He then went over to Fielding who reached for her waist and stripped off the bottom of her suit right in front of him.

"What are you doing?" he said into the sound of the soft surf, unsure of which way to look.

"I'm preparing to make the climb. What do you think I'm doing?" Reaching for a 'dry' bag she finished pulling her feet out of her suit and proceeded to pull on a pair of thick tights, while Buddy turned to face the channel, doing his best to keep his admiring glances undetected. "It's okay, Buddy." She reached for the clasp of the zip at her neck and pulled it straight down in one complete motion. But before his glances could catch all the curves shown off below her two strong shoulders a black T-shirt dropped down to her bottoms. She finished undressing beneath the shirt and quickly pulled on a light pair of shorts.

"Is that all you're going to wear?" Buddy continued undaunted.

"It's going to be hard enough getting up that thing without carrying a lot of unnecessary clothing," replied Fielding, pulling her harness around her waist. Buddy seemed to take stock of the situation. He looked down at her on the beach reaching for a pair of climbing shoes and turned upward to look at the rock-face shaking his head. Fielding glanced up as Buddy finally knelt down beside her. "What is it Buddy?" she asked earnestly.

"That's one hell of a piece of rock, Charlie. Is there anything I can do?"

"Yes there is," said Fielding. She rose, walked the few feet over to one of the bags spread out on the sand, picked out a large belt, and strapped it around her waist. Hanging from it, Buddy thought to himself, were enough tools to start her own joinery shop. She sorted out various lengths of line in front of her and, satisfied that she had located the correct one, made a knot and loop around the main hanger on her harness. She picked up a pair of night glasses and turned back to Buddy.

"Look," she said to him coldly. "You've climbed enough to know what I need down here, someone who can take care of the lines if I fall. How much do you weigh, one-eighty?" she asked, letting a smile sneak out from under her determined look.

"One-ninety-five," Buddy responded also revealing a slight grin.

"Good, then you shouldn't have any trouble." She turned and walked the few paces toward the retreating surf.

Buddy ran up behind her and half grabbed her arm. "Hey, you didn't tell me how much you weighed."

"I know."

"Well?" Buddy began grinning again.

"One-fifty-five," said Fielding turning back to take a long look at the face of the rock with a pair of night glasses.

Buddy looked down at her thin waist hidden beneath the belt and then on down to the black tights and said, "You must be joking!"

Fielding ignored Buddy's poor math and began searching for a route. No specific time limit had been set for this operation but with the sun due to rise in two hours or so, she knew that the clock was not on her side. "Okay. I think I have it," she said finally, handing Buddy the glasses. "I know you'll have someone out here watching for Digger and Doug when they arrive, but I need someone who is not going to be distracted by what's going on behind them to keep an eye on me with these. When I get to the top I want you to wait until you get my signal before attaching the other end of this line to the gear. I will flash my mini-torch down at you when I have the line secured through the pulley, then get the others up as quickly as you can. I'm hoping that Digger will arrive by the time we have our first volunteer up so that the pulling can continue from down here. The rest is up to you."

"Can you wear one of our headsets?"

"Yes, but not right now, Buddy, this is going to be hard enough as it is." Fielding walked confidently over to the left hand side of the beach and reached up.

Buddy was right there beside her. "Good luck, Charlie," he whispered.

"Thanks, I'm going to need it." In three quick moves, she had left the beach. Her shoes already above Buddy's head, she hung out from the side of that rock as if climbing a ladder. Even though he couldn't see a mark in the rock face, somehow Fielding was getting a grip.

Buddy ran back to Bill and Phil. "Bill, here's the night glasses. Take up a position as close to the water as you can and wait for her signal." Bill left to take up his station. "Phil, I want you to keep a look-out for Digger and Doug." He turned back to the cliff face to find the end of Fielding's line was already being handled by Chancey. Buddy went over and took it from him. "Clear the lines behind me, will you?"

"Sure thing," replied Chancey. "Boy, can she move! Did you feel how wet the bottom half of this lump of slate is from all this mist?"

"Yeah," said Buddy not taking his eyes off the distant shadow that loomed above him.

Silence fell among the group as each went about their assigned tasks quietly and efficiently. Bill couldn't help but admire the courage of this climber in front of him. The strength in her fingers was obvious. For her to be able to scale with so few holds to grip onto, and whereas many would have stopped often to spend valuable minutes securing pitons and caribiners every few feet, this girl used them sparingly. Occasionally it would appear that her feet were higher than her head as she searched for a grip and it was obvious, even to the casual on-looker, that the length of line between her and the last secure hanger was considerable. Although this allowed her to save time it certainly multiplied the distance of any fall immensely. The line from her waist ran back through the hangers and on down to where Buddy stood, feeding it from around her waist on up after her, but ready at a split second's notice to catch it and hold fast if she should slip. And slip she did.

Fielding was about eighty feet up moving over to the center of the face when her grip failed. It was a credit to her short finger nails and incredible strength that it hadn't happened before. She had played out the line from the last caribiner by about twenty feet when the line in Buddy's hands grabbed. He wrenched on the line as hard as he could, momentarily being lifted off the ground only to feel a similar tugging from behind. As a precautionary measure Chancey had wrapped another loop around himself to take up any slack. Even from that height as she swung to and fro across the face of that rock, Buddy could hear the tearing and scraping of flesh as she tried to bring herself to a stop. There was no cry of pain, no sharp yell of anguish, just a brief pause in the tension on the line and then, as if gravity had just been turned off, Buddy's line went limp and Fielding regained her footing to began her climb once again.

Lieutenant Fielding was to slip six more times after that and each time, although Buddy had known that he and Chancey could handle the occasional jerking of the line, he knew that her safety depended completely on how well her last caribiner had been secured. He remembered all too vividly an incident during training where the tugging had been severe enough to wrench the piton from its mounting causing the climber, one of his former teammates, to fall the distance to the previous one. By then his rate of descent was such that the next one also sprang from the rock. In eight huge jerks of the line, and in as many seconds, his friend was dead. Maybe the pitons had not been hammered home as far as they should have been for his weight, but once he had begun to fall, there was no time to go back and hammer them home.

Fielding may not have broken any speed records on her climb to the top of that rock of Iran that night, but to do it without making a sound, on wet slate, having to do everything by feel without the aid of a nice sunny day, to Buddy and the others was impressive. Buddy never had cause to be proud of a woman before, he thought to himself, save for the day his baby sister graduated from Yale a couple of years ago. But here was a woman who was intelligent, strong, and fit and maybe could even teach him a thing or too. As he craned his neck up one more time to look at his new found colleague, the cheesy grin belied the fact that he was beginning to accept that maybe looking up to a woman wasn't such a bad thing after all.

Chapter Thirty-Four

The convoy had entered the Straits on a heading of zero-five-zero thirty minutes earlier and was preparing to make the long hundred and twenty degree turn to starboard into the ever narrowing channel around the tip of Oman. The two aging Iranian Frigates had taken up positions about halfway around the turn and even though their behavior was considered by all as aggressive, they weren't actually preventing the forward progress of the five ships. What Commander of Operations Persian Gulf, Tandy, aboard the *Independence* had to decide was, whether to bring the convoy to a dead stop, placing them in the middle of the narrows with little or no control over any drifting into shallow waters, or allow them to continue. In the latter case Admiral Tandy weighed the various scenarios that could unfold. First, and most likely the Iranians may do nothing as the three tankers roll slowly by. The tensions had eased substantially between the two nations and to attack now without any provocation, would be regarded as a needless act of war. Secondly, however, he could not dismiss the possibility of some form of illogical confrontation. Although the channel was some twenty-five miles wide, two small Frigates can still have a big impact on ship movements in and out of the Gulf. By playing a dangerous game of bluff, dodging in and out of the way of large tankers that have no room to maneuver, many a loyal oil company captain would be scared off, begging their owners to avoid the Gulf altogether. Warning shots by either boat would also have the same effect. But to what end and how far would it lead? These were questions that needed analyzing. Signals were being rushed to various Iranian ambassadors in Washington to warn them to stay clear but time was running out and a decision had to be made. Just as he was about to send Fulton an order requiring them to slow to five knots, word arrived that the two Fulcrums had split up. One was heading straight for the turn in the Straits of Hormuz, the

Stork and its charges, while the other had turned toward the Gulf of Oman. Were they going to buzz both Group Six and the tanker convoy or neither, Tandy asked himself, examining the latest reports. If he brought the tankers to a halt now they would be sitting targets. Would the *Stork* have enough warning to shoot down any attack before they came within range of the channel? And even if Fulton had time, they would still be over Iranian air space. Without provocation, how could the captain fire before they launched any Exocets? Admiral Keith Tandy made his decision and sent word to Captain Fulton.

On board the *Stork* Fulton had just arrived in CIC when Commander Lemke handed him the signal from the *Independence*.

"Sound General Quarters!" barked Fulton, taking note of its contents.

"Aye, sir. General Quarters!" Lemke confirmed as he reached for the sounder.

"Closing time for the contacts?"

"Seven minutes, sir," replied Radar Technician Porter.

Fulton grabbed the handset and punched the button for the bridge. "Don, make the turn to port and give me full speed. We need to pull alongside the *Mishtosh* and prepare to repel from the port side." Fulton replaced the handset. From astern of CIC the turbines wound themselves up to full power on the *Stork*, steering left, rolling to the right, made her way past the ten million gallons of crude oil aboard the *Shkirto*. "Dick, call each tanker in turn and ensure that all their crews are up and ready to fight fires."

"Aye, captain."

"Fire control, load and arm all harpoons and Phalanx." Harpoon racks forward and aft began loading, spinning quickly toward the north as the single Phalanx Gatling located just behind the forward superstructure swung round to join them.

Radar technician Porter began his routine of updating the Captain. "Sir, one bogie still maintaining course one-seven-five, range thirty miles."

"Okay," said Fulton, as he took his seat behind master control.

"Two twenty-threes, range sixty miles, still following the Fulcrum, plus three more Migs now closing in on the other Fulcrum and Group Six," Porter reported.

"Is there enough room to get through ahead?" asked Fulton.

"Plenty," replied Lemke.

Fulton sat glued to his full color display as he continued his dialogue with Commander Lemke. "Any IR or homing radar yet?"

"Yes, sir. Trace of homing radar coming up on the Frigates now, weaponry coming up."

"From the Frigates?" Fulton asked.

"Yes, sir, and now from the Fulcrum in return."

"What is this an exercise? Are the Frigates aiming at us?"

Porter interjected, " Not yet, sir, they're turning all their weapon systems on the incoming Fulcrum."

"What are they doing, planning to blow their buddies out of the air? Call it the moment they turn on us."

"Aye, sir. Convoy now starting its turn to starboard. The *Sahand* is on the move."

"Thank you, Porter. Any other contacts?"

"Just the two Tomcats from the *Washington*, the Korean and three Falcons coming straight at us from Bahrain."

"Very well."

"Contact still holding course one-seven-five, range sixteen miles," said Porter loudly.

Commander Lemke was handed another signal. "The Mine sweeper *Lipton* is reporting that the *Sahand* has started to move back across the channel!"

"Perhaps they're going to give us room to get by without altering course after all," said Fulton, wiping a little sweat from his brow.

"Now fourteen miles out, still closing," updated Porter.

"Dick, how far to the Frigates?"

Commander Lemke, who all this time had been keeping an eye on the *Stork*'s heading while preparing the lower helm station, took a quick glance at the scopes. "Five miles. Steering thirty degrees, now zero-eight-two."

"How much room do we have to cut the corner off?"

"About two miles," Lemke responded.

"Tell those tankers to make a sharper turn and head directly for the inside channel marker. I think we've just got enough time to head floating seap-heaps off at the pass." Fulton picked up the intercom to the bridge once again. "Clear the bridge." Far above CIC all the personnel assigned to remain on the bridge were now running the stairs. "Lower bridge station, you have the helm."

"Aye, sir. We have the helm," replied the secondary helmsman.

"Stop the boat! Reverse engines!" ordered Fulton.

"Reverse engines, aye." The rumble of the turbines died momentarily and then built to speed once more as the props began digging in.

Captain Fulton zoomed his screen to the short range radar screen showing all the contacts within a fifty mile radius. "Fire control, I don't want any trigger-happy mistakes here. You fire on my order only and not before."

"Aye, sir."

"Fulcrum now seven miles and closing," Porter's voice beginning to reveal his sense of urgency.

"Still active?"

"Yes, Captain. They've turned on everything they've got."

"At us?"

"No, sir. At their own Frigates."

"All back one third."

"All back one third, aye," the helm responded.

"Fulcrum now thirty seconds away."

"Any locking radar from the Frigates?"

"Yes, sir, but on the Mig, not us. *Sahand* continuing across the channel completely out of our way, Captain."

"Good. Two down, four to go."

"The Mig fired!" cried Porter. "One bogie in-bound." Commander Lemke made a move to Fire Control.

"Not yet Dick," Fulton said firmly holding up his hand.

"It's locked on us, Captain!" cried Porter, as warning tones sounded all over the ship. The stern of the *Shkirto* moved ahead of the *Stork*'s bows.

"Both ahead full."

"Both ahead full, aye."

"Fire FLASH."

"Firing FLASH."

"Hard a-starboard," barked Fulton.

"Hard a-starboard, aye," replied the Helm. As the scope began its rotation the launchers and Phalanx joined in the pirouette, retaining their watchful eye on the in-bound, apparently ignorant to the *Stork's* turn behind the *Shkirto*.

"In-bound bogie, forty seconds to impact," the voice near to a shout.

"Phalanx working," reported Fire Control.

"Any more inbounds?" Fulton shouted.

"Negative, Captain, just the one."

"Fire FLASH two."

"Firing FLASH two."

"Steer two-four-zero," ordered Fulton.

"Twenty-five seconds to convoy."

"Steering two-four-zero."

"Fire FLASH three. On my command I want every single radar shut down including the Phalanx. Give me the count."

"Fifteen seconds to convoy. Thirteen. Twelve. Eleven. Ten. Stern on to inbound now, Captain. Eight. Seven. Six. Five. Four. Three..."

"Now! All radars off."

The inbound Exocet's radar was still attempting to turn the missile to the right when it lost contact with the *Stork*'s radar and flew right through one of the Flight Levy and Alternative System Homers, fifty feet up and eighty feet off the stern of the *Stork*. Fulton counted off two seconds then ordered the Phalanx turned back on and instantly it swung to the right and filled the air with lead. A split second later the Exocet disintegrated, the force of the blast and the debris flying harmlessly into the Gulf.

It was a great move, not one out of the naval book of

procedures for defending a Frigate but nevertheless a move that was later applauded by Admiral Tandy. Fulton had timed his move perfectly. To turn the *Stork* stern on to the inbound, presenting a small target for three or four seconds was Standard Operating Procedure. But shutting down the radar, while giving up any chance the Phalanx may have had of bringing down the inbound, it also prevented the in-bound from using the *Stork*'s own radar to home in on. Left to home-in on the relatively small signature the stern of the *Stork* presented, especially since it had been fired late, the confusing FLASH was sufficient to distract it from its task.

At the moment of impact, Captain Fulton ran up to the port deck with just enough time to see pieces of debris flying around and the -29 Fulcrum scream low overhead turning North up the Gulf. There was no other damage and the *Stork* churned through another hundred and eighty degrees, reduced her speed and regrouped behind the *Shkirto*. The *Sahand* and *Sabalan*, now pairing up on the far side of the turn, remained quiet but watchful. As the *Stork* cruised by the two catalysts Fulton pondered on how their crews had reacted to the attack. Were they cheering or booing? He didn't know and for now, he didn't care.

Chapter Thirty-Five

The three F-16s were closing in on their targets.

"Laser one, this is Yankee-three."

"Copy."

"Your new Vector, zero-seven-three for bogie."

"Roger, zero-seven-three," Major Hinkley replied dialing the coordinates into his navigation computer.

"Target, single Iranian Mig-29 Fulcrum."

"Tally one, nose."

"Threat is leading bogey."

"Roger, Yankee. Tag-one to flight, our bogey is the leading -29 only. Target other two. Wait for my order."

"Nine hundred closier. Tag-two, roger."

"Tag-three, roger."

"Bandits your one-six-five." Sentry's flat voice ever calm in the heat of battle.

"Copy."

"Three will take the southern," Tag three confirmed.

"Just the one hit there."

"Copy." Hinkley's breathing grew stronger as they rolled on to target.

"Estimated mark south."

"Roger. Confirm, tally two. Push it up."

"Two will take eastern," Tag two confirmed.

"Heads up three. Watch out you don't shoot through me."

"Roger, Fink."

"Tallies on all three." Hinkley's HUD's targeting display encircled the Mig. The square box sat firmly in front of him flying directly up the Gulf toward him. He touched the target button and the square shifted to the right a fraction, distance plus five. He touched it a second time and it darted higher. Hinkley reset and armed the first AIM-120A AMRAAM as the distance to target was now down to fifty miles. As he readied his finger on the trigger he considered for a moment why the Fulcrum hadn't made a dash for safety. Surely the Mig's passive radar could see him coming right at him. Perhaps it was preparing to fire. But the Fulcrum hadn't turned on its attack radar; his warning tones would have sounded. He decided to get in closer. "Forty miles," confirmed Tag two.

"Hey, is anybody in burners?"

"Affirm," replied Tag two.

"Everybody out of burners. Target acquisition. Good tone."

The gentle female voice of the computer joined in, "Bingo, fuel. Bingo, fuel."

"Thirty miles," said the flat voice. "Check low."

Hinkley lifted the cap and pressed the trigger with his thumb. "Firing. Fox one. Fox from one." He tapped the target button and the square jumped to the right.

"Roger, fox one." The targeting square moved to his left.

"Closing now," said the Sentry's voice in anticipation.

"Good kill, good kill!" shouted Tag three.

"Pilot ejecting!" yelled Tag two.

"Splash one from one!" Hinkley shouted.

"You're clear."

"Roger, Yankee-three. Tags, knock it off, disengage. Break right."

"Tag-two, roger."

"Tag-three, roger." The targeting on the other two Migs fell off to the east as the three F-16s banked hard away from the threat. Hinkley couldn't believe how easy the mission had been. This had been his first experience of combat conditions against the all new Fulcrum with their first fly-by-wire control systems and up graded avionics and he'd got away lightly. Their radar was certainly as good if not better than his and if the Fulcrum had been carrying any AA-10 Alamos, he could have let one loose thirty miles out, but they hadn't even armed anything. They must have known it was under attack. They had similar cockpit tones to warn the pilots of hostile radar as Hinkley did. Even if all of their systems failed, why hadn't he made a run for it?

These questions and others continued to run through Hinkley's thoughts as the three Falcons made their way back home. It was these same questions that Vice Admiral Pat Swanson would soon be asking his colleagues.

Chapter Thirty-Six

"You are now fifteen miles from the end of the runway," said the calming voice in the headphones of Captain Lu. "Turn to heading two-eight-two."

"I've got another eighty degrees to go and I'm not sure how tight a turn we can make." replied Lu.

"That's okay," replied Corporal Willis, calmly. "Just keep following the aircraft in front of you. We have taken you far enough south to allow you enough room to make the long slow right turn to line up for the runway."

"I see some lights in front of us down there in the Gulf!" shouted Lu suddenly.

"Relax, those lights are American shipping we have on hand just in case. Maintain your turn to the right." Denny Typi crouched between the pilots' seats and waited for the command. "Lower power a little on number three. Increase a little more on number two," and Typi gently manipulated the controls accordingly. As the Captain dropped the right wing again he looked up to see the aircraft in front him bank further to the right.

"Looking good, Captain. Now straighten up on two-eight-two." Lu relaxed the pressure on the rudder, called for equal power and straightened the wings right on the money. If nothing else, Captain Lu knew how to fly. "Thirteen miles from the end of the runway, a little high and drifting left."

"Forty degrees of flap."

"Flaps forty," Denny confirmed.

"Visibility thirty miles. Can you see the runway lights?"

Lu took a good look ahead. "Confirm. Lights dead ahead."

"Will you need the escort from here on?"

"No. We will be okay from here on in."

"Fine. We will monitor you all the way in. Muscat approach is one-oh-six point three, good luck."

Chapter Thirty-Seven

Rear Admiral Bill Lodgers was taking a nap in his quarters. Captain Brad Gurney was visiting with the Air Boss. Commander Henry Reynolds was taking the watch on the bridge and down in CIC the Operations Director was waiting to call in the two F-14Ds that had run escort. On the flight deck two Hornets were taking their turn behind a Hawkeye and an S-3 Viking as they prepared for launch to continue surveillance of the Russian Boats. An SH-3 Sea King departed for rescue alert. A continual conversation had been running between the commercial flight, the Sentry and the *George Washington* to ensure that the Korean crew could continue into Oman without having to ditch in the Gulf. As soon as the aircraft's approach to Muscat was determined Admiral Lodgers changed course by ten degrees to position the Carrier and its support ships much closer to its flight path in preparation for a possible ditching, while permitting the Tomcats to continue escorting duties. Since it had become obvious that a water landing would not now be necessary, the recovery crews were told to stand down and those not on duty retired for what was left of the night.

The Boeing was in the middle of its turn to the right when it passed close to Group Six at about five thousand feet. The two Tomcats broke away from the Korean and prepared to come aboard. The launch area ahead of the *George Washington* was clear. The Hawkeye and the Tracker were just being fired off the forward catapults in quick succession. And it was at this moment, three minutes to five local time the morning of Sunday, the 9th of October, 1994, that the *USS George Washington* and the five other ships that constituted the main bulk of Group Six, died.

Well to say died may be somewhat of an overstatement. But to the officers and crew of the largest ship afloat, it certainly seemed so. Every single radar screen, scope, display and computer terminal went dead. It was as if all the power switches throughout the ship had been turned off simultaneously. Deep in Nucleonics warning lights and buzzers went off everywhere as the primary and secondary evaluators on al eight reactors SCRAMed, driving the rods deep into safety, shutting down the entire power plant. The transfer to back-up steam generation never took place. The main boilers failed to fire up with corresponding effects on steam generation and the main turbines. The helm froze. The entire Communications department went deaf. No reception on any channel as every single receiver and transmitter went inoperative. The NAVSAT dish ceased its independent movement, losing their locks on the sky. All missile guidance information and related defense systems shut down. In fact, apart from a couple of minor exceptions, nearly everything that was electrical necessary for the operational capabilities of the *George Washington* just quit, all at the same moment. The lighting, however, having flickered for a moment, did come back on, although only at half power, and the voice activated phones continued to function.

Men started running and the phones started buzzing as the ship went dead in the water. Commander Henry Reynolds on the bridge jammed the General Quarters alarm button, just as much to see if it worked as to alert the crew, and as the gongs sounded loudly throughout the ship, no longer subdued by the various hums and rumbles of the main engines and aircraft movement, he reached for the phone and pressed the Admiral's extension. "Sir, we've had a major systems failure. We need you on the bridge urgently." Admiral Lodgers did not respond. He was already running down the corridor.

Captain Gurney charged onto the bridge. "What the hell is going on, Mister Reynolds?!" he yelled.

"Don't know, sir. Peterson here is taking the calls," said the Commander turning to his white-faced Lieutenant with the headset on. "Report, Peterson."

"Aye, sir," his voice shaking with nervousness. "Do you wish me to continue taking the calls, sir?"

"Yes! Report Peterson," replied Gurney.

"Fission reports that all is secure, but a total shut down of all their systems has taken place. No steam. Engine room reports back-up boilers have failed to fire up. Auxiliary generators have been started for electrical needs but no forward power and the steam cells for the Cats failed to fill, so launch capability is zero. Bridge?" said Peterson into his microphone briefly.

Admiral Lodgers, a little out of breath, arrived on the bridge. "Did I hear correctly, Brad, no steam?"

"Correct, sir. Continue Lieutenant."

"Yes, sir. Uh..," Peterson, pausing for a moment, tried to sift the information into some kind of priority.

Lodgers reassured him. "Just give us what you know Peterson."

"Yes, sir. Bridge?" Peterson continued. "Radar reports that all, repeat, all systems have stopped functioning. Communications report that we have ceased receiving transmissions completely. Bridge?" he paused for a moment as he listened to the next call. "They commenced calling emergency frequencies but Commander Treedle believes that on preliminary inspection, we're not sending anything either. Bridge?" With every word that was spoken the looks on the faces of those listening to Lieutenant Peterson were turning a deep shade of pale. "We have lost our helm, sir. Lieutenant Commander Otis has taken someone aft to the stern steering station. Bridge? Voice activated phones are working. Air Department reports that the two Hornets awaiting launch have lost all avionics and all flights have been suspended. All contact has been broken with the two Tomcats on finals and we are in the process of waving them off. Air Boss reports he's having trouble switching Cats to manual operation but even if he could we don't have steam to fire them. All landing aids are out of service and the Tomcats only have about four minutes of flying time left. Bridge?"

Admiral Lodgers had obviously heard enough. "Commander Poole, you've got what's left of the bridge. Brad, come with me. Peterson, get a pad and write down all the reports you receive. Mister Reynolds does the tannoy system still work throughout the ship?

"I'm not sure, sir."

"Well find out. In the meantime if anyone wants us, they'll have to wait. I'll call Peterson as often as I can. The Captain and I are off to do a complete inspection. Got it?"

"Aye, sir."

"Brad, grab someone from Admin.' with a note pad to follow us around and tell the rest of the department to split up to the eight divisions and take notes. I want a full report from them, in writing, on the bridge in thirty minutes."

"Right," said Gurney picking up a phone briefly. Within moments, a leading seaman with note-pad arrived on the bridge and proceeded to follow the Admiral and his Chief of Staff on the tour of inspection. Although at the Admiral's pace it could have been termed a runabout.

The subdued lighting everywhere only seemed to accentuate the lifeless feeling aboard. Lodgers made his way through the heart of the ship, ignoring the various departments they passed, preferring instead to head directly for Communications. As they entered the main radio room Lodgers was presented not with the normal chatter of radio operators on duty, but with the shouting and yelling of many of the crew trying to raise anyone on their headsets. Six of the radios that had been pulled from their racks were being examined and tested by various technicians. Commander John Treedle was pouring over a set of his own when the Admiral tapped him on the shoulder.

"Admiral, what happened?" Treedle asked quickly.

"Don't know yet. Got anything?"

Treedle was trying hard not to sound flustered. "No, sir. Nothing. We've gone through every set. Every station is being manned right now trying to raise somebody, anybody."

"Could we hear a response if there was one?"

"I can't confirm that, Admiral. I've even got a Master of Signals working on the black box but still nothing. We can't even hear our own Morse code, so who knows? Maybe everybody can hear us and it's just that our receivers have gone. But I can tell you Admiral, I have never experienced anything like this before."

"Nor have I, Harry. Get someone aloft with a lamp and find out if we were the only one hit. If there's a radio working in Group Six I want to know about it."

"I've already taken care of it, sir."

"Lookouts?"

"All corners, should be arriving now. I had to send runners with them. The portable radios don't work either."

"Great. Keep at it, Harry."

"Aye, Admiral."

"If you hear something, leave a message with Peterson on the bridge."

"Aye, sir," Treedle confirmed. "By the way, sir, do you know what time it is?"

The Admiral looked back at Treedle as if to question the importance of such trivia right now. He thought better of it and glanced at his watch. "Well what do you know, my watch has died as well."

Treedle nodded. "So has mine, Sir."

Lodgers acknowledged the information. "Very well, Commander, carry on."

"Where to next, Admiral?" asked Gurney.

"Your guess is as good as mine," Lodgers replied as they left the radio room. "But whatever we do we must have steam."

"Right." Gurney led the way aft with Lodgers close behind and Seaman Moody bringing up the rear. With every section they passed men were running and orders were being given back and forth as various pieces of test equipment were being forced into service. Two minutes later Admiral Lodgers opened the huge door marked 'Engineering'. All the offices were empty and it was only when they started to climb down into the main boiler area that they found with Commander Robert Medlock. He was surrounded by five engineers, all of whom had their sleeves rolled up, scurrying back and forth as various commands were given. Medlock was lying underneath one of the main fuel pumps.

"Admiral in Engineering!" someone yelled and everybody froze for a second, coming to attention.

"Carry on," ordered Lodgers firmly.

Medlock, from Maine and perhaps the oldest member aboard the *George Washington*, slid out on a dolly from underneath a pump. He had a reputation for not holding to too much protocol, relying more on his 'do it rather than say it' motto for getting things done. Remaining on his back, he wiped the grease off his face. "Morning Admiral. I wish I could give you some good news. Sounds like we could do with some."

"What's the story, Bob?"

"All I know is when Nucleonics shut down, I, along with everyone else, expected one of our two main boilers to spring into life. But they never did. They just sat there. No pressure, no motors, nothing.

"How long to fix it?" asked Lodgers, bending his knees to gain a better look at his engineer.

"Wish I could tell you. We got the generator fired up for limited electricity but apart from that..?" he shook his head.

"Any steam in cells three and four?"

"Sorry, Bill. But you should have enough for one launch each on numbers one and two. Unless you..," his voice trailed off as his question was answered by Admiral Lodgers' expression.

"Commander, you don't need me to tell you that without steam we can't make headway, we can't launch any aircraft, in fact, we can't do anything."

"I know that, sir," said Medlock, with frustration. "I just don't know how long it'll take. We should have full electrical capability in five minutes or so and one way or the other you'll have steam in thirty minutes, even if I have to build a boiler with my bare hands."

"Thirty minutes?" Lodgers questioned. "That long?"

Medlock slid his sled back under the pump. "You want to make that forty minutes, Admiral?"

"Sure don't," said Lodgers, quietly, straightening up. Lodgers, Gurney, and Moody left Engineering and continued to head toward the stern. Among the heavy pumps and steam pipes of the rear engineering space stood the aft steering station. There, as the three arrived on the small platform high above the worm drives and gearing of the rudder, two men stood grinding away at hand cranks.

"Commander Otis?"

"Aye, sir. Didn't expect to see you down here, Admiral."

"Nor did I."

"Well, everything's relatively okay. Seaman Perkins here is in constant contact with the bridge so we do at least have steerage."

"Yes, but it's not much good to us if we don't have any forward speed."

Lodgers turned to Perkins and said, "give me that headset for a moment, will you?" The Admiral slipped it over his cap and found Peterson on the other end. "Any messages for us?"

"Yes, sir. Signals reports that similar failures have been experienced by the *Charlton*, the *Lansing*, and the *Norwich*."

"No radios either, Lieutenant?"

"Not at the moment, sir."

"What about the rest of the fleet?"

"We are attempting to gather information on them now, sir."

"Anything else?"

"No, sir, except that both the Tomcats suffered complete electronics failures before landing and came aboard on hydraulics only. One of them, Shadows Five I think, suffered extensive undercarriage damage."

"Great!" Lodgers mumbled. "Can it be moved?"

"Oh yes, sir. It's being dragged to Station number three now. The Hawkeye and Viking, launched just before the hit, also suffered damage and are trying to make their way aboard now, but it's difficult operating the wires manually. The Air Boss has all available hands top side, but it's a mess."

Admiral Lodgers handed the set back to Perkins, looked back at Otis and said, "Keep at it Commander," and then left to climb the stairs to the main hangers. Lodgers, for all his years, ran the steps in front of Gurney and Moody confidently. "Well, we can't send or receive messages and we may have steam in thirty minutes. Let's see if we can get something in the air." They entered the lower hanger bay area as Lieutenant Commander Ingrams came running up.

"Anything yet?"

"Sorry, Admiral. It seems everything to do with avionics has shut down." Ingrams kept pace with the three as they marched quickly between the numerous ladders and steps around the parked aircraft, toward the forward exit two hundred yards away. The entire hanger was full... full of technicians... full of movement... full of problems. Just at that moment, the lights flickered brighter and behind them Station One began to descend, filling the hanger with the sound of winches and a blast of cold morning air.

"Bob's got the main generators up to speed," said Gurney loudly.

"It's a pity we can't fly one," Ingrams retorted as he kept pace with the Admiral.

"Any helos, radios, anything at all working?"

"Nothing, sir," confirmed Ingrams.

"Commander Davis is top-side, Admiral, if you need him."

"No, that's okay. What can you tell me, specifically?"

"Not much. He checked three Hornets and one Tomcat but all the avionics are dead. He's now checking the Sea Kings and an A-6."

"And you?"

"Same down here, sir. We're all working through everything we have that was operational as of midnight and at the moment it's the same story. All the electronics just seemed to quit working. Hydraulics on some of the older aircraft are okay, but unless you have a volunteer who wants to try a launch on just brute strength, sir...?"

"Even if I did, which I don't, we can't."

"What, sir? Not even in the forward cells?"

"No."

"Boy, what luck."

"What we need is some good luck. So get going and find some Commander," said Lodgers in a soft tone.

"Aye, sir," acknowledged Ingrams as he turned to run back to an F/A-18. A little while later Ingrams continued his checking right down to the very last aircraft, and did indeed find some luck.

Having left the hanger the three made their way to where the red warnings and 'No Admittance' signs began to take pride of place.

"You getting all this, Moody?" inquired Lodgers without turning round.

"Aye, sir. Do you want me to follow you in, sir?"

"Why not? Nothing's working."

A Marine stepped forward and opened the big shielded outer door and then the inner door to the Nucleonics Division. Normally this area was kept spotless, clean and very organized but today was not normal. There were circuit boards all over the floor, tool chests sprawled open everywhere and nine officers and crew working feverishly with testing equipment and replacements.

Captain Gurney called out for the head of the department. "Commander Huffman?"

"Here," came a muffled voice from inside a cabinet. A pair of legs started their backward shuffle and the young Commander, upon seeing Admiral Lodgers and Captain Gurney, jumped to his feet.

"Commander Huffman here, sir,"

Lodgers looked up at the Commander, recalling the College basketball photographs he was shown of this technician the first day Huffman came aboard. "At ease, Mike."

"Aye, sir," replied Huffman, straightening his tie.

"Any leakage?"

"No, sir. I did report all was secure earlier."

"I know. What's the verdict?"

"Well, sir, I'm sorry I can't give you any heat at this time, Admiral, but it seems as though most of our circuitry has, well, failed."

"What do you mean by failed, exactly?" asked the Admiral.

"Well, I'm not sure really, sir. It's tough to do diagnostics when the diagnose programs you're using to nail it down have also failed. All I've been trying to do is locate some replacements that will get us going again."

"Have you?" said the Captain.

"Well that's just it, sir. No I haven't," said Huffman, turning to Gurney briefly.

Lodgers continued, "What do you mean, you haven't? We have stores that are supposed to carry complete sets of spare boards for everything around here!"

"Exactly, sir. First thing we tried. But just like the mains our replacement boards fared no better."

"You mean they fired up and then failed?"

"No, sir. They were already dead before we put them in."

Lodgers couldn't believe his ears. "All of them?"

"Yes, sir. Every single one."

"So, what do we do now?"

"Some of my guys are trying to find which part of the boards failed and which didn't, but as I've said before, sir, that's next to impossible."

"Can you take the good parts from one and use them as replacements for the bad bits on the others?"

"It's not as simple as all that, sir, but we are looking at alternatives."

Lodgers turned and said to nobody in particular, "Let's get out of here."

"Sir?" called Huffman as they were leaving.

"Yes?" Lodgers turning back for a moment.

"Have you been to CIC yet, Admiral?"

"On my way there now."

"I would be interested to know if they've had the same problem with their stores."

"We'll call you as soon as we know."

The trio left Huffman to his own devices and quickly made their way up to the Combat Information Center.

Here again, it was the same story. Instead of low light, bright screens and hushed conversation, the room was bright with disorganization everywhere.

"Admiral?" said Commander Wooten, greeting the three as they entered.

"Any success?" asked Gurney.

"It's just amazing, sir. One minute everything's fine

and the next, nothing."

"Stores failed as well?" Lodgers stated as much as asked.

"Right," Wooten agreed giving the Admiral a quizzical look. "How'd you know?"

Lodgers ignored the question. "What time do you have?"

Wooten rolled his sleeve back. "Well I'll be..."

"You're not the first call we've made today, Frank."

"Well anyway, sir, we used all the back-ups we have and still nothing. I have seventeen civilians in here, all of whom work for the companies that installed all of this and none of them have been able to get anything working again. You might just as well convert this place into a lounge for all the good they've done."

"It's not their fault, Frank."

"I know," Wooten admitted.

"It just seems impossible," remarked Gurney.

"I know, sir, but it's happened. We can't see where we're going, we can't talk to anyone and we're wandering about the Gulf like a piece of driftwood."

"How far to the coast?"

"Ten miles perhaps."

"Any chance of running aground?"

"Don't think so, sir. We were heading North-East at the time this happened. There's a little breeze and the out-going tide might help. For the moment though, all we can do is to hope that we don't drift too close to anyone else in the Group, Admiral."

"Right. Got a line to the bridge?" Wooten handed the Admiral a phone. "Peterson," anything?"

"Yes, sir. Lookouts report four to five enemy aircraft sighted off the port beam."

"I'll be right there. Locate Commander Davis and have him meet me on the bridge." Admiral Lodgers put down the phone and the trio left for the bridge as Gurney made a note to call Huffman.

Back down in Communications Lieutenant Tom Forest approached his chief. "Sir?" he said urgently.

"Yes, what is it?" said Treedle, looking up from the rack he was working on.

"Take a look at this," said Forest holding out two small handsets for him to see.

"The old two-way radios we used to use for emergencies, what about them?"

"They work, sir. Nothing wrong with these at all."

"You're kidding!" remarked Treedle, grabbing the handsets and turning them on.

"No, sir. Having ascertained that everything from Supply was dead, I started going through some of our emergency gear and found these little babies lying on a shelf gathering dust. I grabbed a couple of batteries and bingo!"

"We got any more of these, Forest?"

"Yes, sir. I've got Michaels going through them now." Just then, Lieutenant Peter Michaels came up carrying eight more. "Do they all work, Michaels?" Treedle asked optimistically.

"Yes, sir. Every single one."

"Okay! Michaels, take four of those up to the lookouts."

"Aye, sir," said Michaels, putting the others on the desk nearby as he made for the door.

"Forest, since you found these you can take one of them to Admiral Lodgers on the bridge and one to Commander Wooten in CIC. Then, grab the runners from topside and position yourself on deck where the reception is at its best. Use the four seamen I sent up for yourself, in case you need a runner or two. I'll keep the last radio here."

"Aye, sir," said Forest, picking up another.

"Run a test and then call me as soon as you're in position."

"Yes, sir!" acknowledged Forest and started toward the door.

"Oh, and Tom?" said Treedle, stopping his Lieutenant in his tracks.

"Sir?"

Commander Treedle smiled briefly and said, "Good work."

Admiral Lodgers and Captain Gurney arrived on the bridge. "Billings?" said Lodgers as he took off his jacket and handed it to his aid. "Fetch the Captain and myself a fresh cup of coffee, will you? I assume the coffee machine is still working." Billings nodded as the Admiral turned to the Lieutenant. "Peterson, now what's all this about a sighting?"

"Signalman Price reporting, sir," said Price stepping forward. "Our forward posts have monitored four to five Migs off the port side."

"Let's see." Lodgers took the night glasses from Price and peered through the angled windows on the port side. It took a couple of seconds for his eyes to become accustomed to the relative darkness but even so, he saw nothing.

"There, sir," exclaimed Price pointing to his right.

Lodgers fixed his eyes on the distant twinkling lights before raising the glasses once again. He focused in on five Migs at three thousand feet, cruising at about two hundred knots.

"Any identifications yet?"

"Iranian, I assume, sir," answered Price.

"Have they over-flown the Group?"

"No, sir. Not yet."

"Let's hope it stays that way."

"Admiral?"

"Yes, Peterson."

"Lieutenant Commander Ingrams reports that he has one F/A-18 up and running, sir."

"What?!" cried Lodgers.

"Totally airworthy?" Gurney interjected.

"Don't know, sir."

"Get me Ingrams on the line," Lodgers insisted.

"Aye, sir." Billings came in with two cups of coffee, which were handed out.

Lodgers took a sip of his and, as though refreshed by it's contents and somewhat impressed that something on the GW still worked, took on a more commanding posture. "Now we're getting somewhere. Price, any news on the rest of the fleet?"

"Sir, it appears that every ship has suffered the same kind of problems we have. No power, no radios, no nothing."

"Proximity?"

"The Group seems to be in good shape, sir, except for the Norwich. She's drifted to within one thousand feet of the *Ticonderoga*."

"Damn."

"Commander Davis reporting for duty, Admiral," came a voice from behind.

"Ah, Commander. Report upstairs. I'll be up in a second."

"Aye, sir." Davis immediately headed for the Admiral's deck.

"Commander Ingrams on the line for you, Admiral," said Peterson.

Lodgers reached for the phone. "Ingrams, a Hornet you say?"

"Yes, sir," Ingrams replied.

"How come?"

"Not sure yet, sir."

"Helos?"

"No, sir."

"Well get the F/A-18 topside as quick as you can."

"In progress, Admiral. Should be ready to go in about seven or eight minutes. Are the Cats up yet?"

"No. Listen. I want every hand available to strip that Hornet of everything except a couple of one-twenties. And don't put any more in the fuel tanks than enough for a couple of hours. Everything else is to be stripped off including the Vulcan, and you've got six minutes, not eight."

"Aye, sir."

Peterson interjected. "Air Boss on the line for you, sir."

"Yes?"

"The Hummer's back, sir."

"What do you mean?"

"She was out monitoring the Migs. When we didn't respond they came back for a look see. They're closing back in on the Group now."

"Wave him off. I want him in the air for the time being. Keep him up but signal to him to radio for help."

"But none of our radios work, sir."

"I know that. Get signals to use a Morse light," ordered Lodgers showing signs of frustration.

"But I'm not sure if anyone up front knows Morse code, sir."

"What do you mean by that, Commander?"

"What I mean, sir, is that Morse code hasn't been taught to anyone in the Navy, outside of Signals, for quite a while now."

"Well, that's news to me," Lodgers exclaimed as he looked around at those about him. "What about their radio operator?"

"We'll give it a try, sir, but I'm not sure he's near a window unless he moves forward."

"Then bring them aboard as quickly as you can and get someone up from Communications to jump on their radio and start raising hell."

"Aye, sir." Lodgers put down the phone and turned to Gurney. "I have just been informed that we no longer teach Morse code as a pre-requisite in the Navy anymore!"

"Right, sir. Only Signals covers that these days."

"Great Brad! By the way, the option we discussed on the way up might just be viable. Get down to the fantail and make sure they're ready." Gurney, with coffee in hand, left for the deck. "Commander Poole, I'll leave the, ah, bridge with you."

Up on the Admiral's bridge Commander Brian Davis was watching the lights of five distant aircraft when Admiral Lodgers entered and went over to a cabinet to pour himself a drink.

"Looks like we have some company, sir."

Lodgers looked toward the windows briefly and then appeared to change the subject. "Look, Brian." His voice sounded serious. "Right now I own the most expensive hole in the water ever built. There's six ships out there playing footsy with each other. Four Russian subs creeping ever closer to us and now five Migs banging away at our back door. I need to get some kind of deterrent in the air." Lodgers took a sip and sat down at his desk. "Now normally, as you know, I could still launch you, assuming of course we had something airworthy, by using the cells. However, by shear bad luck Cats three and four were undergoing maintenance and the forward two were discharged just seconds before everything shut down. They took some pressure but not enough for a launch." Lodgers took a another sip from his drink and leaned forward, the light from the desk lamp revealing some worry lines on the Admiral's face. "What I want to know from you is this. At this very moment an F/A-18 is being stripped of everything, including the Vulcan. Except for a couple of one-twenties and half a tank of fuel, you'll be naked. And more importantly, you won't have any wind speed across the deck, either. But with the largest floating runway at our disposal, backing your rear nozzles out over the fan-tail and using just the Hornet's burners, can you get that baby up to speed in three-hundred and thirty yards and into the air safely?"

For a moment Davis looked stunned. "Sir, you want me to launch without using the Cats?"

"That's right," said Lodgers leaning back in his seat. "During World War Two I launched 30 B-25s off a deck, no problem.Yet here I am with the longest floating runway in the world and, nothing. Take your time, Commander. I'll give you two minutes. All you have to do is compute the rate of acceleration of the stripped aircraft, the take-off speed and the length of the flight deck."

"We've never even tried this in San Diego, Admiral."

"I know. But can it be done? I figured if anyone can, you can."

"Can I make a quick call?"

"Certainly," said Lodgers as the buzz of one his phones startled both of them. While Lodgers took his call Davis picked up the other phone and found Hunter, busy with his own problems.

After their respective calls were completed, Lodgers continued. "A bit of good news. We've found some old two-way radios that work and Brad is trying to flash the *Lansing* to find out if they have some too. If they do, we might have ship-to-ship communication. Now then, what's the verdict?"

"It's very tight, sir. Without the thirty or so knots we could normally count on it's too close to call. Besides, locked in the chute our afterburners are up to full power before we launch. But sitting loose on the deck our brakes will never hold us back. And by the time we get anywhere close to full power we'll be halfway down the deck and a definite dunking."

"Good point."

"Is it totally stripped?"

"As much as possible."

Just then the sound of five jets flying low overhead brought Lodgers and his guest running out to the railings.

"Migs!" cried Davis.

"I bet we look pretty dead to them," remarked Lodgers, sheepishly.

"Yeah," agreed Davis.

"At least we have our lights on."

"Yeah, and they might not notice seven of the finest ships of the U.S. navy facing every which way doing two knots, thanks only to the tide!" shouted Lodgers.

Davis looked up at the Admiral, heard the slight despair in his voice and tried to reassure his boss. "But we can change all that if we can get something in the air. How long before we get steam?"

Lodgers looked at his watch in disgust. "Old Medlock told me thirty minutes that's about twenty-two from now." Lodgers looked up at the Migs tailing away and then back to Davis, but he was nowhere to be seen. The Admiral leaned his weight on the rail and looked out at the few small streaks of morning gray creeping in from the east. As five sets of twinkling lights flew past his line of sight and headed on north, Lodgers suddenly felt very lonely. Although at this moment the Admiral was gravely concerned that now all of Iran would know about their problems, he was unaware that so did a few others, including Admiral Pat Swanson, a Sentry, and a Harrier II pilot already on route to the Carrier.

Chapter Thirty-Eight

The streets of this relatively well maintained suburb of Bahrain were clean and well lit and as the wheels of the dark blue Toyota quietly turned down Afdaal Street no-one stirred. The driver stopped his vehicle in front of a small unassuming home, turned the lights and the engine off and softly ran up to the front door, adjusting his tie and cap as he went. After a few seconds of hitting the bell the door swung open.

"Corporal Sanders for Captain Danforth," said the driver to the ever-widening space.

"Come in, come in. I'll be right with you," said a voice.

"Thank you, sir," replied the Corporal, closing the door behind him.

"You know anything about this, Corporal?" asked the voice from the bathroom.

"No, sir. Except that it's a Black Alert."

"Do you know what that means, Corporal?"

"Not really, sir."

"Probably best if it stays that way. Has the rest of my team been notified?"

"As far as I know, sir. There's a phone in the car for your use." Captain Jack Danforth dressed in full uniform, stepped out of the bathroom. The Corporal, having never met the Captain before, looked down at the I.D. in his hand and satisfied that the five foot ten inch, one hundred and eighty pound frame matched his subject asked, "Can I get your bags, sir?" as he slipped the photo back in his pocket.

"Sure, the brown one by the door there." Danforth picked up his cap and a wide but slender metal case and slid out of the door behind his driver. "Okay, let's get going. I've got a hunch a few sailors are waiting for me."

Within twenty minutes the entire team was airborne and heading South.

Chapter Thirty-Nine

The raising of personnel to the top of the ridge had gone well. All of the team, each wearing a micro headset, had been well versed in using the pulley system, and as the lead climber reached the top of the cliff, one of the two equipment bags on the beach had been tied to the end of his line. The kit for the bottom pulley was being put together. The kit consisted of a pulley wheel inside a small but sturdy frame, anchored by a lever and ratchet that angled across the frame at forty-five degrees from bottom front to top rear. An area at the base of the cliff had been cleared, and a small but deep hole had been drilled in the rock face, up at the same angle as the ratchet, using a powerful, rechargeable drill. A very thin, but strong carbon-fiber blade had been unfolded and pushed deep into the wet sand parallel and close to the cliff face. Next, the frame had been carried and placed solidly on the sand between the plate and the cliff with the hole in the rock ready to accept the upward protruding rod. As three members of the team slowly pumped the lever, the upper rod moved up into the hole and the two individual feet attached to the lower rod started to apply pressure to the plate. The more the ratchet was pumped, the harder the top rod forced its way into the hole in the rock and the more it pushed the plate against the weight of the sand. After just eight strokes of the ratchet, the pulley was firmly afixed to the beach. One hundred and eighty feet above the work was much easier. The aerial photographs had revealed some small trees twenty yards from the edge of the cliff, and following a quick dash with some light-weight, non-stretch cord, the overhanging pulley and frame had been raised from below and firmly secured on the edge of the cliff. Fielding had threaded a line through both sides of the top pulley, then dropped both ends of the cord to the team below. One end Buddy had attached to one of four big bags while the other was threaded through the base pulley and out to the beach. One final press was given to the lever when Bill, Phil, Canny and Chancey picked up a portion of the line and walked down the beach toward the surf, hauling the bag quickly up the cliff face.

As the morning light began to stretch across the rocks, it was getting easier for the group to see when to bring the hoisting to a halt. Fielding placed her harness into the empty bag and threw it over the edge. Upon arrival at the bottom, Buddy took the harness out of the bag, strapped it on, rolled the bag up and clipped it to his belt. The pulling team clipped the line around themselves as in a tug-of-war line up and took the strain. As Buddy's feet inched up from the ground, he first bounced up and down on it to test the tension on the pulleys and, having found it secure, gave the 'Go' signal. He swung his feet up on to the rock face and in the time it takes to count to sixty, Buddy had walked to the top of the cliff. Once or twice, one member or another of the pulling team did lose their footing in the wet sand but not enough to slow down Buddy's ascent.

Buddy climbed to his feet as he unclasped his belt. "Good work Charlie."

"I thought I had asked you to take care of things below?"

"You did, but I reckoned you needed more help up here." He then noticed the cuts on her arms and legs. "Boy you look a mess, are you okay?"

"Sure. How long do think Digger will be?" said Fielding, placing a strip bandage on her left knee.

Buddy glanced at his watch. "Maybe another ten minutes or so, we've got time."

"Why wait?"

"Just that it's not safe enough for three of them to lift on their own."

"I know, but how about five of us?"

"What do you mean?" said Buddy curiously, putting the harness back in the bag.

"We can have everyone up here before Digger arrives. That's why we have a double pulley on the top frame, just in case," said Fielding confidently. "Get on that radio of yours and tell one of the guys to get the

spare harness out of one of the bags and put it on."
Buddy gave Fielding a quick questioning glance and
reached for his radio to give the orders. Fielding first
grabbed a couple of rocks and dumped them in the bag.
She then reached in her own and pulled out a shorter
line, tied one end to the bag and holding onto the other
end of the line, let the bag drop to the beach below.

Below, Chancey was already belted up by the time
the bag with two lines attached reached the bottom. He
clipped both lines on to his belt and said "Go." Bill, Phil,
and Canny took the tension from below while Buddy
and Fielding made sure that each line ran smoothly over
each pulley. With three men pulling from below and
Buddy and Fielding pulling from above, Chancey walked
up the cliff even faster than Buddy had. The procedure
was repeated for Bill with Chancey now pulling from
the top. Phil followed suite while Canny released the
pressure on the ratchet, dismantled the frame, put it
away in its black bag, and was just stowing it behind a
rock when Digger and Doug appeared on the beach.
Ten minutes later, following Fielding's change of clothes,
Digger surveyed the scene. It was obvious that leaving
her with the very minimal of cover could be dangerous.
So with gear hidden, mines and weapons distributed
and all headsets, maps and compasses checked, with
Doug carrying their main radio, they all made their way
carefully inland.

Chapter Forty

Davis, dressed in his flight suit, was going through some last minute checks. To Commander Davis, the F/A-18 Hornet was a relatively small aircraft. It handled the bumps and thumps of Carrier launches with ease. But now, as he looked up at the cockpit of his trusty steed parked perilously close to the stern of the Carrier's flight deck, it seemed to loom quite large. The Hornet sat like a white dove perched high on a platform, its wheels chocked from behind, stripped of all unnecessary weight and enough fuel for a couple of hours in the air. The Plane Captain walked around the aircraft with Davis, while Captain Brad Gurney followed hard on their heels.

"Everything's good, sir. Limited tanks, no gun, two AIM-120s only. The automatic take-off and roll equipment is operational. The reverse clip has been removed as you requested, and the seat's pin has been pulled."

Davis continued his walk-around. "I signed off the HUD, how bad is it?"

"This aircraft was under repair for an intermittent HUD black-out and flight-control stuttering problem. The previous crew reported that under five-G pull or more, the HUD began to drop out and that fly-by-wire felt more like a rope. We haven't had a chance to nail it down yet."

"I hope I won't have to pull more than three anyway," said Davis cheerfully.

Lieutenant Commander Hunter ran up to Davis and rocked his hand back and forth. "The numbers are too close to call. You need one-twenty to be safe and if you can get just one favorable gust, it could make all the difference." Davis turned and watched the last few drops of fuel being added. There was no howling gale to shout over, no noisy jet engines blowing about, just the unusual pitch of a ship giving in to the swell rather than powering through it.

Captain Gurney joined in. "I've further reduced your fuel load back to only one hour air time, it might just make all the difference."

"But there's five Migs out there," said Davis.

"I know, but I'm hoping that giving them a dose of radar will be enough to scare them off."

"And if it isn't?"

"Right," said Hunter smiling.

"Listen, what did they say about the thrust parameters?" Davis asked nervously.

"The brakes won't hold you against all that power and if we put chocks under the front to hold you back, they'll never be able to pull them out once the afterburners kick in." Suddenly, there was a sparkle of hope that flittered across the Commander's face.

"You mean, you assumed we wouldn't have full power at the start?"

"Of course! At full throttle the brakes will let go and by the time the burners are up to full whack, you'll be forty feet down the deck."

Davis' voice rose to a near shout in excitement, as he climbed the steps. "Get someone to find three of the smaller chocks, put them in the front, and tell everyone to stand clear."

"But who's going to pull them out?" shouted the Plane Captain climbing up the ladder behind him.

"No-one. With this rugged undercarriage I'm betting that at full power I'll jump right over them." Davis climbed into his seat, received help with his straps and belts and went to work firing up his F-404B turbofans.

"Good luck, Commander," said his PC and climbed down to remove the ladder and prepare for the pre-flight checks.

Although this proceedure is normally carried out while the aircraft is parked, the limited time alloted pushed this requirement back. The PC ran through the checks and responses with hand signals. Davis called for start of APU and fired up engine number two. Confirmed. Start up engine number one. Confirmed, Good to Go. Check hydraulics and Initial Flight Control. Davis worked the stick and pedals moving all flight control surfaces. Confirmed. The PC called for Open Flaps: good. Horizontal Stablators: good. Close Flaps: good. Open

Half Flaps, Set Trim: good. The PC gave the three fingers down calling for Tail Hook, Launch Bar, Speed Brake and Horizontal Refueling Probe: good. Retract same: good. The PC checked the starboard side computer, closed the cover and gave the 'Good to Go' sign. The aircraft was given one more visual inspection by the Final Checkers and the ground crew was ready. Everyone, except Hunter and the Launch Officer had retired to Vulture's Row. The parked aircraft had been moved as far off to the right side as possible, leaving a clear line of sight for Davis right to the end of the deck. Though sunrise was underway, a series of red flares were lit in front of him outlining the left and right side of his path, with six of them marking the bows. At least if he went straight down into the drink, there wasn't any risk of the Carrier running him over. Below, winches had dispatched three teams with rafts to carry out the possible recovery, but Davis had no intention of getting wet. He looked down to his left. The Launch Officer, not quite sure what to do under the circumstances, waited for Davis's salute. Davis obliged. The LO then knelt down and touched the deck briefly to signify the launch, but since Davis was not waiting for a Cat to release him from the hold-back fitting, he went to work on his own launch systems.

"Now to find out how much this old bird can take." He swept the controls to all four corners and checked the radio briefly to see if there was anyone else he could talk to, but it was dead. He gripped the nozzle adjuster and prepared himself for a ride.

This version of the Hornet had been fitted with the latest swing type nacelles, which gave the aircraft greater maneuverability, but it also presented Davis the opportunity to use vectored thrust. By adjusting the control between forward and reverse, Davis hoped to confuse the powerplants just long enough to throw in the afterburners before the GE power units had had a chance to internally hemorrhage. He pushed the throttles up to full power. With the brakes on full, and even with chocks in front, the aircraft began to jostle forward. The two nacelles at the rear of each engine are designed, when switched to reverse, to close in over the thrust's path and force the power forward. As Davis continued to play with the controls, the airframe began to buck from side to side. Brian Davis started to sweat. Too much reverse and he might roll over the rear chocks and into the water below. He continued to move the control in and out trying to locate the nacelles in the middle of their travel, so that half the thrust went on out the rear and half went forward. Davis believed he could dump the fuel into the exhaust and bring the power up by an extra thirty percent before starting the roll, gaining an extra forty feet on maximum power. He pushed the throttles through the top stop and gently eased it into the lower afterburner range. The controls started to shake violently, the nose began bouncing, and the temperatures began closing in on the red lines. The engines started to roar as the whole aircraft began to jump side to side. The brakes were beginning to lose their grip when Davis went for broke. He thrust the throttles all the way to the end of its travel and thought he found the middle setting when, just as he was about to release the brakes, the Hornet bounced right up and over the forward chocks. Before the wheels could crunch back down onto the deck Davis had the wheel brakes off and retracted the reverse blinds. The Hornet was already doing thirty knots. As the Carrier deck slowly began to roll under his wheels, Davis wished he would suddenly feel the reassuring thump of the four 'G' launch, but none came. 40 knots... 50... 60...

"Come on old girl. Get your skates on!" yelled Davis. He was already passing the stack. "Damn this runway's short!" he yelled again, trying to control his desire to test the lift. "Keep it down, keep it down. The less drag, the better." Davis was accustomed to the 'Hands-off' launch that all F/A-18 pilots used when being fired from the Catapults, but this was a one-time effort and his pounding heart was bringing all of his flying experience to bear. By now his eyes had assured themselves of the course to the end of the deck and glued themselves on the speed indicator. "Ninety, one-hundred, one-ten." A quick glance up, and there were the six red flares rushing up to greet him. "The moment of truth," shouted Davis. He tested the stick pulling it back just a little. "There's something there, not much. Here we go!" A quick glance down. "One-fifteen!" THUMP! The Hornet's wheels left the deck with a thump. Immediately the Stall tones sounded loudly. "Gear up!" Davis pulled the stick back firmly. The nose climbed quickly for a second. A quick glance at his rate of climb indicator revealed a minus number. More tones began to sound, signifying altitude below sixty feet. The undercarriage was doing its best to climb into their seats but not before catching a lot of salt spray. He pulled hard back on the stick and put the Hornet into a near thirty degree tail stand. For a few moments she just hung in the air, nose up, her tail just inches from the waves, the engines hissing as they bore holes into the surf. Her forward speed dropped back to ninety knots and as Davis held his breath, trying to blot out the tones that warned of impending doom, he prepared for the worst. Everything seemed to click into slow-motion. His thoughts began to jump around. Would he have time to drop the nose before ejecting, or would he find himself bouncing back off the Carrier's deck? The sea looked black and cold. Perhaps Spreg could send him a copy of the concert during his impending stay in hospital. Suddenly one of the two sets of tones ceased their incessant clanging. His forward speed was still hovering around ninety but his altitude was up to one-twenty and climbing. He pushed forward on the stick slightly and the wings began to bite for more lift. The aircraft was close to a stall but a controlled stall and climbing. Davis let out a loud, "Yahoo!" He couldn't help himself and laughed a huge sigh of relief as his speed began to climb over one-fifty, pushing the nose forward, relying on the first real lift his wings had given him since leaving the deck. The stall tones went silent. He banked to the left and shut down his burners. "Now where are those Migs?" he said as he dialed up his radar. Davis took a glance back down at the Carrier and noticed for the first time the entire fleet floating in disarray. He dialed up his attack radar and immediately the tones sounded. Four Floggers and a Fulcrum flew by five miles to the North. It would have been easy for Davis to turn after them, but he acted with prudence. He watched their lights blinking away in the clear night sky and waited for them to turn on him in anger.

But they never did. The Migs turned and flew off into the distance, checking the coast a couple of times and then disappeared east toward their own border. Apart from a commercial flight landing at Muscat and a Sentry off in the distance, that was all Davis observed as he brought his throttles back to the bare minimums. It was a strange feeling for Davis to be aloft, so close to enemy territory without the normal abundance of ordnance on board. He felt naked and vulnerable and he would continue to feel this way until his wheels touched the deck of the *George Washington* once more,. to the cheers of the entire flight crew.

Chapter Forty-One

For the past hour, Captain Davidson and his crew had continued their monitoring of the various maneuvers carried out by the intruding Russians, and although their antics had been somewhat unorthodox, nothing that Davidson had witnessed was worthy of any further confrontation. The entire formation had increased speed to fifteen knots with the three Russian boats still to the rear of the *Philadelphia*, juxtaposing their positions many times. The lower boat had moved up to take the upper-most position with the other two sliding down to fill the gap. The deeper they went the closer each boat traveled with respect to the other. After ten minutes of this tight grouping the rotation would begin again. And as Davidson continued his scrutiny of the three dimensional display in front of him, Captain Dubrovney, about two hundred feet to his left ordered a decrease in depth.

"Conn, Sonar."

"Yes, Beagle?"

"The lead boat is starting to climb, sir."

Davidson paused for a moment, waiting for the display to confirm Corporal Beagle's observations. "Very well," said Davidson, turning to his Executive Officer. "Mike, stay with him." From the first moment the graphic detail had come alive on the wall of the bridge, the tactical view in front of Captain Davidson had remained relatively the same. Apart from the rear group shuffling positions once in a while, the system had not been given an opportunity to demonstrate its versatility. But now, the observer's view in front of the two leading boats rose higher as the white silhouette and its black neighbor began their climb.

Davidson reached for the button again. "Sonar, any indication that the three Foxtrots are changing their course?"

"Negative, sir. Their course remains constant at three-five-zero, depth five hundred feet."

"Very well." Davidson watched the fathometer reel

off the distance to the surface as he and his companion continued to climb. "Beagle, how close is Group Six?" The Corporal's response was slow in coming. "Sonar, how close is the Group?"

"Uh, unable to establish contact, Cap'n."

"Why not, Corporal?"

"I'm sorry, sir, but I can't seem to locate them. Switching from Passive to Active."

"They're there, sir, but all screws are dead in the water!"

"Heading?"

"Dead-ahead, sir, one mile."

"All ahead flank. Surface the boat!"

"All ahead flank, aye. Ten degrees up on the bow planes," barked Chief Danwall, taking his seat behind the helm.

"Mike, raise the *Washington* on the radio. Confirm their position, anything, just get someone on the line. When you do, I want to speak to them, whoever it is," Davidson said with some urgency. "Chief, you've got the Conn. Take us out ten degrees and bring us around bows-on to the Russian, I want a dominant position on that lead boat as she approaches the Group. When we surface on our new course bring us to a dead stop."

"Aye, Cap'n," said Danwall, stepping up onto the bridge. "Starboard twenty!"

"No response from the *Washington*, Cap'n," Young shouted from behind.

"Keep trying, and someone call home and tell them what's going on."

Beagle's voice rang out. "Hulls ahead, sir. No screws turning, just dead in the water!"

"Distance?"

"Closest is nine hundred yards, sir. Dead ahead."

"You're right there," said Davidson. "Mike, grab the hailer!"

Although the *Philadelphia* was still pounding the surf as the hatches popped, by the time Davidson had finished climbing the ladder, Danwall had taken the *Philadelphia* far enough away from the Typhoon to swing hard left back around, to be bows-on to the intruder.

"Captain, Typhoon surfacing," came over the speaker system just as the engines and the sound of the sea against the hull had ceased.

Neither Harry Davidson nor Mike Young had ever seen such a sight before. Off to the right sat the Guided Missile Destroyer *Norwich*. Further north sat the *George Washington* and one by one the lights of the seven ships, all drifting and pointing aimlessly in different directions, once proud members of Group Six, were counted off.

"Captain, look!" cried Young, pointing straight ahead. Davidson turned to see the Russian Typhoon, traveling left to right in front of them, breaking surf about 50 yards off their bows.

Davidson buzzed the Conn. "Nice work, Chief."

"Shall I plot a solution for the forward tubes?" Danwall suggested.

"Affirmative, all of them. And open the doors. I want them to know we mean business. And if we haven't raised anyone aboard the *Washington* yet get a Signalman up here with a lamp. And call up an AWACS or Bahrain or anyone and let them know what's going on here, if they don't know already."

As Young reached for the intercom, Captain Davidson surveyed the scene. What could have possibly hit the Battle Group to cause such devastation? he asked himself. A Russian sub surfaces and stops within a thousand feet of the ailing fleet to do what? Hit us with our pants down? And since the likelihood of them coming up to actually lend assistance was in serious doubt...

Signalman Watts interrupted Davidson's thoughts as he arrived next to him, taking up a position overlooking the *Norwich*. Just as Davidson was about to start relaying a message he thought he heard an unusual sound coming from the Typhoon in front of him.

"Quiet everyone, listen," Davidson shouted in a whisper. Young and Watts turned their heads as though turning on some inner audio sensitivity. "There it is again," he whispered. "Watts, shine that light on the Russian." Watts swung the lamp around. The powerful beam darted back and forth across the sea for a few seconds settling on the top sail of the Typhoon. There facing the fleet, quite clearly outlined in the morning mist, stood the figure of a large man in uniform.

"He's laughing, sir," said Watts.

"I can see that, Corporal," said Davidson in disgust. "Turn that lamp on the *Norwich* and see if you can raise them. Give me that hailer," he ordered, holding his hand out and Young passed it to Davidson. Before raising it to his lips he watched as Watts swung his lamp back toward the Destroyer. The lamp, with its long lens-like shroud, began flashing its strobe on the superstructure of the Destroyer. Even from this distance, Davidson could see the circle of light reflecting off the area of the bridge. Almost immediately, an equally powerful lamp began flashing its response.

"With the Typhoon present should all messages be coded, sir?" questioned the Signalman.

"Correct. First of all tell them that there's a Russian Typhoon off her starboard quarter, just in case they're all blind."

"Aye, sir," replied Watts.

"Ask them what condition the fleet is in and let them know we've radioed for help." Watts continued his quiet tapping of the lamp as Davidson turned to face the Russian.

"Captain Dubrovney, what is your purpose here?" There were a few moments of silence before the now familiar voice of Captain Dubrovney echoed back across the waters.

"Just taking a breath of fresh air, Captain."

"Would you mind taking it somewhere else, Captain?"

"No, I don't mind at all. As I said before, we're not here to harm you, although I must say, it looks as though someone has been here before us."

"So you have no objection to leaving the area, now?!"

"Hold on one moment, Captain. Let me check with my engineer."

Davidson turned to Young listening intently beside him. "You got a tape rolling on this?"

Young nodded. "Yeah. Watts says that the whole

group has been hit with something and they are very pleased to see us."

"What the hell happened?"

"Don't know. They just said, 'glad to have your radios back'."

"Radios!" exclaimed Davidson.

"Tell them we'll stay right here until we receive orders to the contrary, and that we will relay all messages if required." Davidson turned back toward the Typhoon and lifted the hailer once again. "Captain Dubrovney, there is no need for you to remain here any longer. I am asking you and your confederates to leave the area immediately."

"Very well Harry, we will do as you ask. But I must say, this has been a very entertaining excursion."

"For the record Captain, which course will you be setting, once you have turned around?"

"Oh, I don't know. How about due South?"

"Very well. Any alteration to that course for the first ten miles will be taken as a hostile action and we'll respond accordingly."

"Don't worry yourself, Captain. We will leave you to clean up the mess you have here."

"Thank you."

"It is okay. If I were in your position, I would probably be a little edgy myself too. Have a good morning, Captain." Mike Young put the intercom down and whispered into Davidson's ear.

"You too, Michael." said Davidson before switching off the hailer. He heard another distant bellow of laughter. Mike Young was also smiling as he took it from him. "Thanks, Mike, that was a good dig."

"Yeah well, when I heard that he'd figured out your first name, I thought the least we could do is return the favor." The noise of water churning in front of them caught their attention. The Typhoon, already on the move, was beginning to make a turn to the left. "Mike, get below and keep our bows on that Russian."

"Aye, sir," said Young disappearing below.

Chapter Forty-Two

Most of the operators by now had given way to the host of civilian technicians who, with meters and test sets, had pulled the very heart and soul of the ship out onto the floor in an attempt to get something working. Meanwhile, up on the flight deck, a red jacket who had been keeping an eye on the *Norwich*, turned to his colleague.

"You hear anything, Dick?"

"Yeah, but where's it coming from?" They both began to make a sweep off the Starboard side, but apart from the *Norwich* and the flashing lamp of the *Philadelphia* further out, there was nothing.

"Sounds like it's pretty close, but where is it?"

"Grab a phone and tell the boss."

"Right," said his friend dashing off to find a phone.

"You see anything?" said another voice from behind him.

"No," said Sergeant Woods, "you?"

"Approaching the stern I think." As though watching a tennis match, they looked back and forth trying to locate the source of the sound. In a vague attempt to get a better look, the two men took a few steps closer to the edge of the deck.

Someone yelled, "port side!" Suddenly, about fifty feet off the Port beam, there appeared the cause of the sudden blast of engine noise. Rising from below the level of the deck, with its undercarriage down, as steady as though it were being raised on a hoist, hovered a bright shining Sea Harrier 4-JH/2 bearing the markings of the British Royal Navy. All the look-outs on duty went scurrying as the aircraft swung over the Carrier, the down force from the four nozzles burning their way into the layers of tire rubber that covered the surface. Finally, as the main wheels and outriggers touched down, the Pegasus pushed the Harrier off to the Starboard side and the roar died down completely. Lieutenant Woods watched the pilot climb out of the cockpit, find a couple of built-in toe-holds, step carefully back along the fuselage out onto the wing, and edge down onto the front of a long-range fuel tank. Sitting down for a moment, he kicked his legs over the edge and let himself drop the few feet to the deck below, directly in front of Woods and his colleague, who had run up to greet him.

"Captain Markham Hawksworth reporting. Ask Captain Gurney if I have permission to come aboard would you. I couldn't raise anyone on the radio." Before Woods could respond, Captain Gurney stepped out from the shadows and held out his hand.

"Permission granted, Captain. Good to see you."

"I imagine so. Some senior brass back in Washington heard you had a spot of bother over here and since I was in the area they sent me over to find out what's up."

"Come on inside. I'm sure the Admiral would like a word." As they made their way up to the bridge the lookouts returned to their posts while Woods chocked the wheels.

"Captain Hawksworth, Royal Navy. Pleased to meet you Admiral," said Hawksworth arriving on the bridge. He saluted.

"At ease, Captain," said Lodgers. "Any idea what's going on?"

"Going to ask you the same thing, sir. As soon as your E-2 chaps lost contact and saw you break formation and grind to a halt, they sent word via AWACS to Bahrain and on from there."

"Yeah, we only found that out after we brought the Hummer back on board," said Lodgers smiling.

"Ah, yes sir. Ever since then your Sentry has been pounding the airwaves."

"What were your orders?"

"To come on over as quickly as I could and let my superiors know why you have suddenly become antisocial."

"That won't be necessary now, thank you," said Lodgers. "We now have full radio communication at our disposal, via the *Philadelphia*."

"Is there anything operational on board, Admiral?" asked Hawksworth almost apologetically.

"No, nothing, except maybe the coffee pot and the garbage disposal," he replied as a phone buzzed. They all turned to see a big smile on Peterson's face.

"Sir, Commander Medlock apologizes for the delay and reports that the main boilers are firing up now, and that we should have marginal steam and minimum propulsion in a few minutes." Every one on the bridge let out an exclamation or two, except for Lodgers who reached for the phone himself.

"Medlock, you told me thirty minutes and it's been over an hour," he said in an authoritative tone. "Forget it Robert. I'll make sure there's a little something extra for you in your next wage packet. Tell me, is there something you did that can help the *Norwich* and the others?" He listened intently for a moment then said, "Good idea, get up to CIC and talk to them directly... No, but we have some portables that have the range." Lodgers put the phone down. "Well," he said turning back to Hawksworth, "we can all rest easy. We will at least have steerage. Brad, send that off to the *Philadelphia* and check to see if we have found anything else airworthy. While you're at it, get the Air Boss up to speed. Davis might be close to using fumes by now. And have as much gear refitted to that Hornet as soon as it touches down. We may have to rely on it for sole air cover for a while yet." Gurney nodded and left the bridge. "You in any rush, Markham?"

"No, sir."

"Sorry I can't offer you any tea."

"That's quite alright, sir, don't normally drink the stuff outside of the U.K. anyway. Coffee would be just fine." Billings nodded and left to find a cup. "Any idea what caused this breakdown, Admiral, if I may call it that?"

"You may, and the answer is no. I've been mostly preoccupied in finding ways to get us operational again, but I can at least say that it affected the entire Group all at the same moment, so I assume it was external."

"Well, sir, you may be interested to know that Admiral Swanson has asked that you be informed that a Black Alert was ordered the moment he heard."

"Good."

"Apparently there is a team for such an eventuality stationed in Bahrain and they're on their way now, sir. E.T.A.," said Hawksworth glancing at his watch, "oh-eight-hundred or there abouts."

"Everyone?"

"Yes, sir, the full team. My orders were to check in with my CO the moment I touched down. Before I taste the brew, Admiral, allow me to call in and reassure my boss that everyone's safe and sound, and that you'll be up and mobile here shortly. I'm sure they'll be glad of the news."

"Very well, Hawksworth, and thanks."

As Hawksworth left the bridge a series of bells sounded from the helm signaling the availability of forward motion and a big smile came over Admiral Lodgers' drawn and tired looking expression. Within moments the bridge had taken on a more familiar look as another helmsman, with one eye on the compass and the other on the engine speed, had taken a headset to talk directly to the stern steering station.

"Engine room reporting ten knots available, Admiral."

"Very well. Do we have word from the *Philadelphia* yet?"

"Yes, sir," Peterson interjected. "Signals received confirm safe heading away from the coast, on zero-nine-zero, sir."

"Very well helmsman, steer zero-nine-zero at ten knots."

"Steering zero-nine zero at ten knots, aye," confirmed the helm.

"Sir," said Peterson. "Flight control confirms pressure in forward cells." For the first time in what to Lodgers seemed like days, the *George Washington* was back in business.

Chapter Forty-Three

The room was buzzing with conversation. Admiral Swanson was on the phone at his desk, Latchkey was sitting at the Admiral's terminal, and the rest of Swanson's executive staff were standing pouring over various documents spread out across the boardroom table. Swanson put the phone down and called the room to attention.

"All right everyone, take a seat will you. That was Greg Buntly," Swanson continued over the shuffling of chairs. "He is calling for a meeting of the N.S.C. shortly and wants everything we have." Swanson walked past the table and down to the blank wall at the end of the room where he pressed a switch. The three large wooden panels slid back to reveal a wall-sized map, a map generated not on paper but on a video display.

"John, give us the south-west Asian theater of operations will you?" Latchkey pressed a few keys and the screen burst into life with an overhead view of the entire Persian Gulf region, with Syria, Afghanistan, the Arabian Sea and Yemen at the four corners. "Now we'll add the U.S. portion of Carrier groups only to the GPS II display." A few more lights dotted across the screen. "These lights demonstrate the Carrier and cruiser bases we have in the area and as you can see, we are not receiving any GPS data from the *George Washington* and its support at Gonzo Station. At zero-one-fifty-seven GMT, Group Six was hit with something that knocked the entire fleet to its knees. We don't know the complete extent of the damage but what I can tell you is that they lost forward power, steam generation, and hence all launch capability, all radio communication, and radar. One of their E-2s called it in when they couldn't raise the *Washington*." Swanson left his position by the screen and began pacing around the table.

"Sir, what about those subs?" asked Captain Haydon, Swanson's liaison officer for the Pacific Fleet.

"I'm coming to that, Pete. First, an off-course Korean 747 flew over Iranian air space. Two Iranian Floggers intercepted the flight, pushed it back toward the Straits, and in so doing the Korean developed fires in two engines. We cannot at this time confirm whether the Migs fired on the Korean or not. Two Tomcats from the *George Washington* took up escort duty and followed the Korean down to Muscat airport. Secondly, we had a convoy of tankers coming down through the Straits when they were fired on by an Iranian Fulcrum. No hits were recorded and no-one was hurt. Three Falcons had been dispatched from Bahrain at the first hint of trouble and were ordered to splash the culprit. Fortunately for us we managed to knock it down before it returned across their border and as we speak the *La Salle* is on its way for retrieval. With any luck we should be able to bring the Mig to the surface before the Iranians can mount any resistance. Thirdly, the Korean flew directly over Group Six and just as it did the *George Washington* and the other ships in Group Six were hit with a device that knocked them out cold. The entire group went dead in the water."

"And lastly, as if all this wasn't enough, one Russian Typhoon and three Foxtrots had approached Station Gonzo, as they put it, to visit the area and carry out some maneuvers. We had moved the fleet further north, just over the Tropic of Cancer inside the Gulf of Oman, to put some distance on the Russians but they kept on moving in. At two o'clock one of the Russian boats, no more than a thousand yards from the Group, surfaced for a look-see. Although they were too close for comfort, the *Philadelphia* in attendance has confirmed that no shot was fired from any of the Russian craft." The entire staff sat in disbelief. "So there it is gentlemen," said Swanson finally, "all the current reports are laid out in front of you."

"Action taken so far, Admiral?" asked Lieutenant Commander Patrick Allen.

"A Black Alert was issued immediately and a team of computer engineers we have based in Bahrain is heading to the *Washington* as we speak. HMS *Connington* was in the area so we had a Harrier go over and take a look, though full communications have been re-established through the *Philadelphia*. We are keeping a Sentry on duty over the area until we get them all back under way. I know it's late and it's the weekend," said Swanson returning to his desk, "but I need everyone working on this now. I want complete data reports from AWACS, from the time the tankers entered the Straits until now. I need a full report from the *Philadelphia* as to what activities the Russians were involved in and whether anything could have been let loose by them without our detecting it, plus updates from the Falcons, the *Walden* and *La Salle*. Pete, how quick can you dispatch an UNREP to them?"

Hayden considered the question for a moment and then said, "The *Wendal* is with the *La Salle* in the Gulf. I'm not sure how loaded she is, but we could get her there in six hours maybe less."

"Do it, even if Group Six picks her clean. Okay everyone get to work." The meeting broke up.

Chapter Forty-Four

This area of the coast line, once lush with green vegetation from a now barren underground spring, was just as desert-like as the rest of Iran. And even though the few remaining trees and foliage were a mere shadow of their former selves, they still afforded sufficient protection for the two launchers located within. Fortunately the very same characteristics used to hide the Silkworms were also available to *Gold Seal*, and while the early morning sky had already begun to reach into the upper branches, darkness still prevailed beneath.

About a hundred feet to the south from the first clearing, the team, with heavy black face and headsets, gathered around Phil and Bill as the two returned from their reconnaissance, then all crouched to the deck.

"Two tents, all still sleeping save for a couple of guards, one in the truck half dozing and the other fixing some breakfast at a table between the tents," said Phil quietly.

"There's a loader parked in the trees on the north side," Bill added. "No-one around. We can keep the tents and the food covered no problem. It's just the forty feet or so to the truck that's a little exposed."

"But we're in luck," continued Phil. "The whole area has good ground cover and by approaching from the north, the view from the tents is obscured by the back end of the launcher, so all you have to do is keep the dozing driver out of sight and you should be okay."

"Sounds good guys," said Digger. "Everybody's headset working?" he asked surveying the nodding heads. "All right then. Bill, Phil go and check the other lot while the rest spread out and cover us." The group separated as Digger and Fielding, circling around to the left in-between the trees, edged ever closer to the clearing. Just as Bill had described, a small loader complete with a store of Silkworms had been driven into the trees as far as the undergrowth would allow.

"Crunch time," whispered Digger.

"Right," said Fielding reaching for a detonator. Digger put his hand on her blood-stained arm and shook his head. "I've only let you come this far because there was no cover to speak of back at the rock, but from here on you should stay well clear."

"Look, Digger," she said softly with a little frustration in her voice. "The launcher is here, the mines are here, and I'm here. You can do this if you want, but I'll do it quicker with less risk. All you have to do is keep a good look out. So let me get to work, okay?"

Digger nodded slowly as he watched her turn the power on, push the cylinder into the mine, and twist it gently. Crouching down they walked slowly through the trees to the front of the fully loaded Silkworm transporter. While she lay down on her back to begin working her way underneath the front wheels, Digger crept to the side of the vehicle to take a long look at the launcher out in the center of the clearing. Although the few dents and poor paintwork throughout its length revealed the age and rough handling that these Russian built vehicles had been given, and while similar in shape but considerably smaller than the SS-1 SCUD Carrier, the unarticulated Silkworm launcher, with its eight rear driving wheels and mobile platform, was still a formidable weapon.

Digger appreciated the darkness and shadows that the dawn gave them and though Bill had been correct in his evaluation of the cover the launcher provided from the rest of the inhabitants, the driver now seemed to be alert and active. Digger felt a hand on his arm and turned to see Fielding's smiling face.

"Are you up for another?" he asked.

"Sure thing," replied Fielding unflinchingly.

"Follow me, closely," said Digger, "and keep away from the door mirror." Digger made his move quickly out into the clearing with Fielding close on his heels. They stepped quickly but softly through the tall weeds making for a point just aft of the high stepped passenger door and rolled underneath. Fielding, lying face up, took Digger's pouch from him and pulled out the brick-like explosive and a detonator. She locked it on the number four setting, inserted it into the block, and reached up high above the transmission to the underside of the frame and gently let it grab.

Both Digger and Fielding heard Buddy's voice in their headsets. "All clear. Driver still in his seat." They both rolled out from under the launcher pulling the tall grass back up behind them as much as possible. "Go," said the voice in their ears and the two followed their own footsteps quickly back into the seclusion of the trees. They found Doug and Buddy guarding their retreat.

"All set?" said Buddy, greeting them both with a smile.

"Yep," Fielding responded.

"When do we test them?" asked Digger.

"On our way out," replied Fielding.

"Okay. Phil, we're ready," said Digger into his headset.

"Come on over," replied Phil. "We'll meet you on the west side." The group moved off in single file with Digger leading. After walking a few hundred feet, Phil stepped out in front of them and crouched down. "Not so good Digger," he said as the rest knelt to join him. "Same set up as before with one guy cooking, but there's two mechanics working on top of the launcher and from their vantage point, they can see all the way around."

"Any ideas?" asked Digger.

"Possibly," Phil continued. "The two mechanics are standing in front of the racks facing the rear. Their tool boxes are on top of the cab in front. Now you're totally exposed while they fish tools out from the boxes, but the boxes actually obscure their view of the front grass, once they've returned. And though the cook, standing out in the open, has full view of the area in front of the cab his stores are located in the tent somewhat behind the vehicle."

"Sounds good," said Digger. "Where is their Worm store located?"

"That's the other problem. Bill's checking it out now. All the Silkworms have been off-loaded for some reason and have been set just on the edge of the clearing. Access to them is easy but if they're moved for any reason, anything we leave behind is bound to be discovered."

"Okay, positions everyone. Doug stay here with Fielding while Phil and I take a look," said Digger getting to his feet. Phil led the way through the trees around to the east side of the clearing, and even though all was quiet, Phil stopped at a point about halfway, crouched down and spoke into his headset.

"Buddy, crossing the trail now."

"All clear here," came the response and Phil got up again, crossed the path, and led Digger to where a large stack of Silkworm missiles lay half hidden under a tarpaulin close to the edge of the trees.

Phil pointed to some tire tracks leading away from the pile. "Looks like they unloaded them and just drove off back through the trail they cut into the trees over there on the north side. Do you think they had some trouble with the vehicle itself and took it away somewhere to be fixed?"

"Maybe," Digger replied, "but since they seem to have a lot of tools here, it must have been a major problem for them not to attempt a fix on site, unless... Chancey do you read me?"

"Copy, Digger."

"How many missiles can that truck carry?"

"About twelve."

"Did you happen to count how many were still on it?"

"Eight."

"Thanks. So we don't need to put one here at all."

"Right, what's the good of having missiles if you can't use them?"

"Doug, bring Fielding over to the west side and ask her to prime one for me. I'm doing the next one on my own." Digger and Phil crossed back over the trail to meet Fielding and Doug in the middle of the trees directly opposite the front of the truck. Fielding handed Digger a Porky already primed.

"Just two things, Digger," she said quickly. "I don't need to tell you to place it out of sight, but when you commit, reach up and allow one end to touch first, then one side applying as much resistance away from the frame as possible. It makes quite a loud clunk if you let it bite full face. Besides, even if they're set on low sensitivity, allowing the magnetic base to jump onto the frame may set it off."

"Thanks," Digger said with a wry smile on his face as he walked slowly off toward the clearing. Since the early morning sky was now bright enough to clearly reveal any intruder making steps into the open, Digger took his time. He stood just inside the closest long shadow and watched the two heads of the two mechanics, barely visible as they worked high on the rear of the truck. The cook was in plain view to his right fiddling around with his primitive stove. After two minutes, one of the mechanics turned and made a few steps to the front where three tool boxes sat on the roof of the cab. The Iranian sorted through them for a moment, decided on one and turned to make his way back to the rear. Just at that moment the cook chose to leave his chores and meander off toward the tents. The rest of the team encircled the clearing and watched as Digger, quickly and silently, covered the forty feet to the front of the truck effortlessly, disappearing from view underneath the front axle.

Up to this point everything had gone as smoothly as anyone could have expected and Digger would have had no problem returning to the safety of the trees, if it hadn't been for the clumsy tool-finder above. Just as Digger was gently placing the device up against the gearbox, a mechanic had walked forward to find another wrench and, having chosen one to his liking, pulled it out of the box and proceeded to let it slip from his grasp. It tumbled noisily down through the framework behind the cab and landed with a soft thud right next to Digger, nearly causing him to let the magnetic attraction suck the metal casing hard onto the transmission. But Digger froze, gripping onto the Porky as firmly as he could at arm's length and let the device gently grab the casing.

"Freeze!" ordered Buddy in his ears.

"Now you tell me," mouthed Digger. But instead of remaining still, Digger did the opposite. He picked up the wrench and tossed it out just behind the left front tire and rolled back into obscurity. The mechanic, swearing and cursing at his clumsiness, started to yell something at the cook who by now was making his way back to his stove.

"He's telling the cook to go and find the wrench for him," said Fielding into her headset as Doug and the rest of the team took aim at their respective targets. "The cook is arguing. Too busy. He's a cook not a mechanic," she continued inching closer to the clearing to catch as much of the shouting as possible.

Digger remained still now that the cook had once again regained full view of the area in front of the truck. All the noise and commotion was beginning to disturb the sleeping crews and one by one half dazed, half dressed soldiers began to appear outside the tents, yelling at the mechanic and cook for disturbing their sleep. In the space of a few moments a crowd had developed around the cook, smelling the food and pouring coffee, all apparently oblivious to the fact that the mechanic was still shouting for someone to find the wrench. He obviously wanted someone to save him from having to climb down and find it himself.

The situation was turning nasty. One soldier having filled a tin mug with brew decided to end the verbal brawling by walking over to the side of the launcher to see what he could find. He waved his free arm as if holding a magic wand and the abuse suddenly stopped. The mechanic started to point to an area where the wrench had fallen and even though his volume had softened considerably, he still continued with a chatter consistent with a tired, overworked, underpaid employee trying to get some sympathy. They didn't know that six automatic weapons were now trained on various parts of their uniforms. The volunteer bent down to examine the ground but before he had time to notice anything unusual under the truck, he reached down and retrieved the shiny tool laying in the grass. Standing up he waived it for all to see as the gathering food line applauded half heartily.

Rather than climbing the sides, he tossed it carelessly up to the waiting mechanic who stumbled slightly, grabbing at thin air in a vain attempt in preventing the wrench falling back down to earth. He missed his mark and the wrench fell with a loud clang into the launcher once more. The crowd starting yelling and shouting again as the mechanic looked down around him but suddenly the reflected brilliance in his hand quelled the noise that by now had brought every sleeping Iranian soldier out into the open.

Fielding pushed her microphone away from her lips, turned quickly to Doug and whispered urgently, "the radio, give me the radio." Doug looked back at her in disbelief. They moved away from the clearing as Fielding quickly pulled from her pocket a small black book and thumbed through the pages. "Doug, I'm not calling for help, I'm going to give some." She spun him around and opened his back pack. Grabbing for the handset she changed frequencies, turned the speaker volume all the way off and plugged in her own headset. She thumbed a direction further back in the trees, grabbed Doug's arm and pulled him fifty feet away from the clearing. "Down," she said turning the power on. "Digger, I'm going to call up their local radio to gain their attention. I just hope the radio in the truck is turned off."

"What do you think, Buddy?" said Doug.

"We need something and we need it now before those goons get truck happy," came his response.

"Buddy, tell me as soon as you see a reaction."

"Okay." Fielding started to talk into the handset in an Iranian dialect, her voice was soft and inviting. "Nothing yet," said Buddy. Fielding closed her eyes and moved the handset closer to her mouth. She continued with some form of dialogue that sounded smooth and fascinating.

"Someone's come out of the tent carrying a bag. I think it's a radio," said Phil. "He's shouting something to the guy who found the wrench." While Fielding continued the dialogue, Phil kept up his commentary. "They've brought it over to the food table and someone's playing with the controls. I can just hear a voice coming from the crowd gathering at the table. It's a woman's voice. They're reaching for the handset, trying to make contact I think. Even the two mechanics are climbing down to go see what's up. Everyone's staring at the radio."

"Now, Digger, now!" Buddy's voice ordered over the commentary. Fielding raised her voice a little as though objecting to something. Her eyes were closed. Her head began to roll from side to side as she delivered each line of dialogue. Her face looked snarled and determined.

Buddy shouted, "He's out! He's out!"

"I'm clear," came Digger's quiet whisper. Fielding still continued her one-sided conversation while Phil continued his commentary.

"Each of them in turn are trying to talk on the radio but they're not having too much success."

"Fielding and I are on the west side," said Doug.

"Okay everyone, let's get out of here," said Digger with authority. Fielding's voice began to soften once more and a smile returned to her face. She opened her eyes slowly as she reached for the tuner. The rest of the team, each with the look of appreciation on their faces, began surrounding Fielding waiting for her to finish. She acknowledged their admiring glances with a nod as a beautiful smile broke across her face and twisted the tuner a little further. As her last words died to a whisper Digger arrived. She redialed the radio to it's original setting, put the handset back onto it's mount, and closed Doug's pack.

"Good work, Fielding," said Digger with the first real words of encouragement he had given her since they had met. "I want to hear what you were saying to those guys but more about your bedside manner later. Let's get those Porkies fired up."

"Already accomplished, Digger," she said casually as she zipped up her waist pack, joining the rest of the group returning to their single file formation.

"What?!" said Digger stumbling over her heels from behind.

"I have a little portable. They're all set and ready to go."

"What setting?"

"My orders were to set them for launch prevention."
Digger nodded in approval and made his way to the front
of the line. If *Gold Seal* had secured the area one day
later the Silkworm launch that evening would have been
devastating to tanker shipping in the area but as it was
the entire Iranian outpost was destroyed.

Chapter Forty-Five

The *La Salle*, although carrying somewhat limited salvage equipment, was the only ship in the Gulf that could handle a lift of this size and so had been ordered to make for the southern end of the Gulf, even before the Fulcrum had hit the water. While the diving team prepared URPS for launch, General Quarters had sounded on board the cruiser and all available hands made ready the port-side crane. The signal sent to Captain Tim Connolly warned of possible Iranian maneuvers designed to prevent their salvage work so lookouts had been posted to keep watch for any small local threat as well as possible recovery attempts on any surviving crew. As Lieutenant Bob Greenman, wearing a lightweight shirt and shorts, climbed into the Underwater Repair and Salvage craft to join his fellow diving companion to start the pre-dive checks, the auxiliary winch's hook swung down over the stern ready for the launch. Greenman settled into his prone position next to Lieutenant Victor Manning and donned his headset.

"Give me an audio check please," he said checking the battery levels.

"Roger Bob, we read you," answered control.

"Ready on list one," Greenman confirmed, and the various procedures began. Captain Connolly continued to rush the *La Salle* as directed by AWACS to a point where the Mig had hit the water, passing word to both Greenman and Manning that the expected E.T.A. was ten minutes and to be prepared to dive immediately upon arrival.

Chapter Forty-Six

Everybody on board the *George Washington* had been working feverishly to bring the main systems back on line and even though the ship was once again under power with launch capability, every department had seen the level of activity drop depressingly low. The technicians had exhausted all of the stores and since rebuilding or combining parts was next to impossible, they reluctantly resigned themselves to wait for reinforcements to arrive. Some low-range radio use was becoming available but no main communications, no radar, no nucleonics and no defense systems. Although a lone Hornet was now on station above Group Six, interdiction capability was as yet non-existent. A comprehensive status report was continuing to flash across the waters from the signals deck high atop the tower to the *Philadelphia* for re-transmission via NAVSAT to the Pentagon as the rest of Group Six, having regained some forward propulsion, took up their respective positions around the Carrier.

Out on the flight deck, Hawksworth prepared to climb aboard the Harrier.

Gurney shook Hawksworth's hand. "Thank Captain Smith for me, will you? We appreciate his concern."

"Will do, Captain. I'm sure you would have done the same for us in similar circumstances," Hawksworth replied. "I'm rather sorry I have to leave so soon but my chief wants me back toot-sweet. I just hope that you manage to find out what caused all of this before whoever it was has a go at us."

"So do I," Gurney agreed.

"If you don't mind my saying so, Captain, you look a sight better now than you did when I first came aboard," said Hawksworth cheerfully.

"Yes, well, feeling this breeze bowling down the deck can work wonders."

Hawksworth turned and climbed the steps to the cockpit, the Pegasus 103 sprang into life, the chocks were pulled away and after a signal from the Launch Director the single seat Harrier rolled over the launch area and lifted gently into the morning air nosing north back towards the *Connington*.

Captain Gurney made his way back down to the main communications area adjacent to CIC and found Commander Treedle seated at his desk under a bright light peering down through a microscope at a circuit board.

"Anything interesting, John?" asked Gurney sitting down on the corner of Treedle's desk.

"Not really," replied Treedle rocking back in his chair as he rubbed the tiredness from his eyes. "All I know is that every single one of our twenty-eight radios failed, including, which concerns me the most, the Morse Unit. Our civilian colleagues have already ripped these boards to shreds and told me that basically everything's intact. The only thing that is different from this board here and the one that functions properly is that the memory has taken a holiday and the programs just loop around and around endlessly, as though the mind has been knocked unconscious. Funny thing though, on the Morse circuitry there is no memory or circuit board of any kind, yet it failed as well."

"Perhaps it failed for a different reason?" said Gurney.

"Maybe, but if it didn't, whatever or whoever did this sure knew how to cripple us completely. Did you know that even the Microwave ovens in the galley failed as well?" said Treedle finally looking up at Gurney to reveal the worried expression on his face.

"No, I didn't."

"Well, all I can say is that if we don't find out what caused this and find out quickly, whoever did this might just set another one off at Bahrain and completely cripple our air cover, or incapacitate our ability to secure the no-fly zone in the north. The *Independence* for example could be next."

"I know. What steps are you taking at the moment?" Gurney asked, preparing to leave.

"I've got three of our best guys working on building

a set that can communicate at least with the Hummer if not the NAVSATS directly."

"To be frank, John, it's all a little beyond me how, with all our sophistication and back-up systems, we have to build a set from scratch just to regain our links with head office," Gurney remarked somewhat disparagingly, making a statement as much as asking the question.

"Every set these days is built using various memories that are used to govern and lock-on frequencies to clean audio and to monitor the systems. They've become such an integral part of running radios of all description that once they fail, the entire unit fails. So much for modern technology."

"You mean modern technology is bad?"

Treedle smiled. "The old units we had on the *Sara* relied on steam as much as anything to keep them running. They had no chips, no silicon, just a couple of tubes and some condensers. If she was hit with this thing she may have coughed and spluttered for a moment but then would have kept on going as though nothing had happened. At least the Communications Department would have been able to maintain operations even if another part of the ship had suffered."

"And I suppose we don't have any of those old radios on board any more?" asked Gurney, rubbing the back of his neck.

"Correct, they went out with the Ark, though I hear we did have some old handsets from way back that came through for us. But seriously, our new sets are some of the best in the world and every single sensitive area that may be vulnerable to attack, as you know Brad, is protected to prevent such a thing occurring.

"Well, John, in this case, apparently not."

Chapter Forty-Seven

It had been three hours since Major Barton had left the main road and slowed to under thirty miles an hour, and ten minutes since the warning light had started flashing again. His internal navigation and some dead reckoning told Barton that he still had some fifty miles to go to make the shore line, although at this moment the Major was beginning to wonder whether the coast was where he should head. Any pick-up that could be orchestrated would certainly be conspicuous. He just hoped that as long as his location was kept from the Iranian forces, by the time they had reacted to his rescue he would be out of their reach. However, now that his cover had been torn to shreds, it wouldn't be long before the entire Iranian Defense Force would be sending out helicopters and scouts to track him down. The more Barton chewed over his possibilities, the more he accepted the need to use emergency procedures.

"If ever there was an emergency pick-up needed," he said out loud, "this is it!" He took another glance at his mirrors but still nothing. It had been at least an hour since he'd turned off his own headlights and apart from the large cloud of sand and dust that was his constant companion there wasn't much to see behind at all. Increasing his speed to above fifty once again and keeping one eye on the road and one on the mirror, he pulled the glove off his right hand, reached underneath the dashboard and started to feel around. Somewhere behind the speedometer a switch had been located to activate his GPS. The last time it had been tested was just before he had driven in through a quiet, but risky gap in Iran's back door with Pakistan, but with all the bangs and knocks the jeep had taken since his arrival it was doubtful whether it was going to work at all. As his fingers traced the outline of the small switch hidden between the cables he applied some pressure. As he did so, it sprang into action, bringing with it the bright flash of the oil warning light.

Barton's nerves were frayed, his stomach was empty and his eyelids were fighting back that warm, sleepy feeling that comes to everyone who goes without sleep for too long. He reached inside his jacket and pulled out a small gun-metal flask. Twisting off the cap, he took a long hard gulp and returned the flask to his pocket. In times such as these the taste, more in keeping with the mess hall than the sand, did as much to remind him of his drinking partners as it was to jolt his body awake. Accepting that his fate was probably sealed one way or the other, he forced his mind to concentrate on those few desperate moments driving through the convoy and the sight of the Migs flying low overhead. He pictured the truck and the men hanging out the back. He replayed the tape of the sudden roar of jet engines and the brief glimpse of the two Fulcrums without running lights. Suddenly Barton cried out. "What an idiot I've been. Of course! Why didn't I realize it before?!" His thoughts began to race. Perhaps all his training and experience had put him into Iran just so that he could be the witness to an event that could change the course of history for the entire region. "And I nearly missed it!" he yelled. He reached for the radio. "Rhinestone calling Top Hat, Rhinestone calling Top Hat, come in please." Aboard AWACS 21 some four hundred miles to the south-west the tapes began to roll.

"This is Top Hat, twenty-twenty, go-ahead."

"Urgent for Cherry-Red. Two new storms heading south are suspect, repeat suspect. Started two hours ago. Although the storms are strong, their origin is suspect, repeat suspect. We need a permit. Do you read?"

"Yes, suspect and permit all ready on the way. E.T.A. Oh-nine-thirty."

"Thank you. Oh-nine-thirty. Out."

Chapter Forty-Eight

Although the entire team had been just as cautious on the way back as they had been on the way in, it took them far less time. As they reached the cover of the bushes close to the cliff edge, Digger waited for Fielding.

"What did you mean, you've turned them on already?" he asked.

"I had them both armed and tested while you were waiting to leave the underside of that truck," said Fielding, concentrating on the path ahead.

"But I thought you said that you were going to test them after we've left the area?" continued Digger.

"I lied. They're all tested and ready to go."

"But that could have meant that if I'd have been caught under there and the driver had decide to drive off, I might not be here to listen to this."

"True, but the chance of that happening was pretty slim. Besides, if they weren't working properly I would have needed you to make some adjustments to it while you were still under the truck."

"Great, thanks for letting me know," said Digger sarcastically. "Just for the record, what setting did you leave the transmitter on?"

"Nine."

"Nine?" said Digger nervously, raising his voice in the process and looking around as if to see if anyone had heard him.

Fielding looked into Digger's brown eyes and smiled, "Just kidding." Digger shook his head in disgust.

Phil had already gone ahead and had checked out the area before the team had arrived at the cliff edge. The bags were retrieved from behind the bushes, a line secured for the descent, and Bill quickly disappeared from view over the edge. As Phil, Chancey and Doug followed suit, Digger and Buddy prepared the long line loosely around the nearest trunk, sending both of the long ends down to the beach below. Digger reached into a bag, pulled out a can, and proceeded to spray the bark area at the back of the tree, on which the line would eventually have to slide. In about two minutes the dark mist would turn a somewhat tough bark into a shiny, slippery surface, allowing the rope to be pulled around from either side. While Fielding and the rest of the team sailed down the face, Digger and Buddy lowered the bags and gear and prepared to clear the site. Buddy took the strain of the long line looped around the tree as Digger dropped to the beach. Then from below Phil and Chancey hung to Digger as Buddy loosened himself from the tree, tied an extra length onto the long line, and sailed down the cliff himself. Pulling the rest of the line up from the beach, around the tree and back down again, the team dressed and prepared to get under way.

The retreating tide had enlarged their hide-out considerably and even though it meant that *Gold Seal* would be exposed a little longer when making for the water's edge, the risk was minimal. Canny had climbed into his underwater gear and was heading out into the waves to strip the Dingy of its anchors and fire up it's engines. Chancey retrieved the dismantled lower pulley arrangement and stowed it away with the other gear. Finally, after Buddy had finished a complete check of the area, they all donned their diving suits, checked their pressures, and walked out with the bags swinging between them into the cool waters of the Straits of Hormuz.

Chapter Forty-Nine

The tannoy sounded. "Prepare to retrieve on the starboard side, prepare to retrieve on the starboard side." The *Connington*, having just entered the Persian Gulf only a couple of days before, was stationed in its southern waters and had been carrying out maneuvers when the call had gone out to Hawksworth to check up on the *George Washington*.

The *HMS Connington* was brand new, having been commissioned just three months earlier, and was considered by many as the future replacement for many traditional Carrier duties. About the size of a frigate, she boasted two eight inch guns, two Phalanx gatlings and twin Harpoon launchers. Aft of the main superstructure, in front of the broad landing area that stretches across the full width of the ship, stood the hanger that provides cover and engineering space for the eight Royal Navy Harriers. In all other respects, the Connington is traditional in layout to many sea based V/TOL platforms save for two very conspicuous additions. Located on either side of the hanger deck and looking more like mis-placed masts, two large crane-like arms stretch high into the morning sky. Although these cranes, referred to as 'Hooks' by the Navy, contain no actual hooks, they act in very similar fashion. The end of each crane is equipped with four straight fingers stretching downward and outward each six foot long. On the end of each finger sits a synthetic rubber cup facing inward. In the center, extending down from the crane with a strong grabbing device on the end, is the 'hook' itself. Watching over this grabbing device affixed immediately above the fingers, a video camera and flood lights assist in the operation. Governed by sophisticated computer software, these lifting cranes have the capability of moving from 'Ship Orientation' to 'Spacial Orientation', permitting the movement of the protruding grab to be precisely located up to forty feet beyond the ship's confines and held within an inch or two of a predetermined point, regardless of the ship's pitch and yawl.

Hawksworth had already brought the throttles back from full to slow cruise dropping from eight thousand feet to four thousand when he received his clearance from flight officer Lieutenant Brookings in Launch Control.

"Javelin three, this is Snatch control. Do you read?"

"Roger, Snatch, this is Javelin three, ready to come aboard." Brookings eyed his three monitors keenly. The screen to his left, overseen by his assistant Lieutenant Morgan, displayed the same telemetry as offered on the HUD in the approaching Harrier. The main monitor in front of him was a direct link from the video camera mounted on top of the arm. Lieutenant Nick Brookings readied his sensitive fingers for the two sets of controls that governed the movement of the huge arm, pressed the 'Unlock' and, keeping a careful check of one of five preset computer programs that maneuver the hundred foot crane out over the side of the *Connington*, prepared to dial up the local frequency. The huge arm, stretching somewhat precariously outward, was still locked to the deck, rocking up and down and from side to side as the *Connington* rolled through the gentle seas of the Gulf.

"Javelin, this is Snatch, going Spacial now," said Brookings, reaching for the key marked 'Convert' and pressing it firmly. As the half-ton gyroscope began to spin, four motors, one to each footing of the crane, altered the attitude of the hook with respect to the water line. This action maneuvered the base so that the entire structure began to stand boldly upright seemingly regardless of the movement of the ship, remaining totally motionless with all respects to a fixed altitude above sea level. The main computers that run the altitude of the base, assisted by the horizontal stability of the gyroscopes that maintain perfect control of the arm, are all designed to allow the Hook to act completely independent of the frigate's movement through the water.

Brookings took the controls, fine-tuned the position of the grab, and touched the ship's intercom.

"Divers to starboard side station and prepare to retrieve." Above water line, just forward of the stern on the starboard side, a large door opened revealing one of two rear facing launch shoots for the inflatables. Three divers climbed aboard ready to be thrust out into the warm seas in the case of a ditching. Engine failure was rare at the critical moment of capture, and although not one Harrier had been lost since the *Connington's* first sea trials, the divers were always prepared to rush out to a ditching and grab a pilot from the sinking craft. Indeed, the Royal Navy was proud of their record that, from launch to extrication of the pilot to the safety of the inflatable, had been lowered to just eighty-nine seconds.

"Javelin, this is Snatch. We are Spacial. Ready to receive. Switch to Local."

"Roger, Snatch, switching to Local." Hawksworth touched his radio briefly. "Snatch, this is Javelin on finals."

"We confirm, Javelin. We are ready to receive you on the starboard side," said Brookings. "Our speed... thirty knots, no cross-wind. Transmitters on, you may power Hedges up now."

"Roger. Hedges on." Hawksworth watched his HUD come alive with the two brightly illuminated, horizontal arrows of the Hook Engagement System. Bringing the throttles back to seventy percent, he moved the in-board slide control of the nozzles from 100/00 back to 50/50. The HUD also displayed the static vertical and horizontal lines of the cross-hairs as two bright green arrows appeared from each side, remaining still until the range closed within a thousand yards. Once the HEGES was engaged, the closer Hawksworth came to the grab, the closer the point of each arrow came to the other until they would touch, indicating the perfect location for contact. All the pilot had to do was align his aircraft so that as the arrow heads touched, they would be obscuring the horizontal cross-hair while dissecting the vertical. At this point the grab is ready to make contact with the elevated ball that sits up proud behind the cockpit at the airframe's center of gravity. It is this protrusion that makes this 'H' version of the Harrier very distinguishable to even the most casual observer.

If the aircraft moves beyond the envelope for grab activation, the arrows would overlap and turn red, requiring the pilot to slow the Harrier and allow the ship to move forward relative to its own position. This would bring the arrows back to the head-to-head alignment and confirm grab capability once again. Ideally, as the instructors had put it, the objective for an 'acceptable' arrival inside the landing window is as follows:

1. Your forward speed should slow to equal the mother-ship's precisely when the two arrows touch, while maintaining altitude of 70 feet.

2. Wings level, slightly nose up, the arrows should obscure the horizontal cross-hairs.

3. The arrow heads should touch each other and the cross-hairs simultaneously.

4. The entire procedure should be completed on the first attempt.

The two arrows moved slowly toward each other. They started drifting in tandem to the left, indicating that he needed to use a little left rudder. The arrows drifted back to the middle, dropped below the center line and tilted to the right as the left wing dropped slightly. Hawksworth nudged the nose and the right wing down as his left hand, ambidextrous within itself, continued to tweak the throttles with his fingers and the nozzle attitude with the thumb.

The two arrows were being drawn ever closer together, and even though Hawksworth's attention was fixed on the moving indicators in front of him, he glimpsed out of the corner of his eye at the *Connington*. With its port arm carrying a Harrier out over the side in preparation for launch, the starboard side crane stood motionless in contrast, awaiting to receive. His forward speed had now dropped to forty-five knots as eighty percent of the Pegasus's main thrust was being directed downward through the nozzles at 25/75, punching four big holes into the warm waters just a hundred feet below.

"Looking good, Javelin. Five hundred feet," said

Brookings, beginning his talk-in routine. "Switch to Fine."

"Switching to Fine," confirmed Hawksworth as he dialed up the sensitivity of his HUD. The arrows moved further out and began a more exaggerated motion.

Brookings began to talk him in. "Four hundred. A little high." Hawksworth brought the arrows back up to the center line. "Left rudder. Three hundred. Looking good. A little fast." Hawksworth stroked the nozzle angles to 20/80. "A little high, soften the power." The increased downward angle had increased his altitude but Hawksworth was already on it.

When pilots are first trained for Harrier Squadrons, it becomes obvious very quickly that with every variation of the nozzle settings, power adjustments were necessary, simultaneously. Many a novice, attempting his first simulated landing, found that no matter how many procedures were discussed in the classroom, there was no substitute for the real thing. Slowing from a forty percent forward thrust, the nozzles are lowered, but forty percent power is not enough to take the full weight of the aircraft. As lift is lost, the Harrier loses altitude so more thrust is required. With nozzles at 50/50 and with forward speed too high, the nozzles are increased to the vertical, but at 25/75 a greater percentage of the thrust is directed downward so that as the aircraft slows, it gains altitude. Conversely close to the hover, moving the nozzles aft some five degrees gains forward speed but loses upward pressure.

"Two hundred. Looking good," Brookings continued.

Hawksworth rotated the nozzles to 20/80 and dropped the power slightly to maintain altitude. "One hundred. Looking good. All systems ready."

"Roger, Snatch," Hawksworth replied over the roar of the Pegasus.

"Fifty feet... forty... thirty... twenty.. ten feet," Brookings counted. First the top of the nose and then the canopy appeared on the monitor before him. "Ready for the lights," he said, turning on the floods just above the camera for a better look. "Five feet." Brookings began to manipulate the grab so that it lined up with the approaching stem. The grab was quick and in some ways effortless for the pilot. With quick dexterity, the moment the stem came into view, Brookings lowered the grab to within a couple of feet of the slowing airframe. "Prepare to be received." The ball on the end of the stem protruding up from behind the cockpit of the Harrier was a little low, left and still moving forward at about three knots. With a quick deft flick of the wrists, the grab lowered and reached for the ball and at the moment of contact, the strong grips at the end of the rod took firm hold of it. Within two seconds the four fingers had closed on the body of the aircraft, two each side of the fuselage's hump applying sufficient pressure to stabilize the entire aircraft's movement. "We have contact," said Brookings confidently.

Upon hearing the 'good lock' tones, Hawksworth replied, "roger, contact." He pushed the nozzles to the hover position for the full maneuver to the pad in the event of some failure with the arm, and to relieve the overall loadings on the grab and the crane itself.

"Moving in-board, prepare for motion," said Brookings as the giant arm began to swing the aircraft in over the ship, the huge motors working hard on its own independent equilibrium. "Transferring to Ship Orientation now," Brookings stated as he keyed in the computer governing the crane's functions. The gyroscopes began to spool down and the motors began to return the legs of the crane to the parked position parallel to the ship's deck, a transition left until the Harrier was relatively close to the pad, again to keep the pulling and tugging of the Harrier on the crane to a minimum. "Activate landing gear," continued Brookings.

"Gear activated." The two main sets of undercarriage wound their way down together with the two outriggers. "And locked," confirmed Hawksworth as he gave in to the unnatural movement of the cockpit.

"Twenty feet." Brookings continued, studying the third monitor that gave him a profile of the touch down. The computer landing gave the airframe the softest of thumps as the tires found their target and took the strain. "Touch down, Javelin. All secure."

"Thanks for the ride, Nick, over and out," said Hawksworth gratefully as the engines spooled down. Although one of the most experienced Harrier pilots in the Navy, he admitted that it would still take some time for him to become accustomed to the ride aboard the Hook.

"Well there you are, me old fruit," said Flight Leftenant Chris Booker. Dressed in his flight gear, he climbed the ladder to greet Hawksworth and stuck his head in under the rising canopy. "Beginning to wonder what you look like." Hawksworth gave Booker a smile and finished unbuckling himself. "So how is everything out there in the big wide world? Pretty quiet I hear."

Booker made way as Hawksworth climbed out of the cockpit and followed him to the deck. "Yes, but they're up and running now."

"Good, sir. The skip's on the bridge at the moment holding forth. Said he'd like a word with you in about fifteen minutes." Crews arrived to refuel and check the aircraft as the two walked off toward the hanger area. "So, while you're hob-knobbing over 'brekkers' with the brass I'm taking this puppy back out for another sortie."

"You know there's a briefing at noon today, Booker?" Hawksworth questioned, removing his headgear.

"Aye, sir. I'll be there."

"That'll be a first," said Hawksworth leaving Booker to his buttons and clips. He made his way to his quarters for a quick shower and change before seeing Captain Smith. After his meeting, he was allowed time to eat a hearty breakfast, and he consumed it as though it was his last.

Chapter Fifty

John Latchkey had known where the meeting was being held and had been holding on the phone about ten minutes before his chief had managed to break away.

"Yes, John, what is it?" Swanson sounded tired.

"Sorry to interrupt, sir, but we have just heard from the Iranian Embassy. They are denying any involvement in the incident and said that it was another stunt engineered by their neighbors."

"Well, I guessed that would be their response. Did the report mention anything about retrieval?"

"No, sir. Just that they are carrying out their own investigations and will notify us in due course. Anything I can do, sir?"

"No, thanks. Will you still be at the office later?"

"If you think it's necessary, sir."

"I do. The meeting should be breaking up soon. I'll be back as soon as I can."

Chapter Fifty-One

Upon arrival, Lieutenants Greenman and Manning had taken their craft deep into the Gulf's oily and murky waters, finding terra-firma about a hundred and seventy feet. Greenman, having run the complete check list on the submersible, received the go-ahead and the heading to sweep for the remains of the downed aircraft. Just a few minutes later, right where it should be, the dark shadowy remains appeared before them.

"We found it," said Greenman to the many ears eagerly awaiting the news on the surface. "And it looks in relatively good shape too."

"Great work guys," replied their dive commander. "The winch is on its way." Through the cloudy port, Manning surveyed the scene. Part of a wing had been torn away, part of the tail section had been blown off, the nose was crushed and the canopy was missing, but the unmistakable shape of one of Russia's leading aircrafts came into view.

"He made it out alright," said Manning.

"Yeah. Come on, lets get down to business." Greenman increased the revolutions and steered the craft closer to the wreckage. "How are we going to tackle this, Vic?"

"Take us in a little closer, perhaps there's some convenient damage we can use." Greenman took the craft in closer, hovering gently over the airframe. "There, just behind the cockpit." Just aft of where the canopy used to sit, a large hole revealed part of the structure.

"Will it take the weight?"

"Shouldn't be a problem. It's close enough to the center of gravity, that if we can get the hook under that spar we should be able to take her all the way up in one go."

"Winch arriving," confirmed the Dive Commander.

Greenman peered out of the port. "There it is." He pulled gently on the controls, swinging URPS up toward the cable. As he closed in on the large hook, Manning sent one of the URPS' arms out and in one quick motion, grabbed it firmly in the jaws.

"All set here, Commander. Give us another thirty feet," said Manning.

"Thirty feet, Roger," came the reply and the winch line went slack. Greenman powered up and pushed toward the Mig as Manning extended the arm holding the hook. As they approached the gash in the fuselage, Manning twisted the grips to position the large upside down question-mark so that it would drop down into the airframe. The pitch of the small motors began to shake under the strain as Manning steered the hook into the hole.

Manning released the grip's hold on the hook. "Take up the slack."

"Taking up slack," the voice confirmed. As Greenman backed the URPS away from the aircraft, the cable began taking the strain.

"Looks like a good one," said Greenman as the hook locked itself on to something under the skin of the Mig. "Take the strain."

"Taking the strain," the voice confirmed. The remains began to lift off the sea bed, nose first. Greenman backed the submersible off about twenty feet and pumped water out of the two main chambers to begin the ascent along with the Mig. As Lieutenant Bob Greenman stared out of the small window at the rather chopped silhouette of the Mig-29 Fulcrum being carried aloft, he noticed for the first time the circular identification marks of the Iranian Air Force insignia along the fuselage just aft of the wing. Green outer, white middle and red center. Now, Greenman thought to himself, we will have the overwhelming proof that those Iranians tried to blow us from the water. But something nagged at Greenman's memory as he watched the Mig being winched ever higher, a feeling that something wasn't quite right. The Fulcrum, now one hundred feet from the surface, suddenly stopped rising as their ears sprang to life with the voice of Commander Clarke.

"We have some bogies closing fast. Sit tight, we'll notify you of any developments," and the line went quiet.

"Looks like the owners of that wreck have come to get it back," said Manning as he noticed, even in the dim lighting, the concerned look on his friend's face.

"Migs?"

"Who else?"

"Great, just what we need," Greenman replied. "Here we are dangling at the end of a life line and the Iranians want to play war games."

Chapter Fifty-Two

On the heli-pad, Commander Tom Carlton held on to his hat as the blades of the Sea Hawk gained momentum. Before him, wearing a bright red wet suit and full underwater gear, stood Lieutenant William Zanowski.

"Look, Willy," shouted Carlton over the engine noise. "All you have to do when we give you the signal is to drop down to about sixty feet and wait. We'll give you the direction to the contact just before you drop. Within thirty seconds, light the flares, okay?"

"Aye, sir." Salutes were exchanged and Zanowski climbed aboard. He gave the thumbs-up to the cockpit and grabbed hold as the Hawk's rotors changed their pitch and began fighting for lift. The *Stork* drifted from sight as the pilot flew over the bow and pushed on ahead over the three tankers until, some one hundred yards in front of the British Minesweeper, it banked to the right and dropped down to within inches of the surface.

"Ready!" came a voice from behind as Zanowski felt a hand on his shoulder. "The direction is East, two minutes." Zanowski moved out to the door and sat down on the ledge. He spit in to his goggles and slid the residue over the glass just as he heard the hiss of his oxygen supply being turned on. Taking the mouth-piece and breathing through it, he pulled his flippers tight around his ankles and gave a thumbs up. The water looked warm and inviting.

Zanowski, the relatively young chief diving officer aboard the *Stork*, hadn't had many opportunities to put his training to good use since his transfer to the ship some six months earlier. But now as he looked down at the inviting waters of the Straits some twenty feet below, he couldn't wait to get on with his task. The Hawk had slowed to a few knots, drifting slightly to the right, when he received a firm slap on his tank. "Go!" shouted the voice and he found himself slipping the few feet to the waters below.

The cool chill was refreshing as Zanowski swam

down to the sixty foot mark where he slowed, glanced at his watch, and checked the underwater compass that hung around his neck. As the thirty second mark rolled closer, he reached to his belt, pulled out the two flares, and ripped the tabs. The bright green light didn't stretch very far in the greasy and oily waters but they did their job. Suddenly a large shadow-like mass appeared in the gloom, then the bows of an underwater craft loomed large ahead of him. The diver in the front of the craft spotted the flares, pointed toward Zanowski, and slowed the craft to a crawl. One of his compatriots let go of his grip on the inflatable and swam over to Zanowski who lifted the chalk board to his face and thumbed his hand toward the surface. 'Gold—emergency orders—surface immediately—all hands and gear' the diver read and immediately returned to the craft. Quickly the occupants separated and began their ascent, except for the driver who nosed his transport upward.

Upon breaking the surface, Zanowski was somewhat surprised at what he saw. Two Jolly Green Giants were hovering in close support just feet from the surface with the *Stork*'s Hawk standing off to the west. Within seconds a large basket that hung down from the closest Jolly touched the surface, quickly filled with four divers, and began hoisting them in. Just as the inflatable broke surface, the remaining diver left his charge and swam over to join the others. Again the basket was lowered and the rest of the team climbed aboard. Without waiting for the winch to finish its journey to the door, the Jolly turned west, nosed down, and flew off west toward the coast.

Zanowski had only spent a few seconds watching it disappear into the haze when the sound of the second Jolly's rotors overhead grabbed his attention. Two divers dropped to the surface and climbed aboard the inflatable. The winch was maneuvered into position and the boat was suddenly swinging high above Zanowski on its way north. The Hawk swung in low behind the Jolly and dropped the harness within feet of where Zanowski was waiting. He pushed his arms through the ring and felt the tug as the Hawk carried him up and back to the

Stork. The entire recovery had taken just three minutes from the moment Zanowski had made it back to the surface and all somewhat protected visually from the east by the three large tankers continuing their sluggish journey toward the Gulf of Oman.

Chapter Fifty-Three

"Greenman, we are ready to continue the lift."

"About time," sighed Manning. "What happened?"

"Nothing. A couple of Iranian Migs flew over and around us a few times but nothing serious. We all kept our cool."

"Great," said Greenman, "we were beginning to wonder." He looked at Manning and smiled. "All set down here."

"Roger. Hoisting now," came the reply. The remains of the Fulcrum started to move again and Greenman jumped on the controls to maintain a close watchful eye on its progress toward the surface. Although everything was going smoothly, something was still nagging at him.

"Vic, are you sure you can't see anything unusual or odd about that Mig?"

"Look, let's wait until we get the thing aboard. Then you can do your detective routine, okay?"

"Sure, but I just know it's staring me in the face."

Above them on the *La Salle*, the aft deck was being made ready. The railings had already been dismantled and a couple of platforms that the URPS would normally use were being moved away from the stern. The huge crane hanging over the side was pounding its rhythm deep into the heart of the ship. The loud-speaker announced to those aft of the crane. "Clear the deck. Repeat, clear the deck." Those that had been working on the stern area rushed forward and over to the starboard guard rail and leaned over, each trying to be the first to witness a downed Fulcrum close at hand. Suddenly part of the nose appeared and the cheer went up. The hook came into view and stopped. Four divers swam a line around to the front of the aircraft as it hung down and secured it quickly. They waved their signal and the crane again began to grind the aircraft higher, lifting its heavy burden up to the gunnels as water gushed out from the damage. As the crushed nose cleared the railings, a winch started up on the starboard side and began pulling it inboard, ready for the entire aircraft to be positioned across the deck. Then with a few more subtle movements from both crane and winch, the plane settled down on the stern with neither side of the ship bearing more weight than the other. Again another cheer went up as the Fulcrum touched down and the lines went slack.

"Remember, no souvenir hunters. Okay, batten it down everyone. We don't want it slipping back into the Gulf. All URPS hands to the port side," the loudspeaker continued, trying to be heard over the noise of the men's enthusiasm. A few reluctant sailors left the bleachers and made ready for Greenman and Manning to come aboard. The URPS boarding went smoothly, in fact whatever the record was for battening down the submersible and shutting down the systems, was broken. The skies were clear of clouds and Migs, and everyone who was not actively involved in the running of the ship at that time was allowed to come out and be a part of the group photograph. Lines were being thrown over the airframe while a couple of technicians checked out the armaments to ensure that there was no future risk to life or limb.

It was one thing to capture a plane, another to capture one that had shot at your shipmates. But to capture a relatively new, front line Russian Mig-29 Fulcrum A almost intact was a first, and the crew of the La Salle wanted to make the most of it. And they did. But while everyone gathered around for a closer look, Lieutenant Greenman had made his way up to the port side Phalanx to take a long, long distant look at their new prize.

Chapter Fifty-Four

"Prepare to receive! All necessary personnel prepare to receive helos on the port side," the speaker system shouted across the flight deck. Four SH-3H Sea Kings arrived from off the stern to settle gently on the deck in perfect formation. And as each huge door slid back to their stops, the deck was suddenly filled with long white coats unloading cases and many large trunks from their transports. In stark contrast to all the gray and black on board the Carrier, the thirty-one white coats that ran forward to form three lines of ten seemed, to the other members of the crew, very clinical compared to the oily atmosphere of jet fuel. One white coat left the formation and made his way in through the side door at the base of the stack with a rating leading the way to the bridge.

"Captain Jack Danforth reporting, Admiral. Permission for my team to come aboard, sir?"

"Welcome aboard, Jack, good to see you again. I just wish it was under better circumstances," said Lodgers.

"Likewise, sir. I have already assigned individuals to the rest of the task force and if we can secure them forthwith, sir, we can get to work putting Group Six back on line," said Danforth somewhat severely.

"Of course," Lodgers agreed. "The helos will take your men out under your instructions. Commander Reeves here will show you to your quarters. Anything you need, Captain?"

"No, sir, not unless you have any information on the E.T.A. of the *Wendel*?"

"Ten-hundred hours. When we can talk to the *Wendel* direct, we can probably nail that down a little firmer," Lodgers said with some sarcasm.

"We've brought a portable for you to use in the interim, sir, but we'll do our best to get you fully operational as quickly as we can. May we make use of your flight operations room for a meeting at a time to be determined?" asked Danforth.

"Of course."

"Thank you, sir," Danforth said as though he didn't expect any other answer, then turned and left. The bridge went silent and even though Danforth's somewhat officious attitude appeared too austere for the ragged personnel who had just had a most harrowing couple of hours, Danforth had at least left behind him an atmosphere of relief. Relief that a group of the most qualified technicians, some of whom had actually been involved in developing the equipment aboard the *George Washington*, had finally arrived to dedicate themselves to the task of making the ship a working and viable member of the United States Navy once again. Outside, after a few words from Danforth, the three strips of white broke ranks. Ten rejoined the remaining gear aboard a couple of the Sea Kings while the rest, with some help from some ratings, grabbed the bags and trunks and carried them down to their assignments. Eighteen men and three women went to work on the *George Washington* while nine men and one women flew off to be distributed throughout the Group.

This had been the first full scale Black Alert since the team had been put together following the main-frame shut down on the John F. Kennedy back in 1974, and Captain Jack Danforth and his team were keen to put their expertise to work.

The main objectives for Danforth and his team were three-fold. First, steam for steerage and flight control, second, radar and avionics and third, communications. Danforth, along with three colleagues, donned their radiation monitors and identification badges and waited for the huge steel door to nucleonics to swing open before going in.

Huffman appeared tired and weary. "Captain Danforth, Commander Huffman. Are we glad to see you," he said holding out his hand.

Danforth shook it briefly. "You have a couple of men that can carry some gear down here?"

"Right away." Huffman called out some names and four men followed one of Danforth's to where the trunks had been brought in.

"What I need from you, Commander, is an accurate and precise account of what happened," said Danforth officiously.

"Well, we were on medium register with everything well within parameters when, SCRAM. No warning, nothing. As far as the shut-down was concerned, all eight reactors went quietly to bed. Full Safeties were recorded at eight seconds after initiation. That's it. I immediately located the failure at the primary and secondary controls up here in FCS. The entire set of panels failed all together and at the same time."

"If everything failed, how do you know that they were safe after eight seconds?" asked Danforth.

"Although a lot of damage occurred up here, most of the main frame and recorders below are okay, at least sufficient to provide me with some information. What's strange is that when I pulled the corresponding boards from Supply, as all the other departments did, we found that all of them, apart from a couple of minor exceptions, had failed as well. The entire Supply Department aboard the GW was picked clean, so whatever caused us to shut down wrecked our stores as well."

"Thank you. I will be leaving Commander Rick Norman in charge here. Will you be available to assist?"

"Absolutely," said Huffman.

"Fine. When did you eat last?"

Huffman froze for a second while he dealt with the abrupt change of subject. "About ten hours ago."

"Right, then I suggest you take twenty minutes to go and grab a quick bite, shower and change, okay?"

"Thank you, Captain, I could do with a break," smiled Huffman, but none was returned.

"I can see that," said Danforth and without further exchange left for CIC. Other members of his team were carrying a large case in as he arrived. The crew had relinquished their seats and were now standing about in the middle of CIC observing the procedures.

"Commander Treedle at your service Captain," said Treedle.

"Any conclusions Commander?" asked Danforth as

he surveyed the room.

"None, except that everything we've tried has failed to give us any communications."

"What about the Morse?"

"That's what's so strange. It's one thing to deal with a complete electronics failure aboard ship, but it's another when one includes the Morse unit.

"Are you sure?"

"Yes. We've tried everything to get it working, but to no avail."

"I assume it was working during the sea trials?"

"Oh yes," responded Treedle confidently. "It was working fine, and that was only a few months ago. I know, I carried them out personally. I just can't find out what went wrong."

"Well obviously we need to look into it further," said Danforth matter-of-factly. "Even if you had to build one from scratch, someone could have got something working. Commander Hoover will be taking care of things in here. If you think of anything, see him." Before Treedle could interject, Danforth left CIC for Engineering. Treedle bit his tongue and sat back down in his chair. He watched as Hoover pulled all seven of the main circuits in the short range radar unit, opened up the case they had just dragged in, and, choosing seven boards from its neatly arranged contents, slid them in one by one. As soon as the last one been inserted, he turned the power on and the screen began to glow with that familiar light shade of blue. A cheer went up from the crew that had been standing back watching.

Hoover stood up and raised his voice over the din. "Let's have some quiet in here please. All I've done is re-fire the scope, there's no reception yet." Hoover turned back to Treedle. "If these men have been at General Quarters all this time they must be pretty worn out. When's your next shift due on?"

"Couple of hours."

"Then why not give these men a break and call the next shift a little early?"

"Good idea, Commander.""

"And take ten yourself, Commander, and take the

civilians with you. It's going to take a little while.

"Get going everyone and let your opposite numbers know they should be here in ten minutes, got it?"

In unison they cried, "Aye sir," then left the room quickly.

On the flight deck, two members of Black Alert had climbed aboard a couple of Tomcats parked in front of the stack and were busy fitting new boards. One of them leaned out of the cockpit and yelled down to Commander Davis, who was waiting in anticipation. "Is there a pilot around, Commander?"

"Yes, right here," Davis yelled back. The white coat climbed back down to where he was standing and said, "Fire it up for us will you, sir. Run a complete check of all systems and let me know what you find. I'll be in one of the Hornets."

"Very well," replied Davis climbing aboard. As he looked back he saw another technician running back to where Station Two was bringing an F-14D aloft.

Below, Captain Danforth walked into the engine room, specifically Commander Medlock's office. A rating stood up from behind Medlock's desk and saluted.

"Corporal Tetmyer, sir."

"At ease Corporal. Where's the Chief?"

"Ah, down in the boiler room, sir. Would you like me to get him for you?"

"No, I'll find him." Danforth wound his way down the various stairways to the floor of the engineering space. There seated on an old wooden chair, with both hands stretched back behind his head supporting it, was Chief Medlock.

"I've been expecting you, Captain," Medlock said very sluggishly, not getting up.

"Bad day?" Danforth inquired sarcastically.

"Yep. We have some steam, enough to make way, and electricity pretty much throughout the ship." He paused deliberately. "But without spares, it's just been impossible to do much more."

"If you lost all your computer controls, I'm surprised you did this well."

"We go lucky. Come on your own?"

"Not likely. We're concentrating on the essentials for right now, and since you at least managed to fire up the boilers, you're not first on our list."

"Oh, that's okay, Captain. We'll be ready for you when you have time."

"Tell me, did all the computer software fail or just some of it?"

"Most of it," said Medlock, struggling to his feet. "And if you don't mind my saying so, I'd never have had this problem on the *Iowa* when she first put to sea."

"No computers, eh?" said Danforth actually showing some sign of interest in the conversation.

"Well, this ship is brand new, a month or two out of commissioning. Everything worked in the trials, I made sure it did, and here we are, dead in the water. I spent seven years on the *Iowa* and the only computer we had was a small little thinga-ma-jig that sat on my desk to help me with the duty rosters. If she had been hit with the same electronic buzz that this ship was hit with, the boilers wouldn't even have missed a beat.

Danforth nodded. "Too sophisticated for your liking, eh?"

"You bet. It's all well and good, being able to monitor fuel flow, motor speed, valve temperatures etcetera, except that when the sensors that give you that information fail, the whole unit shuts down, and the entire operation goes in to fail-safe. I told those brass rubbings all this a long time ago when I was allowed to sit in on some prelim' design meetings, but I wasn't asked back. Too old they said, too set in his ways they said. Well, I'm not laughing either, because look who got stuck with the mess. I just wanted to be here when you arrived so I could take my time in my bath before grabbing some grub. If you need anything, Nat Freemont can help you. I'm sure the Commander will do all he can to help you put this baby to rights." Medlock walked right passed Danforth toward the gangway without waiting for a reply, leaving him to ponder Medlock's comments.

Chapter Fifty-Five

The noise from the members of the naval intelligence community that had been asked to join the meeting was considerable. There were many unanswered questions and much information to be gathered.

Admiral Pat Swanson put the phone down, got up from his desk, and walked over to the boardroom table as a hush fell on the room. "Well gentlemen, here's the situation as we know it." Opening up the large teak panels on the wall in front of him, he revealed the giant electronic map of the world and its oceans once again. "The reason we are all here is to discuss the various incidents that surrounded the complete shutdown of the *George Washington* and the rest of Group Six at five fifty-seven in the morning, local time. Black Alert has just arrived and knowing Danforth and his staff, I'm sure they'll be fully operational, or close close enough for horse-shoes, very soon." Swanson looked over to where Latchkey was seated in front of the terminal and nodded. "First of all, let's have a closer look at the Gulf region."

The huge screen switched to an enlarged view of the local areas surrounding the Gulf. "Using GPS, we'll add the main battle groups." A series of blue lights appeared throughout the map. "As you can see, we have all their locations except one. Now, we'll add the rest of our armed forces." A series of white lights were added to the blue, the most noticeable were two flashing red lights, one located in the Gulf of Oman and the other just off the coast of Iran in the north. As Swanson turned back to the map, he looked surprised. "John, what's this up here?" he said, pointing to the flashing red light in the north.

"I don't know, sir," said Latchkey. "Would you like me to make a call?"

"You do that. If it is who I think it is, we'll need to act quickly."

"Yes, sir," Latchkey replied, picking up a nearby phone.

Swanson went on. "When a GPS unit fails or is used as an emergency signal, it shows up as Red. So it appears we may have an emergency signal from one of our agents in the North. Down here at Station Gonzo we see another signifying the distress of Group Six. As soon as they were hit, we were aware that something had happened, and when we couldn't reach them on either the NAVSAT or DEFSAT lines, we issued the Black Alert."

Latchkey put the phone down. "We should hear back in about five minutes, Admiral."

"Good. Phase two of this system is now up to speed, so we can go back and review the data. John let's go back and start her up at about 30 minutes to six local." John Latchkey punched up the instructions as the rest of the group looked on. The NEC, Naval Emergency Council as Swanson had called his senior advisors, all waited in anticipation as a replay of the moments leading up to the hit on Group Six was about to unfold in front of them. To the left of the empty chair at the head of the table sat Peter Pruitt, assistant chief of Naval Intelligence; Rear Admiral Don Walters; John Bradley from the Defense Intelligence Agency; Dr. Frederick Chandler, the founding father of the Black Alert team; and at the end sat Captain Ronald Leemer, Swanson's operational director. On the other side of the table sat Commander Bill Travers, Joint Forces Liaison Officer; Rear Admiral Harold Mitchell, Chief of Naval Intelligence for the Pentagon; Rear Admiral Donald Peterson, head of Research and Development for the Navy and William Crow, the Pentagon's liaison with the CIA.

The image in front of them flickered for a moment then, with a clock in the top right hand corner running local and GMT, the map began its replay. Adjacent to each light a number was displayed corresponding to a list to the left of the screen that described the designation of each position. Two small blue lights could be seen to the north of Group Six, shown as two F-14Ds from the *George Washington*, and the list went on. The AWACS 24 over the Straits, three F-16's inbound from

Bahrain, two ASW aircraft south of Group Six, and a Hummer in close support. Yellow lights designated non-G.P.S. aircraft as relayed by the AWACS. The Korean flight was clearly visible over Iranian air space. One Fulcrum was closing from the north with two Flogger/Fs in attendance. To the east, four more Floggers and another Fulcrum were joining forces and heading out toward Group Six and an Airbus further out, crossing the Pakistan border into Iran; further to the north an Iranian F-15A plus two other Floggers on reconnaissance.

Everyone watched as the screen ran at ten times normal speed and completely replayed the entire sequence of events that occurred over the Gulf. Swanson used a laser-pointer to spot Station Gonzo.

"Remember gentlemen, all enemy aircraft movement is taken from IFF plots only, and the Hoover's data on the sub activity south of Group Six has not been added to the database yet." Every individual at the table leaned forward to concentrate on the screen's activities. They witnessed the Korean 747 being turned back by the Mig-23 Floggers and watched it head toward Muscat airport, flying directly over Group Six. Almost simultaneously the green light, marking the location of the *George Washington* and its tenders, turned Red. Five Migs on the heels of the 747 also flew over the Group. Then, as the three Falcons neared the Straits, a Fulcrum, with two Floggers on its tail, approached the convoy from the north. The yellow light designating the Fulcrum flashed briefly, confirming an attack was under way. As the Fulcrum turned up the Gulf, it ran straight into the face of the F-16s and within moments one yellow light disappeared while the greens turned for home.

"Sir, do you have a moment?" said Latchkey.

Swanson went over to his desk. "Excuse me, gentlemen," he said, walking back over to where his assistant was finishing off his note-taking.

Latchkey spoke in soft tones. "Sir, it's Rhinestone. The CIA is trying to arrange a pick-up via a chopper, but he's quite a ways inland and they're not sure that it would be anything other than a suicide mission."

"Are they sure he wants out?"

"Oh yes, sir. They tried to reach him through the emergency frequencies but there's no response. Any use of GPS under these circumstances is a definite call for help and extrication."

"Very well. Get back to them and find out what they intend to do about him and how long it's going to take. If the answer is anything other than 'now', I'm going to have to pull a few strings. Then get me Byron Davis on the line."

"Yes, sir," said Latchkey and Swanson returned to the wall screen that by now was back in real time.

"Sorry about that. Now tell me Will, what's the latest reaction from upstairs?"

William Crow from the CIA leaned forward. "The President is very concerned about the attacks and is prepared to wait for our comments before asking the Secretary of Defense to make some kind of public statement. The Iranians are insisting that they are seeking peace and help from us and that this kind of attack against our shipping has been outlawed. They're insisting it had nothing to do with them. As far as they are concerned, either our information as to the type and ownership of the aircraft involved is incorrect, or that a rogue pilot was involved." Crow sat back in his chair.

"Well," said Swanson proudly, "we can at least show them it was their aircraft. I have received confirmation that the *La Salle* has located the wreckage of the Mig on the floor of the Gulf and are raising it to the surface as we speak. It will be a pleasant change to actually hold up the guilty Mig and wave it in their faces. But more importantly Bill, do you have any information regarding the attack on the *George Washington*, if it was an attack. Could the other incidents, the attack on the convoy and the visit by the Russians be related?"

Will Crow leaned forward again. "It's too early to tell. We recently received a document, purportedly from the Iranian Government, suggesting that they would be interested in some kind of pact with the U.S. in return for aid. We were in the middle of trying to authenticate its origins when this happened."

"How about you Harry," Swanson asked, looking further down the table. "Any rumors from your sources?"

"Nothing," said Mitchell. "All our energies have been refocused on Iraq as you know. Although we've received this request recently, we've been concentrating all eyes and ears in the north."

"Well, does anybody have any comments about what happened, even if it's mere speculation?" continued Swanson, becoming a little impatient.

Dr. Chandler took off his glasses. "Sir, there's not too much that I can add at this stage I'm afraid. Of course, as soon as Captain Danforth sends his pre-lim's in, I should be able to brief you all fairly extensively, but for now, a couple of things do spring to mind. First, whatever hit Group Six must have been huge, large enough to knock out as many systems as it did, suggesting a hit by a nuclear device. But we know of no such device being detonated. If it was an attack by some other device, then it would have to have been carried in and dropped or delivered by external transport. Unless..."

"Go on."

"Unless it could it have been loaded onto Group Six, before it left port and detonated from within."

"Are you suggesting sabotage?" Walters interjected with just a hint of ridicule.

"Sir, I'm just pointing out the obvious possibilities. Look, having four Russian subs in the area at the time is very suspicious, but the *Philadelphia* reports that no such device was fired from any of them. We have Migs flying overhead, but I'm convinced they are far too small to carry a device capable of such a hit. We also have a 747 in the vicinity, and that's the obvious choice. If it were up to me, I'd get a look at that aircraft and give it a good going over."

"That's a good idea, Admiral, and what about the Russians?" inquired Travers. "Can't they tell us anything about their objectives?"

Crow didn't wait for Swanson. "Good idea. Firstly, Oman has acted very calmly throughout and has offered us all the necessary assistance we might need, through proper channels of course. The passengers are already on their way to Delhi. As far as the Russians are concerned, we were on to their embassy the moment we first heard of their proximity to Group Six and, although the answer did take some time in coming, they assured us that the trials were strictly passive. They apologized if the group commander was a little over-zealous and assured us that action would be taken against him upon his return."

"Will, do you think the Russians could have had anything to do with this?" asked Swanson, taking his seat at the head of the table.

"I find it very difficult to believe in light of recent events, but my gut tells me at this stage not to rule out any possibility. The last intercept reported that the four Subs have been ordered home immediately to face disciplinary action."

"Could they have launched something at us without the *Philadelphia* knowing about it?" asked Travers.

"Negative," said Mitchell. "The *Philadelphia* was on to them from a hundred miles out and nothing was fired from their boats at all."

"Well," said Swanson, "the only aircraft close to Group Six at the time were four Mig-23 Floggers, a Fulcrum, two Tomcats, a Hummer and the Korean 747. I can't give you much information on the Migs, but we can at least investigate the Boeing. It's large enough to carry the heavy payload for such an attack, and it was close enough to be considered a threat."

Travers interrupted. "Perhaps the aircraft itself was one huge jamming device and the engine malfunctions were a ruse?"

"Perhaps, but what did it gain anyone?" asked Bradley, speaking for the first time. "If this really was an attack by anyone, who benefited? If the Iranians were trying to knock out our frigate to create some kind of friction between us, then they succeeded. But then the request for aid would be a phony. If that was their intention, why didn't they use whatever device on the frigate to demonstrate their control of the Straits? If the request, and their latest statements, are correct and it was a rogue pilot, then the Iranians statement is true. The Russian involvement is just what they said it was, none, and I'm back to where I started, trying to figure out who profited from all this. And if it really was the Iranians dropping something from a Mig, then why do it now when they're trying to ease tensions between us? Why not use it against the Iraqis? The whole scenario seems totally counter-productive to anybody, unless some sadistic idiot found a new toy and just wanted to have a good laugh."

"Like the Russians," said Walters wryly, "a good laugh is exactly what they did have, at our expense I might add." There was silence for a moment as everyone considered the point.

"Suppose the rogue was the Typhoon and not the Mig?" questioned Captain Leemer. "That would fit the facts as we know them."

"Yes," said Walters, "but that would suppose that a Russian commander managed to load a highly secret weapon on to his boats without his higher command knowing anything about it, travel all the way to the Adriatic, and set it off inside the boat. If he did that his own hardware would have been hit as well and he'd have to go all the way home in a dead boat. Highly unlikely. And where does he go now? Not back to the welcoming arms of those in Moscow, that's for sure."

"Unless," Mitchell interjected, "the weapon was loaded on for a test against some commercial shipping and, at the last minute, he took it upon himself to try it against our Stars and Stripes."

"Will," interjected Swanson. "Do you have any reports of the Russians putting to sea in any great numbers?"

"No, sir. In fact, I would say the number of Russian ships and subs away from home port right now is at their lowest since before World War II. And besides, considering our current relationship, I believe that if this Commander did turn out to be a rogue, then they would have admitted it before now and put our minds at ease. Yeltsin is not going to let another Chernobyl hang over the Russians' heads."

Another few moments of consideration passed by before Bradley spoke again. "If we turned the coin upside down and assumed everyone's incorrect and it was the Iranians after all, then consider this. Why didn't the Migs, which I understand were loaded for bear when they overflew Group Six, finish us off and sink a major portion of our naval prowess in the area without our being able to fire one single retaliatory response? The whole fleet would have gone under in the space of five minutes and there would have been nothing we could have done about it."

Swanson got up from his seat and walked over to the screen to close the panels. This movement, designed to relax the team from their anguished thoughts, had the desired effect. Taking note of the time, he decided to summarize.

"Good point, John. This is all conjecture at this point, but that's exactly what I needed. It couldn't have been the Russians since the *Philadelphia* has reported categorically that not one single shot of anything was fired. It couldn't have been the Iranians since they didn't have an aircraft in the area big enough to carry such a device. The attack on the convoy could have been a rogue, if we believe the Iranian consulate, but why break a life time habit and believe them now? The attack on the frigate seems to be unrelated to the Group Six thing, yet it happened just before a 747 overflew the Task Force, which it did after going off course into Iranian air space." Swanson paused but no-one said anything. "Fred, when will you receive your first report from the *GW*?"

"In about fifteen minutes."

"Very well, let me know as soon as a replacement Group can relieve them. Don, where's the *Wendel* now?"

"About an hour away," said Walters, glancing at his watch.

"Very well. It's going to be a long night. Harry, Bill, I want everything you have in the way of strange or mysterious communications in that area for the last five days. The rest of us can keep the wheels turning. Keep in touch, we will need to do this again at a moment's notice." Swanson walked over to where his assistant was waiting by the desk, phone in hand.

"Byron Davis," said Latchkey as the rest made their way from the room. Swanson took the phone and put his hand over the mouthpiece and spoke softly. "John, I can see the CIA are going to be difficult. Cut me some orders for *Gold Seal*. I want them ready to go into Muscat and check up on that aircraft as soon as possible." Latchkey nodded and left for his office as Swanson sat down at his desk. "Byron, thank you for waiting. A difficult situation has developed here and I need your help to resolve it."

Chapter Fifty-Six

Major Leonard Barton was nearly falling asleep at the wheel. His constant speed of sixty on the desert roads had kept the adrenaline flowing and the dust flying, and even though he had known it would take a while to mount a rescue, he was becoming concerned that his body was beginning to tell him that time was running out. The morning light had improved visibility and although he had already achieved a good portion of his objective by closing to within twenty miles of the coast, it was beginning to appear to Barton that getting much closer to it was proving to be a problem. After connecting with one of the main arterial roads Barton had headed south, hoping for some luck to take him the remaining few miles west, but he had found neither luck nor dirt to help him escape his pursuers. There weren't too many roads that crossed the front line defenses of Iran to the coast of the Gulf and those that did were watched closely. It was also becoming apparent, as he glanced at his gauges one more time, that another problem was beginning to raise its head. Although the extra large fuel tanks were sufficient to carry him for four hundred miles the consumption of the mighty V-8 was in the lower teens at the best of times and, since he'd been pushing the red line for the last couple of hours, he knew that the gauge would soon be talking to him. However, the proximity device had flashed at him four or five times over the past thirty minutes and he knew that if he lowered his pace, not only would his pursuers make up considerable ground, but it would reduce the time available for his allies to affect a rescue, without coming under ground fire themselves. Play it safe or go for it. Barton considered the alternatives. He might be able to manufacture some time, however unless he came across a convenient all-night Iranian gas station, his ability to make the rendezvous would be severely hampered. He relaxed his foot a little and watched the speedometer drop down to fifty.

Just then the nervous little tingling sensation returned to the back of his neck. Something else wasn't right. What was it he had seen or heard that wasn't fitting in with the way things normally should in this part of the world. A new set of questions and a new set of answers began to dwell on that portion of his mind that his empty stomach permitted to remain operational. If they were really trying to nail him, then why hadn't they put a bird in the air? Why was there no aerial surveillance? Perhaps they weren't trying to catch up with him, just drive him into the teeth of an ambush.

To his right, he suddenly caught a glimpse of what could only be described as a rabbit trail heading west, but he took it. Jamming on the brakes he turned right and refocused his attentions on avoiding the big gullies that were deep enough to swallow the entire jeep. Some were so deep that if he were to slide down into one, the jeep might even roll over. Barton tightened his seat straps and took his time. It was just as well. He had just driven into a mine field.

Chapter Fifty-Seven

The morning sun had already pushed the mercury in the surface thermometer, affixed to one of the external walls of *HMS Connington*'s hanger, beyond the seventy mark. Even though the heat haze from the landing area would have been enough to cause most men to rush for a pair of insulating socks, the men and women who served aboard one of Britain's newest fighting ships were oblivious to it all as the latest two-seat Harrier rolled out into the light of day. The location of the undercarriage on the pad was critical. Since aircraft cannot pivot on the crane, the Harriers have to be located on the pad prior to launch in such a manner so that once swung outboard, they are facing upwind, parallel to the ship's hull.

The chocks were laid down and a ladder rolled up to the cockpit as Captain Markham Hawksworth, dressed once again in full flight gear, walked out from the shadows to be met by the ship's Commander, Captain Dick Smith.

"Care to join me, skipper?" said Hawksworth.

"There wouldn't be any room for our guest," Smith replied.

"That's not what I meant."

"Certainly," said Smith, and the two began the ground inspection.

"Any last minute instructions, Captain?" asked Hawksworth, checking the pods.

"No, not really Mark," said Smith, following along behind. "You can change your mind you know."

"Right. If I did, you'd only have to snap your fingers and ten others would come running up. Besides, what kind of Admiral would I make if I was only good at asking others to take the hazardous duties?" said Hawksworth facetiously. "I heard somewhere that you did yours in the Falklands, sir?"

"Now listen carefully," said Smith, ignoring the change of subject. "Jock has upgraded your short range radar with a device that can lock on to the GPS sending unit and display its location. You might pick up a few others along the way, but where you're going there's only going to be the one and, from what I understand, it's a very important one!"

"It must be if Whitehall has okayed the use of this little puppy," said Hawksworth, walking back to the tail.

"Under extreme circumstances the aircraft may be expendable, but you're not. For what it's worth, we've nearly invested as much in your training and experience as it took to build the Pegasus, but we can build another Harrier, if you follow my drift." Hawksworth grinned to himself momentarily. "Look, there's no use getting yourself blown away over this. Bring him back at all costs, you and the trainer included."

"By the way," said Hawksworth, adjusting his gear. "Supposing he's got company? If this chap's dressed like an Iranian Colonel, how will I know which guy to grab?"

"First of all, Mark," Smith replied, "he's supposed to be alone. If he's not he'll probably be dead. If he is alive, then hopefully he's the only one not trying to kill you. We've given you a complete description of him, plus or minus a beard or two, and you know his code name. Besides, if he's not with his vehicle, the chances of finding him are going to be pretty slim."

"Aye, Captain. Any news on the diversion?" said Hawksworth, approaching the port wing.

"Yes, but it's a little sketchy. Two Hawks and a Jelly Bean have already made for the coast, some hundred miles to the south of where you cross the border. They're going to make as much noise along the coastline as they can for as long as they can and hopefully keep their radar guys busy. If necessary, they'll be assisted by a couple of Eagles from Bahrain. Their AWACS have been told to give this trip number one priority, so they'll be monitoring everyone's position as they talk you in."

"Talk me in?" queried Hawksworth, arriving back at the nose.

"Yes, they've assigned an operator to keep you company all the way."

"Is that it?" said Hawksworth, placing a foot on the ladder.

"Yes, that's it. Good luck."

"Why wish me luck, skip? Anyone would think this is going to get a little dodgy."

"No reason, except that no-one's quite sure whether the diversion will work. The terrain is relatively flat, so even if you hug the deck you won't have any cover from their radar, and there's no saying once you arrive, whether he's there, alive, or otherwise. You might just be walking into an ambush," said Smith with a grin.

"Don't beat about the bush, Captain, get to the real dangerous part."

"Just try not to bang her up too much. It's the only one we have out here," said Smith, holding out his hand. "As I said, good luck."

"Thanks," said Hawksworth, returning the gesture as he climbed up into the cockpit. "There's a lot more room up here than I'm used to, skipper. If this comes off alright, can I borrow it for a Saturday evening?" Smith smiled and left. Hawksworth checked the back seat to make sure all the straps were locked in place, and slid down behind the controls. Having secured himself to his seat, he plugged himself into the air supply and the headset, and dialed up the radio.

"This is Javelin, ready for start up."

"Roger, Javelin. Go for start up." The somewhat larger and more powerful Pegasus 5C began to spool up as Hawksworth ran through his checks with the ground crew. Once operating temperatures had been reached, he pushed the throttle forward.

"Forty percent," his ears counted as the engine began to share it's load with the hook. "Seventy percent." The decreased loadings on the undercarriage were clearly visible to the Pad Chief as the Harrier began to fight back gravity. "Ninety percent, you are cleared for transition. May we proceed?"

"Roger, proceed with transition," Hawksworth confirmed.

"Elevation underway. This is Snatch Control, lifting off now."

"Roger."

"Going Spacial."

"Roger, going Spacial." The gentle rocking sensation completely left the cockpit, as the hook took on its responsibility and swung the Harrier around over the rails and head first into wind. The fingers of his left hand pushed the throttle forward while his thumb rocked the nozzles back slowly to gain forward momentum, decreasing the drag on the crane.

"This is Snatch. Retrievers in position, raise undercart."

"Undercart coming up."

"Compensate for thirty knots. Increase pressure to one hundred percent."

"Increasing to one hundred. Adding thirty knots." Hawksworth pushed the throttles forward to more than the straight hover and dropped the nozzles back to 20/80.

"Ready for launch."

Hawksworth glanced quickly at his engine parameters and gave the order. "Go, go, go." The four cups jumped away from the sides of the fuselage, the grab released it's hold on the ball, and the hook swung quickly up and behind the Harrier.

"She's all yours, Javelin. Hook clear. Switch to one-oh-three point five. Good luck. Snatch out." Hawksworth increased power and pushed back to 30/70 as the airframe's vibration gave way to the familiar whistle of air over the canopy. The Harrier two seater overtook the *Connington*, then with a little right rudder, began to bear off climbing higher as it went. Moments later, as Hawksworth climbed north, he reset the trim to compensate for the lack of a passenger and dialed up the new setting on his VHF. Immediately an unfamiliar voice filled his ears. It was calm and reassuring. It was American.

"Javelin, this is Sentry. Do you read? Javelin, this is Sentry. Do you read me? Over."

"I read you Sentry, this is Javelin. Go ahead."

"Welcome aboard Javelin. Good to have you with us for this one. Would you switch on your signal scrambler please?"

Hawksworth obliged. "Scrambler on."

"Thank you, Javelin. Admiral Swanson has asked us to pass along his appreciation for you joining us for this pick-up, should be a breeze. How's the reception?"

"Perfect," Hawksworth replied.

"You're a little high, drop to two-zero for the time being. We'll tell you when to drop down low." Hawksworth pushed the stick forward, as he pondered what they thought low was. "Heading, three-five-three. This operator has been dedicated to this mission so there shouldn't be any interruptions. By the way, I won't be following normal air traffic protocol on this duty and my name's Willis, but you can call me Dave. When we get close to the coast I will be talking with you pretty much most of the way in and out. This will help you to concentrate more on flying and less on your destination. The forecast is good with average visibility up to ten miles. A little mist is hanging off the cliffs right now but that won't concern us. Our target is some ten miles in-land and should take no more than ten minutes to go in, pick him up, and bring him right out. Currently, there seems to be little or no activity in the target area. The main bulk of Bad Bag, the name we've given this little junket, will be some ninety miles south of you making all kinds of noise. It's going to take us a little time to get everybody in position before you go in, so you can settle back for a while. Our boys should be loud enough to keep their ears away from your task, and long enough, we hope, for you to be on your way home by the time the Nannies realize the rumble. Any questions so far, Javelin?"

"Nannies?" questioned Hawksworth as he leveled out at two thousand.

"Sorry, our pet name for the Iranians."

"What do you call the Iraqis?"

"Rookies. If for some reason our dialogue stops, just say the word 'Sentry' and I'll be right with you. If not, due to a malfunction with your radio or some other annoyance, then turn to emergency frequency one-one-zero. That'll get me or someone up here. It's like our nine-one-one back home. Okay?"

"Roger, Sentry."

"Good. Drop speed to cruise and change heading to three-five-zero, and lose a couple of hundred feet, say down to one-seven-zero, okay?"

"Roger, Sentry." Hawksworth tried to retain some elements of protocol.

"Now, while we have a little time to spare, I'll bring you up to speed on the intended target area. First, the good news. There are three main radar stations we will be dealing with. The first, to the north, is Bandar Khomenyi. They operate a Hawk-Doppler system with a range of a hundred and twenty-five kilometers max. A similar station is located south at Bushehr. They are both used in conjunction with SA-6 Gainful and -12 Gladiator SAMs. The -6's use the old Pulse radar and command guidance and are medium range, thirty kilometers at Mach 2.8 with fair maneuverability. The -12s use the advanced Phased-array Doppler radar. They are medium and long range, up to 150 kilometers at Mach 3 with fair maneuverability."

"That's the good news?" Hawksworth interjected.

"Roger. Your point of access into Iran happens to be half way between these two stations. At the full extent of their radar there is a channel of about five miles that could be considered beyond their normal scope of operation. And the fact that they are both Doppler radar gives us a chance. As you know, Javelin, Doppler is at its best when monitoring aircraft flying straight at the radar, and at its worst when flying a tangent course around its perimeter. Pulse radar is the reverse. Fortunately for us your flight-plan takes us between the two emitters and, coupled with low altitude and diversions, we may get by without being spotted by either."

"So what's the bad news, Sentry?"

"Well, the bad news is two-fold. First, to fly in-between the Doppler radars, you have to fly very close to Karq Island. They also have a Doppler in use and, although much smaller, there's no-way you're going to get through without being picked up."

"And second?"

"Secondly, we have monitored a hostile force bearing down on the area targeted for pick-up. To be more precise..." Hawksworth settled in as his new compatriot began a long detailed description of the objective, cliffs, the descending but open terrain inland and the aspect of various open fissures that were prevalent in the area. Willis continued and since his account was so detailed, Hawksworth found himself picturing the journey ahead, as if watching some in-flight movie. And once the credits had been listed, Willis repeated the journey again.

By the time Javelin was to reach the border he would know exactly what to expect. Unfortunately for Javelin and Willis, they hadn't expected enough.

Chapter Fifty-Eight

For the last three and a half hours the *George Washington* had been classified as 'Dark'. In every department and in all aspects of the repairs, logs were made of the procedures undertaken and the results recorded. Apart from six aircraft that had now been cleared for full operations, the rest of the ship remained in various degrees of disarray. Each member of the Black Alert Squadron systematically tested each phase of their work to ensure that the replacements they had brought aboard would not themselves burn out in the same way. Beneath the rows of navigation equipment each series of circuits was examined and check programs inserted to complete the diagnostic requirements. Behind the bulkheads the huge main-frames sat idle under the draft from the air-conditioners, each awaiting their turn to be fired up and tested.

Within CIC itself the room had filled with sixteen sets of fresh, watchful eyes that scrutinized the continuing work of Lieutenant Carol Chambers as she entered the silence of the unusually bright Combat Information Center for the hundredth time. She was of medium height, had soft blue eyes and a somewhat roundish face with a few strands of natural blonde hair peeking down from under her cap. She had that look of a professional, a thinker, one used to intelligent study, and although the male watchers were anticipating her work, most were somewhat refreshed by seeing an unfamiliar female at close quarters. The long white coat that hid any form she might have had, had full, deep pockets that bulged with the tools of her trade coupled with the total lack of eye contact, left everyone with no doubt that she was dedicated to her task.

She sat down at one of the terminals and logged on. Commander Wooten grabbed a chair and rolled it over next to her.

"How's it going, Lieutenant?" he asked.

Her eyes remained fixed on the screen as her fingers continued to dance across the keyboard. "Not as bad as we had feared, Commander," said Chambers. "There's still a problem with one of the main buffer units but we've managed to drive around it for the time being, and now that this terminal is back on line we should be able to give you some short and long range visuals at least." After completing a series of entries she reached into a pocket and pulled out a small handset. "Chambers to Wallingford, come in."

"Go ahead Carol," came the reply.

"All set here. The CRTs are fired up and I've completed the logging-on test. All systems are up and now awaiting your confirmation that the terminals are on-line."

"Looks good from here. Jack has just finished his go-around at the head-end and reports that the receivers are now revolving nicely with good focus. Go ahead and complete the start-up." Chambers fingers tapped a few more keys.

"Starting up now." Suddenly there was a flicker of blue on the far side of the room. One CRT blinked momentarily and then shone its blue hue brightly into the room. Then the sweeping hand of the radar's watchful eye appeared bright and clear. All eyes had turned toward the activity and a cheer went up from all those gathered as the green operational diode confirmed it's functional ability. Before the cheering had a chance to recede, the other five screens jumped to life and a round of applause broke out. Chambers, still holding the handset to her face, rose to her feet and turned to look past the Commander at the screens on the other side of the room.

"How's it looking?" said the voice.

"A-okay," replied Chambers.

"Good. I'm still a little busy here. Tell Commander Wooten to run the entire sequence of start-ups and if all goes well he can resume operations."

"Aye, sir." Chambers put the radio back in her pocket and turned to face Wooten. "Your men may now resume their stations, Commander. We would like each operator to carry out their own sequence of tests before returning to standard operational duties and report to me if anything unusual turns up."

"Thank you, Lieutenant, we'll be glad to," Wooten replied, trying to encourage a smile from Chambers. None came.

"I'll be working on the Captain's Simulated Visual Command Unit," she said and walked over to the large monitor located at the end of the room, sat down in the swivel chair, and began work.

Wooten turned to face the center of the room and raised his voice over the noisy chatter of his command. "That'll do. We've all had enough excitement for one day. I want you all to hit your posts and complete your primary start-up tests. Once you've received confirmation of full operational capability from your terminal, hold up your right hand and wait for me to give you the okay to bring the main system on line. If your tests are unsuccessful, hold up your left hand and wait for instructions. Okay men, get to it." Everyone made grabs for the chairs and pulled them towards their units as Wooten looked back to where Chambers sat. She was talking into her radio again while the large 40" by 40" computer screen, already alight with the colors and forms of a demonstration run, confirmed to Wooten that perhaps they didn't have long to wait before the hub of the *George Washington* could Command again. He reached for the phone and pressed a button.

"Is Captain Gurney there? This is Wooten in CIC."

A few moments pause. "Yes, Commander?"

"Just running line tests now on all major radar systems. If all goes well, we should have our eyes back in a few minutes."

"Good news. Let me know as soon as you're up to speed will you?"

"Aye, Captain," said Wooten and put the phone down. One by one right arms were stretching into the air. He walked over to the nearest operator, checked the monitor confirming all was ready, and told him to bring the main system up. Moments later, the big round display in front of them burst into life, inducing a quick 'All right!' from both of them. Wooten went down the line as each in turn lit up with all the relevant information required for the operator to fulfill his task. At the end of the row a left hand wandered skyward.

"What's up Greg?" asked Wooten as he arrived.

"Don't know, sir, won't dial up properly." Wooten walked over to where Chambers was busy punching keys.

"Lieutenant, we are looking great. Everything's fine except one of the Honeywell thirty-five hundreds seems to be resisting." Chambers calmly stopped her own investigations and walked with Wooten to where an operator was now standing by his seat. She sat down at the terminal, cleared the screen, and typed in 'RADSYSCHK1'. It went blank for a second and then came up with 'RADSYSCHK1...NON OPERATIONAL'. Chambers rebooted and typed 'DANSEQTEST'. The screen then displayed a list of names and commands totally unfamiliar to Wooten. The list stopped when it showed 'CCK FNTN 3 SX...UNABLE'. Chambers reached for her radio and, after a brief discussion and another reboot, the screen returned to the single white flash of the cursor. Again she typed 'DANSEQTEST' and again the list rolled up, but this time it continued on until reaching a point that read 'DANSEQTEST... COMPLETE'.

Chambers rose and turned to Wooten. "Okay, would you try it again, please?" Wooten nodded at his operator who sat down and proceeded as he had before. The test went well. 'SCANNING RATE, SPEED, FOCUS, KEY1, KEY2, UPSTREAM DATA MIX, DOWNSTREAM LOGIC CONTROL, FINE SCAN, X-TEL REFS, INTROS, CALLERS, DISPLAYS, and finally KEYBOARD TEST and ERROR ANNOUNCERS'... TEST COMPLETE>>... YOU ARE "GO" FOR START UP....'. Before the Commander could voice his appreciation to Chambers, she handed him something.

"Commander, I have a meeting to go to. This credit card-looking device is in fact a pager. We would appreciate that you only use it if you have a major problem, but if you do, press the thumb print and I'll get to you as soon as I can." As Wooten's eyes looked down at the piece of plastic he held in his hand, he couldn't help but glance at the two buttons on the white coat in front of him. Wooten had never strayed from his duty and in fact, on many occasions, had lent advice to his men when their thoughts turned to companionship. He was well respected for his professionalism and the good example he had always set for others. But as he slipped the card into his pocket and looked deep into those blue eyes, he considered that, maybe, after this was all over, he might at least engage her in a sociable cup of coffee.

"Okay, Lieutenant, I'll take good care of this."

"Please do, they're difficult to come by." She turned and left CIC.

High above the deck, some fifty feet higher than the bridge itself and secured with a life-line crouched Global Systems Specialist, Bell. Next to him, with the cover removed from its control unit, sat the dish that provided the communications data from any of the geosynchronous NAVSAT and DEFSAT satellites. These were set up in this region for secure and direct transmissions with the Pentagon and other shipping. Wearing a headset, Bell peered over the drives that ran the table on which the dish sat. He had placed a spirit-level onto the table and was watching it carefully as the motors locked and maintained the dish's aim at the heavens. "Looks good to me. How about you?"

The reply was equally enthusiastic. "Looks in great shape down here too. There she is, loud and clear! All one hundred and twenty-eight on the mains are coming in ten by normal. The emergency lines are open, even the back-ups are as clear as a bell. Good work Art. Can you get down to Avionics and give them a hand? I'm leaving Alan here to finish off the audio."

"Be there in a few. Bell out." He grabbed his level, clipped the cover back on to the control unit, picked up his tool box and made his way down to the hangers just as the tannoy system throughout the ship barked into life.

"Prepare to UNREP, all hands prepare to UNREP." Suddenly hundreds of pairs of boots filled the silent corridors and gangways as they made their way to their appropriate stations. The USS Wendel had taken up station two hundreds yards ahead of the *George Washington* off the starboard bow, steady at 15 knots. The Carrier approached until the Wendel was alongside. The tannoys sounded. "Good Morning Captain Austin and crew aboard the *USS Wendel*. It is a pleasure to be alongside on this beautiful morning. On *Wendel*, standby to receive shot lines forward and amidships. Aboard the *George Washington*, with the proper exchange and signals, send over shot lines forward and amidships."

In the space of about half-an-hour all the necessary stores needed to maintain the Carrier's operational capability had been transferred, including a few extra items ordered by Danforth. The diesel tanks were topped off, some hardware crated for the occasion was swinging on to the deck and the high wires carried an officer on board in the cage. The entire operation went as smooth as silk, but more importantly, it signified, in the minds of most of the men aboard ship, that the *George Washington* and the other ships the *Wendel* serviced that morning were, once again, ready for action.

The tannoy sounded once more, and this time it was the Air Boss with his quick, Ready to Go announcement. "All personel be prepared in proper flight deck uniforms, helmets on, goggles down, sleeves rolled down, check chocks, tire chains, sweep down the deck and check for FOD. Let's go to start aircraft. Start'em up!

Chapter Fifty-Nine

Commander John Latchkey walked back into Swanson's office to find him still busy on the phone. The team was meeting again and this time, instead of coming empty-handed, they had spread out before them the various data that they hoped would help resolve the situation.. Latchkey walked over to the desk and placed a communique in front of the Admiral.

"Okay, Sam," said Swanson, "I'll get back to you as soon as the meeting is over. How long will it take?" There was a pause and Swanson finished with, "Okay, I'll be ready," and put the phone down. Swanson read the note Latchkey had given him, stood up, and walked over to sit in his chair. "Gentlemen, we don't have much time. I have another appointment shortly so let's try and keep it brief. Let's start with you, Peter."

"I don't have much for you at this time, Admiral. It appears we had no warning of the attack on either the Group Six or the *Stork*. All we've managed to gain from the *Philadelphia* is that the four Russian boats insisted on carrying out some maneuvers close to Station Gonzo, forcing Group Six to move further north into the Gulf of Oman. The lead boat, the Typhoon, having separated itself from the other three Foxtrots, then surfaced close to the Group where upon the Russian Captain, loud enough for the *Philadelphia*'s crew to hear, stood on top of the mast and laughed his head off. He was given a firm caution by Captain Davidson and the Russian went below, submerged, joined up with the other boats, and left the area. Captain Davidson requested permission to shadow them from the area but this was denied by Lodgers to maintain and secure defenses." Pruitt sat back in his chair as Admiral Walters took over.

"I have received confirmation that Black Alert has arrived on board the *George Washington* and is affecting a rapid repair to it and the rest of the Group. Although their inventory was extensive, there are a few elements that will have to wait for the *Wendel*. She should be closing in on them as we speak, but I'm sure Fred will have more on that in a minute. Captain Fulton, on board the *Stork*, has confirmed that there were no casualties and no direct hits. Thanks to Captain Fulton's rather unorthodox procedures, the end result was kept to a minimum. As directed by your office, they assisted in the pick-up of a team of Navy Seals while leaving the Straits of Hormuz and the convoy is now safely in the Gulf of Oman. And finally, although they were overflown a few times by Iranian Migs, the *La Salle* has just completed hauling the remains of the Fulcrum up on to her deck, and I can confirm that it is Iranian to-boot!" A murmur of congratulations went round the table. "Preliminary photos will be coming through shortly. As for the *Philadelphia*, I'll leave that up to John."

John Bradley leaned forward and rested his arms on the table. "As of this moment, we can't determine anything positive. If the Russians had launched anything, he would have known about it. The Iranians are insisting that none of their aircraft fired a shot at the convoy. In fact, they are supposedly continuing their own investigations, have even said that if we turn up anything positive as to the cause, to let them know. Yeah right. We now have proof that it was the Iranians that hit the *Stork*. As far as Station Gonzo is concerned we still have two choices. The Russians or the Iranians." Bradley sat back in his chair as Dr. Frederick Chandler, taking a quick glance at his watch, began to speak.

"In about ten minutes, the first group session will be held aboard the *Washington* to ascertain the extent and cause of the damage. As Don said earlier, they have at least brought the ship back to a state of seaworthiness and I will be receiving a full report from Captain Danforth a little later on. The brief call I had with him just before this meeting was the first secure call made from the ship since the shut down. He confirmed the damage was caused by some form of an electronic attack. Every single piece of software aboard the Carrier, and I will assume for the point of this discussion, aboard the rest of the fleet as well, went down at approximately three minutes to six local time. What compounded the attack was that it hit the entire Department of Supply aboard the Carrier at the same time and in the same manner, so that the operators and technicians were basically incapable of carrying out any kind of repair. Whatever hit the ship must be very powerful. All I can say for now is, I want one." A few inquisitive looks flittered around the table. "What I mean, Admiral, is we need to get hold of whatever remains of that device and bring it on home for a good look-see. Perhaps we can figure out how it works or at least determine its origins. If we could let the *Philadelphia* loose to check on the area, we might get lucky. And believe me, gentlemen, we need to get lucky fast. If whoever did this decides to do it again against the *Independence* for example, we will be incapable of responding for a much greater length of time, since Black Alert's own stores in the region have been reduced to zero and will remain so for at least a couple of days." Admiral Swanson looked over to Commander Bill Travers and nodded.

"Well," said Travers, clearing his throat slightly. "We have been able to ascertain a few interesting details from the air force. Firstly, AWACS reports do confirm that it was unusual for the Fulcrums to be followed by the Floggers in such a manner. Just prior to the attack on the *Stork*, the Floggers seemed to be tracking the Fulcrum that led the attack. It was as if they were chasing down their own aircraft. The problem with that is, if current reports are to be believed that the Iranians didn't order such an attack and it was indeed a rogue, why, immediately after the shooting, didn't they try and shoot down the aircraft themselves? Now, perhaps their equipment was faulty or that the range was a little stretched, but the incident as traced by the logs, does not appear, at least at first glance, to be consistent with their current statements. Secondly, it was also strange to air force intelligence that, of the two Fulcrums, one split to fire on the convoy and the other went South and joined up with four other Migs to overfly Group Six. This fact is the first hard evidence that the two incidents are connected. Two Fulcrums from Iran south joined up with four other Migs to overfly Group Six. Not only that, but the aircraft that did fire waited so long that the proximity to the convoy didn't leave much time for the Exocet to maneuver to its target. And finally, it was also unusual for four other Mig-23s to join in with the Fulcrum and overfly Group Six as they did. This was the first actual pass that any of our Carriers have witnessed since the war in the Gulf came to an end. Once the Floggers took to the air from their base at Bam in the southern province, they appeared to head straight for Group Six's location. But, what makes this fly-over particularly fascinating is that their take-off time was some thirty minutes before the fleet was hit, which indicates to me that they knew of the attack in advance." Travers sat back as a silence fell on the room momentarily as everyone considered his comments. "Oh, and one more thing," said Travers, "while I remember. The two Fulcrums had been refueled in the air, about three hundred miles north of the Straits. This fact might confirm that they both had orders for the long flight to Group Six, before the rogue decided to break off."

"Harry?" said Swanson.

"I can't add anything for the moment, Pat."

"Nor I," commented Peterson.

"Well, I do have one comment to make," said Crow. "About a year ago, Admiral Swanson came up with an idea to help with intelligence reports coming out of Iran. He had come across a Commander who had been keeping his family tree somewhat of a secret. He was Iranian by birth and knew the language fluently. With a little encouragement from Pat, he agreed to come over to us for some training and we put him to work for Military Intelligence behind enemy lines, and in the last six months he's been able to keep us well informed of intelligence reports and orders coming out of Tehran. A couple of hours ago, we received a message that he was in trouble and needed to get out, which the Admiral has kindly offered to take care of. But following this call, he again broke radio silence and placed himself in a somewhat precarious position by sending us another message. It says that he saw the two Fulcrums in question, as they over flew a troop convoy he was following, heading toward the border with Iraq, and that we were to assume nothing by the sighting. Specifically, he indicates that there was something wrong with the aircraft and that we are not to, under any circumstance, assume that they were what they purport to be. The message was obviously brief, so hard information, as to what this means exactly, remains sketchy at this time. But you wanted every piece of abnormality with regard to reports or sightings, and this seems to qualify."

"Thank you," said Swanson sincerely. "I appreciate your hard work in this matter everyone. Let me add to all this that we are in the throws of extricating this agent from the field and, as soon as we make contact, his comments we will be forwarded to this committee. Any other comments anyone?"

William Crow spoke again. "Yes, Admiral. I want to pursue some of the findings that Commander Travers has shared with us," he said, turning to face the Commander. "Did the air force offer any hypothesis from their information, Bill?"

"Somewhat conflicting comments were made, sir. Understand of course, these are all very preliminary. Two investigators ruled the behaviors as acceptable. They argued that perhaps one of the pilots was a genuine rogue and he broke ranks and fired. They added that, even though the Fulcrum was not new, it may have had some difficulty firing more than once, misreading the range and flying over the convoy before it had a chance to arm again. They also feel that, considering we were in the area, the chasing Floggers demonstrated reasonable prudence under pressure. Not wishing for any attack by them on the Fulcrum to miss and target our inbound Falcons in error, and escalate any judgments we might make on the situation, they held back. The alternative suggestion, posed by others, was that the Iranians had ordered the attacks in the first place so that somehow they could block the channel with the tankers. The Iranian frigates did move over into some kind of blocking profile, just prior to the attack. Unfortunately for them, the attack was unsuccessful and now they're trying to back pedal."

"But why block the Straits now, when they're trying to open up dialogue with us while we're doing them a favor by dominating their archenemy, Iraq?" asked Bradley.

"Perhaps the rogue was a pilot defecting from Iraq, attempting to swing our attentions back toward Iran."

"Well, if that's the case," said Swanson, "they sure succeeded."

"But our reports show," said Walters, "that their own frigates turned on their defenses at the incoming Migs. Surely they wouldn't have done that if they'd known they were their own aircraft."

"Right," continued Travers, "but supposing this was an overt operation and they had forgotten to tell the frigates what was going on, or that they know we can intercept their radio traffic and may have not have wanted to run the risk of filling them in, for fear we might be onto them."

"Then if they didn't know, why didn't they fire?" asked Bradley.

"Obviously they've installed their own IFF equipment on the frigates, allowing them to dial up the incoming jets and confirm their designation. Once they knew that the aircrafts were indeed their own, they moved out of the way as quickly as they could."

"And what about Group Six?" asked Mitchell. "The Migs could have just been checking us out?"

"Of course," Travers went on. "But in the past, checking us out means getting no closer than five miles. Flying right overhead is considered an act of war and they know that. Which reminds me, at this time we have little on the Korean flight, since the pilot and crew have decided to be particularly difficult and refuse us any information. The government of Oman is helping as much as they can but it's taking time going through channels. Plus the fact that no-one here can trust that their airport security won't walk all over the evidence before we can even get a chance to examine the aircraft ourselves. I can tell you that as far as Cairo is concerned, it left fully loaded with two hundred and thirty-five passengers on board. So all we can assume at the moment, is if the device was dropped, it was dropped by the Iranians."

"So are you trying to say," interjected Walters, "that the air force believes that a huge device, capable of knocking out all the electronics aboard five ships, was dropped from either an old Mig-23 Flogger or a -29 Fulcrum?"

"They're not trying to say anything Admiral," replied Travers calmly. "Just that, based on the preliminary reports on the subject at hand, the Mig solution is the only one that stands up if the Korean is legit'."

Admiral Swanson, who had been quietly taking his own notes to parallel Latchkey's, rose to his feet and walked over to the window.

"So what we're saying gentlemen is that, on the grounds that Iran wanted to block the Straits, they fired at us. But that defeats their own purposes of allowing us in and out of the Gulf to continue the pressure on Iraq. If it was a rogue, then where is he? We've found the plane but no pilot. And if they did drop something on Group Six from a Mig, which seems to me a little far fetched, then why didn't they finish us off when they had the chance? And the Fulcrum that did fire at us instead of turning straight for home, stayed over the Gulf long enough for us to get at it. All this only hours after sending us notice that they're willing to talk peace!" Swanson turned to face his guests and shook his head in disbelief.

Peter Pruitt decided to ease the tension. "It seems to me, Admiral, that considering the Floggers flight plan, they were either part of the initial attack on Group Six or they knew we were hit. They flew over us to see if we could get something up. Somehow Lodgers did get something in the air to chase them off, but I reckon they knew what had happened."

"Maybe," said Bradley, "but they do nail down our own radio frequencies and maybe they overheard the Hummer trying to make contact after the hit and, on hearing no response, the Migs went in closer to check us out."

"Well, I've got one for you," said Pruitt. "I have to assume that the Korean was involved. Let's face it, it was the only aircraft in the air at the time capable as far as we know, of carrying such a heavy load. Why would they wander right into Iranian territory to nearly have their wings blown off when their target was close to their original course? All they had to do was stay on their correct heading and they could have dropped it from thirty thousand feet, and we may never have suspected. Although the aircraft for now is locked away in Oman, we will eventually have an opportunity at inspecting it. Sooner or later we will discover the truth. But for the moment, I believe the two attacks are connected and that the Iranians are behind all of it."

"So what are we doing about all this?" asked Walters. "The press is going to be on us like a ton of bricks."

Swanson made a move toward his desk. "We have an investigating team on their way to Oman now. As soon as we have confirmation of their findings we will, of course, let you know. For now, we must hold back any statements for fear of making any false accusations. So thank you for your comments and we will have another meeting in about two hours. John will let you know." The meeting broke up and left Swanson's office as Latchkey put the paperwork on the table back into some kind of order. "John, after you've finished cleaning up, get hold of Lodgers for me, will you? I want to find out how he's doing, plus, we need him to have the *Philadelphia* do a thorough search for that thing."

Chapter Sixty

The room reserved for aircrew was bristling with activity, but not with aircrew. Not only were the twenty technicians stationed on the *George Washington* making their way in, but so too were the fresh white coats who had just arrived back from the rest of the fleet. And as they waited for the meeting to be called to order, everyone huddled in groups exchanging information and comparing notes. On the two head tables, logic charts were stretched out from end to end, held down with a few scattered coffee cups, behind which a single row of chairs were lined up with their backs against a black board.

Captain Danforth, who had been chatting to a couple of the team members in an adjacent corner, looked at his watch and walked over to where the two tables met. "All right everyone, would you please find somewhere to sit." They all broke from their clusters, and distributed themselves to the rows of small collapsible chairs. "This meeting will be conducted as an open forum so feel free to join in whenever you have something to add. Though initially, I would ask you to restrict your comments to the type and location of the failures, we'll get into the how's a little later. I've formed my own impressions of what happened but first let's hear from you. Art, why don't you start things off?"

Bell, who had taken a seat in the front row, stood up and turned to face the room. "Well basically I found only one type of failure. In every case that I worked on, to coin an old fast-food phrase, every chip on the ship had been fried. Generally, the pre-sets and related were fine and are still functioning, but the minds were gone. The micro-chips, in fact all levels from the P3s to the new ZZs, had been burned out of their sockets. Apart from one or two exceptions not one post was intact. From preliminary examinations, it appears that the silicon itself remained unharmed, but there was no doubt that there were enough wrinkles to force looping at every stage. And as we all know, once a serious loop has been established, it's next to impossible to nail it down for a fix." Bell sat down.

"Thanks Art," said Danforth. "Now a word from Rick, overseeing Nucleonics." All eyes were just swinging around to focus on the middle of the room, when the door opened and in walked Admiral Lodgers and Captain Gurney.

"Excuse me, gentlemen," said Lodgers. "I do hope you won't mind this intrusion, but the Captain and I are rather interested in your findings."

"Of course, Admiral," said Danforth. "Please take a seat."

"Thank you," said Lodgers. "There was a time there, gentlemen, that I was in charge of probably the most expensive hole in the water the world has ever seen, and we are anxious to prevent it from happening again."

"Yes, Admiral, so are we," replied Danforth. Captain Gurney closed the door behind him and followed the Admiral across the front of the room, and took a seat next to him at the end of the table.

"Right. Now Rick, please continue."

"Yes, well, my findings were very similar to Art's with one major exception. After a debriefing with the Commander, I confirmed his findings in that the two floors of the Nucleonics Department were hit with varying degrees. Here, let me show you." Norman made his way to the front of the room, grabbed one of the charts propped up in front of the black board, rolled it out for all to see, and, with Danforth's help, pinned it to the board. The chart he had selected was a profile cut-away of the central part of the Carrier from the base of the stack down to the hull. Taking a laser pointer, he stood back from the drawing and aimed the red laser pointer at the center of the chart.

"Right here, as you know, are where the reactor plants and their support equipment are located," Norman went on, circling the bright red dot around three main areas. "Above, are the two floors that contain most of the control equipment. On the upper floor, where the primary controls for the personnel are located, all of the drams had gone, just as Art has described. I did manage to fire them up again, but everything got caught in a loop. Totally locked with little chance of rectification." He moved his pointer to the second level. "Here on the lower floor only a few boards were touched. In fact, if the control systems could have been brought back on line, I think we could have managed some capability. Fortunately, for everyone on the ship, the emergency control mechanisms for SCRAMing are located on this level. They were still intact and shut the system down without risk." Norman smiled briefly to the gathering and returned to his seat.

"Thank you, Rick. Now to communications. What do you have for us Alan?" Danforth asked, looking over to the left side of the room.

"Mega dittos here," said Corbeth. "All the chips were dead as a Dodo. There was one major exception however that may throw a kink in the problem. There are forty-two main radios aboard the *George Washington*, that handle everything from aircraft movement to the up-links from the birds. They are used to talk directly with D.C. and the front line troops. Those sets dedicated to handling the more important traffic can each handle all of the channels available. Upon examination I found that, although all of the bands were working, including VHF, UHF, side bands, etcetera, nothing was getting through. The operators couldn't get in to use them because the upstream cleaners had gone out in the same way as described earlier. Most of the mains use presets, but the locators, compensators and enhancers had all blown. There was nothing anyone could do without using replacements and, as we all know, there were none. Even the sets on the aircraft themselves had shut down for the same reason. They were all actually still operating but nothing was getting in or out. These days our operational requirements have become so demanding and so sophisticated, to keep the operational intensity of their use to a minimum, that we've packed a whole lot of labor saving devices into them. And for the most part, it was these user simplifiers that shut down."

"Excuse me," said Lodgers. "Since I'm just an old

sailor from the days of rubber bands and steam radios, and since some of this electronic language is a little beyond me, would someone care to put all this into some sense of English that I can understand?"

"Certainly," said Danforth. "There are basically two kinds of memory that all computers run on. The memories, chips or drams as we call them, are the small silicon pads that the memories sit on. These memories are either presets, a type that has it's mind set into the chip permanently, or a type that requires an external power source to keep the memory functioning. Even when the equipment is turned off the small batteries inserted on the boards, similar to those you would find in the base of a camera that operates the light meter, keeps the memories warm, that is, activated. What we are finding here is that all the drams and some of the presets were fried, burned out. And although part of the equipment could still have worked, access to the software using these drams was impossible. Your main radios, for example, were still functioning, but the voice, having been converted into electrical impulses, couldn't reach the set because the surfaces that these memories and controls use, had been damaged."

"Thank you, Captain. Please continue," said Lodgers.

"Yes, sir," replied Danforth and turned back to face the room. "Let's hear from Commander Lelliott covering Radar."

A white coat in the middle of the room stood up. "We are now back up to full speed, thanks to the assistance from Jim and his crew. We had major failures exactly as described by other members of the team, however by using the support units we've brought with us, we managed to fire all the systems up again."

"Good to hear. Now, is there anyone else who has anything to add to the description of the failure?" said Danforth, looking around the room. "Well, okay. I don't think there's too much doubt about where we should be looking. For the Admiral's benefit I will preface this by summarizing our capabilities so far." The room relaxed a little as Danforth launched forth.

"Way back, when computers were first used to run data on our early nuclear tests, we found that all the computers, although housed in safe bunkers miles from the blast, kept failing within milli-seconds of initiation. We termed the energy from the tests that fried the chips as an Electro-Magnetic Pulse. The high levels of EMP, that were generated from nuclear explosions, gave us cause to be delighted. If ever we were to drop one on an opposing force, their electronics would be knocked out at a far greater range than the blast's force. However, this was short-lived since we realized that if the roles were reversed, our forces and our ability to communicate with each other would be just as vulnerable. A hit on any part of the U.S. would cause incredible levels of damage, not only due to the blast and the high levels of radiation, but any chip that was being used to handle our defense and communications systems, essential to combat any attack, would be fried by this EMP. So, the first thing we had to do was to design and build a device that could generate EMP so that we could ascertain the combinations of materials necessary to shroud our military hardware to ensure that they would continue to operate under such an attack. We did. The largest generator that exists at the moment is currently being used by the DoD research center in San Antonio, head quarters of AFEWC, the Air Force Electronic Warfare Center. We found that by pulsing large magnetic fields, a strong EMP can be generated, similar to those emitted by nuclear devices. The resultant tests proved that substances such as gold, lead, steel and even cast iron were in various degrees impervious to such pulses, and we proceeded to surround all of our sensitive equipment throughout the entire military community with these materials, where vulnerability dictated and costs permitted.

Up until now we have maintained a high confidence in some of these materials to ward off any such attack." At this point Danforth slowed his dialogue down as if to drive home the point. "But it seems to me, at any rate that what we were hit with here was an attack by a pulse, that pushed right through our shrouds and fried our equipment, just as though our systems had no protection at all. This, gentlemen is most disconcerting. If someone has found a way of penetrating our hardening techniques at will, every single ship, aircraft, and in fact every piece of military hardware down to a simple field radio, would now be vulnerable to such an attack. It is indiscriminate and devastating, and if we don't find a solution quickly, we will all be running for shelter. My only doubt is that, if EMP was used, I find it hard to accept that the device could have been built small enough to move yet powerful enough to shut us down completely, not to mention light enough to load it into an aircraft." Danforth paused for a moment as if trying to imagine such an instrument. "Does any member of this team have any information that in some way conflicts with the EMP scenario?"

"I do", said Norman. "As I mentioned earlier, unlike other departments, I found that the damage was confined mostly to the first floor of Nucleonics. On the second floor, where most of the main programs run, the damage was minimal to say the least. Yet it is my understanding that the protection given to the entire department is consistant on both upper and lower levels. So why was the lower level less vulnerable?"

Bell spoke up again but this time remained in his seat. "I had some anomalies too. Up where Sperry's turntable governs the stability of the dish I found very little damage at all. The cut-offs shut down when master control stopped listening. Once the up-links were established again, I just turned it on and there she was, loud and clear."

"My exception is a big one," said Corbeth, almost interrupting. "The whole point of back-up systems is that they are supposed to work, even under complete power failures, and the black box that the navy still fits to even the most sophisticated Carrier, such as this one, is one such device. We call it that because at the end of the banks of radios, located in the heart of the communications department, is a little black box. Underneath it is a simple Morse sending unit. It has no chips, no enhancers or cleaners that might prevent its operation under such an attack. It is a bolt-standard piece of equipment, exactly the same as fitted to ships built before the war. When the Commander on duty realized the total incapacity of his department, he grabbed an experienced signalman and fired up the Morse Code unit, just as I did. Nothing. Absolutely nothing. Using Audition they could hear the signal generated from the hand-set, but nothing came back on program. Now the amplifiers also suffered under the attack so he by-passed them and went to a straight signal using battery power. Still nothing. When I first arrived at the Morse unit, I immediately checked for tampering. I took photographs of the conduit and looms. However I found no reason to suspect any. The key was fine. I asked an operator to send in plain language to any Ham in the area. He did. Nothing. I even sent a simple SOS and even though I could pick up a lot of junk out there, I couldn't get anything back. I can tell you that what worries me is if EMP can knock out even a simple Morse unit, then we're all going to have go right back to the drawing board." At this point, a young looking female stood up.

"Yes, Lieutenant," said Danforth.

"I was assigned the *Norwich* and though they had similar failures as experienced here, the Morse was fully operational. They began sending a coded distress as soon as they were hit and received immediate confirmation that help was on the way." The Lieutenant sat down.

"Anyone else?" asked Danforth, looking toward the rear of the room. After a few moments pause, a deep voice made everyone turn.

Garry Sharp, the team's liaison officer, was propped up against the back wall. He was tall and thin, with that air of someone who has taught at University for most of his life. His deep voice carried the room with ease. "I'm not happy about the cause of this devastation either. The size and shape of this device concerns me immensely and any hypothesis that I might make about such a device would be purely conjecture at this stage, I'm afraid. I might be able to shed a little light on a few of our apparent contradictions however, concerning some of the anomolies.

First, Art mentioned that up around the antenna area, he found a few circuits that were still intact, even though they were on the outside of the ship and very exposed to any external attack. "As I understand it, these few chips were located in a control box, mounted directly underneath the turntable extremely close to where the motors that drive the table are located? Now a couple of years ago I worked on the Stanford project where we spent an awful lot of time trying to find other materials that could stand up to large amounts of EMP. We did find a couple. However, they were even less available, heavier, more cumbersome and even more expensive than the ones we use today. But one of the spin-offs we found was that if a strong in-phase magnetic field was activated close to the controls that had been hardened, though itself a threat to cause damage, somehow these fields actually dissipated the test pulses and rendered some of them harmless. The EMP seemed to find it harder to break through other local fields than it would without the fields being there in the first place. I think that we might find that the magnetic fields generated by the motors close to the control unit, may actually have helped save it from failure rather than improve the destructive potency of the attacking pulse." Captain Danforth, listening intently, sat down. "This research unfortunately was discontinued due to a lack of funding at the time, although I believe Professor Adams from MIT is now working to investigate this discovery further."

"Secondly," Sharp continued, "Rick's work in Nucleonics has shown that the reactors SCRAMed due to failure of the major controls up on the first floor, leaving most of the main drivers down on the second floor, undamaged and fortunately for all of us, allowed them to continue their work. Now I'm not totally convinced of my conclusions and I am not here to cast doubts against any member of our team, especially Rick, since he's relatively new to our group. But if I recall correctly, there were a few design changes that were canceled at the last minute, during the building of the *George Washington*. One being that the extra density added to the walls surrounding the reactors aboard this ship was meant to be twice the normal thickness for both floors, that is two feet thick, immediately above the reactor and full width, four feet, lead lined, steel reinforced for the containment area itself. The original plans called for this security to be built up to and including the second floor only. At the last minute, while budget activity was adjustable, the level of containment was increased to include the upper floors. The implementation of the addition was, one, going to delay the launch, and, two, since the containment was nearly half finished, it was decided, to over-ride the change and build as per original specs the lower floor as protected as the powerplants, but not the upper floor. Now as you can see the pulse, if that's what it was, had difficulty penetrating the lower floor. But due to the reduced security surrounding the upper level, it is perhaps clear to see why it succumbed so easily." A quiet murmur went round the room.

"And finally," said Sharp, shifting his position slightly, "this last comment must be considered as purely speculative, Admiral. I do have an idea concerning why the Morse unit failed." Admiral Lodgers, who had been playing close attention up until now, managed somehow to raise his level of concentration on Sharp's comments even more. "I know that Alan has covered all the bases internally, but I have a thought for you. We have known for some time that the more sophisticated and sensitive that radars become, the more prone they are to outside interference. The emitters and antennas that abound these days aboard surface ships of all nations, are a testament to the ever-increasing ability everyone has to watch and listen in on everyone else's activities. I don't think there's a radar technician who hasn't been told to completely strip down his unit and find out why his receiver keeps blurring or ghosting signals, even when the equipment is brand new and recently installed. This can also go hard on the men, since the civilian counterparts, sitting just a few feet a way from them, do absolutely nothing all day while earning a salary, three, four times more than they are. Indeed, many of the engineers used to be in the navy. We trained them and the private sector steals them away. This does nothing for morale. So anytime a sailor can fix something, without having to turn to his civilian watchdog for assistance, he'll jump at the chance, whatever the risks. Although solutions such as these have been hard to quantify at times, there have been a few reports of radars beginning to lose their contrast, as though they were some fault with the units themselves. Even the civilian technicians have had cause to scratch their heads at times, trying to track down the cause, especially since these same civilians had a hand in testing the units at the plant before overseeing the installation. But the initial tests are carried out in a very sterile environment, a complete contrast to the competition some of these units have to put up with from their neighbors located in panels inches away. Under these new conditions some ship personnel have taken to various unorthodox and unofficial tweaking procedures to improve their equpment's performance. And I believe that this is not the first case in this area to suggest human intervention.

"I'm sorry Mister Sharp," interjected the Admiral, "but I don't see what this has to do with the Morse Code unit."

"I'm coming to that, sir. There have been two other reports where, with so-called best intentions, an operator has taken it into his head to carry out certain tasks that would be regarded by the rest of us as reprehensible. Indeed on one of these occasions, one of only two that were actually reported, a senior officer on duty not only came up with the idea but recommended to his youngest and brightest recruit that he, the recruit, carry it out. During tests with simulators and land based masts, technicians are sent up to help secure the series of antenna that may have been damaged in the wind or fail in some way. Through a series of requests that had been made, particularly on recently commissioned ships, we have found that many radar units were not performing within parameters, very similarly in fashion to weather damage. The resulting action often led to a volunteer offering to go outside normal operating procedures to affect repair."

"If we accept that image-ghosting began to prevail

aboard this ship, it is only reasonable to assume that the same events may have occurred. While most of the ship is asleep, during some quiet, graveyard shift, a radar operator, with permission to use the head, would quietly leave his station and climb up to the aerial mast and locate the emitter for his own station. Invariably, he would find that the antenna used to transmit the Morse Code signals had been placed in such a way as to interfere with his radar's operational capability, either being set too close or in some way that causes ghosting. Now all our discerning sailor, equipped with a pair of pliers, would have to do is snip the leads off the Morse antenna and tear it off completely. Let's face it, when will the Morse unit ever be used again? And besides, it's not even part of his department. If Communications want to keep their Morse unit working properly, then they should keep a check on it. Low and behold, when he returns to his station, he finds that all his problems have cleared up. Reporting the problem had little or no effect during trials, since the ghosting effect only seemed to occur once in a while, Murphy has proven that. Suddenly one day, the *George Washington* goes to General Quarters and he's stuck in his seat. When the ship went black he knew that the Morse unit would be tried but there was no way that he could replace the broken antenna without leaving his post due to the G.Q. So he keeps quiet about the whole thing, especially since there is no proof that it was him. Why own up to it? Meanwhile, not far away in communications, a frustrated commander was bashing away at the key and concluded, because the failure apparently occurred at the same time as the rest of the radios, that it had also failed for the same reason. If I'm not mistaken, Admiral, right now, somewhere on this ship, either on duty or perhaps lying in his bunk, is a Radar operator quaking in his boots, with a very long piece of antenna wire stuck under his mattress."

Captain Gurney sounded pesimistic. "Wouldn't he have got rid of it by now?"

Gary Sharp was up to the task. "He may not have had a chance. First he may have carried out his little scheme very recently, and even if it wasn't, what would he do with it? Be caught trying to throw it overboard? I don't think so."

A round of chatter broke throughout the room as Captain Danforth rose to his feet. "Very good Gary, I'm sure we can find someone to run up the mast and check Mister Sharp's theory out," he said, glancing briefly in the Admiral's direction. "Time to get back to work. If there're no other comments, please return to your posts and I will be round to visit with you all independently before deciding on our next course of action. Thank you, everyone, good work." Danforth proceeded to shuffle the pile of papers strewn out in front of him back into his brief case as the rest of the team, chattering amongst themselves, filed from the room.

"Captain Danforth," said Lodgers, quietly walking up to him. "May I ask you a couple of questions?"

"Certainly, Admiral."

"I still don't understand why all of our stores went as well."

"Well you see, Admiral, the chips we needed were not, for the most part, the pre-sets. They were the drams that had to be constantly powered up to retain their memory. The boards in your Supply department were exactly the same. They have little batteries inserted on the boards to retain the memory, even when in storage. They were hit just as if they were in use."

"You mean a computer can be damaged, even if it isn't turned on?"

"Exactly."

"So this applies to our aircraft as well?" asked Lodgers.

"Most certainly. The fact that the aircraft was down in the hanger made no difference. If there was a chip on it, as all of them have, from radio, radar, to the fly-by-wire controls, you had no capability."

"So," said Lodgers, thinking that he'd found a chink in the solution. "How did we manage to find a Hornet that worked okay?"

"I thought you were getting round to that, sir. I wondered about that myself. Upon examination of the repair logs in the workshop, I found that one of your Hornets was going through a major electronic systems examination due to some malfunction as reported by the pilot. The fact that it was a Hornet, with total fly-by-wire systems, perhaps now is obvious. Because the entire aircraft uses chips to keep the aircraft flying, all of the boards are accessible and removable. Due to the performance problems, all the operating memories had been removed from the aircraft to be checked, leaving the aircraft totally naked and devoid of all boards. Once the shift had finished, all of these boards had been put away in the very thick lead-lined safe provided for such circumstances, and it was obviously well up to the task. Once the attack was realized, your engineers were ordered to check all aircraft. So they opened the safe, slid the boards back into place on the Hornet, and found that, except for the radios that were left on board, all the systems fired up immediately. The original problem still hadn't been rectified, but under the circumstances, they were considered secondary to the task at hand."

"I see." nodded Lodgers with a smile.

"Incidentally, just to enhance the point, if you had a couple of W.W.II. Swordfish on board, they would have remained fully operational throughout the attack and they could have been launched without the use of the Cats."

"I know, but they wouldn't have been much use against the Migs." nodded Lodgers. "And the portable radios we found?"

"Unharmed, simple solid state, presets only."

"Maybe we should get some more of them."

"Maybe. And by the way," said Danforth, "I would be equally fascinated to learn how you managed to launch that Hornet without any steam propulsion?"

"I'll introduce you to our hero before you leave. As for now, we're going to instigate a search for that nervous radar tech and then hit the sack for a while. Will you be contacting Admiral Swanson with an updated report on all this?"

"Yes, sir, as soon as I've packed up things here."

"Good, then we'll leave you to it." Lodgers and Gurney made their way to the bridge and ordered the Marine Guard to run a complete inspection of all living quarters.

Chapter Sixty-One

To the East, beyond the end of the runway markers, about a mile from the main terminal, a dirt road weaves its way around the outside of the perimeter fence. Although the mix of barbed wire and wood were high in places, it was obvious that upkeep of the airport boundary was not on top of the security's priority list. This disrepair was due largely to the complacent attitude Oman had toward its friendly neighbors on this side of the Gulf, and even though it accepted flights directly from Iran, its ability to police the incoming tourists was so complete that hanger areas were not considered important.

Amidst the dust and blowing sand that swirled above the road that morning, a well camouflaged school bus turned right and headed south toward the huge hangers that began to loom large in front of it. Behind the wheel of this dusty transport a fifteen year old boy wrestled with the controls, nurturing the engine to maintain its popping and banging, not by subtle and deft movements of the choke and accelerator, but by shouting in Arabic. His constant yelling was as much amusing to those hiding between the seats as it was disconcerting. Noise to them was a betrayer, a signpost as to their activities and movements. But to this boy, as their contact had put it some thirty minutes earlier, it was the only way, the youngster believed, he could prevent his livelihood from breaking down altogether.

The bus appeared empty. But to the boy, his cargo of greasy looking overalls hiding between the seats was somewhat comforting. It was the first time he had ever carried anyone that looked ready to help rebuild the engine if it blew up while he was on the road. But while he was in his element, his cargo was not. It was a strange awakening to the passengers that amidst the foreign tongue that had filled the confines of the bus for what felt like an eternity, they were all suddenly brought to their senses by a change. The volume and pitch of his dialogue never faltered or hesitated, but there, in the midst of this onslaught of what Digger later described as the longest, continuous Arabic profanity he had ever heard in his life, they understood in plain English, the unmistakable order, "time to disembark." The shouting returned to its native dialect as the bus bounced to a halt just inside a large shadow thrown off by the hanger nearest the fence.

Digger thrust a wad of money into the boy's out-stretched hand and *Gold Seal*, minus Fielding, disembarked. No sooner had the last foot left the remains of the stairwell than the bus began to cough and splutter its way into the mist, leaving behind a large cloud of blue smoke.

"They've got to be blind to not know we're here," grunted Bill as they ran the few yards to the fence. But before the second-hand had managed to claw a full sweep around the dial, they had cut the wire, crawled under, and found refuge in the hanger's rear doorway.

Digger peered in and saw a number of small air-craft. He shook his head, walked down to the rear wall, peered around the corner and ran down the alleyway between it and the fence, the rest hot on his heels. The gap between them and the next hanger was about twenty feet and they crossed the distance easily. There was no door in the rear of this building so Digger led the team around the far end and up to the first entrance that they came to. He took a quick look through the pane in the door. Inside, occupying every inch of space, nose out, looming so large that it appeared to touch the roof, sat a Boeing 747, with huge letters painted along the body that read KOREAN AIRWAYS. Digger gave a thumbs up to the rest of the team and looked at his watch.

"Five minutes," Digger said, glancing at his.

Dave peered in through the window, to watch for signs of movement. "Any idea whether it'll be a chopper?"

"No. All I know is that we'll be provided transport of some kind out of here."

"I don't see any movement inside," said Buddy.

"Nor do I," echoed Digger. "It would help if the lights

were on. Okay, Buddy, go in with Dave and see that we have room to work." They gently opened the door and were no sooner inside, when each had found refuge behind some freestanding racks. Buddy took a quick look around and noticed the office area. Just inside the main hanger doors, a mechanic was sitting behind a desk reading a magazine. Buddy couldn't see anyone else, so he signaled Dave to let the rest in. Just as they were spreading out amongst the shelving units, a bell sounded, the overhead lights flickered into life and men started wandering in the front. *Gold Seal* retreated into the shadows and prepared to defend their positions. From their pockets large and small automatic weapons were drawn, as Bill and Phil took up point guard. Digger watched between two crates as one of the mechanics appeared to be walking in their direction. Bill dropped to his knees behind some large boxes and the rest took their cue. The casual footsteps on the hard concrete floor grew louder and Bill slid his gun onto the shelf in front of him. The mechanic stopped for a moment on the other side of the rack from where Bill was standing, and then, still searching the shelves, he wandered right around behind the rack to see Bill bending over a shelf in front of him. The mechanic opened his mouth, as if to cry out, but no sound was heard. Phil put down the two-by-four, as the man slid to the floor. Digger brought over a blanket and covered up the body while Bill moved a couple of items on the bottom shelf and pushed the unconscious mechanic onto it and with Digger's help, maneuvered the boxes so as to conceal their work. Phil was already back up front ready for the next one, but thankfully none came.

Six thousand feet up, ten miles to the West of Muscat airport, Captain Robinson was preparing his all black, twin-engined aircraft. The paintwork was military dark green with no seats inside, save for a couple of extras up front right behind the cockpit.

"Make smoke on the port side," said the Pilot.

"Making smoke," confirmed his co-pilot, as the local frequency was dialed in.

"This is Captain Robinson of the United States Air

Force calling Muscat. Come in please." The speaker crackled for a moment, followed by a rather officious voice whose English left a lot to be desired.

"Go ahead, American."

"We were on a flight to Bahrain when an engine began to overheat. We have four passengers and request permission to land."

"Negative American, we have no permission to give you on landing at this time."

Robinson let a grin cross his face. "We have only one engine, we request permission to land immediately."

"Negative American, we have no permission to give you on landing. You are hurting our pattern and must leave the area."

"Whether we put down on your runway or crash into your terminal is up to you, but your airfield is the only safe area to land, so we are landing, whether you want us to or not," said the pilot as angrily as he could.

"You are breaking airspace that we are restricting. You have no permission on landing!" The voice was taking on its own tone of desperation. "One moment, please while I check with my superiors."

"Look Muscat. We won't land anywhere near your terminal buildings. All we need to do is land, do some minor repairs that we can fix ourselves and take off again."

"Repair yourselves?"

"Yes, repair ourselves."

"And how long would this repair be taking?" said the voice, relaxing just a little.

"About ten minutes. It's an oil leak. We just need to replace an oil seal and be back on our way. If you want to send out a couple of trucks to watch over us, that's okay with us. Now do we get permission or not?!" Robinson raised his voice to a shout at the end. As Robinson waited for the radio to respond he lowered the extended undercarriage and lined up with the runway nearest to the main buildings.

"American, this is Muscat airport. You may land on the right runway. A marked vehicle will escort you around to the repair area. You will fix and then you will take off again, yes?"

"Absolutely, yes. Just tell your men to keep their distance away from the aircraft. The engine is very hot and may explode at any time."

"You are running the risk of a fire, Captain?"

"No, not if you leave us alone," said Robinson, trying his own brand of relief. Smoke was pouring out of the port vent as the Captain brought his aircraft in toward the runway in a very exaggerated fashion. Both rotors were still turning as the port wing dropped, gained altitude for a moment, and then straightened. Again the port wing dropped, and the gyrations continued all the way down to the concrete. The long, extended undercarriage touched once, twice and then finally took the weight as the brakes were applied and the huge blades spun down to an idle. A car with a big red flashing light appeared in front of them and Robinson steered his craft to the right, following it all the way back to a series of hangers at the South-Easterly end of the airfield.

By the time the short haul passenger aircraft with smoke still bellowing from the cowling had pulled up in front of the huge doors, most of the maintenance workers inside the hangers had wandered out to watch the action. It was here that *Gold Seal* grabbed their opportunity. Digger and Buddy, keeping their eyes on the front desk, walked quickly up to the flight of steps that led up to the rear exit of the Boeing. They both climbed up the steps quickly, checked to see if there was anyone aboard, and moved into Coach. It took them two minutes to search the plane. Neither the galleys nor the aircraft had been cleaned since it was last occupied. Waste paper, cartons of milk, miniature soft drink cans, and napkins littered the seats and floor. In the first-class cabin it was even worse. Digger started to make his way back to the door, just as Buddy came down from the lounge.

"It's a mess up there," said Buddy.

"I bet. Did you see the fire damage as we came in?"

"Yeah." Digger followed Buddy out of the rear door and down to the concrete once again. In the shadows, around the perimeter of the aircraft, their colleagues watched the front and back. All except one. Chancey, fully exposed to the main door, was halfway up a ladder feeling around inside a maintenance hatch to the inboard starboard engine. Buddy found a flight of steps propped up against the largest entrance into the cargo hold. The huge door above them had been latched open, and they climbed aboard. Any luggage and cargo that may have been on the aircraft had been taken off. The entire length of the partitioned compartments was empty.

"Check around, anything you can find," said Digger as he looked at the side wall next to the door. He took a couple of steps to the switch on the wall that operated the door from the inside while Buddy began searching the floor area. The cover of the switch had been removed and there, between two terminals, was strung a small piece of copper wire. He pulled out a miniature camera from his pocket and took a couple of close-up photographs of the switch. He knelt down to the edge of the door and began feeling the area where the door seal sat proud of the ledge. As if he knew where to look, Digger ran his fingers around the lower corner of the door seal. Suddenly, his fingers caught on something, and he peered down to see what it was. A piece of tape was stuck to the inside edge of the groove that the door swung down into. Digger rose to his feet to find Buddy ready to leave.

"Find anything?" said Digger.

"Just a tear from a blanket, a suitcase handle and a small piece of convoluted hose," answered Buddy, holding out his find. "Could be part of a breather kit.

"That's great, mate, now let's get out of here." Digger followed Buddy back down the ladder and took the few quick steps to the shelving units. Phil moved out of the shadows and gave the thumbs up, just as Chancey came softly over.

"We've got company," Chancey whispered, just as a few of the workers that had given up on the excitement outside began strolling back into the hanger.

"Any luck?" Digger inquired and Chancey held out a small round cylinder with a control device attached.

"Good, let's go." They ran to the benches, each grabbing a tool from the hundreds that lay strewn about, regrouped in the middle of the hanger, and began sauntering casually out the main door, right past the locals, toward the twin-engined craft under repair. A crewman, standing out on the wing, saw them coming and began walking back toward the fuselage, just as both engines began to fire up. A huge side door slid open. The group, containing their eagerness to break in to a run, continued their stroll toward it as smoke began to belch out of the port engine. Two large trucks appeared from nowhere and pulled right up in front of and behind the aircraft, blocking it in completely.

"Let's go," cried a voice from the doorway, the engines building in momentum.

Digger was first to sprint to the rope ladder as the rest followed suit. He climbed up and yelled at the eager arms helping him aboard. "What the hell are we going to do now? We're totally blocked in."

"I know, great isn't it," came the reply. The rest of *Gold Seal* climbed quickly aboard with Buddy bringing up the rear.

"All aboard, Captain," cried the crewman into his headset, and then shouted to the group, "now hit the deck and hold on." They did and grabbed at wall struts. Digger took stock of the situation, climbed to his knees, took a quick glance out of one of the windows to see how close the surrounding vehicles were and then took a couple of steps toward the cockpit. The entire aircraft began to shake as the oversized blades began winding up.

"I understand that, Muscat," said the pilot loudly, "but we have finished our repairs and we insist that you give us permission to leave."

"We've got company!" the navigator yelled, "assault weapons, the whole nine yards!"

"Make smoke!" ordered the captain.

"Making smoke," the co-pilot confirmed. Digger took a look out to the left. Clouds of smoke were billowing out from somewhere under the wings but the trucks were not moving. In the distance, closing fast, five or six armed troop Carriers were racing across the grass toward them. Digger reached for his weapon. If those trucks don't move in the next thirty seconds, he thought to himself, then this whole exercise is going to turn into a blood bath. He felt a hand on his arm.

"Relax," said the voice. Digger turned to see a fourth crew member smiling at him. "We've got the whole situation well in hand." Digger looked back out of the window. Through the smoke and fumes, he saw the engine on the end of the wing begin to rotate upwards. The vibration and noise increased to an almost deafening level. He crossed to the starboard side and saw that the other engine had also rotated and was now pointing almost vertically. The pitch of the blades shifted, and the aircraft leapt vertically off the tarmac, throwing Digger to his knees. Almost immediately, the engines began swiveling slowly back toward the vertical, as the aircraft gained altitude and forward momentum. Digger climbed to his feet and joined the aircrew again.

"Ten knots." The co-pilot was calling out the airspeed and manipulating the engines' angle of attitude. "Twenty knots... thirty... fifty... eighty." The engines had already receded to a forty-five degree angle. "One hundred knots." Digger returned to a window to see what was happening below, but all he could see through the plumes of smoke still gushing from the wings were a few tiny dots scattered across the airfield. Digger made his way back up front.

"This is Eagle One to Fat Cat, Eagle One to Fat Cat," said the pilot.

"One-twenty," continued the co-pilot.

"Roger, Fat Cat. We have all eight pieces of luggage on board and have cleared the airfield. E.T.A. twelve-hundred hours."

Digger returned to the navigator. "I didn't know any of the Osprey's were operational yet?" he said, raising his voice over the noise.

The navigator looked up and pushed his earphones back on his helmet. "Nor did we," he said laughingly. "One minute we were carrying out a few exercises in the Middle East, hoping to drum up some orders for this baby, and the next, we were told to come and pick you up."

"But I didn't think the Osprey could land conventionally!"

"Bell fitted the extended undercarriage before we began our tour of duty over here, just in case we needed to land without rotating the power-plants."

"Well, it certainly fooled our friends out there."

"Thought it would."

"It could have turned nasty, you know," said Digger.

"No, not really. The Oman people may be very protective of their airspace, but they're basically friendly with the U.S. and not about to open fire; at least that was what we were told at our briefing. And I don't believe the Pentagon would have approved this mission if they thought they were going to lose her to some small arms fire. It's the only one we've got."

"Well, this little junket looked pretty risky to me."

"Just ol' thumper at the controls showing off a little. He's been dying for a chance to prove her worth."

Just then, Buddy, Phil, and the others joined Digger up front.

"Hey, what a deal," said Buddy, patting the navigator on the shoulder. "What do you say, Dig, we should get one of these?"

"Right!" Digger turned to face the crew and said, "Way to go guys," and *Gold Seal* gave them a big round of applause.

Chapter Sixty-Two

The *La Salle* had just completed her docking maneuvers at the navy dock yard at Bahrain. The main bulk of the crew had assembled on the aft deck. A couple of deck hands were preparing the cables around the Fulcrum in preparation for the hoist, and just as the huge harbor crane swung over the stern, one of the men slipped. He was making his way on top of the fuselage forward from the tail section, when he lost his footing and tumbled to the wing below. He didn't hurt himself seriously, but while he was being attended to, Lieutenant Greenman, who had witnessed the fall, climbed aboard the wing and examined the area of paintwork where the crewman had lost his footing. Greenman was surprised to find that it was neither damp nor greasy, rather it had a somewhat sticky texture. Greenman yelled for someone to get him a scrubbing brush similar to those used for the decks. Captain Connolly, who had run forward to check on the condition of his man, shouted up to Greenman.

"What is it, Lieutenant?"

"I'm not sure, sir, but I think we have a problem here," Greenman replied. "It's been bothering me all this time, and now I think I know what it is." The injured crewman was being helped off the aircraft as the brush arrived. Greenman took it and began scrubbing the paintwork around the airforce symbol immediately behind the wing-root. "Sir," he yelled down to Connolly, "I think I know what he slipped on. It wasn't salt water or oil, it was paint!" And as Greenman continued to scrub over the circular insignia of the Iranian Air Force, the paint began to peel right off. "Look," he cried, "I knew there was something wrong with this pile of junk." The more he scrubbed, the more the circles disintegrated, revealing another set of markings underneath. "These larger rings were hiding the original set underneath. Looks like the work of someone in a hurry." As Greenman continued to scrub, the circles peeled off to reveal a green triangle. He looked down at the Captain but he was no-where to be seen. He was already back in Communications making a call to the his Commander-in-Chief.

"Yes, sir. I don't need to check the book, I've seen enough of them in my time. It was probably due to contact with the salt water that the insignia just peeled right off... Thank you, sir... Aye, sir. No doubt about it, the original owner's insignia was underneath. It's quite clear, sir. It's an Iraqi Mig, not Iranian.

Chapter Sixty-Three

The Naval Advisory panel was meeting again in Swanson's office, all except for Admiral Swanson. Admiral Walters was sitting at the head of the table as the latest reports were discussed.

Walters looked around the table. "Pat has asked me to run the latest by you and get your impressions. I take it you've all seen the findings?"

"A small piece of blanket and a rubber hose?!" said Crow, shaking his head. "You sent in a team of Seals to break in to Oman airport, running the risk of the whole thing blowing up in our faces, and all you found was a piece of blanket and a small length of rubber tubing?"

"Take it easy, Will," said Walters, "nothing's going to blow up in our faces. Besides, this was all cleared with your superiors, and personally I think our boys did a great job. Now, let's get down to business. The switch had been tampered with. There was a simple bypass that would have enabled the guy to open up the door while it was still in flight. And the tubing may well have come from a portable oxygen supply. They also discovered a fragmentation device, inside one of the engines. Before we go into all of this in more detail, any news from Cairo, Will?"

"As a matter of fact, there was," said Crow, settling down. "Apparently, it left late by about ten minutes with a full compliment of crew and two-hundred and thirty-odd passengers. Although no-one noticed anything unusual in the loading bay, one report from traffic control did suggest that they thought it used every inch of the runway and then some to get airborne."

"Okay," said Walters. "So let's assume someone with the device was on board. Why would the aircraft go so far off-course when the original flight plan took them pretty close to Group Six in the first place?"

"I don't know," said Bradley. "But what's more to the point, how could he have accomplished such a feat?"

"I don't follow you." said Walters.

"Let's say the guy, or guys, managed to have loaded this device onto the aircraft and stowed away without anyone noticing. And let's also say that they managed to set some incendiary devices in some of the engine nacelles. How could they ensure that the aircraft would fly exactly over the fleet? I mean, as if that's not enough to swallow, the odds of them flying right over Group Six under any circumstances is just too much to accept, especially when no-one could have known in advance that the Group was further North. And when you compare it to the actual flight path, nothing could be further from the truth. Not only did the aircraft not even come close to Group Six, but it flew off into no-man's land and was nearly shot down as a consequence."

"Well, it's obvious things didn't go according to plan," said Pruitt sarcastically.

"Okay," said Leemer, "let's just discuss the plan. How were they expected to know when they were close to the Group? What was the point of going to all this trouble, relying on a plan so flimsy? Supposing they never get close to the Group, what do they do? Abort and try another day? Hoping to drop the aircraft a few thousand feet by setting fire to a couple of engines is too far fetched for me. I agree with Brad, the whole thing seems absurd."

"The thing I can't fathom," said Crow, "is how, after everything went wrong with the flight, they managed to succeed at their task in the end anyway. Boy, were they lucky!"

"We don't know for sure that the 747 was involved at all," Walters insisted.

"As I say, they got lucky."

Walters wasn't convinced. "Could the items found on board be coincidental?"

"Not likely," Crow replied. "These guys knew what they were doing."

"Okay, then what?" asked Bradley.

"They push the thing out of the door, and then he or they jump," Crow went on.

"Jump? That would put them right in the middle of the fleet?"

Crow was trying hard to remain consistent with his thoughts. "They don't jump straight away. They wait until the aircraft's cleared the fleet and close to the coast."

Pruitt intervened. "You remember the reports about the Migs flying up and down the coast for a while afterwards, they could have been looking for them."

"In a Mig?" asked Walters.

"No, but at least they could find out their location."

"Pretty dangerous, don't you think?" asked Bradley. "Can you imagine someone opening the doors at that speed? The turbulence would blow them right into the tail. I just can't picture them maneuvering this thing out the door by hand?"

"Okay, so there were four or five of them," agreed Leemer. "What's the difference? It could have been possible for them to have pushed it out of the door and jumped later."

"Wait a minute," said Bradley. "How did they close the door?"

Crow continued. "The door must take at least ten seconds to close, so the last one out just threw the switch and jumped."

"But the open door must have caused a terrible drag," Bradley insisted. "The pilot must have known something was wrong."

"Yes," said Crow. "But the aircraft was turning toward the airport anyway, and the pilot and crew were so busy dealing with the fires and keeping control of the plane, that they may not have been able to tell the difference."

Just then, the phone rang on Swanson's desk. John Latchkey got up from his note-taking and answered it.

"All I'm saying," continued Crow, "is that it is possible. It is too coincidental for it to be there, right over the fleet, just at that moment they were hit."

Commander Latchkey, having finished the call, approached Admiral Walters. "Excuse the interruption, but that was General Wilson's office."

"And?" asked Walters, turning toward him.

"There seems to have been some problem with the

Mig the *La Salle* raised earlier today."

"Don't tell me, we've lost it?" Leemer interjected.

"No, sir. It's just that we've found that the Mig's paintwork is a little suspect. It appears that the Iranian Air force were not the original owners. Under some fresh paint we found the insignia of the Iraqi Air force."

"You've got to be kidding!" Walters exclaimed. The rest sat back in disbelief.

"No, Admiral. It's been confirmed," replied Latchkey.

"Does Pat know about this?"

"I don't think so, sir. That was the purpose of the call."

"Well, wherever he is, track him down and get this information to him immediately."

"Aye, sir," said Latchkey, leaving for his office.

"Good grief!" said Bradley, leaning forward in his chair.

"You know what this means don't you?" said Crow. "It means that we've been fooled all the way along."

"So the Iraqis hit the convoy. But what about Group Six?" asked Walters.

Crow threw his pen down on the table. "Maybe it's all beginning to make sense now. The Iranians were following those two Fulcrums for some time, because they couldn't nail down who they were."

"But the IFF units showed that they were Iranian aircraft?" said Walters.

"They did. The Iraqis probably scrounged one from a downed Iranian Mig a long time ago."

"Well, I'm glad we found this out now," Walters said, somewhat relieved. "Immediately after Group Six was hit, the N.S.C. ordered a squadron of B-1Cs into Bahrain from Germany as a show of force against the Iranians, but now we'll be ready to go back and finish the Iraqis off."

John Latchkey came back into the room. "Sir, I've sent a message to Admiral Swanson regarding the Iraqi Mig, and while I was on the phone this memorandum came through. It was for the Admiral's eyes only."

"Give it here, it may be important." Walters took the

sealed envelope, opened it, and read it carefully, as the rest of the group leaned forward in anticipation.

"What!" cried Walters.

"What is it?" asked Bradley urgently.

Walters cleared his throat. "This is part of a memorandum sent from the Assistant Bureau Chief of the CIA in Connecticut to his Director, dated over a month ago. It reads as follows:

'Regarding Project EXEMPT. I can now confirm that this device can penetrate current hardening techniques and the trials you requested will be going ahead as scheduled. The developer of this device in Connecticut has followed your security requirements to the letter and is now awaiting the third payment.'

"You mean this thing was developed in the U.S.?" cried Bradley.

"It certainly looks like it," said Walters, throwing the paper down on the table in disgust. "And, more to the point, we've known about it for some time!

"Mister Crow, I will be informing the N.S.C. of this discovery immediately, assuming they don't know already and, if I were you, I would find out everything your agency has on this device and have it on my desk in no less than forty-five minutes. Now move it!"

"Yes Admiral," said Crow sheepishly and hurried from the room.

"The rest of us will meet back here then for one more go on this thing before we grab some sleep. John, get me Admiral Morehead on the phone. I need a meeting with him now, and get a line to Pat. We need to talk."

Chapter Sixty-Four

Save for those on duty in the Communications Department, nearly everyone had gathered outside in the morning sun around the various buildings that constituted the Bahrain Air Force base. About three thousand feet, five miles away to the north-east over the Gulf, the first black spot could be seen turning on to finals. As it loomed larger, a second dot came into sight. The leading B-1C lined up with the runway, lowered its undercarriage, and prepared to be the first Lancer ever to touch down on Middle East soil. Its nose rising higher as the extended swept wings with full flaps began to show signs of the vortex sweeping up from the tips. As the Lancer crossed the grass the rear wheels reached down for the runway, letting out a screech as they found the tarmac. The nose wheel followed suit as the nacelles on the four F101-GE-102 turbo fans opened and the roar of the reverse thrust momentarily ceased the vocal interest of the spectators. No sooner had the sleek bomber slowed and turned onto the taxi-way than the second and then the third B-1C touched down. The three gathered closer, following each other like three Praying Mantises, rolling along to the far end of the airport. As they came to rest in formation, many of the off-duty air crews walked over to greet them.

Chapter Sixty-Five

Colonel Bob Standford and his crew were tired. The eyes and ears of the Persian Gulf had remained vigilant for the last fifteen hours and as the coffee pot made the rounds once more throughout the aircraft, the adrenal glands tried to fire up again.

The large computer image in front of Standford depicting the northern coastline of Iran, began high-lighting the positions of the Harrier and the helicopters. Standford took a quick look at the entire field of operations, assessed the priorities and sat down. "Willis, any change?"

"No, Colonel. Javelin's managing to stay under the radar on Karq Island, but they will pick him up eventually."

"How long before he's out of Karq Island's range?"

Jennings checked his data. "About another two minutes or so."

"Maybe this is going to turn out to be Rhinestone's lucky day. Javelin's E.T.A. is seven minutes. Let's go everyone."

Jennings spoke again unexpectedly. "Hold on. Looks like Rhinestone's got company."

"Well, get on the stick."

"Yes, sir."

O'Grady's voice sounded in Standford's ears. "Colonel, just heard that relief is on the way. Head for home?"

"Sure. Okay everyone, we're heading home so we've just got time to get Javelin in and out before we hand over."

Chapter Sixty-Six

"Javelin, the decoys are now in position. Any tones?"

"Negative," replied Hawksworth.

"That's good news. However, it does appear that a reconnaissance party has closed in on the GPS location."

"Any weaponry present?"

"Unknown, but we can assume that they'll have something aboard. Three miles to the coast. Are you ready to make the run?"

"Roger, Sentry. All set here."

"Altitude?"

"One-fifty."

"Change heading to zero-four-three, altitude fifteen hundred feet, and increase to maximum speed."

"Roger, climbing to fifteen hundred," Hawksworth confirmed as his altimeter climbed above the one-zero mark.

"Keep all radar devices turned off. We will monitor all activity in the area for you."

"All radar systems still off, roger." The Harrier two-seater felt good under him. No vibrations and little noise except for the quiet hiss of the Rolls-Royce purring behind him, the rush of air over the canopy and the reassuring voice of the Sentry. Even if the dialogue was a little too casual for his liking, Hawksworth maintained a high degree of confidence for the mission's outcome. The cliffs loomed up in front of him but he held his altitude.

"From now on there is no need to reply to our commands unless specifically required to do so, Javelin. We have detected low level surveillance from the north. Change heading to zero-eight-five." Hawksworth banked hard to the right, as the G indicator climbed over 6.

"Reduce altitude to twelve hundred. Change heading to zero-three-five. Distance to target is fifteen miles. The weather is good with visibility up to ten miles, heat haze restricts much beyond that. There is no ceiling to speak of. Change heading to zero-two-five. Twelve miles to target. Maintain altitude. Jamming is underway to the north. Change heading to zero-three-seven. You're looking good, Javelin. Target now eleven miles. Terrain dropping to five hundred feet, reduce altitude to seven hundred. The target area has shifted a few hundred yards to a deep crevice in the rock, the deepest of which runs about a hundred feet. Target now ten miles. Change heading to zero-three-two. At present our decoys are helping to keep radar concentration away from your area. We are now monitoring some aircraft movement from Bandar Khomenyi, one hundred and twenty miles to the north. Target now eight miles. Change course to zero-two-four. You may activate your GPS signal locator now."

"GPS locator now functioning," said Hawksworth.

"Are you receiving a good signal? The sending unit has been running on batteries for quite a while and the signal is weak."

"Reception intermittent."

"If it fails, we can guide you in close enough. Change course to zero-two-seven and slow to three hundred knots. Range five miles. It's pretty much heads-up from here on in. Bogie contact, one hundred miles to the north. E.T.A. to you is about seven minutes. How's the GPS tracking?"

"Strong."

"Standing by Javelin, and good luck."

"Thank you, Sentry." The flashing beacon on Hawksworth's HUD had become more consistent, straight ahead about three miles. He pushed the nose of the Harrier a little closer to the terrain, and began to take note of the surface beneath him. It was definitely undulating and here and there, separated by sections of mounding dunes, the rock presented several deep gashes. Some were very narrow and not very deep, but a few were two hundred feet wide or more and at least a hundred feet deep.

"Two miles to target," said Sentry, and Hawksworth dropped down to fifty feet, pulled the nozzles back to 60/40, and pushed forward on the throttles. Suddenly, out of the corner of his eye to the right, he thought he saw something dark. He took a quick glance and saw a jeep with at least two men inside, desperately trying to bring their jeep mounted machine gun to bear. He dived to the right and curved back around to the left, the beacon falling back to the center of his display. Then he saw an armored troop Carrier to his right.

"Sentry, this is Javelin. There's a lot of folks roaming around down here."

"Heavy?"

"Small arms fire, nothing big as yet."

"Thousand feet to target."

"They must be all over it by now."

"Can you confirm any prisoners present?"

"Negative, Sentry. Two more jeeps scurrying about. Coming up on a deep gully now. Target dead ahead. Slowing. Over the gully now. It runs south-west to north-east with a high rim on both sides. There's a lot of vehicles down there, they've opened fire!" Hawksworth pushed the throttle wide, banked hard to the left trying to clear the rim of the gully and rotated the nozzles to gain some acceleration. He felt small arms fire in close proximity and banked to the right. "Looks like they may have some anti-aircraft too."

"Maybe Rhinestone left the scene before it got too crowded."

"Roger. I can stay above the rim to the north-west. It will take them a few minutes to drive all the way up to the top." He glanced out both sides of the canopy and, failing to see any threat, looped hard around to the left back toward the trench and slammed the nozzles into 80/-20. With a nose up attitude, the Harrier, some hundred feet above the rocks, dropped its airspeed from a hundred and twenty knots down to zero. The nozzles went back to 100/00 and the trainer, in full hover, leveled out. Hawksworth, maintaining a high state of vigilance, rotated the aircraft to the left in an effort to make a full three-sixty sweep.

"Mig-25 Foxbat now five minutes away."

Suddenly, off to the north, a red flare began to burn brightly in the desert. "I have a red flare burning about five hundred feet to the north," cried Hawksworth, pushing the nozzles back. "There's someone down there. He's on his own and waving a shirt or something. Going down to investigate." Hawksworth dropped the power and the undercarriage and brought the Harrier down on the north side of the smoke below the edge of the gully. "He's injured. I'm going to have to get him."

"But..," was all Hawksworth heard as he pushed the canopy switch, pulled the plugs on his air supply, hit the buckles, and threw off his helmet, leaving the engines running at idle. The large one-piece canopy swung up and away to starboard. He climbed over into the rear seat, unbuckled the rope ladder from the straps, placed the grabs on the edge of the front cockpit and let the ladder unroll itself to the ground. In a couple of seconds he was on the desert floor. About forty feet away, clutching his left arm and limping was a man wearing the remains of a uniform.

"Come on, man, get the lead out!" The shirt that the man had been waving was torn and ripped, parts of it bandaged around his left arm. Hawksworth ran over to him. "Come on ol' man. We've got about one minute before the locals arrive."

The man's voice was rasping and his leg was bleeding heavily. "Sorry."

"How's the shoulder?"

With every step he winced with pain. "Surface mainly."

"Can you put weight under your armpits?"

"I guess so."

Hawksworth let go of his arm, stepped in front of him with his back to Barton. "Stretch your arms straight over my shoulders, palms up." Barton laid his arms over Hawksworth's shoulders and then twisted his palms up, letting out a groan as he did so. Hawksworth reached up with both hands and pulled Barton's arms down in front of him. Barton let a deep groan. The resultant maneuver lifted Barton's feet off the ground. Hawksworth shuffled as fast as he could to the base of the nose wheel. "I know this is going to be tough, but I have to get you into the cockpit." Hawksworth let his passenger gently to the ground, put Barton's hands onto the ladder and yelled, "now climb!" Barton made every effort to lift himself up but he was painfully slow. Bending down further, Hawksworth stuck his head between Barton's legs and lifted him up. "Come on old son, we've got to get out of here." Somehow Barton managed to lift his one good leg and place his foot on a rung. Hawksworth climbed up around his injured colleague, past the air intake and fell as much as jumped into the cockpit. "Come on, Rhinestone, just one more hurdle!" cried Hawksworth, reaching down and grabbing him by the collar. With one almighty effort, as though it could have been his last, Barton pulled himself level with the sill. Hawksworth grabbed for Barton's belt. "Now put your bad foot in there, your good foot over there and pull yourself in." Hawksworth pointed to the two footholds in the aircraft's side but it was no use, Barton was doing his best but for the pilot it was still too slow. Hawksworth grabbed one of Barton's arms and pulled with all his strength. Barton screamed in pain but at least was now half in and half out of the cockpit, his bad leg kicking in space. Hawksworth steered the legs over the edge as the spent body flopped into the rear seat. Barton let out a another groan of agony as his feet found the floor. "Get those belts done up pronto and hang on!" yelled Hawksworth as he threw the rope-ladder overboard, pulled on his headgear, grabbed the straps and pushed the throttle to the stops. The Pegasus roared into life and quickly the wheels rose from the ground just as the canopy closed tight around them.

"Javelin, this is Sentry do you read? Javelin, this is Sentry do you read?" The voice was urgent.

"I read you, Sentry."

"Move it, Javelin you've got company!" The voice in his ears was smothered by the sound of a low flying jet engine passing very low and very fast just overhead.

"Bad Bag accomplished, now get me out of here."

"Turn east, zero-nine-zero. Anti-aircraft fire in the vicinity." The Harrier climbed out of the rift, swung to the left and pushed eastward, Hawksworth juggling the optimum nozzle angles for maximum forward speed.

"Your over-zealous Mig is now banking to the west trying to turn on you."

"Roger." There was no telling how far the ground troops had managed to climb out of the deep trench.

"Negative radar, Javelin. Turn off your GPS locator. Turn right on heading one-seven-five. Increase to maximum speed. The Foxbat is attempting to turn on you. Boy do these guys need training. By the time he gets back to where you were you'll be long gone."

"Let's retrain him later, okay?"

"Ah, roger, Javelin. Turn right on heading two-zero-zero. Maintain altitude. Mig One's tightening his turn, Javelin. His range to you, now three miles. Four minutes to the coast."

"I've got positive Infra-red," said Hawksworth as the tones began to sound.

"He hasn't fired yet, Javelin."

"Sorry Sentry, but I'm turning on my radar and defensive systems."

"Roger, Javelin. Three minutes to the coast. Mig One now trying to close, Javelin. Bogie south. Change heading left to one-nine-zero. Increase altitude to one-zero." Hawksworth pulled back briefly on the stick, banked to the left, and armed his flares. "Two minutes to coast. Increase altitude to two-one-zero."

"Mig One has lock, he's fired, firing flares, taking evasive action," Hawksworth reported relatively calmly, letting go of the first batch of flares. He cranked the nozzles to hover and banked hard to the right. With the Pegasus's exhaust now hidden by the back of the Harrier, the threat locked on to the hottest object it could find, the flares, ignoring the Harrier altogether. The tones went silent.

"Inbound detonated, good work, Javelin." Hawksworth rotated the nozzles back to the full aft position, pushed the power up to full and rolled the Harrier to the left. "Change heading to one-eight-zero. Mig One still closing distance. One minute to coast line. Mig Two on track, forty miles." The tones sounded again in the cockpit though this time it warned of a radar-seeking missile.

"He's fired again, Radar tracking. Slamming on the brakes."

"What? Where are you going to dodge to? There aren't any trees around." Hawksworth repeated the process as before, but this time he fired off two blocks of chaff.

"How high are the cliffs ahead?"

"About fifteen hundred feet. Coast line dead ahead. Time to impact, twenty seconds."

Hawksworth had brought the aircraft down to one hundred knots, and with the nozzles in the fully forward position, 80/-20, he lifted the nose, gained two hundred feet and stalled the Harrier in mid-air just over the rocky coastline. For the first time, the voice broke from it's calm reserve almost to a shout. "Five seconds, Javelin! Four... Three," the voice continued its count as Hawksworth felt gravity grab the stalling aircraft. Jamming the throttle hard against the stops once again and pushing the nozzles aft, the Pegasus attempted to deal with the falling Harrier. It fell backwards on its tail briefly, enough for it to fall below the cliffs ragged edge. The power plant, now on maximum thrust shook and shouted as it attempted to grab hold of the aircraft in mid-air. Just as it was about to roll off to one side, Hawksworth dropped the nose, rotating the nozzles that now clawed their way to the horizontal just fast enough to catch the Harrier in the full hover. It was a brilliant move. The missile shot right over the cliff and on out into the Gulf. As if drawn by some sadistic desire to witness the carnage the Mig followed suit a few seconds later, right over the top of Hawksworth and his passenger.

"What happened, Javelin? Are you okay?"

"Roger, Sentry. All okay."

"It passed right through you!"

"Over me actually." Hawksworth let the Harrier's systems go to work. He accelerated once again bringing his heading further North toward the Mig.

"Mig Two, south." The short range Magics came on line and confirmed the acquisition on the Mig-25. "Javelin, break off, your heading now one-eight-zero."

Hawksworth shook his head. "Are you trying to tell me that I can't have a go at him?"

"Sorry, Javelin." Hawksworth banked hard to the left allowing his lock to catch up to the Mig. The tones sounded and the Mig flinched for a moment in disbelief that the Harrier was now behind him, then turned hard to the east, heading for safety.

"Are you sure we don't need an exhibit for the prosecution?" remarked Hawksworth disappointedly.

"We're sure, Javelin, thank you. Climb to five-zero on one-eight-zero with E.T.A. expected before nine local. I will inform Bahrain to expect you."

"Uh, Sentry?"

"Yes, Javelin?"

"Thank you. We must do lunch sometime."

"Right. How do you Brits put it? Nice doing business with you anyway. By the way, how's Rhinestone?"

"Don't know, haven't heard a peep out of him since he climbed aboard."

Twenty minutes later, Captain Markham Hawksworth touched down at Bahrain. Two ladders were run up the side of the cockpit with two medics in attendance. By the time Hawksworth had pulled out the headset lines and air supply, unstrapped himself and prepared to look behind him, his passenger was already receiving aid. For the first time Hawksworth realized that his suit and hands were covered in blood and reached for a rag from one of the assistants to clean his hands. Turning in his seat to see how his passenger had coped with the bumpy ride, he saw blood all over what remained of his colleague's pants, a bandage over what turned out to be a bullet wound in his shoulder, and a nasty looking gash in his leg. He looked dead. He was dead. Dead tired. He had slept through the whole thing.

Chapter Sixty-Seven

Swanson's committee was back in force as before. Admirals Walters, Mitchell, and Peterson along with Bradley, Chandler, Leemer, Travers and Crow had all taken their usual seats with coffee and an occasional pipe or two. William Crow had just completed his report to the consternation of all, especially to Admiral Peterson, who by now was voicing his displeasure and pacing the room. "We were not only hit with the most devastating weapon since the atomic bomb, but the development of it was carried out within our own borders. I think it reprehensible that this kind of thing is going on under our very own noses. Don't we have any control over this sort of thing any more?"

"I understand your concern," said Walters from the head of the table, "but we must tackle this as quickly and efficiently as possible. Now what do we have?"

Mitchell tried to sound optimistic. "We at least have the name and location of the manufacturer, Admiral."

"Yes," said Crow, "and the DIA are at this time attempting to contact that company to obtain a current status."

"So what are we going to do with Iraq, Admiral?" Mitchell asked.

"We are not sure," replied Walters. "Now that we have identified the Iraqis involvement in the attacks against our convoys in the Straits of Hormuz and possibly Group Six, the N.S.C. may advise the President that strikes deep in Iraq may soon be necessary."

"But wouldn't it be prudent to strike immediately while the irons are still hot Admiral?" Crow insisted.

"Perhaps." said Walters. "As a matter of fact, they're meeting to discuss this very point as we speak. Now let's get down to business. Fred, we have ordered the *Independence* to maintain the highest levels of defense possible, but do you have any ideas as to what we can do in the interim to protect ourselves from another attack?"

"Not really, no. Even if we tried to triple the layers of hardening material around all of our computer systems, which at the moment would seem to be an impossible task assuming we had the supplies, which we don't, and assuming that room within the equipment was available to carry out such a task, which it isn't, we don't have one of these weapons to use as a test bed to find out whether all the work would actually make any difference. So for the moment all our department can suggest is do our best to ensure that no unidentified aircraft come within a ten mile range of any grouping of our forces, and that we disperse our ground units and navel task forces to such wide areas that no single weapon could penetrate more than one ship at a time."

"But that's impossible," said Peterson.

"Exactly," said Chandler.

"So what you're saying is," Peterson continued, "if they decide to drop another one on our bases in Saudi Arabia, they could walk back in to Kuwait, or even Saudi Arabia for that matter, and there wouldn't be much we could do to stop them."

Chandler leaned forward. "If they hit one of our key air bases, that's correct, Admiral. At the very least it would get very messy."

"Did you manage to get hold of Admiral Swanson?" asked Pruitt.

"We did," replied Walters.

"And what was his advice?"

"His only question was whether we had found its remains."

"But we haven't," said Leemer. "For all we know it's still aboard one of our ships. Considering the Admiral's question, wouldn't it be prudent to do a thorough search of Group Six?"

"Yes, but let's wait until they get up to speed," said Walters. "Our boys have enough to deal with in getting themselves organized without tearing themselves apart internally. But I will agree, it is something we will have to carry out shortly. The *Philadelphia* has orders to begin a close inspection of the immediate area around Group Six until Admiral Lodgers considers it prudent to allow her to broaden it. As soon as we hear anything gentlemen, we will let you know. Until then I think some sleep is in order. Back here at oh-seven-hundred."

Chapter Sixty-Eight

Major General Larry Pullman returned to his office, put the note he was carrying into his desk drawer, and yelled for his duty clerk.

"Collins?"

A young Corporal ran to the door. "Yes, sir?"

"First get Captain Branden and his crew, then get me General Wilson on the line, on the double."

"Yes, sir," the Corporal replied and disappeared.

Just then, Captain O'Grady knocked on his door and walked in. "You wanted to see me, sir?"

"Yes, Captain. Glad to see you made it back okay. Take a seat will you? I know you've had a long trip but I need to take care of a few things first. The Brit had a good go-around, eh?"

"Apparently, sir, but Colonel Standford would know more about that side of things," said O'Grady, taking a seat in the corner.

"Yes, well, the Colonel should be joining us shortly. How's the Major doing?" asked Pullman, returning to his desk.

"All things considered, General, he's doing fine. From what I hear the Iranian troops were about five minutes from finding him." Another knock at the door and Colonel Standford walked in.

"Glad to see you back safe and sound. Take a seat Colonel. I'll only be a couple of minutes," he said, looking at his watch for the second time since O'Grady had arrived.

"Captain Branden to see you, sir," said the Corporal at the door, and a relatively young looking pilot entered the General's office.

"Branden, how many hours do you have on one-thirty-fives?"

"About six thousand, sir."

"Ever flown a C-137?"

"A General's transport?"

"Correct."

"About forty hours, but none of them had a General on board at the time."

"Well, now you're going to have the chance. General Wilson is over at Ad-Damman and a couple of his crew have gone down with food poisoning or something. It shouldn't be more than a day before they're well enough to get over here, but unfortunately that's too long for the General. So, for the time being I've offered to send a crew over to bring him in this afternoon. Get your flight crew ready and report to the CH-3 outside in five minutes."

"Yes, sir, will that be all?" asked Branden.

"For the moment, although I'd like you to report to me upon your return so you can brief me on how it went. If you do well, we might consider using you in this capacity more often," said Pullman.

"Yes, sir," replied Branden with a tone of eagerness in his voice.

"Carry on then."

"Ah, yes, sir," said Branden.

Pullman went over to the door. "Corporal?"

"Yes, sir?" came the reply.

"I don't want to be disturbed."

"Yes, sir," the Corporal responded and General Pullman closed the door to his office.

Chapter Sixty-Nine

The dark blue, unmarked van sat quietly in the shadows. Up ahead, where the lights of the main thoroughfare sparkled in the rain that washed away the grime and dirt of the day's commuter traffic, the flashing red light that swung in the wind over the junction continued its steady heart beat. But to the four dark-suited occupants of the van, all was well.

A radio crackled in the front. "The mark is on his way, he's just clearing the club now. He's lost quite a bit of dough, so he's tired and preoccupied."

A dark figure appeared at the window. The glass slid lower in response. "All set?" a voice whispered. The driver nodded. "Okay. Keep it tight and make it clean. No noise. No fuss."

"Right," said the driver, starting the engine.

The radio crackled again. "He's reaching the corner of Farmington and turning toward you... now." Up ahead the figure of a pedestrian appeared briefly under the lights and then dropped from view in the darkness. Again the radio spoke. "Six car lengths, he's searching for his keys." The driver swung the nose of the van out a little and checked the rear. No traffic from behind. "Four car lengths," said the speaker. "Light gray suit. Okay, nice and easy. His car's four up from you. The red Porsche." The driver twisted the wheel and drove out into the road. "Two car lengths, take your time." The van crept up the street rolling by two cars. The radio crackled again. "He's walking out now. He's found his keys. Go, go, go!" The driver had timed it well. With a stab on the gas and a stab on the brakes the van pulled right up alongside the man fitting the keys in the door of the Porsche just as the van's large side door slid open. Two men jumped out and grabbed his arms, spun him around and tumbled him into the van. The two climbed back inside, slid the door shut and the van moved up two more car lengths where it stopped again.

Again the shadow at the window and again it slid

down an inch or two. "See you back at home plate," said the figure. The window slid back up and the van moved off toward main street. In the back of the van with his mouth taped and his wrists handcuffed a small, well-dressed figure sat between the two large suits. The man on the right was reading him his rights, while the other lifted a phone from its receptacle.

"Home plate, this is the Bagger."

"Go ahead."

"We've picked up our package and we're on our way in."

"Good condition?"

"Oh, yes."

"Home plate out." A second van joined in the five minute journey. Leaving the main flow of traffic they turned into a courtyard, through some high gates and into a large disused warehouse. As the two dark vans pulled up to the far end of the building the huge wooden doors closed behind them. Except for a desk and a couple of chairs illuminated by the headlights, the rest of the warehouse was barren. Three men climbed out of the second van and stood guard as the first emptied. There was no discussion, no talk from anyone. The small man in the light suit stood out amongst the dark jackets, suits and ties that pushed the captive over to the desk. The tape was peeled off his mouth and the handcuffs removed before being steered to one of two hard chairs in front of the desk. One of the men from the second van came over and sat down at the desk, turned on the small but bright, downward facing lamp that sat on one corner next to a solitary phone, pulled out from inside of his dark wool jacket a wallet and laid it open on the front of the desk. The headlights were turned off and a hush fell on the room.

"My name is Pimsleur, Frank Pimsleur," said Pimsleur in a quiet but firm tone. "I work for Government Intelligence. Your name is Baker, David Baker, and you are Vice President of the Energy Research and Development Center in Hartford." Baker, lit from the neck down, sat motionless and unflustered by the proceedings. "Your company has developed a device that can penetrate the various hardening materials used to protect computers from electro-magnetic attacks. Your development has continued under the guidance and supervision of the CIA, and as such, we are grateful to your company for the success that your organization has had producing this device. Mister Fuller here," he said, turning to his left, "is a senior officer of that distinguished agency, and his authority supersedes any that Mister Brownwell, your CIA contact up until now can demonstrate. In fact it was our plan to have Mister Brownwell present for this meeting, but unfortunately we don't seem to be able to locate him at the moment."

"Although the CIA has no official jurisdiction here, Mister Fuller is here at my request and that of Special Agent Gorni of the FBI who stands behind you." From the shadows a dark suit stepped into the brightness and laid his identification alongside Pimsleur's. The folded wallet flipped open to show the big blue letters of the FBI Identification on one side with its photographic counterpart on the other. "We are confident that you will be able to provide us with all the information regarding the location of any such devices that have left the confines of your installation in Hartford." Baker sat motionless, staring at the opened wallet. "Even though you personally are not being charged with any specific crime at this time, I should point out that you and your company are still listed as official guardian of this research, and that an act of treason has been committed. One of your devices has somehow found its way into the hands of a foreign government, where it was recently used against American armed forces. We have traced this device back to your company and we are holding you ultimately responsible for the resultant damage, damage that we estimate to be in the region of two hundred million dollars. Unless you can tell us right now where and to whom your company moved this weapon, you will be taken from here and charged publicly with treason. Do you understand?"

The beads of sweat that were forming on Baker's forehead began to glisten in the shadows. "I do," said Baker.

"Now, we don't have a great deal of time to get into the finer points of diplomacy, so I'm going to ask you to be specific, detailed and brief. This entire meeting is being taped so don't concern yourself about being misquoted. Now, the information please."

Baker leaned forward into the glare revealing, for the first time, the sallow complexion, the furrows on his forehead, and the bags under the eyes of a man deeply troubled. His voice was soft but nervous. "I just knew something was going on. We were told, for security reasons, that Mister Brownwell was our only contact and that everything concerning Project EXEMPT was to go through him. The preliminary tests had been completed and we needed a further payment. He told us that funding cuts were being discussed and that we had to act quickly if we were to receive the balance of the monies due. In July Mister Brownwell told me that if we could get a field test sponsored we would not only get the balance due, plus a hefty bonus, but also a large order for a thousand of them, starting at one million dollars apiece depending on the size."

"What do you mean by size?" asked Pimsleur.

"The bigger they are, the bigger the range and the more they cost."

"You mean you can make them to various specifications?"

"Oh, most certainly," said Baker. Pimsleur took a quick glance up at Fuller. "Well Brownwell said that his chiefs had made contacts with various high ranking officials of the Armed Services and a test was going to be laid on in the Nevada desert somewhere. The day that he would take delivery would be the day we would receive a cashier's check for the balance plus a bonus. But I just knew there was something fishy going on."

"When did you first suspect?"

"When he said the CIA would handle all aspects of delivery and that none of our personnel would be allowed to go along on the trip."

"Why did this make you suspicious?" asked Pimsleur with a less officious tone.

"Well, we have to charge these units up before they

are used and it is necessary to check the levels of charge within the unit before discharge is permitted. Not that it is dangerous you understand, just that for a satisfactory test we would want the highest levels possible."

"And how did you answer his request?"

"I argued that we needed to be present at the testing but he insisted the CIA was going to take care of everything. I then told him that the longer the unit went before discharging, the weaker the overall effect."

"Wel, I can assure you, it worked just fine." Pimsleur announced. "What did you do next?"

"All we could do. Carry out the charging process before being loaded on the truck." Just then, a figure entered the light and whispered in Pimsleur's ear.

"Just remain in your seat Mister Baker." Pimsleur turned out the light on the desk. From behind Baker, the large wooden doors opened and a dark blue limousine rolled into the warehouse. The doors were closed behind it, the headlamps turned off, the desk lamp turned back on as all eyes focused on the driver who stepped to the rear door and opened it. The crisp white uniform of a member of the U.S. Navy stood out in sharp contrast to the dark figures that surrounded Baker. The officer accepted the other seat close to the desk.

Pimsleur continued as though nothing had happened. "Now then, Mister Baker, you were saying?"

"Yes, well," he continued more visibly distressed than before. "Ultimately I didn't object to his team taking delivery because he did arrive with the check, which, by the way cleared the bank okay and he did have plenty of support."

"What do you mean, support?"

"Well, there was a big truck, an armed troop Carrier and three jeeps. They had just come from the nearest army post."

"Were there any soldiers present?"

"Oh yes, in fact I was introduced to one of them, a Colonel Withers I think."

"And what papers did they present to you?"

"All very official I assure you. They were signed by the Director for Counter Intelligence at the agency and his field chief."

"Do you have their names?"

"No, but I have the papers in my safe back at the office. I can show them to you if you wish?"

"We wish. And then what happened?"

"Well. We got the fork-lift out and started the loading process."

"How big is this thing?" said Pimsleur.

"About the size of four of these desks, two up, two down, side by side. Anyway, I went to call the bank and confirm the validity of the check, leaving my chief technician to oversee the loading, arriving back just in time to see them pull out."

"And that's it?"

"That's it. Look, the agreement was to follow Mister Brownwell's instructions to the letter and we did that. I haven't done anything wrong, I've got the papers to prove it." Baker paused for a moment, and then added in a more apologetic tone. "I want to call my lawyer."

"You'll be permitted to call your lawyer once we have the documents." Baker reached in his pocket and pulled out a handkerchief and began wiping his face. "And what did this thing look like, exactly? Round, square, black, red, what, and how much does it weigh?"

Baker began to sweat even more so. "Each Exempt weighs in about a ton and is fitted into a large metal frame with steel panels secured around it to protect it from the environment. It looks rather impressive, pity really."

"What do you mean, pity?"

"Well, under the orders for preparation we were given, they were each covered in wood paneling to make them look like large wooden..."

"They!?" exclaimed Latchkey jumping to his feet. "What do you mean, 'they'?"

"Oh. You obviously don't know then. The orders called for two EXEMPTS to be delivered that day, not one."

"And you delivered two?!"

"Of course."

Chapter Seventy

The SH-3 Sea King had just lifted off from the deck when Cats one and two were made ready.

"Ready to launch S-3 Viking," said the launch commander into his headset.

"Launch S-3," ordered the air boss. The Viking was thrust toward the bows of the ship as the next aircraft rolled into place.

"Ready to launch KA-6."

"Launch KA-6," came the reply and the tanker roared down the chute.

"Ready to launch E-2C."

"Launch the Hawkeye."

"Ready to launch EA-6B."

"Launch EA-6." The launch commander for Cats three and four broke in.

"A-6s ready to launch." The air boss looked toward the fan tail as the two fully loaded Intruders were readied on the stern.

"Launch Cats three and four." First one then the other A-6 swept across the angled flight-deck and into mid-day sun.

"Ready to launch F-14s." On the bows two F/A-18 waited their turn behind the Tomcats.

Ever since the *George Washington* had been brought back to operational status, Admiral Lodgers had instigated full air cover and the deck crews were making up for lost time. Up on the bridge both Lodgers and Gurney watched with pride as the Carrier once again thundered with the sound of afterburners.

"Captain Danforth reporting, sir," said Danforth upon entering.

"Ah, there you are Danforth," said Lodgers turning away from the windows. "We all want to thank you for the expediency and efficiency that you and your men completed your tasks here at Group Six."

"Thank you, Admiral," said Danforth. "I hope we won't be needed again, sir."

"Don't we all. If you ever need an extra vote for funding to keep your team well equipped, just let me know," said Lodgers, shaking Danforth's hand. "Are you and your men ready to leave?"

"We are, sir."

"Very well. Good luck and a safe journey," said Lodgers, returning to the window. Danforth made his way back down to the deck to where his men were gathered around three Sea Kings that were winding up on the stern and prepared for the trip home.

Chapter Seventy-One

The CH-3 carrying Captain Branden and his crew touched down close to the C-137, and just as their feet touched the ground General Wilson and his entourage surged out of the main building.

"Boy," said Branden to no-one in particular. "He certainly carries a lot of men with him, doesn't he?"

"Sure does," replied his co-pilot.

"Come on, we mustn't keep the General waiting," said Branden, signing off the helo to the ground crew and making for the steps up to the flight deck. The General and his men were making for the rear door, except for a Colonel, who followed the trio into the cockpit and arrived just as they were settling in.

"Good afternoon, Captain."

Branden looked round. "Sir?"

"Welcome to General Wilson's flight," said Colonel Klugge.

"We appreciate the opportunity to help out, Colonel."

"The General is pleased you could come over on such short notice. We just need you to get us to Bahrain as quickly and, most importantly, as smoothly as possible, okay?"

"Yes, sir. We know this part of the country like the back of our hand."

"How long will it take?"

"About twenty minutes tops, Colonel."

"Good. If you should need to talk to me for any reason, just press the button marked 'cabin' by the intercom, and I'll come up to see you what you need. We don't disturb the General with routine matters. Any questions?"

"No, sir, we're all set here."

"I'll leave you to it, then. You may take off as soon as you are ready," and the Colonel left the cockpit. The C-137 taxied out, turned on to the main runway, and took to the air smoothly.

"Hey, this is easy," said Branden. "We're used to carrying three hundred thousand pounds of cargo, making this feel like a kitten in comparison."

"Yeah," agreed his co-pilot. "I bet the General doesn't carry more than a few bottles of scotch and an overnight bag."

"But you have to take into account all the go-fers he brings along with him. Must have a staff of at least ten, plus a few Marines."

"Well, a General gets all the beni's."

"Yeah. What a cushy number, eh? I bet the pilots who shuttle him around don't go hungry. The best food and easy shifts. Must be nice seeing the world and then flying home to check in with the wife and kids every month."

"You would have thought," said his co-pilot, "that with all the traveling they do they would have gotten used to the food in these parts."

"Maybe. But maybe they always eat the General's left-overs and for once they went on the town, stuffed their faces with local chow and threw up all over their nice clean uniforms."

"Yeah and maybe they're in the General's bad books right now, and if we do a neat job of ferrying him over we'll get asked to take over the job permanently!"

"Ha, ha. Wouldn't that be just what the doctor ordered?"

Chapter Seventy-Two

Out amongst the rocky dunes where the mine fields began, five miles from the last of the 'Do Not Enter' signs, two Israeli jeeps trundled slowly along. The maps of the area still marked the old Jordanian trails that were in use when they ruled over this part of the country, so the few that still ventured out into this part of the wilderness did so at their own peril, since most of their retreat was spent laying mines.

Standing on the front seat and holding on to the windshield, the guide kept his eyes glued on the two sets of tire tracks that stretched out before him in the sand. The tracks twisted and turned among the rocks and imaginary obstacles, reassuring the navigator that whoever had been driving through here before him had known where to go. The two jeeps had just risen over a particularly high hump in the ground when the passenger stretched out his arm bringing the jeeps to a halt. Before them, with its axles buried in the sand, sat a small Israeli army truck. The six men grabbed their rifles, climbed out of the jeeps and walked slowly toward the vehicle, checking to the left and right for any signs of movement. The passenger, leading the expedition, walked slowly up to the side of the truck, took a gentle step up onto the running board, and looked in through the broken window.

"There's two bodies in here," he said to another soldier standing by. "Get them out." He stepped down and walked to the rear. "Lieutenant, check underneath for signs of tampering." His driver began checking under and all around the vehicle.

"Anything?"

"Looks clean," said the soldier, getting to his feet.

"Okay, make some room," and the rest found what little cover they could. He reached up, grabbed the handle and slowly twisted it. Nothing happened. He gave it a tug and opened it a couple of inches. He ran his fingers up and down inside the door and, feeling nothing out of the ordinary, swung the door wide. "Okay, see if you can get this thing started." He turned and made his way back to the jeep. As the two bodies were being removed from the front of the truck and the hood lifted, the Colonel reached for the handset.

"Reconnaissance party three to H.Q. Over."

"Come in Colonel," the speaker replied.

"We've found the truck."

"Are you sure it's the same one?"

"I'm sure. The two occupants are still in the front. We are removing them now."

"And the cargo."

"Gone, I'm afraid. The weight was obviously too much and it got stuck in the sand. They must have had a terrible time trying to off-load it."

"Any signs of life at all?"

"I don't think so."

"Thank you, Colonel."

Just then, one of his men came running up to him. "Sir, one of them's still alive."

"Hold on," said the Colonel into the handset. "One of the men may still be alive, I'll get back to you," and put it back on its hook. He grabbed the first-aid kit out of the jeep and rushed back over to where the body had been laid out in the sand. The uniform was that of an Israeli officer and he had been beaten severely. His eyes flickered and his mouth quivered, and even though the signs of life were obvious, death was not far away.

"He's trying to say something, sir," said a Corporal and the Colonel bent over the body, as the wounds were being attended to. "You are among friends," said the Colonel in Israeli pouring some water between the bruised lips of the stricken man. The mouth began to move. His eyes opened. "Who was it, Colonel? Who did this to you? Can you give me a name?"

"Naa..," the voice murmured ever so quietly.

"Yes, yes. Go on," begged the Colonel.

The mouth attempted it again. "Naa... Saa..," the voice coughed.

"Naa, Saa?" the Colonel repeated.

"Nash... Anal... Sss..." What little volume his throat

could muster was dwindling fast.

"Again, again!" said the Colonel, moving his ear ever closer to the lips. But this time there was no reply. The mouth quivered one last time and, although the eyes remained opened, they turned cold and motionless. The Colonel climbed to his feet and returned to the jeep to call in the news. The two bodies were laid gently in the back of the truck, the engine fired up, and a tow-rope tied to a bumper. Within minutes the truck had climbed out of the deep hollows it had made for itself and, following an about-face, the convoy prepared for the return journey.

Chapter Seventy-Three

The decision had been made, the air crews briefed, and the orders given. Radio traffic had confirmed to those that knew Air Force dialogue that a complete compliment of strike aircraft had already taken to the air for the trip to Baghdad from various bases throughout Saudi Arabia, including F-15s, -16s, -117s, assorted Jammers and Refuelers, soon to be joined by the trio of B-1s from Bahrain that were already heading north toward their targets.

Air Force and Naval maneuvers were not, however, restricted to the northern end of the Gulf. South at Bahrain the base was also alive with activity. The mess hall had been converted into a large meeting room. Near the main doors to the left at the top-end of the room two head tables with chairs sat on a raised platform. On the far side, away from the doors, a single row of tables displayed a fine array of appetizers while to the rear a fully stocked bar had been set up. The rows of seats that filled the remainder of the room stretched back to the single fire exit. A few orderlies were milling around, setting up food and serving drinks to Colonel Bob Standford, Captain Michael O'Grady and the entire compliment of AWACS 24 as they made an early start on the refreshments. Admittedly the crews were tired, but they weren't going to miss out on an opportunity for some brunch, especially since they were guests of General Sam Wilson.

A compliment of Marines, the same command that had taken over the *Jardavian* the previous evening, walked through the propped open door and immediately joined in the festivities. A few minutes later, together with the crew of the Osprey, Digger, Buddy, Bill, Phil, Canny, Chancey, and Doug sauntered in, not in overalls or wet suits, but in the Navy uniforms of which they were so proud. The unfamiliar sight of white in the mess was a welcome opportunity for Captain O'Grady to demonstrate his ability to make any newcomers to his dining room feel at home. He watched them gather for a moment by the stage as though waiting for a reservation when, with beer mug in hand, he left his colleagues and walked up to greet them.

"Captain Michael O'Grady at your service," said O'Grady with an Irish smile. "May I be the first to welcome you to Madam O'Reilly's munch and crunch."

"Thank you, Captain," Digger responded. "General Wilson invited us to a luncheon meeting here today, but it looks as though we may be a little early."

"Not at all," said O'Grady. "You have the right room all right, Lieutenant Commander. Don't take the limited numbers here present as an indication of a lack of interest in the General's pending visit. It's just that most of the crews have to be persuaded to come in here 'cause the fare normally provided to us lesser mortals in the Air Force generally comes from a can." O'Grady's audience returned his smile. "However, today we have brought out our finest china and cleaned out Pully's, I mean General Pullman's refrigerator, so you shouldn't be poisoned to death at least." Just then O'Grady noticed someone limping through the door. "Excuse me please, my assistance is required elsewhere," said O'Grady, making his way over to where the injured crewman, propped up by a British pilot was standing. "May I be of some assistance?"

"Thanks awfully, old chap," said Hawksworth. "My friend here has just been through a harrowing experience, but insists on being present at this get-together, something to do with orders I understand."

Barton leaned on the door-jam for a moment. "I can manage, thanks," he said with a gasp.

"Of course you can," said O'Grady, putting an arm under Barton's shoulder. "But if you have permitted a Brit to prop up a wing to this point, the least you can do is allow a fellow compatriot to take you the rest of the way."

Barton took O'Grady up on his offer and hobbled toward the nearest chair. "Would someone be good enough to get me a drink," Barton grunted, stretching his bad leg out in front of him as he lowered himself to the seat.

"Good idea," said Hawksworth, walking off to the bar. "But I'm not sure this place is likely to serve anything other than lemonade."

"Now wait just a minute," said O'Grady, catching up with him. "We have one of the finest watering holes this side of the Mississippi and I defy anyone to order something that we can't mix."

"Markham Hawksworth," said Hawksworth as they arrived at the bar.

"Michael Patrick O'Grady," said O'Grady, trying to keep pace with his British counterpart. "And who's our injured crewman?"

"Him? Oh he's Major Barton, late of your Navy, so I gather."

"Navy? Then what's he doing in an Air Force uniform?"

"It's all we could find. His previous attire was destroyed by gunfire."

"His luggage was shot up?"

"No, he was wearing it at the time," said Hawksworth, turning to the steward awaiting orders. "One scotch and water, one lemonade on ice and," turning back to O'Grady, "your poison, Captain?"

"Oh, I'll have another beer thanks, and you can stick it in here," O'Grady said, shoving forward his mug. "Lemonade? I thought you were going to order something stronger by the way you were carrying on."

"Not at all, I'm still on duty and will be on my way as soon as the party, ah, this meeting is over." The drinks arrived and Hawksworth, leaving O'Grady to his own devices, carried the scotch over to Barton. "Here you are, Major. I trust it's to your liking." Barton took it gratefully and sipped. He nodded his approval and Hawksworth sat down beside him to view the new arrivals. Navy and Air Force uniforms intermingled. Some making for the bar, others the food and all Hawksworth could do was accept the somewhat egotistical habit of his American counterparts to throw a party every time they shot down an aircraft. The room soon filled with the sound of voices, chinking of glasses, and the occasional bout of laughter. And as Hawksworth looked around he wondered at the fact that, individually, any of these men could be sent against the best that the rest of the world had to offer and they would all come out on top. But put them altogether in one room and they looked just like any ordinary bunch of guys throwing a party for one of their colleagues.

At this point his attention was drawn back toward the main door as two Generals entered the mess and stepped up onto the podium. A steward arrived to take their orders as three other officers took their own respective seats toward the left hand end of the stage. Some more drinks were served when finally a Colonel stepped up onto the stage, checked in with his supierors, and called the meeting to order.

"Gentlemen, if you'd care to take your seats please." A few last minute helpings of food and drinks were snatched from the trays and the crowd spread themselves in their respective huddles throughout the room. The Colonel's order also signaled two Marines from the base's security unit, that had been standing near the entrance, to close the door. "Sergeant, you may bring in the prisoners now," and the two Marines stepped aside as four Iranians, in various degrees of repair and under armed guard paraded around to the rear of the room. "At this point, I would like to introduce you to, for those of you who are new to Bahrain, our Director of Operations, Major General Larry Pullman. General?"

Pullman, who had taken a seat in the center next to General Wilson, rose to his feet and cleared his throat. The room went silent. "Thank you, Colonel. I know many of you are perhaps wondering why I have asked you to join me this afternoon for this meeting, especially since there are some crews here that had no direct bearing on the recent attacks on our shipping. But we feel that we are all working for the same company here and whether directly or indirectly, you have all been responsible for the successful defense today of our operations in the Gulf. I should add that the four Iranians present were part of continuing attempts by their country to lay mines in the area, and, thanks to the members of *Gold*

Seal who are with us today, the *Jardavian* and its crew will not be hampering our progress through the channels any more." A smattering of murmurs rang round the room. "I should also add that these prisoners do not speak a word of English and have been invited here by our Naval colleagues. We will try to be as brief as we can, considering the fact that we have just commenced proceedings once again against Iraq, so we will all need to be back at our stations shortly. But in closing I would just like to welcome all of our other guests to this meeting and introduce to you, for those of you who have not had the pleasure of getting to know our Commander of the Asian theater, Lieutenant General Sam Wilson. General?" said Pullman, turning to his boss as he sat down.

"Thank you, Larry," said Wilson, climbing to his feet. "Could I ask that all ratings who have kindly volunteered to serve the food and drink this afternoon, and anyone else save for the Marines not directly ordered to be present, please leave." The seven ratings quickly made their way from the room and, as the last one left, the door was closed by one of the armed guard. "Some of you may be thinking," continued Wilson, "that the reason you have all been invited here today is to celebrate the downing and capture of a Mig-29 which, as most of you know, is on display down at the dock yards. But when you consider the actual series of events that occurred today in the Gulf Region, not only to the frigate *Stork*, but also with regard to the attack on Group Six early this morning, outside of the Mig, there hasn't been too much to celebrate. The first thing I want to make clear is that everything said in this room this afternoon must be considered to be privileged information. Every single one of you already know that something happened to Group Six, and so as to contain the problem, it is so ordered by the Pentagon for all those present, that you consider this meeting as ultra-sensitive and that nothing of what is discussed here today may be passed on to any fellow crew member or officer. Indeed, we ask that you resist any temptation you may have from even discussing this subject any further with those who are present. If any of you are overheard discussing the content of this meeting for any reason after today, you will be considered in violation of the terms of your employment and will be dealt with accordingly." If any of General Wilson's audience had not been paying attention to this point, they were now.

"Now before we continue, just to ensure that everyone is present, I would like you all to stand and, as I run through your names, would the various commanders ensure that no-one sits that is not their own direct responsibility. The entire room came to its feet as the General picked up a clip-board. "The head table here is accepted," and the four Air Force and two Naval officers sat down. "Colonel Standford and his team aboard AWACS twenty-four." Standford and his team sat down. "Captain O'Grady and the flight crew of AWACS twenty-four." As General Wilson continued through his list the corresponding commander surveyed the men around him as each sat down in turn. "Captain Danforth and his team." After each name Wilson paused to allow those called to be seated. "Commander Davis and his Navy colleagues representing Group Six. Captain Chuck Fulton from the *Stork*. Major Barton. Captain Hawksworth. The members of *Gold Seal*. Captain Branden and his crew. Colonel Klugge and the rest of my staff. Captain Dan Hinkley and his wing men. And finally, Captain Davidson of the *USS Philadelphia*." General Wilson surveyed the room and upon seeing that everyone was seated, took a quick glance at his watch, a quick sip of water, and walked around to the front of the stage. "Now that we've ascertained that we're all here, it's time to get on with it. First, allow me to appraise you of some interesting developments with regard to Iraq and our current intentions...

Chapter Seventy-Four

Sprawled out on a thousand acres of prime real estate, halfway between Baltimore and Washington D.C., Fort George G. Meade sat like a caged bird awaiting its daily feed. What was once a single office in a small Munitions building, had grown to become the Headquarters of the largest Intelligence Community in the world. Though larger than over 130 other cities and towns in the state of Maryland, it fills to immense proportions once the morning commute gets under way. From the truckless Baltimore/Washington Parkway thousands of locals stream into the huge parking lots that nearly double the residency of SIGINT City. It has its own power station, shops, bus service, police force, travel agency, bank, Doctor's surgery, library, telephone exchange, and even its own barber. But the location of this city cannot be found on any map. Its function or costing is not listed on any Government budget. Indeed, the very existence of the Puzzle Palace has only been acknowledged by Federal officials in the last ten years and, even today, despite its size and power, no law has ever been passed prohibiting the National Security Agency from engaging in any activity.

Commander John Latchkey and Colonel Ken Trist climbed into the back seats of the unmarked Ford and prepared to move out. This prearranged meeting was taking place in front of an all-night store some four miles from the main gates.

"What's your state of readiness, Colonel?" asked Latchkey, fastening his seat belt.

"The DIRNSA has ordered a full alert and as we speak, two thousand of our troops are deploying around the entire perimeter."

"May we take a look?"

"Of course. Corporal," said Trist, raising his voice, "back to the office." The Ford turned right, mingled with the relatively heavy traffic for this time of the morning, and headed off toward the loop that would take them under the freeway and on to Fort Meade. "The entire facility is laid out in such a way as to make unauthorized entry impossible," Trist continued. "My orders are to maintain the highest degree of security at the Agency and, stick to you like glue." Trist smiled as he looked down at the proximity between him and his naval colleague. "Unusual to see a Navy man carrying a side arm, Commander?"

"This is a pretty unusual business, Colonel," Latchkey replied.

"That's for sure. I've checked with our traffic personnel and there have been no vehicles large enough to carry such a device as you have described into our complex in the last 48 hours, so if the NSA is their objective, they won't be carrying out their mission from the inside."

"What's to stop them just driving up to the gate in the truck and firing it off right there and then?" asked Latchkey.

"We've moved a gate patrol up to the outer perimeter."

"How far away from the main gate is that?"

"A couple of hundred yards."

"But we need to protect the Agency up to a mile, maybe two!"

Trist rolled his eyes at the prospect. "Have you any idea what it will take to secure a two mile area?! You're talking total evacuation of probably forty commercial operations and at least three hundred private dwellings, not to mention completely blocking off the parkway to traffic in both directions! We'll have everyone from the local stations to CNN out here in droves in no time at all!"

"What vehicles do you have available at Meade?" asked Latchkey, pulling out a small notebook from an inside pocket.

"Commander, Fort Meade is a fully operational base, you name it and we've got it."

"Good, get me this phone number will you, we'll be needing some help." Colonel Trist picked up the car phone, dialed the number, and handed it to Latchkey.

After a brief conversation, Latchkey handed the phone back to Trist and continued his train of thought. "What about a low fly over?"

"There's no possibility there either. The entire airspace is restricted and no-one is allowed to fly over the Agency under any circumstances."

"But Colonel, we're not talking about taking photographs or dropping a bomb and getting away with it. We're talking about an aircraft large enough to carry a one ton device. The pilot isn't worried about being shot down or being sent off to jail for the rest of his life. There are some Iranians out there who have orders to hit the Agency and they're not going to concern themselves with the consequences, just the deed itself."

"Two squadrons of F-4s are already up and running so I don't think we'll have any problem," Trist said confidently.

"Forgive me, Colonel, but when was the last time that the NSA has been threatened from the air?"

"Well I'm not sure that it ever has," replied Trist.

"That's my point." Latchkey leaned forward. "A couple of basic questions. How close is the nearest air corridor?"

"There are two, in and out of Friendship International. One to the north and one to the west, both of which are at least seven miles away."

"The edge or the center?"

"What do you mean?"

"Some corridors are up to three miles wide. Are they seven miles away to the edge of the corridor or closer at the limit?"

"Seven miles to the edge," Trist responded curtly.

"Have any aircraft ever wandered outside the lanes?" Latchkey asked as if he knew the answer already.

"I get your point, Commander, but what can we do about it?"

"I'm not sure we can do anything about it at all, but air traffic control certainly can."

"What are you going to try and do now, John, close every airport in the area?"

Latchkey sat back in his seat and looked out at the

flickering shadows that accompanied the Ford on its journey. It had started to drizzle and the soft rain mingling with the occasional street lamp gave Latchkey a sense of isolation from all the threats. "No, that would bring too much attention, but maybe your Director's authority could persuade them to restrict the lanes a little to give us some breathing room. But even at that distance an aircraft could leave the lanes and still be within range in a couple of minutes, so maybe it's not worth even pursuing."

"How much time do you think we have?"

"We're not sure. Admiral Swanson told me to expect anything anytime from now on."

"That's pretty loose, isn't it? Don't we have any harder information?"

"With the best ears in the world listening out there I was kind of hoping that you could get me some."

"What do you mean? I'm in Security, not Signals. You probably know more about what's going on 'round here than I do. For all I know you're wearing one of our official pagers.

"That's an idea. No, the Assistant Director will have someone buzz you."

"Covered all the bases, eh?" whispered Trist, nodding his approval.

"I hope," said Latchkey. "The Admiral figures that the most likely time for a hit should be around zero-six-hundred, or thereabouts."

"How does he figure that?"

"Just a guess but twelve-hundred hours GMT seems as good as any."

"Sounds good. Well, that might just give us a enough time to close ranks."

The Ford turned right onto Savage Road and even though Latchkey had expected to see a large complex, the few lights that burned in the main building were enough for him to realize he had underestimated the immense size and proportions of the National Security Agency. At first glance, it would be easy to assume that they were approaching the main buildings of the Social Security Administration or perhaps even the CIA headquarters, but even they, as Latchkey was soon to find out, were juniors in contrast. The nine story structure was only the centerpiece of over 1.9 million square feet of operational space that constituted the NSA's top seat. Depth perception at this time of night was difficult at best and Latchkey was surprised that the closer he came to the tan structure with its three story A-shaped attachment, the further away the buildings appeared to be.

The Ford came to a stop at what appeared to be an arbitrary spot and three armed guards approached the vehicle. The driver wound down his window, but before he could reach for his identification all four doors of the vehicle opened, followed closely by an order instructing everyone to climb out. The light rain was minimal, yet everyone on duty was dressed as if they were expecting a storm. Hoods, gloves and thick parkas were the order of the day. The three climbed out.

"I'm sorry, sir," said a Sergeant close to Latchkey's elbow, "you'll have to leave your side-arm with us." Latchkey obliged. "You can retrieve it from us when you leave, sir."

"That's okay," said Trist with an overruling tone. "He's with me."

Four other uniforms appeared and checked the inside of the vehicle, opened the trunk and hood and even shone a couple of high powered lamps underneath. Off to the side someone nodded. "You may continue, Colonel," said the Sergeant, and the three climbed back into the Ford.

"Good work, Colonel," said Latchkey as the car moved on.

"Secure means secure, Commander."

"You know," Latchkey pondered, "there is one other area that we ought to consider."

"What's that?"

"Well, if they were going to attempt an air attack, then this thing is certainly going to knock out all the computer assistance on board the aircraft itself. There's no way they can hit us without hitting themselves, unless they drop it from more than ten thousand feet."

"So what are you saying?"

"They're either going to drop it out of a door from a high altitude or, more likely, they may have decided to use an aircraft that doesn't rely too much on computer chips to stay in the air. They could detonate it inside the plane, hoping to take out some of our Phantoms as well. That way they might reduce our pilots to flying on hydraulics only and have a chance of keeping the device to use again."

"Do our pilots know about this?"

"Probably not."

"Then that's job one."

Chapter Seventy-Five

General Wilson took another glance at his watch and another sip of water. "So, gentlemen that's basically the order of events that took place today, and now to continue. Permit me to share with you some of the latest information we have regarding the field of electronic warfare. As most of you know, following the discovery of EMP, the scientific community went to work to create a device that could generate these pulses so as to test our hardening techniques. Although this task was difficult and required the best scientific ingenuity available, once EMP could be generated at will, running the tests and finding the correct amounts of shielding materials necessary to protect our equipment was, by comparison, easy. Since then, we have had to bear the cost of installing these hardened covers around all of our front line equipment, so as to maintain operations in the vicinity of a nuclear attack or, as we suspected might happen, a separate attack of EMP used by a nation capable of developing such a weapon. The only nation as far as we know that has this capability at the moment is Russia, so it's a pretty safe bet that they have a similar device. Whether or not they've managed to come up with a miniature version of the fifteen ton unit we use to generate EMP is another question." At this point, the door opened and in walked Admiral Swanson. Wilson looked somewhat relieved to see the Admiral and smiled as he gave way. "Gentlemen, allow me to pass the discussion over to Admiral Pat Swanson who has just flown in direct from the Pentagon to fill us in on the latest developments."

Swanson climbed up onto the stage, listened intently to a quiet whisper from the General for a couple of moments, and then, as Wilson returned to his seat, moved to the front of the stage. "Thank you, General. I apologize for my seemingly untimely entrance, but we did fly out here as quickly as we could. As it was, the journey from Washington only took about two and a half hours, but I would have still preferred to have been here at the start of General Wilson's meeting, and," turning briefly back to face the General, "I thank him for covering for me in the interim." A few faces turned in disbelief as they wondered which mode of transport had made such a dash. "Now I should start, since the General has brought you up to date with phases one and two of the Magnetic Pulse story, by bringing you all up to speed on phase three." Swanson's voice was slow and deliberate.

"A few hours ago I was notified, for the first time I might add, that the next step in EMP development has been accomplished. A device has recently been developed that can generate EMP in a form that can penetrate nearly all forms of our hardening techniques. Developed not, however, by military experts under the supervision of the United States Government, but by a private organization under the watchful eye of one of our intelligence agencies. A member of the leading team of designers, a Doctor Adams who had worked on the original tests, upon retirement went to work as a consultant for a small but industrious contractor in Connecticut. The operators of this company built, and eventually delivered, not one but two Extra-Electro-Magnetic-Pulse-Transmitters into the hands of this agency for testing. These devices, known as EXEMPTS, were to be driven to Nevada where they, under the supervision of a couple of senior ranking officers of this Agency, were to be tested. In reality, one of these EXEMPTS was taken to the dock yards in New London and placed on a small cargo vessel bound for Israel. The three individuals who had planned this operation flew to Tel Aviv in time for its arrival to receive a hefty payment that the Israelis thought was to be deposited in the account of a dummy company, set up by the Agency to handle delicate transactions such as this. Unfortunately we've had to inform them that this account, in fact, was a private one, set up for the sole purpose of providing financial security for the three ex-agency officials. Needless to say we can find no trace of these individuals since the transaction took place two days ago. The Israelis, thinking that they had top U.S. Government approval to test this device, decided to take it down to the Negev and use it against some tanks that were about to be retrofitted with new technology. Unfortunately the device never arrived at its destination. Late last night, as it was being transported South in the heart of the city of Tel Aviv, the truck carrying the EXEMPT was hijacked." A murmur filled the room briefly and Swanson took this opportunity to take a sip of water. Just as he was refilling his glass there came a knock at the door. Swanson nodded and the door opened. A note was thrust into the Marine's hand and the door closed again.

"What is it, Sergeant?" said Swanson.

"An urgent message for you from Washington, sir."

"Good," replied the Admiral, taking it from him. Swanson read the note keenly as he sipped his refreshment and then folded the message into his inside pocket. "So. We believe that somehow this EXEMPT was taken to Cairo, loaded onto a Korean 747, and, by setting fire to two engines, a group of terrorists brought the aircraft down low over Group Six and set the device off." Swanson walked to the edge of the stage and delivered the next few words even more slowly and deliberately. "I would like to add that the very individuals who are responsible for dropping this device on Group Six, the same individuals who were part of this giant conspiracy, employed by those that wish to see us damaged in any way, shape or form, and lose credibility throughout the Arab world, are in this room at this very moment!" Murmurs ran through the room as eyes turned on the prisoners. "And even though we can bring these perpetrators to justice, what concerns us most is that there is another EXEMPT out there somewhere and we need to retrieve it as soon as we can. Until we can find out it's exact location, we will have to assume that another attack could come at any time. To that end we have put all of our forces on full alert and have ordered all of our field commanders to restrict air traffic around our land and sea bases in the area. The note I just received has confirmed that only one EXEMPT was shipped to Israel and that a reliable source has recently managed to pass on to us the possible location of the second one."

Chapter Seventy-Six

After a complete tour of the perimeter the Ford pulled up sharply at a gap in the fences.

"Good morning, sir," said a voice from a cloud of condensation through the dropped window.

"How're things looking, Len?" asked Trist leaning forward.

"Busy. I've just completed a tour of the fences. There're eight hundred men spread out around the outside and another five hundred on the inside. I've put four extra senior squads on permanent foot patrol around the outer and four on the inner, including the extra back-up you requested."

"Good, did you call FANX?"

"Yes, sir. I've sent a couple of extra squads over there, just in case."

"Get a jeep for me will you? I'm taking the Commander to my office."

"Right, sir," the Major stood up straight and saluted. The window slid shut.

"FANX?" inquired Latchkey.

"Friendship Annex over at the airport. A small facility but we need to cover all possibilities."

The Ford made a few sweeping turns before pulling up at the curb of the Main entrance, as two more armed guards reached for the door handles. Trist and Latchkey climbed the dozen steps up to the glass doors.

"This is Gatehouse One," said Trist. "Let's get you signed in." Trist pulled out something from under his uniform as two Federal Protective Service Guards in blue uniforms approached them and checked the Colonel's face against the plastic-laminated, color-coded, computer-punched security badge. They saluted and pointed to the right. They passed through another set of glass doors into a plush waiting room where a young man appeared with some paperwork.

"Make this quick," said Trist. "I'm his sponsor. John, just routine. I've got a couple of quick calls to make. Be right back." The young man sat down with Latchkey and filled out a 'Sponsor' sheet. A few moments later Trist returned.

"All set?" Trist asked.

The young man pulled out a 4 1/2-inch by-2 1/2-inch red and white striped badge and pinned it on to Latchkey's lapel.

"Would you sign for the Commander, Colonel?"

Trist took the clip-board and signed in the appropriate places. "All right, let's go." Latchkey followed Trist back through the glass doors to meet with the blue uniforms once again. They repeated their checks and this time, after noting the legitimacy of Latchkey's badge, let them pass through a corridor into the lobby of the Headquarters' building. Latchkey was impressed by the long mural that ran down one wall, depicting a variety of employees, some wearing headphones, to others collecting signals from satellites, and for the first time since arriving on the premises, witnessed a declaration as to where he was, since even the badge he was wearing simply stated 'One Day'. At the end of the passageway the huge Agency seal dominated the wall. Containing over twenty thousand hand-cut cubes of Byzantine smelt glass, the four-foot diameter seal depicted an Eagle standing guard on a blue background, clutching in its talons an ancient skeleton key. A key for unlocking the codes of the world's signals while guarding its own. Around the outside just three words sparkled in the dim lighting; NATIONAL SECURITY AGENCY.

A left turn and they arrived in the Tower's lobby, decorated throughout with paintings of all of the Agency's former Directors. "If we had more time I'd give you a tour," said Trist, returning the salute of another guard. "These elevators take you down to the Cray or up to Mahogany Row where DIRNSA resides." They continued on through another set of glass doors that connected the Tower with the Operations center until they arrived at what could only be described as Main Street. Longer than three football fields, 'C' Corridor took Latchkey past every conceivable service that a town could need. But before he had a chance to digest the full extent of the hallway, Trist turned down a side passage and out an exit-only door to where a covered jeep waited with a driver.

The sudden change of climate, from warmth to cold-wet, was a refreshing change as John Latchkey ducked into the back seat. Trist sat in the front and grunted something to the driver. The journey took them away from the main tower toward a series of buildings that were more reminiscent of a barracks, past a line of trucks, a sharp left turn into an alley and the brakes pulled the jeep up outside a plain looking door. Moments later, Latchkey was following Trist down a short corridor. No quiet solitude and armed security here. Trist, with Latchkey at his shoulder, turned right through a pair of double doors and into a large Communications Center. Latchkey felt as if he had just walked into a maxi version of a Carrier's CIC. A Sergeant appeared with a note book and tried to keep pace as the Colonel made for an office at the far end of the room.

"What's the latest, Menkin?"

"Sir, the entire command is on full alert as requested. A second check-point is in place at the far end of Savage, the perimeter is clear and five aircraft are on station. The Assistant DIRNSA is in-house and wishes us every success. He apologizes for not being here in person to greet you Commander but his energies are being spent concentrating on the problem at hand, and any information that can clarify the situation will be forwarded to you directly."

"Good," said Trist, taking up station behind his desk. "Any word from Admiral Swanson, Dick?"

"No, sir. But DIRNSA is flying back from Europe, should be here in the early hours."

"Let's hope it's all over by then. Have Bren' get me General Painter on the line, urgent." The Sergeant made to leave. "Oh and Dick, coffee Commander?"

"Yes please, white, sweet."

"Two coffees, and make mine high-test. What else can we do, Commander?" As Trist sat down, Latchkey walked over to look at one of the group photographs hanging on the wall.

"I don't know, Colonel." He looked at the happy smiling faces sitting around a much younger Trist, a setting similar to a couple of squadron shots he had in his own office, and felt a cold chill run down his back. All those cheery, carefree days seemed to Latchkey so far away. And now that the threat of major damage occurring to this Agency was so close, it was difficult for Latchkey to even remember their faces.

One of two telephones on the desk rang. "Trist!" Latchkey wandered over to another photograph and stared at it for a moment, but the subject was soon lost in his thoughts. "Commander, it's Captain Erikson."

Latchkey took the receiver. "Yes, Captain, any luck?" Trist watched as the Commander once again pulled the note book from a pocket and began scribbling. "How long will that take?" Trist watched Latchkey at work. The Commander had admitted that he had been pushing paper for the last couple of years, but the man looked calm and capable. Stress was no stranger to this sailor. "Colonel, it's all set. All we need from you is an ETA."

"ETA?" Trist asked, looking at his watch.

"Estimated time of accident."

"Ah. Zero-five-ten?"

"Captain, you should receive a call at zero-five-eleven or thereabouts. By the way, do you carry a cellular? Oh. Channel two, fine. Look forward to meeting you." Latchkey put the receiver back on its hook and the note pad in his pocket. "He's all set. He reckons the best location would be smack on top of the bridge, wherever that is."

The phone sounded again. "General Painter on the line for you, sir." While Trist warned the General about the threat to his aircraft in the area, Latchkey's knees let go for a moment and he suddenly realized how tired he was. Just another couple of hours. Just two more hours he reckoned and he could get all the sleep he needed.

"Right," said Trist, reaching for another telephone and punching a button. "Bainbridge, get your legs in gear. We need you in flame-proof jonnies, hard hat, gloves, and boots. I expect you in full flight behind the wheel of an empty tanker, outside my office in three minutes!" Trist put his hand over the mouthpiece, stood up and turned to Latchkey. "We have two tankers, one is full and the other a third. We don't really have the time to drain it."

"That'll do. Can you rustle up a small timer with a bang on the end of it?"

"Right. Bainbridge, grab the Dodge and a pair of goggles, you're going to need them." Trist pressed another line into service. "McBee, you've got three minutes to grab a couple of flares and a remote and join Bainbridge outside, got it? Good." Latchkey's look stopped Trist in his tracks. "What is it?"

"It's got to be two miles or nothing. If we don't have the room to work, they might still..."

"Okay, Commander," replied Trist with a hint of resignation in his voice. Menkin brought in two cups of coffee. "How long does it take to make coffee around here?" yelled Trist to no-one in particular. Both he and Latchkey took a large gulp from their respective cups and made for the door. Suddenly both Trist and Latchkey's faces took on a most distasteful grimace. They stopped, turned, gave each other a questioning look, dumped each other's cup's contents into a handy waste bin and charged for the exit.

"Sergeant Menkin!" Trist yelled over his shoulder. "We will be needing you and your platoon's services."

"Yes, sir!"

"Two trucks and a dozen flares, on the double!"

"Sir!"

In the corridor Trist turned to Latchkey briefly and said, "Now's the time to test this base's efficiency once and for all." He pulled his handset from it's belt Carrier. "Get me Major Franks." They passed through the outside door and into the night. "Major, how many men do you have that are not already being used on patrol or gate duties?"

A crackle sounded in his set. "Six hundred, if you include those off-duty or sleeping."

"I don't care where they are or what they're doing. Get every available up and running at the double. You know this is a full scale alert. I want you to place a circle of men at a two mile radius around this base."

There was a brief pause. "But, sir," said Franks. "That would be a line of men, ah..."

"Twelve miles long, I know, Major. But we don't need to cover every inch of ground, just every road, track and trail."

"Yes, sir."

"Prepare your men and use every vehicle available, bus them if necessary and have the first batch in the front compound ready to go in five minutes on my command, got it?"

"Five minutes, on your command, yes, sir."

"Good." Trist put his radio away. "Five minutes is pushing it John but for once we're going to find out if this Fort can really perform like one." Just then a large, green army tanker truck pulled up next to the Colonel's jeep. The driver jumped down looking more like a fireman than a soldier.

"Ah, Bainbridge there you are," said Trist, walking around him, examining his equipment. "Very good, Sergeant."

"Orders, Colonel?"

"Right. Your orders are to drive on to the Parkway, get this old tub up to its maximum speed and have an accident with yourself on top of the overpass."

"Sir?!" said the Sergeant with a gulp.

"Don't worry Bainbridge, this tank may be old but it's well protected. All we want you to do is to smash it up a bit, nothing fancy."

"Bainbridge smiled. "Roll it over, sir?"

"Just make it look like an accident. You've got some help. It's raining so the road is nice and slippery and the bald tires you guys love to drive on should make it real easy for you. We'll be in convoy so there won't be any public vehicles near you. Check your radio and get ready to pull out. This is a diversionary tactic and we need to totally block the freeway. Oh, and Bainbridge."

"Sir?"

"You seen McBee?"

"Yes, sir, he's in the truck."

"Well, get him over here. I don't want him going up

in ball of smoke too. Don't get out of the truck until we get to you. We'll have our boys on the tanker within seconds, so just hang tight."

"Hang? Right, sir."

"Just make it look as messy as you can. Do your best, just don't kill yourself, Sergeant." Trist attempted a smile. "Good volunteers are hard to find."

"Yes, sir," Bainbridge replied and climbed back in the tanker. McBee climbed out of the passenger seat and ran up, saluting.

"Staff Sergeant McBee reporting with equipment."

"Bainbridge, wait for us at the main gate." The Sergeant drove off just as three troop trucks arrived.

"McBee, get in the back of the jeep."

"All set here, Colonel," shouted Menkin, leaning out of the window of the lead vehicle.

"You in front of Bainbridge," Trist responded crisply. "The other two, at least fifty yards behind. I don't want any public vehicle getting anywhere near that tanker, got it?"

"Yes, sir."

"Good, Bainbridge is waiting for you at the gate." The trucks rolled off. The radio crackled in the jeep. Trist reached in and grabbed the receiver. "Trist."

"Major Dover here. We should be ready to move the first wave out in about two minutes. Where's the first priority?"

"Start on a line two miles from the start of Savage and then work both left and right from there. I want groups of five stationed every twenty feet across the main roads and at every other road that closes within the two mile limit. No civilians or vehicles of any kind will be permitted through.

"Right," said Dover as Trist put the hand set back on its hook.

"Time to go. John, you ready for this?"

"Ready as I'll ever be," said Latchkey, climbing in the back. Trist's driver fired up the engine as the colonel climbed aboard and drove quickly out to the main gate. There, the four vehicles were waiting for the word.

Trist waved his arm above the canopy and the trucks

began to follow. "Pete," said Trist, turning to his driver. "Stay sharp, we'll only have one shot at this. Take me down to Major Kuehn." A quick sprint around the front parking attendant's gate, down Savage Road to where the jeep ground to a halt as the same three familiar faces greeted them.

"Colonel?" said the Sergeant, lowering his head to jeep level.

"We're moving out." A new face appeared. "Major, have some of your men move out to a new location. Dover should be here shortly with the first crews, we're forming a two mile perimeter. From now on, no-one is permitted to enter until I return, got it?"

"Yes, sir, no-one. Do you want us to evacuate everyone in the area?"

"Not until I give the order. I'm hoping that won't be necessary. There's been a chemical spill and the entire area must be sealed until further notice."

"But we haven't heard of any spill over the radios, sir?"

"You will." The noise of diesels filled the air. "Let's go, Pete." The convoy moved off and headed for the on-ramp.

Chapter Seventy-Seven

Swanson turned and sat down on the head table. "Let me now turn to the so-called attack on our convoy. As you know, we rely on our IFF and AVID equipment to identify aircraft, and in this case the units aboard the Migs informed us that the Migs were Iranian. However, thanks to an observant midshipman aboard the *La Salle*, we now know that the downed Mig was a Fulcrum, operated not by the Iranians, but by the Iraqis." Again murmurs circulated the room. "If nothing else these events will teach us perhaps to rely a little less on electronic identification than we have in the past. Obviously the Iraqi IFF unit was substituted for an Iranian one, and it was this substitution that, as intended initially, led our thinking in the wrong direction. However, the attack on our shipping did tip the balance in Washington earlier today and, as you may well know, a full scale bombardment on Baghdad has now been initiated. Our objective is to contain the Government of Iraq and to secure the entire region. F-117s were dispatched a couple of hours ago along with our B-1s. No-one from the *Independence* is here today since they've been asked to step up the vigilance on the no-fly zone, prepare for air-to-ground attacks on the six tank battalions that are threatening the marsh-lands and increase our defense capabilities. It has not been a good day for us, but we anticipate that with our renewed attacks on Iraq we should be done with aggression in this region once and for all." A rumble of agreement echoed from Swanson's audience as a more relaxed atmosphere developed.

"To be more specific about the attack on Group Six, somehow, someone managed to get himself and the EXEMPT loaded into the cargo hold of the Korean 747. The plan was to wait for the appropriate time and set off some fragmentation devices in two of the engines, causing it to lose altitude. We are not exactly sure how they expected to bring the aircraft down close to Group Six, unless the pilot was involved in the mission, but they did. Fortunately for us something went wrong. Either through a system failure or due to some error by the pilot the flight found itself inside Iranian airspace and the locals immediately sent up a couple of Migs to push it away from their airspace. It appeared for a moment that the Migs, used to escort the Boeing back on course, had fired on the Korean. But upon examination of the engines on the 747, it was obvious that this had not occurred and the items that we found in the cargo hold helped us work the rest out.

So this is how we believe they carried out their mission. There are two sensors on each cargo door to warn the pilot if any are not secured shut. After removing his oxygen supply, with the aircraft now down to some three thousand feet, he wired around the door switch so that when he pressed it into service, the warning in the cockpit was not activated and prepared himself for a very exciting few moments. As the door rose up and out into the slipstream, the rush of air and subsequent turbulence must have been tremendous. He reached down and stuck some heavy duty tape over the other sensor located inside the door sill. He then had to maneuver the device close to the door and, again, even though much of this does sound rather arbitrary, push it out just as he flew over the fleet. The Korean flight managed to make it into Muscat airport on the remaining two engines, and what exactly happened to our saboteur or saboteurs after that is not known at this time. Perhaps he, or they, jumped off the aircraft once it had touched down, or perhaps left the aircraft using chutes while it was still over the Gulf and ditched somewhere near the coast.

Much of this is guess work, much of it summation. But you may be interested to know that we acknowledge, as many of you have already worked out, that it couldn't have been any of our Iranian guests here since they were under lock and key at the time of the attack. No, I admit, it is with a sad heart that I inform you all that the saboteur, the individual who was given the primary task of attacking Group Six with such devastation, is not only in this room at this very moment, but is wearing the uniform of the United States Air Force as well." That did it. If minds had begun to wander in the mess that day, Admiral Swanson had certainly regained their attention. Everyone sat in amazement as they looked about them trying to work out who the traitors were, and it took a couple of moments before the noise level returned to a hush.

"Gentlemen, I know this must sound rather incredible to you, but to ensure his presence here today we had to make sure that he joined us under the pretense of a celebration. General Wilson put you all through the role call not to ensure that those not invited had left the room, but to confirm the fact that all those responsible were indeed here and secured. The Marines by the way are not here to watch the prisoners, although keeping an eye on them is necessary. No, their purpose is to ensure that no-one leaves the room until this meeting is over. Putting an armed guard at the exits earlier may well have aroused their suspicions and caused them to try and leave before we had really got underway. But with the prisoners here, their arrogant confidence in our inability to trace their involvement in all this has been their downfall. Sergeant, you may now bring in the rest of your men." At this point the door opened and in walked ten Marines, with rifles in hand taking up positions around the room, specifically at the main door and at the fire exit at the back of the room.

Now all eyes were on the Admiral. Everyone in the room couldn't wait for him to reveal the perpetrator, but Swanson took his time. "I don't think that the Iraqis had much time to plan the attacks. Perhaps some Palestinian, hoping to do the dirty on Israel and make them look bad in our eyes, took the truck in Tel Aviv and was surprised to find that his catch was a far bigger fish than he expected. We're not sure of how they discovered the use of the device or even what its capabilities were, but use it they did. The Colonel and his driver accompanying the vehicle were beaten so badly that they eventually succumbed to their wounds, a tragedy when you consider that all they thought they were carrying was some new kind of ammunition. But somehow the perpetrators did gain enough information on how to use it, and shipped it to Cairo. The whole exercise was designed to lead us to believe that the Iranians had fired on our convoy and hit the fleet when in fact it was the Iraqis all along. I should add that Captain Davidson and his crew aboard the *Philadelphia* carried out an extensive search of the floor at *Gonzo Station*, but apart from a few pieces of fragmented sheets of steel, they found nothing. Perhaps after detonating, it self-destructed before hitting the water, though no-one heard any explosion at the time. All we can hope is that the second one, which we believe has been located close to a large installation in the south, will be found in time.

And so it befalls me to ask our armed guard to arrest the four traitors who made all this possible, the pilot and crew of the KC-135 tanker." Suddenly those that were seated around Captain Branden and his crew were all over them. Bill and Phil who had been sitting closest to the crew grabbed the pilot and navigator. Five marines jumped forward, restrained the flailing arms, slapped handcuffs on them all, and as a few well aimed punches found their marks, a few groans were heard.

"We didn't do anything," shouted Branden. "Admiral, you're making a mistake!" The four crewmen were dragged from their seats and pulled over to the side of the room, where everyone could see them.

Swanson raised his voice. "All right everyone, please return to your seats. As you can see our Marines have the situation well in hand." The room returned to some semblance of order. "Well Branden, if that is your given name, all I want to know is, why?"

Branden struggled. "Why what, Admiral? I didn't do anything! We were up at twenty-five thousand feet, nowhere near the Korean!"

"No you weren't, you had your co-pilot fly the tanker while you were aboard the 747."

"That's ridiculous, sir. We had all arrived back from leave yesterday and were ordered up not long afterwards."

"Yes, your signature is on the log sheet, but no-one

remembers actually seeing you."

"I was here all the time, believe me Admiral, it's the truth."

"Look, since the situation with the Korean and the attack on the *Stork* was taking up most of their time, AWACS 24 have no firm record of your location at any-time during your flight, except for when you carried out the actual refueling process some fifty miles north of Muscat airport. Apart from that we have little record of your actual route."

"But we were there, Admiral. Captain O'Grady can tell you that I spoke to him at least twice during the transfer!" Captain O'Grady made a move as if to say something but the Admiral motioned for him to remain seated. Branden was getting edgy. He stepped forward slightly as if to face his accuser directly. "Admiral, why is it that you can't trace our whereabouts during our shift? All you have to do is go and read the GPS reports and you'll see that we flew no further south than maybe twenty miles north of Muscat."

"We've already looked at them but your GPS unit wasn't working or something and you're entire flight is nowhere to be found."

"Admiral, this is ridiculous. I'm telling you I was flying the -135 when the hit occurred. We were waiting to refuel the AWACS and circling around at about twenty-five thousand feet."

"How do you know the hit took place if you were up at that altitude?"

"Uh, I got it from someone on base after we re-turned."

"And where did the refueling take place?" asked Swanson.

"I don't exactly know, the whole flight was pretty routine for us. All I can remember is the quarter moon and the lights of Group Six below." The other members of Branden's crew began to pull against their restraints but no-one took any notice.

Swanson's tone suddenly became more serious. "How did you know it was the fleet?"

"I know Group Six when I see it."

"Even at twenty-five thousand feet?" asked Swanson deliberately.

"Yes, even at twenty-five...," suddenly Branden stopped in mid sentence, his face seemed to go pale and a bead of sweat broke out on his forehead.

One of Branden's men said softly, "You idiot."

"You are right to be concerned Captain," said Swanson sitting down on the corner of the table. "You told us earlier that the farthest you flew south was to a point twenty miles north of Muscat airport, yet you have now told us that you saw the lights of the Group Six sailing below. This means that you were right, you weren't on the Korean flight at all, you were flying the tanker just as you say. However you slipped up when you said that the furthest south you flew was twenty miles north of Muscat because you flew right over Group Six. Group Six had moved no farther north than due east of Muscat, we have the radar tapes to prove it."

Branden began struggling again but the strong arms of the marines held him at bay. "But it was you who said that the farthest point south we went was...,"

"I know what I said," said Swanson. "I told you we had no record of your route and that we could not prove the tanker was anywhere near Group Six at the time it was hit to give you an opportunity to get out of the situation altogether, and you took the bait. But you slipped up when you admitted you saw the lights of the fleet 'below'. Not, 'way off to the south', but 'below' which meant that you did fly over the fleet. I told you that AWACS was busy and failed to check on your location, but that was another lie I'm afraid. Colonel Standford noticed your GPS unit wasn't working so he had one of his team keep an eye on your route by radar just for the record. He confirmed your location over the fleet at the precise moment Group Six was attacked and passed this information on to General Pullman. Captain Branden, you just talked your way into proving that you are a liar." Everyone in the room began chattering quietly, all except Branden who just stood there in disbelief. "You thought that by disarming the GPS unit aboard your KC-135, we would not be able to prove exactly where you were, at any given time, unless of course we were watching you. Of course our radars had you plotted for the entire journey but you hoped that while everyone had their eyes glued on the Korean flight and the Mig movement in the area, no-one would notice you that far south. And even if they did, you were part of the normal traffic expected to be there. But in the last hour, while you were ferrying General Wilson over here, General Pullman had a chance to go through the -135 that you used last night with a fine tooth comb, and he found three things. First, by some clever ingenuity, you had assigned yourself the only tanker that has the capability for carrying cargo. Maybe it was you who caused the other two AWACS aircraft to be taken off line, but nevertheless, you managed to be allotted the KC-135C with the large side door, ideal for a drop such as this. Secondly, the scratch marks close to the side door ramps are fresh and fit the dimensions of the device perfectly. And thirdly, we had not used your particular aircraft for any purpose, other than refueling, for a long time. And although there's no reason to use them for refueling, both the door mechanisms and runners have been used very recently."

"It's all coincidental, Admiral," cried Branden. "Nothing you've said proves anything. Believe me, we've got nothing to do with this."

"I'm sorry Branden, but you're wrong. Although you went to great lengths to disguise it, the failure of the GPS unit was caused by outside interference and not by any malfunction. Yes, you were ordered to prepare to refuel both AWACS 24 and the Tags, and that you were told to keep clear of the area under siege over the Straits. But taking such a wide berth, close to the fleet, aroused our suspicions. There was absolutely no need for you to be that far south. Colonel Bob Standford aboard AWACS 24 who first discovered the anomaly between his radar and the lack of your GPS readouts, called General Pullman on his own secure line. You had disconnected your GPS since you couldn't afford the risk of General Pullman noticing your GPS indicator going too far south on his video map display and ordering you to remain this side of the Straits.

"But Admiral," Branden shouted back. "You've just told us that whoever did it was aboard the Korean flight, and since we were on board the KC at the time, none of us could've done it. Besides, you said only one man was a traitor, and all my crew were with me."

"Yes, none of you were on board the Korean, because the Korean fiasco was a blind! There never was anyone in the cargo hold of that Boeing and you know it."

"That's ridiculous," cried Branden. "You said you found an oxygen supply or something proving that someone had been in there."

There was a long pause. "We are getting careless, Branden," said Swanson, stepping down. "I said we found some items in the hold and that he was on oxygen, that's all."

"But how would you have known he was on oxygen if you hadn't found something?" cried Branden, beginning to lose his cool.

"What else would he have been on at thirty-three thousand feet?" Swanson added lowering his voice to almost a whisper. "Besides leaving behind a piece of breathing hose is a little obvious don't you think? What did he do, cut a piece off before he jumped?"

Branden's voice became quiet and firm, trying to match the Admiral's. "I don't care, you can't prove a thing."

"Oh yes we can, Branden, besides, that's not the half of it. Searching back in our files we find that all of you actually requested to join tanker squadrons. Now, it's very rare for anyone to actually request tanker duty, but for each of you to be the rare exceptions makes the coincidence a little unbelievable." Swanson slowly walked ever closer to where Branden was standing. The closer he came, the tighter the grip the Marines took on Branden. "Boy you really had to push it back to your rendezvous point with the F-16s didn't you, and you only just made it in time. Before I ask these fine Marines to throw you in a cell for thirty years, answer me one thing. What I don't understand is why you did it?

Perhaps you were offered a lot of money for your deeds?"

"Money's got nothing to do with it!" shouted Branden.

"So, why?" asked Swanson, stepping ever closer. Branden's eyes were fired up as he bit his lip. "We're not saying a thing."

"And who, may I ask is the 'we' you refer to?" Swanson continued getting even closer to Branden, as though goading him into action.

"The who?"

"Yes, the who?" The Marines began dragging him toward the door.

"Me and the crew."

"Just you and the crew?" Swanson repeated. "No I mean what nationality?"

"Why.., Iraq. "

"Hold on Sergeant, drag them back over here will you, I don't think I'm finished with them yet." The Marines obliged.

"Listen, you traitors, I want you to hear this from me," Swanson smiled, nearly breaking into a laugh. He glanced at his watch. "In about ten minutes from now Baghdad will be leveled to the ground and you will have lost any hope you may have had of continuing your stupid little games and your foolish little attacks against us." The Admiral raised his voice, allowing his hatred to show. "Once and for all your entire nation will be flattened to the ground and your mighty leader, that Saddam Hussein of yours, will be dead. Dead and buried and there's nothing you can do to stop it, so you might as well resign yourself to the fact that you're going to spend the rest of your life behind bars."

"We still have one ace up our sleeves," said Branden quietly with a sneer.

"Oh yes? And what may that be?" said Swanson, moving within a couple of feet of Branden. The Marines tightened their grip even more, if that was possible. "I won't tell you the where but I will tell you the when. Before the sun is at its highest," said Branden coolly.

"So now we know the when. The where is to disrupt the next shuttle flight."

"Florida, eh?" said Branden, with a grin.

"Right," said Swanson confidently."

"Florida!" cried Branden laughing in Swanson's face. "You're way off base. When we let the other one off, it'll be the biggest attack on your government history has ever seen."

For the first time Swanson was visibly shaken. "Not Florida?"

"No, and there's nothing you can do that'll make me tell you either."

Swanson's voice had fallen to almost a whisper. "But where if not NASA?" The momentum was clearly shifting away from Swanson.

"Close but no cigar, Admiral," gloated Branden.

Swanson turned and walked back toward the podium shaking his head and whispering, "close but no cigar. NASA? NASA? NASA?" over and over to himself.

Branden shouted after him. "And it's going to be big, real big."

"Big? Real Big?" repeated Swanson, turning back to look at the Captain.

"Yes. The United States built the thing and it was going to be used against us eventually. Now the tables are turned and you're getting some of you're own medicine. How do you like it, Admiral?"

Suddenly Swanson revealed a look of relief, as though the last piece of the puzzle had finally fallen into place. "Thank you Branden, you have been most helpful. Everybody stay where you are," said Swanson, turning for the door. "General Wilson, we need to make a couple of phone calls, urgently. No-one is allowed to leave the room until we return. General Pullman you'd better come too," and the three left the room hurriedly. The mess hall filled with discussion. Branden and his colleagues were pushed up against the wall and searched, while a few crew members made threatening advances. Others nearest the back walked noisily to the bar to refill their glasses.

Chapter Seventy-Eight

The plan was in motion. Trist was yelling orders back and forth on the radio as Corporal Smeed was attempting to maneuver up behind the tanker. Menkin had waited for a couple of stragglers to catch up and then shot off in advance. Bainbridge, doing about fifty, had taken up position in the middle of the two lanes, with the other two trucks following at a safe distance, one in each lane hard on the heels of Trist's jeep.

"As soon as you reach the crown of the bridge, Bainbridge, do your thing." The convoy climbed the last few feet of slow incline to the highest point when Trist yelled, "Now! Bainbridge, now!" Smeed applied the brakes as the tanker suddenly swerved to the right. Trist yelled some obscenity when the tanker, even more suddenly, swerved back to the left with such severity that it went up on three wheels, riding for a few moments like a stunt drivers finale. Just before it went crashing through the guard-rail, the huge tanker rolled gently over on to its side. Sparks flew as the sound of crushed metal filled the air, the tanker coming to rest inches from the barriers. No flame as of yet. Latchkey instinctively glanced back through the plastic window to see if the two trucks were getting too close, only to find they had already stopped, blocking the oncoming traffic.

The Colonel jumped out as soon as the jeep ground to a halt, McBee hard on his heels. "Commander, you stay here." Other footsteps joined the rush to the tanker. Latchkey climbed out and watched the Colonel climb up on to the cab and lifted the door. Four more hands came to his aid as a limp Bainbridge was lifted out. McBee had sprinted to the back of the overturned vehicle and was busy taping his equipment to one of the rear pipes. A stretcher was brought to bare as Bainbridge was lowered to the ground and the area around the tanker cleared. McBee began unscrewing one of the vents and gasoline began trickling out. Soldiers were piling out of the leading truck, running across the road to divert the on-coming traffic toward the off-ramp leading up to the bridge. Trist arrived breathless back at the jeep and picked up the handset. "McBee, is everyone clear?"

"If you've got your men out, sir, we're clear here."

"Go ahead, McBee, let her rip!" McBee continued to open the vent and a large gush of gasoline erupted from the nozzle, spilling out all over the road and quickly flowing into the gutters. "Get out of the way man," yelled Trist. McBee didn't need any prompting, he was already at full sprint toward the jeep. Trist reached into the jeep and picked up a small transmitter.

"Now, sir," yelled McBee. Trist pointed his arm at the tanker and the flares burst into life. The bright red glow sparkled and spat its embers all over the road. For a few anxious moments the two volatile substances continued their antisocial behavior and Colonel Trist gave McBee a questioning look, just as a spark finally made contact. The vapor ignited and the sheet of flame ran quickly off in the direction of the flowing fluid, gaining strength and momentum as it went. A roar quickly built at the nozzle head as the flame tried to make contact with the liquid, but with the existing ignition consuming so much oxygen it looked as if the tanker might get away unscathed. But the quantity of fuel inside the tanker had been minimal, and with the tanker on its side the nozzle's position was too high to drain anywhere near all of the fluid. The rate of flow suddenly dropped sharply, permitting a gap to form between the top of the onslaught and the opening. The burning vapor rushed inside the tanker and with a large explosion that sounded more like a crack than a bang, the tanker split its sides, and the air was consumed with a huge fire ball and clouds of smoke.

The tanker crackled and burned, lighting up the cool night air. Indeed, Latchkey had to take a step away from the inferno. Even at his safe distance the heat was intense. He looked at his watch, estimating the time it would take for the emergency services to be notified, but the sirens were already within ear-shot. Behind him the traffic was doing its best to make way for the two fire trucks that were screaming up the road behind him. One of the Army trucks was already pulling clear as the fire-fighting vehicles came to life in front of him. Firemen appeared from everywhere and within seconds, foam was being sprayed over everything. The level of activity was impressive.

"Commander Latchkey, I presume?" shouted a voice behind him. Latchkey turned around to see a huge man dressed in full bunker gear wearing a grin and holding out his hand.

"Captain Erikson, thank you for being so prompt," replied Latchkey.

"Not at all. We were already en route before the first call came in. After our earlier discussion, I rang the assistant DIRNSA and he supported everything you required. The Colonel around?"

"Sure is. He's on the other side of the freeway, directing traffic I think."

"Good, I have to check in."

"Captain," said Latchkey, catching Erikson's arm. "The longer you can leave this wreck smoldering, the better."

Erikson surveyed his crews progress. "How long do you need?"

"That's just it, we don't know. We need to keep a two mile perimeter secured around Fort Meade for at least an hour, ostensibly to keep people away from this chemical spill, but in reality there is a much more dangerous threat in progress and we just don't know when it'll be over."

"We'll do our best."

"A squad will be with you at all times. Once you leave you won't be allowed back in. I'm sorry, Captain what you see is what you get."

"The driver?"

"He's fine, sitting in one of those trucks."

"How can I reach you?"

"Call Trist, I'll be nearby."

"I hope you can get this wrapped up soon. I'm going to have Hazmat experts and cameras all over this place, trying to get in and find out what the hell happened."

"The troops can handle crowd control and as far as the Hazmat people are concerned, tell them that the Army has pulled rank on you and no-one can inspect that tanker until you get the okay from them."

"But they'll start quoting from the state requirement lists."

"Captain, you are the only one privy to this due to your military service background. I don't care what trouble we get into breaking local ordinances, the fines are nothing compared the trouble that's brewing. Just give us as much time as you can. Just refer all inquiries, from state and local police, to the Army."

Just then Trist arrived, red faced and sweaty. "Captain, your men seem to have everything under control."

"As ordered, Colonel."

"I trust the Commander has filled you in?"

"Yes, sir."

"Hold off as long as you can. Refer all inquiries to the United States Army. You can reach me, as always, on my private line, okay?"

"Yes, Colonel." Erikson looked as though he was going to salute but thought better of it.

"Come on, John, we've got work to do." Erikson wandered off toward the now smoldering remains as though he had no particular place to go, while Latchkey and Trist joined McBee and the Corporal in the jeep. A quick U-turn around the fire trucks and the four sped off the wrong way down the freeway, past the trucks and along a two hundred stretch of hard shoulder down to the on-ramp. Trist was back on the radio once more, barking orders and receiving up-dates as to the construction of the perimeter. Just as they rounded the turn at the bottom of the slope the jeep was confronted by a huge vehicle blocking the entrance. Someone was flagging them down.

"What is it, Jack?" yelled Trist as the jeep slid to stop.

A head stuck itself inside under the jeep's canvas. "Message from Admiral Swanson for Commander Latchkey, sir. 'Confirmed destination your area, definately around noon GMT, good luck.'"

"Looks like we're on the hot seat Colonel," said Latch-key.

"Sure does," he replied. "All set Jack?"

"All set here, Colonel," and the Colonel waved an arm. The group of soldiers parted in front of the jeep and the occupants hung to their straps as they rushed off to check up on the rest of the troops that now surrounded SIGINT city.

Chapter Seventy-Nine

Just as many members of the audience were coming close to carrying out some form of judicial sentence on Branden and his crew, Admiral Swanson and General Wilson came back in the room and climbed up on the small stage. The room fell silent once more as everyone returned to their seats.

"Well gentlemen, it seems that Captain Branden here may have given us a clue as to where to look for the remaining device and Generals Wilson and Pullman are now organizing the recovery. The one piece of information we weren't sure of was where the other unit was going to be detonated. Thanks to Branden here, I think we might have a handle on it. We already had a security team on site ready to contain the situation but now they can be fully prepared. They haven't got much time, but I think they'll make it. Branden, you said around noon and that's forty-five minutes from now Military time. How about it Branden? How about the National Security Agency?"

Branden was too shaken up to hide his anger. "You'll never find it, besides, even if you do, Admiral," barked Branden, almost spitting the words out. "You may have made the biggest blunder of your career. Your name will go down in history as the Chief of all that's pure murder in the Gulf."

Swanson stepped down and walked over to talk to Branden personally, but this time his accuser was met by subservience rather than confidence. "What do you mean, blunder?"

"I just mean that you, all of you," said Branden, surveying the rest of his accusers, "have made such a blunder, that it will make the United States look like the big blustering fools you really are, and it serves you right."

"And how is that?" Swanson inquired somewhat concerned.

"Never mind. But you'll see. You'll all see what stupid fools you and your government are made to look like. Even if you do blow up our capital city you'll never get our fearless leader. We will rebuild again, whatever it takes, and you'll walk away with your tails between your legs."

"You won't have anything to rebuild by the time we've finished with you." Swanson boasted, returning to his confident mannerisms. "As we speak the entire downtown area, including all of the tank forces in the Southern and Eastern region, are being annihilated."

"And the main ammunition and fuel dumps?" Branden asked somewhat crestfallen.

"By now, gone," said Swanson, with a hint of pride. "And," as he turned his back on Branden, he glanced at his watch. "I think I can say, without too much fear of contradiction, that apart from a couple of divisions way up in the north, our combined forces have brought the entire Iraqi government to its knees for the last time. I wouldn't be surprised," continued Swanson, climbing back on the stage, "that whoever is left alive in your administration is on whatever's left of your phone lines trying to arbitrate some kind of surrender. Tell you what I'll do, Branden," said Swanson, turning to look at the Captain again. "I'll ask the Colonel to call General Pullman from the mess phone here and get some kind of update on how the so-called war is going." The Colonel got up and went over to the wall phone in the corner of the room. "Perhaps, once you realize that you have no home to return to, assuming you thought there was some kind of way out of this mess, no pun intended, you'll all confess to your treachery? While we wait, you can perhaps tell us how it is that you thought you could attack our fleet and expect to get away with it?"

"I'm not saying anymore." said Branden quietly.

"Yes, perhaps Branden you've said too much already." Branden turned away from Swanson and began staring at the floor. "We were on to you long before you arrived for this meeting," said Swanson, resuming his confident style. "As I've said before, if you had not wanted us to believe that the Korean flight was used for the drop, then your men wouldn't have been so clumsy as to leave evidence behind for us to find. Plus, there would have been ample time to pull the tape and wiring from the door switches before jumping. So we concluded the whole thing was a decoy. Someone wanted us to find evidence of tampering. An unused Iraqi fragmentation device was even discovered in one of the engines. In fact, the flight over Iranian air space was essential, since it was probably one of your pilots who set off the fragmentation devices using a transmitter. But to us, leaving evidence behind was either very sloppy, or very clever. I wasn't totally convinced of which, until we had managed to search your aircraft. To do it without you knowing, we needed to get you out of the way for a little while. So General Wilson and I cooked up a little food poisoning. His crew didn't suffer from anything and, in fact, should be landing here shortly."

Just then the Colonel put the phone down and announced proudly, "Admiral? It's all but over. We hit them with so much force in such a short space of time that the entire Iraqi government is in shambles. The Iraqi tanks are retreating from Kuwait and the downtown area is a mess. We did lose two aircraft, but the rest are safe and on their way home."

"Good," said Swanson with pride. "So there you have it, Branden. You and your men can now go to the lock-up in the knowledge that your efforts to slow us down have resulted in the kind of retaliatory strikes that have reduced what was left of Iraq to a pile of rubble in the desert." At this point the entire room was shocked as Branden and his three colleagues burst out laughing. Swanson reacted. "What in heaven's name do you guys find so funny. I've got a good mind to let these boys here string you all up right here and now!" yelled Swanson as some of those previously seated made moves toward them.

"Admiral," said Branden, calmly stepping forward slightly. "I must admit that we had planned to leave here after the United States forces had finished flattening Iraq, assuming of course that you all fell into our trap. But unfortunately for us, you were one step ahead of us, but only one step."

Admiral Swanson stepped back down from the stage quickly and made advances toward Branden. "What do you mean, trap!?"

"What I mean, Admiral is that you've all fallen into our trap. Whatever happens to us is immaterial now, but what happens to our nation and our cause is important and will continue on. If I'm not mistaken, you're powerless to stop what has happened. We have been fighting with our neighbors on and off for the last hundred and fifty years and now you have helped us in our goal of walking in and taking over." The Admiral's face was beginning to turn red. "You look a little worried, Admiral, and so you should be. My friends and I aren't Iraqi, we're Iranian by birth and proud of it!"

"What are you saying?" said Swanson, wiping his brow in disbelief.

"We couldn't believe our eyes when Hussein decided to move his tanks closer to the border with Kuwait! It was just what we needed to tip the balance!"

"What?!" cried Swanson.

Branden tried to quell his own excitement. "I am saying that when we said we were Iraqi, like you, we weren't entirely accurate either. We are Iranian, and all of you fell into our trap and laid the Iraqis to rest. With all the troops we have assembled along their border, I wouldn't be too surprised if our aircraft haven't already dropped troops in on the capital, preparing for the arrival of our tank divisions. Before you can get your aircraft refueled and rearmed, we will occupy Baghdad once and for all and there is not much you can do to stop us. The attack on your fleet was a sufficient final catalyst to force you to move against Iraq, considering his troop movement and everything. And although the plan was pretty hastily conceived, I think we did a pretty good job of it." Branden was obviously proud of himself.

"And what about the attack on our convoy?" said Swanson quietly.

"Well, we thought that if we flew Iraqi marked aircraft at you, you might get suspicious and resort to your normal dialogue of threats and excuses and take no action at all. But if you found an Iraqi aircraft disguised as an Iranian it would convince you to move, and move quickly, against an Iraqi plot. We thought that you would believe a scheme you uncovered much more than one we presented. We believed that what looked like the truth, presented to you in the form of your own discovery, would be much more convincing than one we tried to engineer directly. Your ego sold you on a plan you thought you'd discovered by yourselves, much easier than anything we could have done from afar. We had hoped that the Korean decoy would keep our work going, but that's not important now. You all love conspiracies, so we gave you one, and you went for it hook, line, and sinker. You fell into our plans, and Iraq is now ours." Branden returned to the wall and leaned up against it, as though the deed was done and there was nothing left to say.

Some of the crowd were getting anxious, but Swanson waved them back to their seats. "Well, I'm sure everyone here appreciates your candor," said Swanson, returning to the table for another sip of water. "Branden, you were quite right when you said we didn't have any proof. Nearly everything we had up until now was purely circumstantial, so I had to play this little charade to force a complete confession out of you. We needed some hard evidence, so I had to let you think you had the upper hand, and you have just given us all the details of the plan we needed, and in front of a few witnesses I might add."

"What?!" cried Branden, struggling against his captors one again.

"And so as to put everyone's minds at ease, let me say that we have not fired one shell against Iraq this afternoon, at least not yet at any rate."

"But the radio traffic confirmed that all hell was breaking loose!" Branden exclaimed.

"That is true, it had. But some of the more active radio traffic you heard was added for your benefit. Yes, we are flying in seven squadrons to Kuwait to ward off the recent advances the Iraqi tanks have made toward the border. And we are planning to build a very strong defensive force once again, against the Iraqis. But our reasons for improving our strength in the region is not only for Kuwait's benefit. Officially we need to have strong military capability in the area to fight off any more stupid attempts that Saddamm may make on the oil fields of Kuwait. But the real reason we are bringing in our big guns is that we want to ensure that you, the Iranians, will not have a prayer in crossing the border now, or at any time in the future to take over your arch-enemy. Once we realised the attack on Group Six was Iranian based, we knew that we had better keep a close eye on you. For the rest, that's all it was, radio traffic," said Swanson with a smile.

"You bastard!" yelled Branden. "You wait, in a few minutes, we'll hit you so hard that you'll wish you'd stayed at home!"

"Thank you, Branden. So, we've still got some unfinished business. Before you're taken away from this place to a nice tight little cell somewhere away from any possible attempts by your colleagues to rescue you, I will at least give you a brief summary of what we have discovered, and in that regard, I must admit there are a couple of things I have neglected to mention."

"Listen. To make this work, you had to make sure that we captured one of your aircraft. I wonder how many volunteers you had for that mission?" Branden didn't answer. "We made a quick examination of the Fulcrum we retrieved and found that, even though the aircraft had been badly damaged in the tail section, the rest of the aircraft was relatively intact. Internally we found that most of the systems had been stripped out of it including the radar. So much so in fact, that we were surprised that it could have fired anything at all. It was probably damaged beyond repair and so you decided to try and use it for a one-way trip. Your pilot was pretty brave. We thought it strange at the time that he didn't turn immediately for home after the attack, instead choosing to head down the Gulf right into the teeth of our F-16s. This maneuver was one of the first to make me suspicious. The fact that you used paint, which would eventually have totally peeled off if we hadn't discovered it when we did, really got my attention." Swanson cocked his head sideways to emphasize his sarcasm. "Now really, Branden, water soluble paint was just a little bit much. Besides, why paint the thing at all if you hadn't intended for us to get a much closer look? I must admit, however, that having your frigates turn on their attack radar at the in-bound Fulcrum a neat touch. Though it appeared strange at the time, you hoped that as soon as we thought the Mig was Iraqi, it would all fall into place. Fortunately though, not for long."

Swanson turned face forward to the room. "By the way, I would like to express my personal thanks to Major Barton here," pointing toward the bandaged, outstretched leg in the front row, "for confirming the irregularities, after being snatched from Iranian troops by Captain Hawksworth of the Royal Navy. The two Fulcrums were first monitored by our AWACS over Iranian airspace, but the Migs had been flying so low that we had difficulty confirming their point of origin. When we discovered the Iraqi insignia on the side of the downed craft, we went back to examine the tapes and concluded, just as they hoped we would, that they had made it across the border from Iraq without being spotted. In reality, they had to make it into Iraq without being seen before doing a a complete about-face and coming up for air, just enough for it to look like just another radar-evading flight from Iraq. Fortunately for us, we had someone on the ground. Major Barton had been driving his jeep deep inside Iran when he saw the two Fulcrums as they happened across a convoy he was following, and, correct me if I get this wrong, Major, saw them flying south-east, away from the border with Iraq. The Fulcrums, you see, had orders to make it to the border, turn 180 degrees and increase altitude to appear on our radar. Even our AWACS have trouble below 100 feet at long range. The route made the initial sighting consistent with Iranian jet movement, but later confirmed to us that they could have indeed come from Iraq. However, you forgot about the second Fulcrum. Just before the attack on our convoy it broke off with his partner and joined up with another squadron of Iranian Migs for a little re-con' of Group Six. Now, how could it have done that if it, like it's partner in crime, had come from Iraq?" Barton remained motionless as Swanson took another sip from his glass. The room remained totally silent as they waited for the Admiral to continue. "The most obvious factor that brought my attention to the doubtful origins of the Fulcrums was that, and here's a point you, being a KC pilot should have made clear to your leaders, both were refueled over Iran. No, don't try and tell me that Iranian tankers can't tell who they're refueling, even if they are disguised." Swanson looked at Branden as though expecting a response but none came.

"Why send two up in the first place you ask. I'm not sure. Perhaps the Fulcrum had been stripped or damaged so much that they weren't sure that its IFF would work properly. Or that both were intended to be involved in the attack and the second one chickened out at the last minute, but whatever the reason, it blew your cover."

"But long before the -29s had been picked up by our watchful eyes in the sky, Major Barton had already questioned their intentions and sent a word of warning in our direction. The Major realized that to see two Fulcrums fully loaded with Exocets heading not toward the Gulf but away from Iraq, that something was wrong. If they were Iraqi then, what were they doing over Iranian air space with anti-ship armament rather than air-to-air guided missiles? No, certainly not, they would have chosen to fly down the Gulf rather than over Iranian air space. Or they were Iranian. If so, then either they were going in the wrong direction, ie. why fly overland to the south when you have bases much closer to the intended area of attack? Or more common and more likely, they had headed toward Iraq to monitor Iraqi border activity and were now on their way back home. So again, why were they loaded with Exocets? On top of this, the Major knew that the Fulcrum is an air-to-air combat platform, not normally given to air-to-ship duties."

"Then Major Barton realized that what was also missing was a procedure, a habit that had not been broken since he'd arrived in Iran. A procedure that should have taken place, but didn't. Whenever an enemy aircraft approaches a convoy, and I mean any convoy anywhere in the world, most convoy commanders would be informed by radio of enemy aircraft movement in the area. The first thing a convoy would do in such circumstances is to scatter, break ranks, but nothing of the sort happened. The convoy kept trundling along as though all was well, and it was. This helped the Major confirm that of course, these were Iranian Migs not Iraqi. But it didn't take our man in the field long to realize that something else was wrong. He knew that whenever friendly aircraft flew overhead the hundreds of troops on board the trucks, with nothing to do but ponder their fate, would always, without exception, cheer and wave their rifles in the air. As these two Iranian Fulcrums flew over the convoy, not only did the convoy not scatter, but there were no cheers from the troops either. This probably meant that the convoy's commanders had been informed that a secret mission was under way and not to pay them any heed. The word was passed back to the troops to keep their heads down and ignore the aircraft completely. The convoy should either scatter or cheer. Not doing either was a red flag to our Major here. To the onlooker this might seem trivial, but to Major Barton's trained eye, the two occurrences were a disturbing contradiction, especially when you consider that there are Iranian airbases closer to the border than his location. As soon as I received his report I made plans to hold this meeting and made tracks for Bahrain as quickly as I could. Once our men from *Gold Seal* had reported in with their findings on the Boeing to me there seemed little doubt that it had been used as a diversion."

Swanson sat back down on the table and for the first time sounded a little tired. "My main concern was how anyone could dictate the flight of a commercial airliner, acting as a decoy, to fly right over our fleet. It couldn't have worked if the *George Washington* had still been on location at Station Gonzo, they would have been too far off the flight path. So that's where the Russians came in. Now, I'm still not sure whether they found out about the plan, or got involved in some kind of financial deal in return for a look at the weapon, you Iranians are very short on cash right now. But anyway, they did get involved and most likely offered to retrieve the unit after it was fired off just before it hit the surface. Perhaps in return, they even offered to nudge Group Six a little further north to help the KC-135 with the drop."

"I say this with no criticism of Captain Davidson, whose lone sub was preoccupied with fending off one Typhoon and three Foxtrots. While the Russian leader kept us preoccupied close aboard the Group, one of the other three went down to the ocean floor and retrieved the spent and somewhat damaged device. I'm sure that the Russians are singing their praises at the moment on the marvelous new toy they now have in their possession. But with any luck, we'll have one too. Now the commercial aircraft chosen to act as decoy in this thing had to be steered to the right location. This meant that either the Korean pilot or the third officer was in on the act. Considering the radio traffic I will assume that it was the latter who deliberately fixed the radios and fed in sufficient errors into the INS to ensure that the aircraft flew into Iranian airspace. It would not surprise me to find that a Korean engineer has just come into a lot of money, resigned from his job and is about to take a trip around the world."

Swanson paused and Branden took this moment to try and disrupt the Admiral's momentum. "Figured it out all by yourself, did you?" said Branden sarcastically.

Swanson turned briefly to face the traitor. "When playing bridge there may be only one lay of the cards that would suit your being able to complete the contract. The trick is to assume that the cards are actually distributed to the opposition in the manner necessary to make the contract, and, ignoring the odds, play the hand accordingly. So what I did was to assume that the Iranians were behind all this and see where it led. It demonstrated to me that the Korean going off-course could have been deliberate, and under the guise of escorting the Korean 747 out of Iranian airspace, your country-men carried out the only course of action that could guarantee that the flight steered directly for Group Six. Making it appear that the Migs had fired on the 747 was clever, probably it was one of your pilots who detonated the flares ensuring a good location for the wet landing. And I'm sure that, with perhaps only one engine running, your original intention was to bring the aircraft down near Group Six so that the incapacity of our Carrier force to help with the rescue would eventually be made known to the public, causing us further inconvenience. But fortunately for us, the 747 made a safe landing. Had the third device gone off, the resultant lack of power would have certainly sealed its fate."

"Having established a train of thought, the other pieces of the puzzle started to fall into place. Following this line of reasoning we must consider that contacting our government with a plea for help, as they did yesterday, had to be nothing more than a smoke-screen. If it wasn't genuine, then what other purpose could be served? There were initially two Fulcrums flying together, but after a somewhat doubtful refueling, they split up and went their separate ways, one to hit our convoy and the other to check out Group Six. Two Floggers were hard on the heels of the first, under the guise of trying to demonstrate to us the Iranians' doubt as to their origin, and the written request for assistance, sent yesterday, certainly gave us reason to accept their excuse of a rogue pilot. But it was the second Fulcrum that gave you away." "If the second Fulcrum was in doubt, then why wasn't the first? When the first changed its identity, we went back to examine the second. I'm sure the orders were to simply get close to Group Six and check it out, but your over-zealous Iranian commander, probably disobeying strict protocol, couldn't resist overflying the Group soon after the attack. They would have only done that if they had some prior knowledge that the fleet were incapable of retaliation. In fact, that was the second thing that happened in all this that didn't make sense and I probably would not have been suspicious at all, if those Iranian Migs had not come so close to the Group . But when it became clear that not only the first Fulcrum gave us ample time to shoot it down, but that we weren't receiving any complaints about our picking it up from the bottom of the Gulf either, I began to see a little clearer. Incidentally, the Mig pilot was probably picked up by one of the inflatables we saw scurrying around that part of the Gulf at the time. And as far as the EXEMPT is concerned, I'm in no doubt that whoever delivered it into the Israeli's hands made a connection with the opposition and sold the information about what it is, how to use it, and its limitations."

"Just to wrap things up here, I apologize if this meeting went on longer than expected, but as you can see there was a great deal to be done. But since we are not at war with Iraq, yet, there was no immediate hurry. I'm sure some of you thought it was strange, that we would go into Baghdad in broad daylight, and I thank those of you who were suspicious for keeping quiet about it. I know you're all eager to return to your units but I would like to add that we have indeed sent some of our forces into battle already. They were sent to monitor the border area between Iraq and Kuwait, to watch for any aircraft that might stray into our airspace."

"Branden, you can be rest-assured of one thing. If we do go into Iraq again, it will be solely because the Iraqi government has still not complied with the cease-fire agreements, not because some sneaky neighbor tries to trick us into it. Get them out of here. Sergeant, take them away."

Struggling against their captors Branden and his crew were escorted from the room, followed closely by the other Iranian prisoners. Swanson ignored Branden's look of hatred and addressed the room. "Remember everyone, you must never mention anything that transpired at this meeting today to anyone, not even to your immediate superiors. When asked about it, just say that it was some over-pompous Admiral wanting to celebrate the downing and capture of a Mig. Dismissed." Swanson sat down on the edge of the table and wiped the sweat from his brow as the room exploded in cheers and applause. As the occupants noisily exited from the room, a few offered congratulatory comments to the Admiral as they departed. Swanson stepped down from the stage, wandered over to the bar, bounced some ice into a glass and poured himself a long scotch. General Wilson was close on his heels.

"Want one?" asked Swanson quietly with a yawn.

"Yes please." The last remaining stragglers filtered out from the room as Wilson climbed aboard a stool and watched his friend fix the drinks. "Pat, I must say, that was one of the most brilliant pieces of modern-day detective work I have ever seen in my life. I know you had told me to disregard anything you said today, but there were a couple of moments there when you even had me going, I can tell you. At one point, I thought you were even going to hit him. Boy, what a great grandstand play that was."

Swanson passed the General his beverage. "It's amazing what holding your breath for a couple of minutes can do to make you look flustered. I'm just concerned about the other EXEMPT. If we don't find it in time..?" Swanson shook his head.

"Well," said Wilson. "Pullman just told me that the Iranians are putting up a bit of a struggle. Once they realized that we were not bombing the hell out of Iraq, they sent in some aircraft toward the *Independence* and *La Salle*. They're even threatening to blockade the Straits again. We may be in for some retaliation."

"What bothers me," said Swanson, pouring himself another drink, seemingly ignoring Wilson's comments, "is whether we are we going to get to it in time. It sounded as though they were planning to let it off very soon. I just hope we're going to make it."

"If not Kennedy, then, where?" asked Wilson, gently.

"Boy, was I wrong," said Swanson, taking another sip. "The source we had only managed to blurt out a few sounds before he died, but they sounded like Naa, Saa. But while I was churning things over in my mind on the flight over, it occurred to me there was another possible solution and I called my aid to get things moving. Why would they fly it or drive it all the way down to Florida, I thought to myself, when there were many more juicy targets to be had closer to home? If you had a device in the north-east that could knock out computers at will, where would you go? If not NASA, then where? Our source for the second location had only managed to blurt out a couple of letters, before he died, which sounded like NASA, but it dawned on me he could have been trying to say NSA. When he laughed at Florida, I knew it had to be, so I called Washington to be prepared."

"Oh my God," whispered Wilson and took a gulp from his glass.

Swanson sounded tired. "If they manage to hit that installation the damage to our communication network world-wide will be catastrophic and cost us billions to fix. The trouble is, even if they do find it in time, I have no idea how we can prevent those idiots from discharging the device. They only need to see us coming, press a button and poof, the entire communication links, that everyone from the President on down rely on, would be destroyed without even making a sound. I just hope we're not too late. Come on, finish up, I've got to get back." Wilson downed the remainder of the scotch and walked with Swanson out of the officer's mess toward the main exit to the airfield.

The brilliant sunshine streaming in the door made Wilson squint. "I hope the next time John calls me with one of your requests, it won't be to use some unknown crew for ferrying purposes."

"I'm sure this will be the one and only time, General," said Swanson, straightening his tie.

"Are you sure you want to fly back now? You look as though you could do with some sleep." They walked out onto the tarmac, and there, about a hundred feet away being gassed up and preparing for service, sat an all-white SR-71 Blackbird, dressed with the blue NASA stripe.

"Pat!" cried Wilson. I thought we'd got rid of those?"

"So did I," said Swanson, mustering a smile. "But when General Tupper heard of the urgency he told me to get ready for the flight of my life, and it was."

"Bit of a contradiction in terms, isn't it?" Wilson remarked, grinning profusely.

"What do you mean, Willy?"

Wilson turned to look at Swanson, cocked his head to one side, and said slowly with a questioning look. "A white Blackbird?"

Swanson decided to ignore the remark, lifted a bright red suit off a peg in the entrance, and began climbing into it. "I thought we officially scrapped them all too, but as you can see someone with some foresight and just a little bit of extra scrambled egg on his cap managed to salvage this three seater for NASA Research, before they were all ripped to pieces. Actually they operate six other all-black Blackbirds, this one's just to test a new paint at very high temperatures. "

Wilson assisted with some of the zippers. "Well I'm sure you'll have a pleasant flight," handing him the large red space helmet.

"Right, besides there's nothing more I can do here. See you Don, and thanks for everything. We couldn't have done it without you," and Swanson shook Wilson's hand.

"Don't mention it, Pat," Wilson shouted, as Swanson walked off toward the warming craft. "Except, if there is a next time, I'm going to bring some heart pills."

Admiral Swanson joined the rest of the flight crew and climbed aboard, and within moments it seemed the Blackbird roared down the runway and disappeared westward toward its first refueling point.

Chapter Eighty

There were no signs of moving vehicles, no pedestrians walking, not even a dog barking. A curfew was in effect and it took Latchkey's thoughts away from the diversion and back to the reality of what could be the second ever attack by a foreign nation on American soil. But this time the attack would not come in the form of a few shells from a Japanese submarine's gun, but from a device that could cause irreparable damage to the monitoring systems of the most expensive concentration of computer equipment in the world. And it was up to Latchkey and Ken Trist to ensure it didn't happen.

The jeep came to an abrupt halt, jolting Latchkey back to the task at hand.

"What the hell's going on here?" yelled Trist, reaching for the handset again. "Dover, you read me?"

"Dover here."

"Get some guys down to the end of Savage. It feels naked out here."

"But, sir you said..."

"I don't care what I said. I wanted my crack staff out in the field, but I still want warm bodies all over the place, especially our front door, got it?"

"I'll have a couple of squads there in five minutes."

"Make it two! Trist out. Good grief, do I have to think of everything myself?" Latchkey guessed that Trist had to, but that he had better get his own devious mind working just in case. The jeep brought them back to the exit door close to the Communications Center. Trist and Latchkey went in, leaving the Corporal and McBee to their own devices.

"Right!" yelled Trist as he entered the room. "What's the latest anyone?" A rather trim girl ran up with notebook in hand and followed Trist toward his office, reading as she went.

"Major Dover reports that two-thirds of the entire area has been sealed off with the remaining areas to be completed by zero-five-fifty. Major Kuehn has confirmed that the entire bridge area has been sealed off, and that requests for phone lines to the Department of the Army and Army Intelligence are coming in from state police and eight news agencies already on the scene. And you have a phone call waiting for you in your...," she was prohibited from finishing her sentence, as she found herself walking into the door-jam of Trist's office.

"Thank you, Staff, but I know all that already. Get me a fresh brew, will you please." He picked up the phone. "Trist here." Latchkey turned and watched the thirty or so individuals out in the main room diligently carrying out their duties. He left Trist and walked out and around two of the large banks of communications equipment. No-one looked up to see who he was or take their minds off their immediate task. Phone lights were blinking and buzzers sounded, but everyone appeared to have everything well in hand. If only they knew, he thought.

Trist came out of his office. "That was the General. Your boss has just been on the phone to him and wanted to ensure that we were doing everything possible to keep this thing contained."

"There's not much we can do now but wait, I'm afraid," said Latchkey.

"Yeah. Come into my office and grab a fresh cup, it may be a long night." Just as Latchkey was about to follow Trist, one of the five girls sitting by a phone bank called out.

"Sir, our air cover has a contact, an intercept with a Learjet."

"Send it over," ordered Trist as he rushed into his office. Latchkey entered the doorway and listened to the dialogue coming from the speaker on Trist's desk. Sharp in its delivery and a little muffled, but the dialogue was clear and familiar to Latchkey's ears.

"Learjet, Learjet, this is the United States Air force. Come in please." No response. "Learjet, Learjet, this is the United States Air force. Do you read me, over?" Trist looked up at Latchkey but the Commander shook his head.

"This is Captain Freemont, go-ahead."

"What are you flying and where are you heading, over?"

"We are flying a Learjet bound for New York from Chicago, over."

"What is your flight plan?"

"Currently at ten-zero, heading zero-nine-five."

"Why is your altitude below one-five-zero?"

"We have a planned stop-over in Pennsylvania."

"You are heading directly for a restricted area. Change heading to..."

Trist reached over and turned the volume down. "It's going to be like this for quite a while."

The speaker sprang back into life. "Sir, there's some more traffic. Radar is attempting to track something big and low coming in from the south. There has been no response so far so a couple of F-4s are heading out to take a look."

"Colonel," said Latchkey. "Would you mind if I grabbed a radio and took a walk back outside? You and the flyboys have everything buttoned up, and I feel like grabbing some air and taking a stroll."

"Where to?" asked Trist, reaching into his draw and pulling out a handset.

"Down to the checkpoint to check up on Savage Road."

"Sure, I'll tell my guys to expect you." Latchkey took the handset, slipped it in his pocket, and went out to the main office where he'd left his flashlight.

"Thank you, Colonel. I'll find my own way out." Latchkey left the control room, found his way back to the main entrance and went out through the glass doors. His eyes soon became accustomed to the night sky and even though it was dark he found he could see quite well without the use of the flashlight. The two big guards who had opened the doors to the Ford when he first arrived, were waiting for him.

"Good morning, Commander," said one of them.

"Good morning," Latchkey replied.

"Allow me to escort you across the parking lot, Commander."

"Okay," said Latchkey and the two of them walked

out onto the front access road, across the grass and on toward the beginning of Savage Road proper.

"Any news on what's happening, sir?" said the young soldier, trying to sound as off-hand as he could.

"What do you know, Corporal?" inquired Latchkey.

"Not much. Just that all hell's broken loose and we'll spend the rest of our working lives breaking rocks if we let any unauthorized vehicles near this place."

"That's about the size of it, soldier," said Latchkey, realizing for the first time his legs didn't have their normal spring. "Not only must we not let anyone in, but we mustn't let them get closer than two miles."

"Is it nuclear, may I ask, sir?"

"Yes, you may ask, and no, it's not. No-one's life is in danger on this one Corporal, but the lives we're left with won't be worth much if we don't catch them on their first try."

"Sounds pretty bad, sir."

"Oh, it is, Corporal, it is. Even if we catch these guys, the consequences of their attempt will have far reaching effects that will no doubt change the entire shape of our defense capabilities."

"Is that good or bad, sir?"

"Good question. No-one will know that for quite a while, I'm afraid. The entire defensive role since the beginning of time seems to be to ward off the newest form of attack. Once we have found a way of protecting ourselves against a particular form of insurgence, some Charlie goes and discovers a new way of breaking through it. So then we trundle off and find new ways to combat the latest technology until the next one comes along, and so on, and so on."

"But we have the finest defense systems in the world, Commander," said the Corporal with pride.

"Do we?" There was no reply and the last few steps to the little gate house were quiet ones.

"There you go, Commander," said the Corporal. "Anything else I can do for you?"

"No, thank you." A Sergeant stepped out of the small building to greet them.

"Sergeant, this is Commander Latchkey, out for a stroll."

"That'll be all, Corporal. Strange kind of night to be taking a walk, Commander?"

"Not really, Sergeant. It's been a long day and there's not much else I can do at the moment."

"And where will you be walking to now, sir?"

"Well I thought I would take a wander down to the end of Savage to see how they're doing."

"Very well, I will call them to expect you."

"Thank you, Sergeant, I think the Colonel has already done so."

"That may be, sir, but we have our procedures. By the way, stick to the road, Commander, the fence is wired." The Sergeant stepped back in the shadows and Latchkey continued his stroll down the lane toward the first road block. Looming large in front of him was another entrance that he hadn't seen on his trip in. Two large posts stood on either side of the road, each topped off with a video camera. The twenty foot high fence on both sides looked dangerous, and it was. As he passed through the entrance he saw a large notice. He turned his flashlight on it briefly and read:

'Cyclone fence. The taking of photographs, making of sketches or the carrying out of any reproduction in this area is strictly prohibited under penalty of law.'

John Latchkey continued on his way. After twenty feet or so he came across another fence, a wire fence with wooden posts planted in a bed of green asphalt pebbles. And finally, after another twenty feet, a second Cyclone fence, again with the obvious warnings. He heard a noise behind him and turned quickly around to be immediately blinded by a bright beam of light and deafened by the bark of a very close and angry dog.

"You alright, Commander?"

"Oh, yes, thank you. Just going for a breath of fresh air."

"Right, sir." The lamp was turned off and within a second, both the owner of the flashlight and the dog had disappeared into the night.

John Latchkey took a deep breath and resumed his

pace, surprised at how much the patrol had startled him. He must be getting old, out of practice and condition for this sort of thing. The road began to veer to the right, and he pondered on what evils may await the N.S.A. Was there anything else he could do? His boss had given him his orders. Stop and secure. Well, they had done all they could on the ground and it was up to the Air Force for the rest.

The trees on both sides were thin but close together, and as the road meandered he noticed long shadows stretching across his path. As he rounded the curve he finally caught a glimpse of a large truck parked across the road and as he drew closer, he saw a figure standing out in front of him. A flashlight shone in his direction and then faded. A few moments later it shone again, but this time it moved toward him. Latchkey's radio went off in his pocket with a buzz that the entire neighborhood would have heard. He pulled it out and pressed the key.

"Latchkey here."

"Commander, this is Trist. Have nailed down the bogie. It now has a fighter escort, but they still can't seem to raise the crew on the radio. They're flying directly at us. If they don't change course before they close within three miles, the F-4s have orders to open fire. Want to come and join in the fun?"

"No, that's okay."

"Well, whatever happens the pilot will have a lot of explaining to do, assuming he gets out of this alive."

"How close is it?"

"Ten miles, five thousand feet."

"Remember, two miles minimum!"

"Yeah, right. Maybe the idiot's got a death wish."

"Well if he does, it better not be at our expense."

"I hear you, Commander. Give me a call on your way back."

"Okay, Colonel, see you shortly." John Latchkey slid the handset back into his pocket. He suddenly had a feeling of deja vu. Why was this scenario so familiar to him? He was just trying to make some kind of connection when the flashlight arrived.

"Commander, Sergeant Porterfield. We were told to

expect you."

"I'm sorry to be such a nuisance. I know you guys don't like pedestrians wandering around with all this security going on."

"You're right, sir. But seeing how you're helping us out, sir, I think we can handle it. Anything in particular we can do for you, Commander?"

"Not really. I thought I would see how you're doing."

"Very good, sir." The two continued to stroll toward the road block. "Great diversion we have going, Commander?"

"You mean the fire?"

"Yeah why, we have more than one diversion going on?"

"No, but..," Latchkey's mind began to focus in on something. Some of those light bulbs Professor Bono used to preach about began to shine away through the fog in Latchkey's mind. He reached for his radio. "Colonel Trist, this is Latchkey."

"Go ahead, John."

"Did your guys examine every vehicle inside the two mile perimeter?"

"No, we didn't have time. We have a team doing just that right now but it's going to take..."

"Never mind. We've been so busy setting up our own diversion, we may have been falling for one ourselves. What's the news on the bogie?"

"Still on course."

"Tell the Air Force to get it down and arrest its occupants, I think it's another damn decoy."

"A diversion to what?"

"The end of Savage Road must be blocked off completely. If those nuts have used their heads they would have moved the vehicle with the device very close to here long before now and all we did was turn our backs on them." Latchkey waited for the reply but none came. "Colonel?!" he shouted.

"He's rang off, sir." Latchkey was just about to shout into the radio again when his ears came alive with the unmistakable sound of gunfire. Latchkey grabbed Porterfield by the scruff of the neck and pulled him into the trees to the left.

"Porterfield to Control. Zap one, repeat Zap one." yelled Porterfield into his handset.

"Zap one, roger Porterfield, assistance on the way."

"I'm fifty yards up the road from Stop One and we just heard four shots. Wait. Now the truck's motor's running. Someone's moving it."

"Is Commander Latchkey with you?"

"Affirmative, he's right here."

"Good, remain where you are and get off that road, assistance is on the way, out."

The Corporal put his radio away. "You okay, Commander?"

"Sure am. Your rifle loaded?"

"Of course."

"Whatever vehicle comes by, we must shoot its tires out. Now get over behind that tree and as it goes by, use half a clip on the front tire, the rest on the rear."

"But Commander, how do we know..?"

"Just do it, Corporal. Don't wait for my signal, just open fire at will." Latchkey drew him up against a tree, not ten feet from the road. "This should provide enough cover, oh and Corporal?"

"Yes, sir?"

"Don't miss." Before the Corporal could say anything else, Latchkey had dashed across the road into the trees on the other side, just as a pair of headlights stretched up the road toward them. The sound of a large gas engine grew steadily louder. Latchkey threw himself down wind from the oncoming lights, pulled his hand gun from it's jacket and released the safety. He was right handed, so he was going to have to work his way around the tree counter-clockwise. The noise grew nearer as the engine screamed its way up through the gears. It was a large van with small wheels. A hundred feet, ninety, eighty, seventy. He had twelve shots so he could only risk six on the front. Fifty, forty, thirty, twenty. The bright headlights caused him to squint. NOW! he shouted to himself. He let off six shots in quick succession. Another sound caught his ears as Porterfield's gun echoed his. Latchkey refocused on the rear. NOW! More shots rang out. There were a couple of loud bangs, followed by a huge hissing sound as the air was crushed out of the rubber by the weight of the vehicle.

Suddenly all hell broke loose. From somewhere up ahead a voice cried out. From Latchkey's vantage point he could see two streaks of light flash though the air, the projectiles hitting the van head on. The explosions were deafening. The fire ball lit up the sky revealing large pieces of the cab and front end flying off in all directions. The blast knocked Latchkey back behind the tree momentarily, but as he fought against the furnace of heat, he climbed back up onto the road. The front of the van was completely destroyed. A dozen soldiers arrived from nowhere and began dowsing the flames with extinguishers.

"Porterfield, you okay?" Latchkey shouted as the Corporal, putting away his weapon, came up to join him.

"Sure am."

"Give me your radio." The Corporal handed it over.

"If you want to talk to the Colonel, press three."

He did.

"Trist here."

"This is Latchkey. Is everything okay? Is everything still working?"

"Sure is."

"Great."

"I'll be there in about thirty seconds."

"Call your road blocks to secure all exits and stop any vehicle trying to leave the area, shoot to kill if necessary. I think there's a fast car on it's way out of here."

"Right. Stay where you are Commander, I'll be right there."

"Good shooting Corporal."

"Anytime, Commander," said Porterfield, shaking the Commander's hand eagerly. A crowd of sirens and flashing lights arrived. Colonel Trist jumped down from the lead vehicle as two more trucks squeezed by the smoking ruins and sped by Latchkey down toward the road block.

"I grabbed everyone I could," shouted Trist, running up. "You okay?"

"You bet, but I'm not so sure about the driver. Everything still up and running?"

"Sure is."

"How did he get through?" They looked over at the damaged wreck lying on the edge of the road and noticed what was left of an inscription.

"An ambulance?" said Trist, shaking his head.

"I'm sure it was already inside the two mile limit before I arrived here."

"Corporal," said Trist, pointing a finger toward the road block. "See if you can be of some assistance."

"Yes, sir." The few flickering flames of orange died down leaving the fire truck's white lights to illuminate the carnage. Trist and Latchkey walked toward the remains as five soldiers approached the rear of the ambulance.

Trist's radio buzzed again. "Stop One to Trist." The voice was slow and deliberate.

"Trist here."

"Three dead and one injured I'm afraid, Colonel."

"Who were they?" said Trist turning away from Latchkey.

"Simmons, Reece and Lodner, sir. Rudy got it in the arm but managed to hit a car as it raced away from here."

"Give the man a medal and tell him a real ambulance is on its way. Trist out."

Latchkey handed Trist his radio. "Colonel, the attack is over. Tell the perimeter to turn inwards and not to let any vehicle escape. There's no-one left in there so it would be great if we could get their escape route." Trist barked a few sharp words into his radio and joined Latchkey at what was left of the front of the ambulance.

A Sergeant yelled from the trees. "All secure here, Colonel. We've found the remains of two bodies, both dead."

"Okay, Commander," said Trist, putting his radio away. "Let's see if we've won first prize." They walked back around to the rear of the vehicle.

"Booby trapped?" Latchkey suggested.

"Doubt it, but we'll make sure just in case. Bowery!"

barked Trist. A Lieutenant came running up.

"Sir?"

"The van may be rigged. Clear the area and check it out."

"Yes, sir." Bowery yelled for the area to be cleared as Trist and Latchkey walked off into the trees.

"Your Corporal Porterfield handled himself pretty well back there," said Latchkey.

"Pleased to hear it. Might give him a chance at another stripe. You handled yourself pretty well too, Commander."

"Where the hell did all that fire power come from?"

"I had an independent unit stationed in the trees as a final back-up in case anything did get through. Small stuff, nothing that destroys any vehicle completely."

"I'm glad you did."

"So am I. I just wish Simmons, Reece and Lodner had been so lucky."

"It was more than luck that stopped this lot from succeeding."

"Right," said Trist, turning to face Latchkey. "Just the kind of luck that Admiral Swanson found when he chose you to come down here."

"Perhaps."

Lieutenant Bowery came running up.

"Yes Lieutenant," said Trist.

"Not sure, sir, no traps from what I can tell, but there's a large item of cargo in the back, still relatively intact."

"Come on, John, let's go take a peek." The two walked out of the trees and over to the open doors. A huge crate about six foot wide and seven foot high stretched right up to where the front used to be.

"Well?"

"Bingo," said Latchkey. "Still has the company's name on the side."

"What do we do now, John?"

"The first thing we do is move this crate more than two miles from here as quickly as we can."

Trist yelled at Bowery and a truck was brought around to the rear. Within moments, a winch had been attached to the grabs on the crate and with some help from a couple of ramps and some strong backs, the EXEMPT was hand-winched into the back of the truck. "Take it over to FANX back field area and stay with it until I send someone over to relieve you. No-one gets near the thing unless I personally give the okay. Got it?"

"Yes, sir."

"Good."

Bowery left.

"Right, next?" Trist continued.

"Tell Captain Erickson he can go home. Get a tow-truck out to bring the tanker back here and call your men in."

"Right," Trist replied, as they turned to walk on down toward the road block. He pulled out his radio. "Trist to Control." He paused, awaiting an answer. "Trist to Control," he repeated louder. "That's funny, my radio's dead." There came a shout from the Lieutenant. Trist turned to look back.

"What is it?"

"My radio's given up the ghost, sir." said the Lieutenant, running up with radio in hand.

"Funny, so's mine." He tried Latchkey's but that was dead too.

Latchkey nodded. "The radios were in close proximity to the crate."

Trist looked confused. "So?"

"It obviously leaks."

Trist looked back at Bowery. "Lieutenant, see if any of your men have a radio that works for me, will you?"

"Yes, sir," said Bowery and left.

"Good grief," said Trist. "It leaks?"

"Guess so. The longer you leave it charged the smaller its effective range." Bowery returned with a handset.

"Good work, Lieutenant, you found another that works?"

"Yes, sir."

"Good, then get on with it." Bowery handed him the set and left. "Looks like we got lucky at any rate. They could have stopped at the road-block and set it off right there, it's only about half a mile to the Cray and Platform's head quarters."

"For all I know," continued Latchkey, "it's been so long since this one was fully charged that they figured they had to get to within shouting distance or the whole trip would have been a waste of time."

"No power left you mean?"

"Right." Latchkey suddenly felt very tired.

"Let me call in the news and get a few wheels rolling." He lifted the replacement to his mouth. "Trist to Control."

"Control. Go ahead, Colonel."

"Call the Assistant DIRNSA and let him know that we have the item in custody. Then call everyone else and tell them the show's over and take the Agency off full alert status."

"Will do, sir. Oh, Colonel?"

"Yes."

"Major Kuehn just called in to say that a speeding vehicle attempted to break out through the perimeter without permission."

"And?"

"And he reports that two prisoners are being brought in for questioning."

"Great news. Trist out." Trist put the handset back in his pouch. "You hear that? We've got 'em."

"It's a pity your men didn't come away as unscathed." Trist didn't answer. He pulled back his cuff and checked the time. "Your watch has probably died too," said Latchkey calmly.

"Well, would you believe it."

"So's mine."

"Boy, what a gadget," said Trist, looking back over his shoulder as they continued. "We don't want too many of these falling into the wrong hands, things could get decidedly heavy."

"You're right there. Strange thing is, it was in the right hands to start with."

"You mean this thing is one of ours and we let it get away?"

"That's right."

"Can you imagine what it could do if it were dropped on some of our warships in the Pacific or the Persian Gulf?"

"Yeah, pretty devastating, eh?"

"Any idea how it works?"

"Beats me."

"What a gadget," Trist replied, softly.

"Yea," echoed Latchkey wiping the sleep from his eyes. "Unfortunately however, we're not the sole owners any more."

The two continued their stroll up the road. Latchkey looked up at the fresh dawn breaking across the sky and saw the new moon smiling down at him, as though it knew all along that everything this day would be okay. Maybe, thought Latchkey to himself, but what about tomorrow?

Epilogue

Everyone who had attended the meeting at Bahrain Air Base that afternoon were on their way home. AWACS 24, with a fresh crew returned to the skies to continue its constant vigilance in the north. Major Barton flew back to Ohio for a debriefing while the remaining Allied Forces in the Gulf resumed normal operations. The Iranian Government immediately withdrew an earlier offer to open fresh lines of communications and within an hour, in the middle of the afternoon, two Iranian frigates had closed in to block off the Straits of Hormuz to further shipping activity just as a convoy of tankers, led by the *Stork* entered the channel. At the same moment, a Pave-Hawk, returning to the *Stork*, and two F/A-18s on their way back to the *George Washington* were engaged by four Mig-23 Floggers and a Mig-29 Fulcrum. The Hornets, joined by two F-14D Tomcats from the Carrier, drove back the Migs, but not before one of the Hornets was hit by cannon-fire. During the engagement, two Iranian Floggers were shot down, three explosions were reported coming from an area east of the Straits where two Silkworm launchers were located, and a United States Los Angeles class nuclear attack submarine, armed with ten Tomahawk cruise missiles, surfaced in the Persian Gulf. The remaining Migs immediately broke off their brief engagement while the *Sahand* and *Sabalan* retired to a safe distance away from the channel. Although the pilot of the Hornet was seriously injured, the aircraft remained airworthy and continued its journey back to the *George Washington* where, thanks to a new on-board landing system, returned to the Carrier safely. Ten hours later, after everything throughout the Gulf Region had settled down, a Marine Master Sergeant aboard the Carrier found a long length of antenna under a Radar Technician's locker about the same time that a dusty Range Rover was being driven out of Oman. On Monday, the 10th of October, the News of the massive build up of American troops in Kuwait hit the Newspapers. And, in January of 1995, an unofficial spokesman revealed that the Republic of Russia was beginning work on a brand new form of defense capability.

Glossary Of Terms

A-6: Intruder. Many versions were built from this all purpose strike aircraft, eg. Tankers and the Electronic Jamming version EA-6B.

AMRAAM: AIM-120A. Advanced Medium Range Air-to-Air Missile. Began its development in 1975. Features minimal propellent smoke. Range 28 nautical miles head-on and uses active radar proximity fuse. Now one of many Fire-and-Forget choices available.

ASW: Anti-Submarine Warefare.

AWACS: Airborne Warning And Control Squadrons.

Black Alert: A highly trained team of computor engineers, on call 24 hours prepared to fly to all parts of the world at a moment's notice to assist with any major shut-down of computors and related support equipment.

Blue Thunder: Term used to identify missions, Silver Flag, Desert Storm, Cover Charge, etc.

Bobblies: A form of wool hat generally knitted by hand. The top would feature a tuft of wool in the shape of a ball. Referred to as a Bobbly Hat.

Cats: Catapault, the steam operated system that fires aircraft off Carrier decks. Modern Carriers with angled decks operate four catapaults, two off the front, two off the angled deck to port.

Chish and fip: A term first coined in 1874 by the reverand A.J. Sooner. One Sunday he arose in the pulpit and announced, "Let us preal and nay, and confess the dongs we have run." From that day forth, whenever the first letters of two words used in conjunction with each other are transposed, it is called a Spoonerism. eg. "Go fly a boat," becomes "Go buy a float."

CIC: Command Incident Center, the hub or nerve center of most modern fighting ships. All systems can be operated from this room buried deep in the heart of the ship.

CINCPAC: Commander-in-Chief Pacific Forces.

CINCARA: Commander-in-Chief Arabian Ocean Forces.

Conn: The area designated as the bridge of the submarine. On early designs, the bridge was located inside that part of the sumarines's structure above the deck: The Connington Tower or Sail. Though the captain may be elsewhere on the boat, an officer must be in charge of the bridge at all times.

Cover Charge: see Blue Thunder.

DEFSAT: Defense Satellite.

DIRNSA: Director of National Security Agency.

Doppler radar: A system that relies on movement toward or away from the emittor. As the emittor sweeps the change in distance to the radar is dermined by the Doppler shift and shows up to the operator on the screen. Aircraft movement to the left or to the right of the radar, keeping equal distance to the emittor will have little or no Dopplar shift and will be difficult for the operator to discern.

EA-6B: see A-6.

EXEMPT: Extra-Electro-Magnetic-Pulse-Transmitter.

Exocets: Air-to-Ship missile. A fire-and-forget munitions carrier that uses both radar and infra-red as targeting methods. Manufactured by the French.

FALCON: F-16D Fighting Falcon, single seat, single engined interceptor.

FLASH: Flight-Levy-Alternative-System-Homer used for ship defense when under attack from infra-red homing missiles. A series of canisters that upon firing emit high levels of bright light that hopefully distract the infra-red targeting missile away from the ship.

Flogger: MIG-23ML Flogger-G. The Soviet Union produced approximately 600 per year entering service in 1973. This single seat, single engined, variable-geometry intercepter has a maximum speed of 790 mph.

Fly-by-wire: Aircraft design that does not rely on cables or hydraulics as the primary method of elevator, stablator, rudder control. Instead, stick and rudder movements are converted into electrical impulses fed into a computer system. This system drives individual motors that control aircraft attitude.

FOD: Foreign Objects and Debris. Routinely ten or twenty deck crew are required to visually sweep the deck and pick up everything that may hinder aircraft operations. A simple washer or bolt can be sucked into an air intake and totally destroy an engine.

Foxbat: Mig-25M, Russian built, single seat, twin engined interceptor.

Fulcrum: Mig-29 Fulcrum-A. Designed to counter the F-15, the Fulcrum fell short. It is more comparable with the F-16. This single seat, twin engined top-of-the-line Mig has a top speed of 760 mph.

GMT: Greenwich Mean Time. Although Greenwich Observatory used to be the Center for what otherwise would be referred to as "World Time," today's military time goes by its given name—"Zulu Time." For the purposes of the non-military reader GMT was chosen.

GPS: Global Positioning System. Ground based units that take coordinates from Geosynchronous satellite stations to provide acurate location information to the user down to 10 feet.

GPS II: Permits senior ranks to keep track of unit leaders in real time by using the GPS' location to trace plots on area commander's electronic maps at HQs.

Hawkeye: The given name for the E-2C Navy AWACS.

Hedges: Hook Engagement System. A computor system that assists a Harrier pilot in the approach to the Engagement area by using a series of lights that shine off the HUD.

Helix Mix:: A mixture of Helium and Oxygen that divers use to permit a more lengthy stay at great depths.

Hornet: The F/A-18 CD Multi-role combat airframe, though not as maneuverable as the F-16, it can deliver a variety of ordnance. This single seat, twin engined fighter and strike aircraft is replacing many F-14s and most E-2s.

HUD: Head-Up-Display. A system that reflects key flight management data to the pilot via a specially treated glass mount. This system keeps to a minimum the amount of time a pilot has to spend looking down at his/her instruments. The HUD is located in direct line of sight forward, raising the visual vigilance that pilots need to maintain.

Hummer: An in-service term to describe the E-2C Hawkeye, a more modest version of the E-3B 707 AWACS.

IR: Infra-red.

Kip: A term used when the intention is go to sleep for eight hours with the undeniable possibility that he/she would be lucky to sleep for an hour or so.

LSO: Landing Signals Officer. A senior pilot that stands with his support staff close to the ramp is in charge of every landing or Pass and it is his job to wave off any approach to the Ramp that is outside of normal perameters and to score each Pass to be given to the pilot during his debriefing.

Mother: Call sign for the *George Washington*'s Traffic Control.

Meatball: The series of red and yellow lights, located on the aft port side of a Carrier, that aids pilots visually to line up their aircraft to the Ramp. This system will soon be replaced by a Laser based unit.

MUT: Miniature-Underwater-Transports. 6 feet long, 3 feet wide, these transports, using a single water jet system can move up to 6 knots underwater, 20 on the surface. Strapped in using a harness, the diver is carried half behind the MUT using his legs to steer.

Nacelles: A set of two movable covers that together cover the rear of the aircraft's engine's exhaust. When applying reverse thrust each cover closes in over the end of the exhaust forcing the thrust forward.

NAVCOM: Naval Communications.

NAVSAT: Naval Satellite.

NSC: National Security Council.

Ouija-board: Details a minature version of the Carrier Flight Deck and cut-outs of aircraft, permitting Operations and Maintenence to keep track of which aircraft are parked where on the deck, so that as aircraft leave and arrive back on the Carrier, space is alloted.

Pass: Landing attempt.

Pegasus: The unique powerplant of the Sea Harrier. The four moveable exhausts, two on each side, permit the aircraft to change from hover to forward flight. Smaller nozzles located above and below each wingtip and on the nose and tail give the pilot accurate aircraft attitude control at low speeds.

Phalanx: An M61A1 20 mm Vulcan Gun mounted on a self steering, self targeting system. Protected under a tall white encasement, the Phalanx once turned on, will indescrimanently shoot down anything that comes within range, friendlies and bandits alike. Although the *Stark*'s captain was heavily criticized for not having the Phalanx turned on when it was hit with an Iraqi Exocet that slammed into the side of the ship while on duty in the Persian Gulf, the United States was not "at war" with any nation at the time. No other ship had orders to leave the Phalanx turned on at the time due to fear of friendly fire accidents. Yet with 8 seconds warning the *Stark* was supposed to have defended herself against one of the most advanced anti-ship weapons available.

Phased Array Radar: A radar system that uses many signal generators rather than one. The disadvantage of having a single radar emitter is that the signal sweeps, either 360 degrees or back and forth depending upon search design requirements. To check a certain area for bandits the operator has to wait until the sweep has been completed before he/she can determine activity. A Phased Array radar has up to 100 radar emitters that fire off in sequence all in the same direction eg. forward of an aircraft since most airborne Phased Arrays are located in the nose.

Porkies: A type of ordenance that uses vibration to set off the detonator. The amount of vibration needed to set off detonation can be adjusted remotely.

Pulse Radar: A radar emittor that can monitor large objects flying across (eg. left to right) its target area. When an aircraft makes course directly at the emittor, due to the low cross-signature or frontal area, the operator will have little chance of tracking it until it has overflown the tower. Pulse radar systems generally have lesser range compared to Doppler equivalents.

Ramp: The stern of the Carrieraft of the landing area.

Rogue: "An individual varying markedly from the standard," in this case from standard operational procedures as laid down by the Iranian Air Force.

S-3: A twin turbo-jet, four seat aircraft designed for Anti-Submarine Warefare.

SAPS: Signal-Algorithmic-Processing-Systems. An intregal part of the data processing systems aboard a submarine that aids Sonar operators to discern and distinguish sounds. Every sound underwater has a particular pattern or signature and the sound library with records of all known ship and submarine types, screw size and configuration helps determine what each sound is.

Sail: Conning tower. Submariner term for that part of the boat above the deck.

Signals: A branch of the service that specializes in communications.

Sarnies: An abreviation of sandwhiches.

SATCOM: Satellite Communications.

SCRAM: Super-Critical-Axe-the-Manila. In the early days while conducting experiments with nuclear fission, the Uranium rods would be lifted and then lowered into the coolant by the use of Manila braids. If, once the rods were raised the reaction began to get out of control and the temperatures rose above red line, the term SCRAM was used. This cry from an operator would mean: Cut the Manila, the plant is going Super Critical! So someone would grab a blade of some description, envariably an axe, and cut the strands. The nuclear rods would fall back into the coolant and all would be well. SCRAMed is the same term used in past tense.

SIGINT: Signals Intelligence.

Silkworm: Description of Russion built Surface-to-Ship missiles that can be launched from mobile units using a crew of 4 or more. Dated weaponry with a range of 30 miles using radar targeting.

Sortie: Bombing mission—though may be used as slang for any flight operations.

Tag: Squadron designation. Mission call-signs are issued for each sortie.

Three wire: There are four cables used for arresting aircraft upon landing on a Carrier deck. An LSO will give the highest marks to landings where the aircraft's hook engages the third cable, the first is nearest the back of the ship.

Topo: Topographical.

Tomcat: F-14B, twin seat, twin engined, swing wing, multi-roll aircraft.

Toot-sweet: A British pronunciation of a French term meaning "quickly."

Trumpets: An affectionate term for the Motorbikes made in England—Triumphs.

URPS: Underwater-Repair-and-Salvage-craft. Though

design and dive perameters are from the 70's this craft still performs well for salvage and repair work for the Navy while abroad. With a crew of two, it requires shore lines to mother ship as it cannot run independently without air supply and electrical power for props and external grabs.

Viking: S-3 ASW aircraft.

VTOL: Vertical-Take-Off and Landing.

Vulture's Row: The port side open deck of the Tower or Stack that off-duty crew can spend time watching Carrier Deck operations. Named after the possible sadistic nature of some crew who want to watch accidents happen from the stands.

Way-point: A point permanently designated into the Internal Navigation System of any modern aircraft, military and civilian. This point is designated, not so much as where on the planet it is, but where this point is in relation to the start point or "zero."

About The Author

Julian Hudson, though born in England, had always been fascinated with the power and might of the United States Navy. The day the *USNS Stark* was hit, killing 37 officers and crew, he decided to put pen to paper, and from that moment on Julian has spent most of his spare time working on Black Alert. He believes that some designers of military hardware have lost sight of how much we rely on computers and electronic hardware to fight our battles for us. Through this story Julian hopes to bring to our attention that one day, if our computers do fail, we will have little or no capability to ward off any serious attack.

WATCH FOR THESE NEW
COMMONWEALTH BOOKS

	ISBN #	U.S.	Can
❏ **EPITAPH FOR A CLICHÉ,** Susan L. Zimmerman	1-55197-012-0	$4.99	$6.99
❏ **SAND DREAMS,** William Allen	1-55197-002-3	$4.99	$6.99
❏ **DEATH BY CHARITY,** Carol Ann Owen	1-55197-020-4	$4.99	$6.99
❏ **DAYS OF THE MESSIAH: PHARAOH,** Ehab Abunuwara	1-55197-004-X	$5.99	$7.99
❏ **POOLS OF ANCIENT EVIL,** Eric E. Little	1-55197-008-2	$4.99	$6.99
❏ **DEMANITY DEMANDS,** Eric Tate	1-55197-018-X	$5.99	$7.99
❏ **NO TIME CLOCKS ON TREES,** Gary Lilley	1-55197-020-1	$4.99	$6.99
❏ **FOR YOU, FATHER,** Jennifer Goodhand	1-55197-016-3	$4.99	$6.99
❏ **JOURNEY TO SPLENDOURLAND,** L. J. London	1-55197-024-4	$4.99	$6.99
❏ **I.R.S. TERMINATED,** Charles Steffes	1-55197-137-2	$4.99	$6.99

Available at your local bookstore or use this page to order.

Send to: COMMONWEALTH PUBLICATIONS INC.
9764 - 45th Avenue
Edmonton, Alberta, CANADA T6E 5C5

Please send me the items I have checked above. I am enclosing
$_____ (please add $2.50 per book to cover postage and
handling). Send check or money order, no cash or C.O.D.'s,
please.

Mr./Mrs./Ms._____

Address_____

City/State_____ Zip_____

Please allow four to six weeks for delivery.
Prices and availability subject to change without notice.

WATCH FOR THESE NEW COMMONWEALTH BOOKS

Admiral Pat Swanson becomes the ultimate detective when the largest and most modern fighting ship afloat, the Aircraft Carrier, *USS George Washington*, goes dead in the water just off the entrance to the Persian Gulf. With misinformation and red herrings at every turn, the Admiral nevertheless manages to discover who the real perpetrators are, captures the device and puts the culprits behind bars, all in just one day!

Search with Swanson, through the myriad of intelligence and electronic data, spot the clues and solve the puzzle before time runs out, for he knows this is not just a matter of life and death, but, if not contained, one that could change the future policy of Naval design forever.

Black Alert
AT GONZO STATION

by

Julian Hudson